RISING TIDES

RISING TIDES

A. M. PORTMAN

CETUS

Contents

To Philip,
My Love

Belgrand Bay
N
The Ans
Lev
The Cairn
Sornia
Hedda
Smuggler's Port

Pentz
The Isles
The Teeth
Valenna
Raymouth
Elldon
Campos
s Point
ehead

Stones

A wild, fishy reek rose from the black void below the rocky ledge on which he stood. He nudged a pebble toward the edge with the toe of his boot, watching as it rolled over the lip and disappeared downward. As he leaned precariously over the gaping hole, he waited for a sound to echo up from the darkness, but there was nothing.

The Hole in the Campos, he said to himself. *That's what they called it.* He wasn't sure what he expected to find—a cave or a ditch, perhaps. What he found was what they said it was, an immense hole in the ground. It seemed to bore straight through the Campos, or down to the very center of the world, for all he knew.

The hole appeared to have formed at the bottom of one of the many pools that were common in the area. Shrubs and stunted trees grew at the margins, with a wide circle of bare rock and pebbles around it where water had once been. He imagined the surrounding pool draining through the hole like water drains from a leaky bucket.

He knelt and brought his face as close to the strange opening in the ground as he could manage without toppling in. The void below was large enough to swallow a carriage. He squinted into the depths as the cool, musty air wafted upward, chilling his skin. The shadows were too deep for him to make out any shapes in the darkness below. *Wait...* His eye caught a faint gleam of light far beneath his feet. *What was that?* he wondered, peering into the void.

"Tobias!" a voice came from behind him, startling him so much he nearly fell in. "Stay back!"

He sat back on his heels, trying to catch his breath from the sudden fright. "Damnit, woman!" Turning to look, Tobias saw a portly figure hustling toward him. "You nearly killed me," he chided. Returning his attention toward the hole in the ground, he glared down into the deep shadows. Again, there was a twinkle of light, a glitter of gold against the black. Finally, it stilled long enough for him to focus his eyes on its shape. It looked to be a shining, golden orb with a slit of black in the center. He stared at the strange form, blinking at it. It winked back at him.

"Get away—" she began, but her words broke off into a high-pitched shriek. Tobias only felt a sharp, bone-shattering pain clamp down around him, and everything turned black.

* * *

Kneeling beneath the shadow of the tall elms of Greywood Manor, Adella set the smooth fieldstone down onto the others at her feet. The rain pattered on her oilskin cloak as she rose and looked down onto the pile; buried beneath the rocks and soil lay a rough-hewn coffin, empty save for two sets of carefully folded clothes. *Mother...* Her fingers could still feel the soft velvet of the riding habit she'd selected from her parents' wardrobe, the rough canvas of her father's patched breeches and jacket from his campaign trunk. *Father.* The items would take the place of bodies; her parents had been lost at sea that spring. Tears stung Adella's eyes as she recalled the moment in Raymouth when she'd been told of the wave that had destroyed their ship. They never made it home; this was the best she could do.

The loss of her parents had never really seemed real through her travels over Belgrand Bay; it wasn't until she returned home and they weren't there that the pain of it truly hit her. Though she always tried her best to bear it, the weight of her grief hung like a stone in her heart. This ceremonial burial of their belongings had been her attempt at letting some part of it go. She wiped a tear from her cheek.

Beside her, Kol set a firm hand upon her shoulder, the warmth of it seeping into the flesh beneath her cloak where the rain couldn't reach. "I sometimes forget you're grieving," he said quietly, "you bear it so well."

"Even so," she sighed, "that doesn't make it any less heavy."

"Burdens are heavier when you carry them alone," Kol replied, then stepped aside as Armand approached, holding a small bunch of wildflowers.

Adella looked them over, then drew out a sprig of lavender blossoms. Holding it to her nose, she inhaled the heady fragrance for a moment, the scent bringing to mind quiet moments spent sipping lavender tea with her parents. She blinked her eyes clear and dropped the lavender onto the stone pile. "Goodbye," she whispered, her voice little more than breath. Kol followed her lead, dropping a stalk of yellow mustard flower.

"Goodbye," Armand said, his voice cracking with more than age. "My friends." He set the remaining handful of blooms onto the stones.

They stood in silence as the warm, misty rain filled the grey evening with haze. Eventually, Adella took the first step and turned away, facing the solemn silhouette of Greywood Manor. The fieldstone mansion was nearly all that was left of Elldon town after the attack by the Sornian army that spring; they had crossed the Campos between the two countries and invaded the frontier of Valenna, burning down Elldon. Thanks to Kol and his quick change of allegiance, the manor had been spared. "How do we rebuild?" Adella asked, more to herself than to either of them. "After everything that's happened."

"The same way we did this," Armand replied. "One stone at a time."

1

Hedda

Teressa held Lucas's hand as they stood at the iron rail of the balcony overlooking the port city of Hedda, the waters of Belgrand Bay churning gloomily in the distance. Storm clouds hung low above the rooftops, dark and heavy, as the rain began to fall. Lucas squeezed her hand in the rising wind that whipped their hair and tugged at their clothes. Turning to look along the railing, she watched Matei pull something out of his waistcoat pocket.

"What is he doing?" she asked. "Why are we out here?"

"Just watch," Lucas replied, and a smile spread across his face. "You'll see." The breezes blowing in from the sea ruffled his freshly-cropped blond hair. Gone was his traditional Valennian queue; the change was an outward sign of his new allegiance to Sornia. Beyond the city, a streak of lightning lit up the sky, followed by the loud crack and rumble of thunder. They turned back to watch as Matei stood motionless, eyes closed and arms raised skyward. In one hand, he clutched the double-pointed crystal, glowing with a faint white light in the gloom beneath the storm clouds.

"Nothing's happening—" Teressa began but stopped short, her breath caught in her throat. Around them, the wind stilled. She felt a lifting, pulling sensation at her skin as the atmosphere around them shifted. Beside her, Lucas's cropped hair began to float on end. She noticed a gentle tugging at her scalp as her ginger ringlets wafted weightlessly up in the damp, rising air.

The world seemed to shimmer oddly around them, but Teressa couldn't understand what she was seeing until her eyes focused on a single droplet of water suspended in the air before her face. Slowly, it floated up toward the sky. She put out her hand, placing her fingers over the liquid mote as it drifted upward. As the droplet rose, it met her skin, wetting her palm as any ordinary raindrop would, but it traveled in the wrong direction. Water glistened in the air around them as tiny spheres of fallen rain rose gently, back toward the clouds. Teressa watched in amazement. *It's raining upward,* she realized.

Far beyond the city, a flash of light caught her attention. Lightning spiraled, twisting and twining around itself, steadily up toward the swath of black clouds above the dark and heaving waters of Belgrand Bay.

Matei fell to his knees upon the hard stone of the balcony floor, pressing a palm to his forehead as the rain reversed its course, falling downward once more. The lightning flashed back down into the dark waves from which it had ascended. In only a moment, everything had returned to its natural state, the raindrops once again falling on their faces.

Teressa stepped cautiously toward Matei, who knelt on the balcony, but Lucas put out a hand to stop her. "Is he all right?" she asked, her voice hushed.

"He'll be fine," Lucas replied. "It just tires him for a while." He turned toward her, taking her hands in his as he grinned widely. "Can you believe it? We've recovered the Heart of the World. And it's ours to use."

"It's amazing," she admitted, tucking back strands of loose hair. "But what do you plan to do with it?"

"We're going to restore the Andolinian Empire. Reunite the colonies," Lucas said, a hopeful look crossing his face. "That's why we need him." They both glanced over at Matei, who seemed to recover as he rose tentatively to his feet. "The glory of Andolin," Lucas added quietly, "resurrected at last."

"Valenna will never agree to join Sornia," Teressa countered.

"I know," he replied. "We won't give them a choice."

She released his hands. "What do you mean?"

Lucas grinned, his green eyes creasing at the corners. "We're going to conquer Valenna."

Teressa followed Lucas down the long corridor of the Royal Palace, passing finely carved alabaster pilasters that lined the walls. She wasn't sure how she felt about everything that had happened lately, but there was one thing she was certain of. *This place is beautiful.* Since she had come to Sornia, her life had taken a fortunate turn. It had seemed bleak, at first, adrift in the little boat in the stormy sea for nearly an entire day, just Lucas, Matei, and herself, before being rescued by a passing fishing boat and brought to this port city of Hedda.

She didn't understand the relationship between Lucas and Matei; she was only told they met in a tavern. *Does it matter? After all,* Teressa told herself, *many friendships begin that way. Did it matter that he was Sornian?* Even Adella, much to Teressa's dismay, had apparently made friends with a Sornian, even after he'd led the attack on their hometown of Elldon, on the frontier of Valenna.

Her relationship with Lucas, and his friendship with Prince Matei, had elevated her to a higher social rank in a way she didn't yet understand. Apparently, Lucas had won the favor of Matei's father, King Berento, and now received preferential treatment in the Sornian court. Because of this, Teressa barely had to lift a finger, but Lucas deflected and changed the subject whenever she tried to ask him about it. She tried not to wonder how a Valennian could have managed to earn such favor within an enemy country. After such a hard life of manual labor, she was enjoying this well-earned rest. If it meant that she and Lucas could be together in a way they never could when she was working for his family, then she was willing to make this new country her home. Strings of pearls clinked at her wrists as she grabbed the soft silk brocade of her skirts and hurried to catch up. Lucas offered her his elbow, which she took, enjoying the small gesture of affection that she had never received at Greywood.

Ahead of them, Matei stopped before a set of mahogany doors and turned toward Teressa. "You will meet many people here. I must warn you, it will be hard to tell friend from foe. Take our lead, and do not say too much about Valenna. Leave that to us." Matei turned and reached toward the doors but paused, glancing back at the two of them again. "While it is important that we are seen attending this event," he added, his voice taking on an enigmatic tone, "please, don't do or say anything out of the ordinary. Just... act like you belong here." Lucas nodded. Teressa could feel her palms starting to sweat, and she released her skirts to keep from staining them.

"Don't worry," Lucas reassured her. "Just do as he says, and everything will be fine."

Matei pulled open the doors and the three of them entered. The dining hall had been set with many tables, which were already crowded with brightly-dressed guests seated under massive candle-lit chandeliers. On the far side of the vast space, sitting at a long table set apart from the others, was a very large man dressed in colorful brocade, a golden circlet sitting atop his shorn head. Seated around him were many beautiful women of various ages. "King Berento," Matei whispered, nodding in his direction. "And the Royal Consorts."

Act like you belong, Teressa reminded herself while she followed along behind Matei, her hand gripping Lucas's elbow tightly. She had never been one to be invited to lavish social events. *How can I possibly belong here?* she wondered. *No, I can do this.* She took a deep breath. *Just... be yourself. But quieter. And don't drink too much wine.*

Teressa's heart leapt into her throat as King Berento motioned for Matei and his friends to approach. The wooden heels of her pointed shoes echoed loudly in her ears as they crossed the spacious hall and stood before the King.

"My son!" King Berento said proudly, rising from his high-backed chair. "You have proven yourself. I wish all to know that this Prince of Sornia has earned his place beside me!" The King lifted a hand into the air in a grand gesture. "Come, show us the treasure you've recovered. Show us the Heart of the World!"

"Yes, Father," Matei said, bowing his head before turning to address the room. Teressa stood aside, watching as he placed his hand inside the large pocket of his waistcoat to bring out the double-terminated crystal. A gentle, white luminescence emanated from the stone as he held it carefully on his palms and lifted it up for all to see. "The Heart of Mundil!" he announced. The room erupted with cheering.

"You've earned that treasure," King Berento said, the voices quieting as he spoke to his son. "And my thanks go out to your friend here as well, for all he has done for Sornia." Lucas bowed in response. Teressa waited for the king to acknowledge her presence, but he never did. She stood by as the three men made conversation amongst themselves until he dismissed them without even a glance in her direction, though she had to admit it was a relief to her nerves.

The rest of the evening passed pleasantly, and Teressa thoroughly enjoyed being here on the opposite side of the social order from where she had been relegated in Valenna. The serving girls filled her cups with polite smiles, while the men admired her in her finery. *How different things are for me here,* she marveled. She began to feel more comfortable in her new station and freely made small talk with the other well-dressed ladies at her table, until they started to ask questions about Valenna and she had to defer to Matei. She resisted the second glass of wine. *Or was it the third?* She couldn't remember. As the final course of the supper was served, however, the ambience was ruined when the pair of doors slammed open suddenly, crashing into the walls.

A courier in a travel-worn greatcoat entered; his wide-brimmed hat fell to the floor as he ran across the vast space toward the King's table. The courier dropped to his knees. "Your Majesty," he began.

"Forgive me, terrible news. Crown Prince Gio," he lowered his head toward the floor. "He is dead."

* * *

Teressa wandered aimlessly across the vast, newly decorated solar room, as the sea breeze blew in from the open balcony. It had nearly been a week since the Crown Prince's funeral, during which time the palace had been abuzz with speculation regarding his death, but now things had begun to return to normal. Many well-dressed men and women lounged on plush sofas or stood in groups, trying to outdo each other with gossip. From one side of the space, the scent of jasmine emanated from a tea service on the buffet table.

She stopped before a glass-paneled cabinet, her eyes roaming over the various precious objects inside. Figurines carved from jade, exquisite blue-and-white Madorran porcelain, and silver and gold candlesticks glistened from the dark wood shelves. Her gaze settled on an unusual disc-like object on one of the higher shelves, displayed on a little wooden stand. She rose to the tips of her toes to get a closer look.

"Leveret's Key," Matei said, walking up behind her. "Useless now, of course," he added smugly.

Teressa didn't take her eyes from the Key, studying the wavy lines etched into its surface. "Why keep it, then?" she wondered.

Matei looked at her incredulously, his distorted reflection showing in the glass of the cabinet. "It's solid gold," he replied snidely.

Teressa heard footsteps as Lucas came up next to her. "We might need it again one day." His tone was quiet, almost somber.

"Why do you think that?" she asked, looking up at him.

His gaze held hers as he searched for an answer. "I don't know," he finally admitted. "I just have a—" His eyes shifted from her to the golden disc in the cabinet, and grew distant. "A strange feeling."

Teressa stood there, staring blankly at the shining object as it brought to mind the events that led her here. When she had escaped on the ship's boat with Lucas and Matei during the battle at sea, Teressa had left Adella behind on *The Tigress.* She had been plagued by guilt over it until only days ago, when she had seen *The Tigress* moored at Smuggler's Port. One of the crew had informed her that her friends had made it safely to the Capital. "I wonder how Adella is doing," Teressa said quietly.

"I'll let you know when I find her," Matei replied.

Teressa turned to face him. "What do you mean?"

"I have people searching for her," he replied.

"Why?" Lucas asked, his forehead wrinkling in confusion. "What do you want with her?"

"I want my seventy gold coins," Matei grumbled. "Along with my honor as a prince." His expression hardened into a scowl. "I did warn her of the consequences if she escaped," he stated plainly. Teressa glanced nervously toward Lucas, who returned the look with a frown.

2

Awakening

The din of shouting and the roar of a stormy sea surrounded him as he looked around in the dark chaos. He searched for a familiar face amid the people that rushed by with blazing torches, passing him without so much as a glance in his direction. *Papa...* he thought. *Where's Papa?* A large hand grabbed his elbow tightly.

"There you are, my boy—Shh, don't cry." A kindly face bent down toward him, and he looked up into a pair of dark eyes, as warm and comforting as solid ground. *Papa.*

"You must be brave," his father continued. Something heavy pressed into the belt around his waist. "Take my knife and keep it on you, do you understand?" The man's brow furrowed deeply as his tone became more urgent. "If anyone gets too close, use it. Shh, no tears; we will meet again." His father smiled through glossy eyes. "Just keep it on you. Borrowed things always find their way back home."

From somewhere behind him, the piercing sound of a woman's scream cut through the noise of clashing metal. In an instant, his father was gone and he found himself once again lost and alone, looking on helplessly as bodies fell around him in the tumult. Blood pooled on the planks at his bare feet, seeping warmly between his toes.

A sudden onslaught of cold water slammed him across the planks and pressed him against the rail, pulling at him until his legs dangled over the side of the ship. As the wave abated, he clung there, coughing out seawater and calling for help that never came. A second surge hit him again, washing over his head, pulling his hands free from their grasp.

He plunged down into the midnight sea, the icy chill stinging his skin, settling deeper into his body. Finally, he surfaced, desperately gasping the cool night air. High above him, the mast of the ship was engulfed in a blaze of lashing flames, the heat of it warming his face briefly before cold water crashed over him again. The last thing he saw before sinking back down into the darkness was a series of glistening, gilded letters carved into the prow above him: *The Seaborn.*

Kol awoke with a gasp. Throwing back the quilt, he sat bolt upright. His pulse pounded in his ears; the damp nightshirt clung to his heaving chest as he tried to catch his breath. It had been a full two weeks since his dreams last disturbed his sleep, which he figured was due to the comfort of his new surroundings. Though he slept lightly, expecting each peaceful night to be interrupted by an attack from the Campos, he did so while atop a soft mattress with goose-down pillows in his own bedchamber at Greywood Manor.

Swinging his feet down to the floor, he took a seat on the edge of the wood bedstead. Judging by the black sky out his window, dawn was some time off yet. The coals in the fireplace still cast an orange light. He picked up his knife from the little table beside his bed, unsheathing it and turning it over in his hands. The wood handle was well-worn, polished to an oily grey with age. Despite the years of wear the knife had endured, a faint but familiar marking could still be seen on the base of the blade, which he had taken to be a maker's mark. He rubbed his thumb over the small etched letters: *A S.*

When he had left the orphanage all those years ago, this was the only thing they had returned to him before he departed. He kept it with him ever since, save for the time he had loaned it to Adella, as it always seemed to come in handy. Though he knew it was a silly thought, part of him imagined it to be good luck. Now, he wondered why. *That dream...* It was different than any he had before, more in-tense, more life-like. *What did it mean? Could it have been... A memory?* He dressed quickly, stuffing the knife into its customary place in his boot top, and walked out of the chamber.

Kol came down the stairway overlooking the foyer of Greywood Manor, catching glimpses of his dark reflection in the mirrors as he continued down the hallway. Inside the candle-lit parlor room, Adella sat at her desk, looking over Teressa's letter. Kol had noticed her studying it many times, searching for new meaning in its brief mes-sage. Teressa had only written to inform Adella that she had survived the battle at sea, along with Lucas, and that they were safe, but won't be returning to Valenna. While Armand was ecstatic at the news of their safety, Adella's reaction had been more tempered, more pensive.

"You're up late," he commented quietly. "I thought you went to bed already."

"I did," Adella replied. "I'm not up late, you're up early." Her long hair had been pinned into a bun and she was dressed in canvas knee-breeches and riding boots, ready to start the day. She turned to look up at him. "Is everything all right?"

Kol thought it over. He hadn't expected to find her awake at that hour, but realized how grateful he was to see her just then. "Yes," he replied. "It is."

"Good." She folded the letter up and tucked it away into one of her desk's little shelves. "Let's get started."

The faint light of dawn crept over the meadows behind Greywood, shining pale upon the circle of tents and the people as they worked in the cool morning air. Adella scanned the group of riders before her as they readied to depart, and noticed one man struggling to keep his horse still long enough to mount up. "The reins, Jacoby," she called out, frowning as the horse turned circles around him. "Use the—Oh, for heaven's sake." She strode across the dewy grass and, taking hold of the leather reins under the muzzle, steadied the horse long enough for Jacoby to climb up into the saddle.

She released them, sighing as the animal trotted off happily without any cues from its rider one way or the other. "Use the reins!" Adella called out again. She knew the spirited chestnut mare was not a good match for him, but they didn't have any horses to spare. Misses Asher's group had not yet returned from their excursion in the Campos.

"I don't think Jacoby knows how to ride," Kol suggested as he walked up beside her. Jacoby was Misses Asher's youngest son. Though the man was around the same age as Kol, Jacoby apparently led a simpler life working the land on his mother's smallholding, and doing little else.

"You'd think he would've mentioned it before now." Adella pulled out from beneath her arm a leather notebook she had lately taken up the habit of carrying around. She flipped through the pages and made marks in it with a brass pencil.

They walked over to the northwest field, where several people were practicing archery on targets leaned against the tall elm trees that sheltered Greywood. Kol followed along behind Adella, absent-mindedly watching the arrows hit or, more frequently, miss their targets.

"Put your arrow to the other side of the bow," Adella instructed quietly to one young blonde woman whose arrows were missing their target completely. The woman only looked at her blankly. "Here, may I?" Adella asked and, after receiving a nod, guided the arrow into its proper place above the woman's other hand. She stepped back and the archer let the arrow fly, striking the wooden target dead-center in its little painted circle.

Adella opened her notebook and flipped through the pages. "Miss Bligh appears to be a natural," she commented as she wrote. They continued on down the line of archers,

stopping behind one man who seemed to be paying more attention to the people around him than his target. "Fix your stance, James," Adella said to him. "Square your hips."

"Could you come over here and show me?" James asked, clearly trying not to smile at his own cleverness.

"I'll show you," Kol offered, cracking his knuckles as he stepped forward.

"Ah, no—" James laughed nervously. "No need for that." He corrected his form and loosed an arrow, striking the target just outside the bull's-eye. "See? I've got it now."

"Well enough," Adella admitted, once again writing in her journal and continuing onward.

"What are you writing?" Kol wondered. "Do you keep notes on everyone?"

"Mhm," she replied, her hand still scrawling notes.

He arched his brow. "Even me?"

"Of course." She flipped through the book. "I record your pay here, for one."

"And what else?" he asked, glancing at the open pages.

Adella tucked the book back under her arm. "It's private."

"Oh." Kol smirked. "So it's a diary."

"It is not—" Her words were interrupted by a low rumbling as the ground beneath them jolted sideways. Adella lost her balance and was thrown off her feet, notebook tumbling from her hands. The green grass rose up quickly toward her face as she hurtled toward the ground, squeezing her eyes shut in anticipation of the impact. Instead of slamming into the hard dirt, however, she felt firm arms catch her by the waist. "Oh," she breathed, mind blank with surprise when she found herself looking up into Kol's keen, black eyes, so close that she felt his breath on her skin. He seemed to be studying her face as his gaze shifted from her eyes to her mouth. "That was close," she said quietly, warmth flooding up into her cheeks.

Kol gave a small laugh, a grin tugging at the corners of his mouth, as he helped her back to her feet.

She tucked back a strand of hair that had fallen into her eyes and looked around. A couple of the horses had spooked and were running loose, and her neighbors were all picking themselves up off the ground or clutching at the tents for support. "What was that?" It reminded her of the turbulence at sea during their previous voyage aboard *The Tigress*.

Kol retrieved her notebook from the grass and handed it back with a shrug when the soil beneath them trembled again, though less violently this time. They stood motionless, not daring to move again. Finally, after it had passed and everything had quieted, they heard shouting coming from the direction of the manor.

"Miss Adella!" Armand ran across the grass toward them and stopped to catch his breath. "Come inside," he said, still huffing. "We've got visitors... From Raymouth."

Kol made his way through the crowded space as the residents of Elldon mingled among their returning neighbors. "Did you feel the quake as you arrived?" Kol asked one of the new guests. The man was perhaps ten years older than himself, and well-dressed with a neat wool hat and a jacket of bright green velvet. The long queue of his light brown hair had been set into a curl.

"We did," the man replied, looking about the room. "I haven't felt ground tremors like that since my travels in Andolin."

"Mister Martin," Adella said, weaving her way across the large gathering room of Greywood Manor. "It's good to see you again."

"Lady Grimless," the man said, taking her hand and pressing it briefly to his lips. Kol grimaced. "Forgive me," Martin continued, raising an eyebrow at her riding breeches. His eyes lingered on her boots caked with horse manure. "I didn't recognize you. I'm sorry to hear about your parents, but am glad to see that you are well. We received the news in Raymouth that Elldon is to be rebuilt, and we're here to help."

"You have perfect timing," Adella replied. Her words were earnest, but she cast a pensive look at Kol. "You are all welcome here at Greywood."

Kol had spent enough time with Adella by now to recognize the meaning behind that glance. *A change of plans.* They had been preparing to head out into the Campos that morning to search for Misses Asher's scouting party, which had been expected to return the day before. Kol didn't think the delay had been long enough yet to be too concerned, but Jacoby was eager to set out to find his mother. Of course, the Lady of Elldon couldn't leave now, with the new arrivals to attend to.

Armand joined them. "I'd better put some tea on. Come," he said to Kol, "give me a hand with the trays."

"What is it with Valennians and tea?" Kol wondered as he and Armand made their way to the kitchen at the back of the manor.

"Well," Armand began, warming up for a discourse, "it started when the Madorrans arrived in the Bay from across the sea..." He squinted one eye thoughtfully. "Fifty-some years ago? We began to trade with them, and suddenly all things Madorran became fashionable. Their hairstyles, their porcelain... and their tea especially. It's become a custom here." He stopped to turn toward Kol. "Isn't it like that in Sornia?"

"No," Kol replied. "The Madorrans are looked down on, being foreign. Anything that is not of Andolinian culture is treated with suspicion."

"The Empire is long gone," Armand commented. "The Sornians should let it rest." A look of concern settled over his features. "They do still drink tea though, right?"

Kol laughed.

In the large gathering room of Greywood Manor, Adella sat on the button-tufted sofa, lost in thought while she watched the sun set in vibrant streaks of gold and red through the open windows. Most of the guests had withdrawn for the night after being fed and given a place to sleep, some in the various spare rooms, some in tents with the rest of their neighbors behind the Manor. The July nights had been warm and comfortable after the rain moved on, and the air was perfumed with the balmy scent of kitchen herbs wafting in on the light breezes from outside.

Her thoughts were on Teressa; she wondered how her friend had survived the battle, and what she might be doing at that moment. *And why in the world would she stay in Sornia?* The letter Teressa sent had been brief. *Mysterious, even.* Adella couldn't help but wonder if her friend had been unhappy at Elldon. *Was it something I'd done?* Adella thought about the other people who had left her suddenly throughout her life, disappearing without explanation. Lucas's betrayal of Valenna, and his involvement in the attack on Elldon, had come as a complete shock. *And before that, Rogero.* Years ago, he had confessed his feelings for her; she spent that night with him because of his pretty words. They must've been lies, she had come to realize, since he was gone when she awoke the next morning. *And not a word from him for an entire year afterward...* Adella shook her head to clear the thought away. There was nothing that could be done about it now; Teressa was gone. *Oh, Tess... I hope you know what you're doing.* Adella was startled back to the present when Kol and Armand entered the room, chatting between themselves.

"What luck," Armand said, turning toward Adella. "The more hands, the lighter the work."

"Yes," Adella replied, trying to smile in acknowledgment. "But..." The pantry was running out of necessities that were still in high demand in Raymouth. *Flour, sugar,* she remembered the list she wrote out earlier. *Oil... Tea.* That was a hard one to do without, if only for morale. "We'll have to feed them, and there hasn't been much game for hunting in the Campos lately." Kol took a seat beside her, letting out a loud breath as he leaned his head against the sofa back.

"True," Armand admitted. "And they'll want better accommodations, if the rain blows in again. But we need building supplies. Everything's been destroyed." The three of them sat silently, mulling over the situation.

"I didn't mean to overhear..." Mister Martin stepped out of the shadows from the hall and entered the room, a glass of wine in hand. "But I think I can help. I'm expecting a shipment—a broad order of dry goods and high-demand stock meant to completely replenish my shop." He took a sip of wine. "It will be arriving at the port in the western Campos."

"That'd be what they call Smuggler's Port?" Armand asked.

"That's the one," Martin replied. "I have a cargo ship coming in from Madorrah. I must meet them there at the docks to sign for the goods, then transfer them to another vessel to send onward to Raymouth." He turned toward Adella. "From there, I can have it all carted here to Elldon for our use."

"You would do that?" Adella asked in disbelief. She knew Henry Martin to be the wealthiest man in Raymouth, having inherited his mother's mercantile company when she passed years ago. He had moved to Elldon to open a new shop only months before the Sornians attacked. Adella assumed he would simply stay in Raymouth like many other residents from Elldon; the idea that he would donate such a massive sum of goods to rebuild the town was completely unexpected. "I will pay for the supplies on behalf of the town," she offered, "if you can manage to get it here."

"I will, I promise you." Martin took a drink from his glass. "But I admit, this is my first shipment coming directly from Madorrah. I've never been to this Smuggler's Port, and, to be honest, I'm not used to traveling unless by carriage." He laughed at his confession.

"How are you with a bow—" Kol began, but shut his mouth as Adella elbowed him lightly in the ribs.

"You couldn't sail out from Raymouth?" Armand asked.

Martin shook his head. "They are allowing incoming ships now, but things aren't fully back to normal. There was nothing available to charter."

"There's no way around it, then," Adella replied. "You'll have to cross the Campos."

"If I'm just heading dead west," Martin reasoned, "perhaps I could manage it on my own."

"No." Adella shook her head. "It isn't safe to travel alone; I don't allow it of anyone." She pressed her lips together. "I'll talk to the others in the morning, and get a group together to take you." She turned to look Martin squarely in the eye. "It will be dangerous, you know."

"My life could stand a little excitement," he said, a bit too enthusiastically. "Oh!" he continued. "I just remembered. When I was at the docks, I saw your beau there." He fumbled around in his jacket pockets before pulling out an envelope and handing it to her. "I mentioned I'd be heading here next, and he asked me to give this to you."

"My beau?" she muttered, brow furrowing as she scrutinized the handwriting on the letter. "You can't mean Captain Declan?"

Martin nodded as he swallowed the last of his wine. "That's the fellow," he said, pointing a finger for emphasis. "I know him well enough. He would've taken me aboard, but his ship had only just made port. Decent man."

Adella frowned, setting the letter down unopened. "He may be that, but he's not—"

"Pardon me," a soft voice came from the hallway. "Lady Grimless?"

Adella turned to see a woman standing in the shadows. "Come in," she replied. "What is it?"

"The well..." the woman began hesitantly. "There is no water. It's gone dry."

"What do you mean?" Adella asked.

"There's no water," the woman replied. "Our buckets come up empty."

"It hardly seems possible, with all this rain..." Adella muttered. "We'll have to get water from the stream, then." It sounded simple, but the stream was at least an hour's walk into the Campos. Not only that, but it was seasonal, and wouldn't be there much longer as it dried up during the summer. "Ask Benson and Carrick to bring up the empty barrels from the cellar and load them into the smaller wagon," Adella continued. "Then, have Benson go with you to draw water first thing in the morning. Take weapons, and use the northwestern path," she instructed carefully. The other woman nodded. "Thank you, Miss Bligh," Adella said, and the woman disappeared into the shadows of the hallway once more.

Kol and Armand passed a look between them. Wondering what it was about, Adella raised a brow at Kol questioningly, but he only smiled. Martin then excused himself to retire for the night, leaving the three of them sitting in quiet contemplation.

Adella looked at Declan's letter on the sofa beside her. Finally, she gave in and broke the wax seal. Unfolding the paper, she looked over the scrawling, elegant script, and her eyes skimmed over words she never expected to see. *Who does Rogero think he is?* she thought angrily, her cheeks burning as her pulse flared. Jumping from her seat, she crumpled the letter into a tight ball and threw it across the room at the fireplace. "I'm going to bed," she said as calmly as she could through her teeth, then walked out of the room, leaving Kol and Armand to themselves.

Kol looked over at the ball of paper as it rolled harmlessly away from the hearth. Adella had missed her target. As he stared at it, he wondered what words it could possibly contain to cause such a reaction. *And from Declan, no less...* A sinking feeling hit his gut.

Beside him, Armand sat quietly, arms folded on his round belly. "Why don't you tell her?" he said at length.

Kol's gaze shifted from the paper up to Armand. "About the teacup I broke this morning?"

"No, you dolt." Armand rolled his eyes up toward his bushy grey eyebrows, stifling a smile. "That you have feelings for her."

Kol crossed his arms and looked away. "I don't know what you're talking about," he muttered, though his words didn't sound convincing.

"Suit yourself, but—" Lines furrowed across Armand's brow, deepening the folds and hollows above his eyes. "Tomorrow is never certain for any of us; best not to leave anything unsaid."

For a moment, Kol wondered if the old man spoke from experience. Then, biting his thumbnail, he looked back toward the letter on the floor.

Armand followed his line of sight. "It would be improper to take a peek, I suppose," Armand reasoned, tipping his head toward the ball of paper.

"Seemed like a private matter." Kol leaned forward on his elbows, eyes focused intently on the letter. "None of our business."

"Right," Armand replied. "Would be a breach of trust."

"Exactly." Kol tapped his thumbnail to his teeth. "I would never..." His words dropped away unconvincingly.

"No, no," Armand agreed, drumming his fingers on his arm. "Never."

The following morning, Kol rose early again, and knew what he needed to do. He wasn't sure why Adella hadn't brought it up herself, but he was certainly the best choice for the task. He could find his way across the Campos, and he knew what he would be up against with the Sornians. Though the residents of Elldon put on brave faces, none of them were experienced fighters, save for the few that were old enough to have seen real battle, like Armand. Since Adella needed to stay to oversee Greywood, Kol knew it was up to him.

He entered the crowded kitchen where Adella sat at one table, absent-mindedly pushing a spoon around in her breakfast while studying the Codex. Armand and Jacoby sat beside her, eating in silence. Kol grabbed an empty bowl, helping himself to a thick liquid that bubbled in the pot over the hearth, and then took a seat beside Adella.

"Adella," he began, pulling her attention away from the pages of the Codex. "I will do it. I'll take Martin across the Campos."

Adella shook her head. "You don't have to do that."

"I know the way," he countered. "And I know the enemy." Kol leaned in on his elbows toward her, lowering his voice. "You know it should be me."

"I can't ask you to do that."

"You aren't," he replied. "I'm offering."

Adella studied his face for a moment, then reached out hesitantly, her fingertips stopping just short of his forearm. "Kol..." She seemed to be searching for words, then finally let out her breath in resignation. "Just be careful."

A smile tugged at the corner of his mouth as he noticed the small gesture, and the concern in her voice. He wrapped his broad hand around her fingers. "Don't worry," he replied. "I'll come back in one piece." He managed to keep his tone even, though he could feel his heartbeat rising at the warm touch of her skin. He glanced around to see the others at the table watching him intently. Adella released his hand and cleared her throat, looking down to turn a page in the book.

"What's there to worry about?" Armand asked gruffly as he turned his attention back to his breakfast. "I'm coming with you."

"Uh," Kol started to protest. The knee injury Armand suffered at the Cairn wasn't fully healed, and may never be. He still walked with a limp. Not to mention, he was supposed to be retired. "Shouldn't you stay here? After all," Kol said, keeping a straight face, "you're really old."

"Listen here, you little—" Armand began, pointing a finger, and Kol's shoulders shook with suppressed laughter. "Oh, you think you're hilarious?" Armand muttered.

"No, Armand," Adella interjected. "I need you to go into Raymouth and deliver a private message."

Armand brightened. "A special assignment, is it?" He stood, slapping his hands down onto the table in enthusiasm. "You can count on me, Lady Governor Grimless," he put a hand to his heart, bowing slightly as he spoke her full title with relish. "I'll get my boots, just give me a horse. Jacoby!" he called out, alarming the young man. "Get me a horse ready." Jacoby scrambled out of the kitchen without a word, leaving his breakfast behind.

"Wait," Adella said, pulling an envelope out from beneath the Codex. "You'll be needing this." Armand took the letter, studied the name written on the front, and hurried away.

"Who will you take with you?" Adella asked.

Kol shook his head. "Just Martin and myself. Fewer travel faster, and are less likely to be seen." He didn't want to say it in front of the others, but Kol didn't want to take away any more people from Greywood. They would need as many hands as possible if the Sornians were to attack, and the uneasy feeling stirring in his gut told him it will happen soon enough. *And Misses Asher's party is still missing...* Nobody mentioned it, but he knew they were all thinking the same thing.

* * *

Adella pushed aside the heavy tapestry curtain to let the midday sunlight in through the large windows of the main gathering room. In the green fields behind the manor, Kol was giving Martin a leg-up onto a chestnut mare. Adella turned quickly from the window and made her way down the hallway toward the back entrance. The morning's tasks had taken longer than she realized, and she wanted to see Kol and Martin before they left for Smuggler's Port. Though it was a dangerous journey for anyone, Adella felt especially uneasy at the thought of Kol returning across the Campos and traveling so close to Sornia, where he was wanted for treason. She couldn't let him leave without her saying goodbye. *Goodbye and thank you, at the very least...* Perhaps there was more she'd like to say to him, but that would have to suffice.

Adella stopped in front of the rough oak door just as it swung open. James entered, blocking her path as he shut the door behind him. He, like his younger brother Jacoby, was a broad, robust man. Though she had known them both for years, as they would visit Greywood whenever their mother came to pay rent on their smallholding, Adella often had to stop and think which brother she was addressing. Though they were generally alike in appearance, Jacoby had blue eyes and a cheerful demeanor, while James had the same brown eyes as their mother, and was known for being rather flippant.

"Miss Adella," he began. "I want to have a word with you."

"I'm sorry, but it'll have to wait just a moment," she replied and edged around him, reaching for the door handle.

He leaned back against the door. "My mother is still out there," he reminded her. "Or did you forget?"

"I did not," she replied. "But really, I must—"

"You and your hired soldier were supposed to search for her." His voice was calm but laced with suspicion. "What happened?"

"There's been a delay. Listen," Adella replied, lowering her voice to speak candidly. "The pantry is nearly empty as it is, and now with all these added people—if we don't replenish our stocks soon, we will have to abandon Elldon. Our little foothold here at Greywood is all that stands between the Sornian army and Raymouth... Or all of Valenna."

"Even so—" James began.

"She's right," a voice interrupted from the hall as Jacoby appeared in the doorway. "We have to defend Elldon. That's what Ma would want."

"Says who?" James asked.

"Our farm is all we have," Jacoby countered. "You know that. We can rebuild it. Or would you rather stay in Raymouth?" He stepped closer to James, squaring up with him. "Or would you rather join our father, drinking the days away at the Ivy Crown?"

With a glare, James held his brother's gaze. Then, he relented. His shoulders drooped as he let out a weary breath.

"We're all worried about her," Adella said gently. "Choose someone to go with you and take the last two horses. Search as far as Compass Point." He nodded and opened the door to let her pass. As Adella looked to the fields in the west, she saw that she was too late. Kol and Martin were gone.

3

Greywood Manor

When the Heart of Mundil was stolen, The Lady of the Deep sent forth her Twelve Calamities in retribution. The first calamity to come forth was sickness, which deftly worked to cut down the numbers of her people. Out of the west the first calamity spread, a red plague that robbed me of my kin.

The second calamity to darken Mundil's horizons was a rising of the tempests, which washed the lands with her waters. It fell upon my homeland in an onslaught of rain and winds, which destroyed our crops and drove us away with hunger.

The third calamity to befall the children of Mundil was the summoning of the Pelkimund...

Adella stopped, pointing with her finger to mark the place in the text while she tried to recall what Jago had told her. *The sea wolf,* she remembered. *Or wolves, in this case.* She looked back down at the page. *Its brother, the Haramund,* she continued to read silently, *or the sea horse, followed behind.*

The fourth calamity came without warning; the rising of the tides. Lady Mundil holds thirst in one hand and drowns with the other. In her anger, she sent her deluge to break upon the cities of her people. Even now, the waters still rise. None are safe.

The fifth calamity was a sundering of the lands, as Mundil shuddered at her awakening... Awakening... Adella repeated to herself. *No, that can't be correct.* She made a note on a spare sheet of parchment, sketching out the double pictograph with the dull lead of her brass pencil.

She sat at the dining room table with the Codex open, sheets of loose parchment spread out under the glow of the candelabra. For the past few days, she had renewed her efforts at compiling a dictionary of the Old Andolinian glyphs, if only to keep her mind busy. Though Greywood Manor had more people in it now than it ever had, she had never felt so alone in her own home. Her parents' bedchamber had been cleared out for use, and their belongings had been stored away or donated to her friends and neighbors, but every piece of furniture, every empty corner, still held their memory.

Adella had often buried herself in her self-appointed work, doing so in the quiet hours of the day when she wasn't busy with daily chores or overseeing more important tasks. Comparing the Old Andolinian glyphs with the Modern Andolinian script in the Codex, she labored to match each symbol with its translation on parchment. She was delighted when she suddenly realized the significance of a particular symbol, which revealed the deeper meanings of many other glyphs recorded in the hefty tome. With the dictionary she was creating, she hoped to be able to decipher the charcoal rubbings that she had made in the tomb within the sea cave that spring, when Prince Matei had taken the Heart of the World for himself.

As each new calamity arose, she continued, *it joined the others; none relented. The sixth—* Adella stopped reading once again as the high-pitched barking of a small dog broke her concentration. She sighed, and reluctantly rose from her chair.

The stars in the night sky overhead seemed to shine with an unusual intensity as Adella crossed the broad swath of grass behind Greywood Manor. She walked past the glowing coals of the campfire, surrounded by the tents of her neighbors. Adella followed the sound of the dog's yapping westward past the encampment, weaving between iron tripods set over spent cook-fires and around clothing lines that held drying laundry, to where a boy stood, a dog in his arms, staring out into the wilds of the Campos.

"Is that you, Nicolas?" Adella asked, peering at his partially-illuminated silhouette. The boy was the son of the blacksmith Benson, and the youngest person in Elldon at present.

"Sorry, Lady Grimless," he replied, trying to whisper loud enough to be heard over the continuous bark of the little terrier. "Molly's in a state, I don't know what's got into her."

"Who's on watch tonight?" Adella asked.

"Papa," he replied, pointing into the distance.

She looked out over darkened plains. Though all seemed calm and quiet, it left her feeling on edge. No calls came from the nightbirds, and even the insects seemed to have fallen silent. "Go to your mother." She put a hand gently on his upper arm and leaned down to look him in the eyes. "You both need to get inside the Manor. Do you understand?" The boy nodded solemnly, but hesitated. "Go," she urged, shooing him away. He turned and ran off toward the camp, with the dog still yapping in his arms.

Adella returned to the encampment, where many of her neighbors slept in their tents. Searching for any who were still awake, she found a group poking at coals in one of the smaller campfires and hurried over to them.

"Wake everyone," she whispered to the nearest person. An elderly, bearded man rose at the sound of her voice. "Quietly. Tell them to arm themselves and find cover."

Adella set the stock of her crossbow on the edge of the overturned camp table, her finger lightly resting on the iron lever. Her two fingers, which had previously been broken during the scuffle at the Cairn, were still too tender to wield a bow, so she had taken up the smaller crossbow of the two that had come into her possession during her travels. Unlike heavier crossbows that required a spanning device, she was able to load this one quickly with one hand. Still, her arms were getting sore from the weight of it. As the hours crept by with no sign of activity from the Campos, she was starting to wonder if all she'd accomplished was to rob everyone of a full night's sleep. Glancing back at her neighbors, she noticed the pale light of dawn just beginning to tint the inky sky behind Greywood. The windows of the manor were all black, every candle inside had been snuffed and the windows and doors hastily barricaded. Those of Elldon's residents who were willing and able to fight were, like herself, hunched down behind tables, crates, or other cover with bows, hunting spears and pitchforks at the ready. She yawned and tried to decide which she would prefer more, her warm bed or a hot cup of tea. Figuring she had erred and had better send everyone back to sleep, Adella lowered her crossbow behind the table and began to rise to her feet.

A flash of movement caught her eye as something dashed out from a stand of trees off to the southwest. The shadowy form moved over the darkened fields before being obscured behind a rise in the land. Adella dropped back down to her knees. "Archers, make ready!" she called out. Soon, she could hear the pounding of hooves in the distance, and her heart echoed their pace. Due to the shorter range of her weapon, she had chosen a place at the front, hoping the thick oak table she hid behind would protect her from the arrows of the Sornian horse-bows. Adella startled at a shuffling at her side. In the dim but growing light, she saw Miss Bligh kneel down beside her, with bow strung and arrow nocked.

"I thought I might join you," Miss Bligh whispered.

"I'm glad of that. But please," Adella replied, glancing at her sideways, "fix your arrow."

Miss Bligh gave a nervous laugh and moved the arrow to the other side of the bow. "Ready now."

As they waited breathlessly, Adella's mind raced with anxious thoughts. She wondered what she was doing here, facing Sornian soldiers with only a small band of townsfolk. The woman beside her was a seamstress, Adella recalled with dismay. Feeling woefully unprepared, she scolded herself for not sparing Greywood any horses; she regretted sending Armand to Raymouth, and, most of all, she wished she'd sent anyone other than Kol off with Martin across the Campos. As the galloping horses drew closer, however, all those thoughts cleared away.

"Hold," Adella instructed, loud enough for those behind her to hear. She was familiar with the general skill level of the group, and knew it would be worse due to nerves. She watched the leading horseman break forward from the group, hooves pounding across the dewy grass toward them in the wan morning light.

"Now!" She raised her crossbow and aimed at the oncoming rider, hoping it was high enough to miss the poor creature beneath him without going over the man's head. He drew back an arrow on his bowstring as he came riding fast upon them, so close now that she could hear the blowing of his horse's breath. Adella pulled the lever.

Just as her bolt was released, the rider let his arrow fly, and it lodged into the table right below Adella's face with the sharp crack of wood. In the confusion of the moment, she couldn't tell if it was due to her bolt or someone else's arrow, but the rider fell out of his saddle and was trampled by the horse that followed. Adella ducked back beneath the table and pulled a bolt out of the quiver at her side to reload.

Bringing up her crossbow once more, Adella peeked out over the landscape, prepared to see the riders coming down upon her. To her surprise, they had ridden no closer to the line of cover set up in front of the encampment. Instead, they curbed their horses and ran parallel along the defenses as they let loose their arrows into the group. Taking aim at one of the last riders, she squeezed back on the lever, and heard a cry of pain beside her.

Adella ducked down and saw Miss Bligh hunched over beside her, cradling her head in her arms. The woman's left hand covered her ear, and as Adella noticed blood trickling between her fingers, a cold dread flooded over her. "You're hurt!" Adella exclaimed. Miss Bligh attempted to sit up, but Adella put a hand on her shoulder. "Stay down, don't move," she ordered.

Peering over the rim of the table, Adella watched the last rider gallop away. Horses wheeled about over the field before her, leaving a trail through the dewy grass as they returned the way they had come. They left their dead behind, and the riderless horses followed after the retreating group.

Adella turned her attention back to her companion, who still clutched the side of her head. "Let's take a look," she said softly, trying to hide the concern in her voice. Miss Bligh slowly removed her bloodied hand, revealing a slice through the shell of her ear. Adella sighed with relief that it wasn't worse.

Miss Bligh looked down at the blood on her hand. "Damn," she winced with watering eyes. "That stings."

"You're extremely lucky—" Adella began, but stopped when she heard an uproar coming from behind. Turning to look, she saw the others hoisting their weapons in the air, cheering.

"Are they gone?" Miss Bligh asked hopefully.

"For now." Adella rose to her feet. "Come, Miss Bligh. Let's get you looked after."

"Rosalind," she replied, wiping her hand on her skirts.

Adella blinked at her. "What was that?"

"My name," she replied. "It's Rosalind."

Adella waited by the rear entrance to Greywood, bolting it shut behind her after the last of her neighbors made their way inside. They passed down the central hallway and entered the main parlor room, where everyone had gathered to regroup.

An uneasy feeling overcame her. *It could have been worse...* Only Rosalind and two other people had been injured, and, barring infection, all would survive. Benson had stumbled home from the field only with a bruised temple, and the other had been grazed in the shoulder by an arrow. Adella watched as the blacksmith's wife tended to the wounded with skillful hands. *It could have been much worse.* She couldn't help but wonder why it hadn't been. *Why hadn't there been more of them?* She had seen the numbers the Sornians had in their encampments in the Campos, yet they had only sent a small group of horsemen to make a pass and then retreat. *But why?*

"I want to thank you," a voice beside her began, drawing her out of her thoughts. She looked to see the heavy-set blacksmith standing beside her with Nicolas, who still held the little dog in his arms. "I thought I heard something out there, but wasn't sure..." Benson shook his head, strands of dark hair dangling loose over a forehead encrusted with dried blood. "I stopped to listen, and that's all I remember. Thank you for looking after my son."

Adella gave a tired smile. "It's Molly we should be thanking." The blacksmith and his son nodded their gratitude and walked off to join the others, who were recounting to each other the exciting events of the morning. Rosalind sat on the sofa, describing the attack from her perspective to a young man that tended to her ear. She would let them enjoy the small victory, Adella reasoned, but then they would have work to do to prepare Greywood for another attack.

4

Parting

*T*he sixth calamity, Adella ran her finger in the Codex while she read, *was the turning of the Heart of Mundil, and with it the corruption of the one who held it, as Leveret grew in his folly.* She recorded the new symbol, along with its meaning, in the dictionary she was compiling. *The seventh calamity to beset Andolin was an omen, terrifying and strange as the sea filled with fire...*

Adella stopped as a loud clinking sound caught her attention. *The sea filled with fire,* she repeated, putting fingers to her temples as she tried to concentrate despite the noise. *No, that can't be right...* Defeated, Adella looked over at Rosalind sitting across the table, vigorously stirring sugar into her teacup. It took the young woman some time before she noticed the pointed look on Adella's face and gave up her assault on the porcelain.

Rosalind cleared her throat and set the spoon down gently. "Sorry," she whispered, tucking a stray blonde curl behind her ear.

The eighth calamity, Adella continued to read, *was the turning of the minds of her people, a plague of madness among those nearest to her waters. The ninth was the warning of the plants; the point of no return. The tenth calamity caused much unrest,* she read on, determined to finish the page, *as the dead were seen again. The eleventh was the rising of Guardian, who surfaced from the deep waters to enact the will of Mundil. The twelfth and fi-*

nal calamity, the fall of Andolin. The Empire is broken. This record was writ-ten by the hand of Paloma, scribe of Andolin appointed by His Majesty, High King Daw Claer. May Mundil have mercy on us all. At the familiar name, emotion welled up in her throat.

"Paloma wrote this," Adella remarked softly, recalling the tomb of the woman deep within the sea cavern. According to the legend of Leveret and the Heart of the World, the Heart had been buried with Paloma. It had been one thing to see the remains of a woman who had lived so far back in Andolinian history, but now, to see the woman's own words that had been written when she was alive, it was a differ-ent feeling entirely. *Her living hand wrote this,* Adella marveled, placing her fingertips gently over the pictographs. She felt a personal connec-tion to Paloma now that she had this small glimpse into her life. *She wasn't just a legend,* Adella thought. *She had a life of her own. The modern translations,* she realized, *must have been added to the Codex much later.*

"Who?" Rosalind asked, wrinkling her brow in confusion.

For a moment, Adella considered telling her Leveret's story and ex-plaining how it related to the recent events, but Rosalind returned to clanking her teacup while she shoveled in more sugar.

"Never mind," Adella said wistfully. She wished Kol were there; she had grown accustomed to his presence as a quiet but good-humored companion. It had been weeks since he left, and she felt his absence keenly; she preferred his conversation and advice over anyone else's, and Greywood seemed empty without him. She imagined his crooked smile, his dark eyes, and the way she felt when he would stand close. Her pulse rose as she became lost in her thoughts. The pencil fell from her hand and clattered to the floor, startling her back to the present. "Damn," she whispered.

"Uh," Rosalind said awkwardly. "Are you all right? You look a little flushed."

Adella didn't have a chance to respond before voices echoed down the hallway. One in particular could be heard over the others. Adella closed the Codex and looked up with widened eyes. "Misses Asher!"

Adella hurried down the hall with Rosalind at her heels. They emerged into the large gathering room of Greywood Manor to see Misses Asher dropping her rucksack to the floor while she plopped down onto the antique sofa. Her traveling companions likewise looked tired and disheveled. Misses Asher's two grown sons, James and Jacoby, had returned as well.

Misses Asher leaned back, rubbing the thin skin around her temples. "We lost Tobias," she said matter-of-factly. Her grey hair hung half-loose, half-pinned up on her head.

"To the Sornians?" Adella asked.

"I don't know what it was," Misses Asher replied. "He got too close to the Hole in the Campos. Something grabbed him, pulled him in." She looked up at Adella, her brows drawing together over her lined eyes. "We tarried there for days, trying to find a way to get him out." She shook her head sadly. "It's too deep. Nothing we could do."

Adella considered the older woman's words. She had not seen this so-called Hole in the Campos herself, only heard her neighbors speak of it grimly. "Where, exactly, is it located?"

"Just northwest of Compass Point," Misses Asher replied.

Adella frowned. "By the saltwater pool?"

Misses Asher shook her head, loose tendrils of hair waving about her face. "There's no pool there. Just the hole." The woman looked exhausted, so Adella did not ask any further questions, only nodded.

James stepped forward to speak to Adella. Though he kept his voice low, there was an edge to it. "There's something you need to see."

The afternoon sun warmed Adella's skin as she crept beside James through the tall grass, drawing beads of sweat from her skin. They slunk down onto their bellies at the ridge's summit, and she pulled a spyglass from her haversack to get a better look. Below, a fire burned in the center of the open field, with a tall column of smoke streaming upward. Arranged haphazardly around the campfire were several plain canvas tents. She swept over the view through the spyglass and stopped at two men to the south, emerging from a patch of small trees and shrubs. Adella watched for a while as they tossed armloads of branches into the fire, the bright orange flames growing higher as dark smoke billowed up into the blue sky.

"What can they be doing?" Adella muttered under her breath. James motioned for her to follow, and they retreated down the hill.

"I'll put a group together, and return tonight," James said, following Adella through the summer grass as they made their way back to the manor. "Take them by surprise."

Adella chewed her lower lip. "No," she said finally. "Let's not be hasty. We don't know what they're up to."

"I don't mean to be disrespectful," he began, "but perhaps you're not the one who should be making these decisions." He stopped in front of her, cutting off her path. "It was my mother and myself who took charge of Greywood while you were gone."

"And I appreciate that," Adella replied, stepping around him.

He grabbed her by the elbow. "Why should I defer to you, anyway? You have no experience in this sort of thing, being just a lady."

Adella wrenched her arm free. "And you're just a farmer. These aren't gophers we're dealing with." His eyes widened as a look of pain flashed across his face. "But you're right," she admitted. "Valenna's been at peace for over a hundred years, save for the uprising at Enth. Not one of us here is experienced in war."

"If only your father were still here..." James muttered.

His comment stung like salt in a wound as she heard her own wish echoed carelessly back to her. Without a reply, Adella turned and continued walking.

"Armand fought at Enth, didn't he?" James asked, following closely. "Perhaps he will know what to do."

She shook her head. "Armand hasn't yet returned from Raymouth."

He frowned at the news. "It should've only taken him a day. We could really use him here. Aren't you concerned?"

"I sent Armand to Raymouth to get him *out* of danger." As far as Adella was concerned, Armand had more than fulfilled his duty to Valenna over the course of his life, and with only a limp to show for it. She would not see him die on the frontier; she had lost enough of her loved ones already. "He has many friends there," she assured him. "The fact that he's not back yet probably just means he's finally enjoying his retirement." She smiled at the thought. "If I know Armand, he's having a drink at the Ivy Crown as we speak. And he's certainly earned it."

Adella and James found Misses Asher on the sofa of Greywood's large gathering room as the golden light of evening slanted in through the windows.

"So, what were they doing?" Misses Asher asked.

Adella shook her head. "We don't know yet."

"I think we should attack now," James exclaimed. "There were only a few of them; we could reduce their numbers with little risk to ourselves."

"And I think that would be hasty," Adella added. "We would be leaving Greywood vulnerable."

James turned toward his mother. "She thinks we should give them ample time to attack us again."

"It may be a trick to draw us out," Adella explained. "I don't want to risk it until we have a better idea of what they're up to."

"A trick?" James crossed his arms. "The Sornians aren't that intelligent. You give them too much credit."

"You're wrong about them," Adella countered, turning toward him. "Kol, for one, is the cleverest man I know."

"You would think that," James said, his nose wrinkling with disdain, "since he follows you around like a lost lamb, but that only proves my point."

"That's what I *pay* him to do—" Adella began sharply, but bit down on her lips. She composed herself with a deep breath. "You don't think their behavior seemed at all suspicious?"

James glared at her. "My only suspicion is your apparent affinity toward Sornians."

Ignoring his comment, she turned back toward Misses Asher. "So, you see our dilemma," Adella said calmly. "Attack now and perhaps fall into a trap, or wait and possibly give them the advantage." She tapped a finger to her chin thoughtfully. "There are simply not enough of us; we could do with an army of our own."

Misses Asher's face brightened at the thought. "Can't you ask Queen Ellinora to send us troops?"

"I thought of that," Adella replied. "I sent a letter to the Queen with the request weeks ago, but haven't received a response. I think she may be traveling."

"We can't wait," James replied.

"He's right," Misses Asher said. "We can't wait. The Sornians are certainly plotting something... It's too bad Elldon doesn't keep troops of its own, like they do at Pentz."

"What did you just say?" Adella blurted out.

"I said..." Misses Asher began slowly, "it's too bad we don't have troops, like they do at Pentz..."

"They have troops at Pentz," Adella repeated.

"The Lord Governor of Pentz keeps a standing regiment," Misses Asher explained. "They don't really do much now that the Northern Hostilities have ended, but they keep in training. They're mainly ceremonial now," Misses Asher went on as Adella nodded with encouragement. "Guarding the estate or walking in parades and the like..." Misses Asher's words tapered off while she considered what she was saying. "But he may be willing to hire them out to us, given our situation."

"Exactly!" Adella replied. "And Pentz is only a short sail from Raymouth." Though she didn't like the thought of leaving Greywood with the growing threat of another attack, she knew their numbers weren't sufficient to take on the Sornians. Without reinforcements, defeat was only a matter of time. But if she were to try this new plan, she could be back in only a few days, at most. "Do you really think he would hire them out?"

"Certainly," Misses Asher assured her. "Lord Endlebridge would do anything for the right price." She thought for a moment. "I will come with you. I've been to Pentz many times, and I've met the Lord Governor myself. My niece works as a maid at his estate." She grinned at her idea. "So, it's decided. We'll make ready tonight, and we'll leave first thing in the morning."

"I'll be along in a moment," Adella replied as the older woman hurried away. She knew she would have to leave someone in command of Elldon while she and Misses Asher were gone. Though she and James had been at odds lately, he always came through admirably whenever she asked anything of him. There was no denying he had been indispensable in the defense of Greywood while she'd been gone. He may be contentious at times, but had proven himself dependable nonetheless.

"Why are you looking at me like that?" James asked nervously.

A smile spread across her face. "I'm going to leave you in charge."

He raised his brows. "You are?"

"On one condition," Adella replied. "Don't do anything hasty while we're gone, you must promise me that. Your task here is defense, not attack. Do we have an agreement?"

He tilted his head to one side. "Yes," James said earnestly, his posture straightening with pride. He held out his hand. "I give you my word, my Lady."

Adella took his hand, and they shook on it. "You know, James," she began, her voice taking on a softer, solemn tone, "my father often gave me bits of advice that I hardly paid any attention to, as I thought I wouldn't need it for quite some time." She shrugged in an attempt to hide the pain that the memories rekindled. "But, I still remember…"

she continued, "one evening, as we sat in his study upstairs while he recounted his most daring escapades as a cavalry officer. I voiced my admiration for his leadership and the dauntless cavaliers that were always ready to charge headlong into danger, sabers swinging." A smile played at the corner of her mouth. "And he said to me, 'If you learn only one thing from my stories, let it be this: There is a time for action and a time for patience. The hardest test of leadership is to discern one from the other.'"

"I will keep that in mind," James promised.

Adella entered her bedchamber to find Misses Asher sorting through the open wardrobe and laying petticoats across the bed. "Do you know how many times recently I've wished I'd been wearing breeches?" Adella asked, pulling a tapestry bag from beneath the bed.

"We're going to the wealthiest port city in Valenna, aside from the Capital," Misses Asher replied, holding up a silk caraco jacket and inspecting it carefully. "Not some dusty frontier town. If you wear that," she eyed Adella's form-fitting breeches disdainfully, "you'll draw a lot of attention, and not the good kind. Here, pack this," she offered, shoving the caraco and a matching skirt into Adella's arms. "Valennian scarlet; the same shade the regiment wears."

"Fine," Adella sighed, and stuffed the clothes unceremoniously into the bag.

"And bring loads of gold," Misses Asher advised. "We may need it where we're going, and the bank in Raymouth is still closed from the ague."

"Closed?" Adella's brow furrowed. "Oh, no..." she muttered. She had given what little remained of Greywood's gold and silver reserves to Kol before he left, and was depending on stopping by the bank in Raymouth in order to pay Armand's monthly pension on his return. She had banknotes, of course, but they were not always a welcome form of payment. Adella knew both Armand and Kol preferred coin.

"Bring your jewelry, then," Beatrice said, seeing the dismay on her face. "We may need to use it for bartering."

Adella pulled open the drawer of her little vanity table and dug through old letters, pieces of ribbon and other odds-and-ends until she found a small wooden box. She pulled it out and rifled through the contents. Misses Asher gave a small gasp when Adella pulled out a gold chain adorned with little pearls and a perfect, sea-blue topaz. "This was given to me by Captain Declan," Adella reminisced. "Years ago," she added pointedly.

"We all thought you would marry him," Misses Asher commented.

"So did I," Adella replied, watching as the older woman admired the piece of jewelry. "Doesn't matter now."

"Right," Asher agreed. "Now that you're Lady Grimless, you'll have to marry a noble."

"That's not what I meant," Adella muttered, frowning at the thought. She handed the necklace to Misses Asher. "You take that one."

"I can't," she countered. "What if I lose it?"

"It's yours now." Adella smiled slightly. "You're free to lose it if you wish. But try not to; you may need it if we're separated." Misses Asher offered her thanks and eagerly fixed the chain around her neck. Adella continued to look through the box until she came to a familiar object, glowing red in the light from the window. Lifting it by its heavy gold chain, she pulled out a large ruby wreathed in gold and diamond.

"Your mother always wore that one," Misses Asher remembered, her voice growing solemn.

"Except when she was traveling," Adella replied softly. "Which is why it's here with me, and she isn't." She touched its glossy red surface. Taking a deep breath, Adella lifted the necklace and fastened it around her neck. She then slipped on the little gold and peach-colored coral ring that she had gotten used to wearing after Kol had returned it to her. This item, she had no intention of trading away. Though the ring itself was a gift from Captain Declan, she appreciated the trouble

Kol went through to see it safely back in her hands. She didn't want it to have been for nothing. Then, she slipped a few more gold rings and chains into her draw-string purse along with what was left of her silver pieces.

The faint light of a dreary dawn lay over the fields as a misty, warm rain played upon Adella's face. Her right hand drew back an arrow on her hickory longbow, and the tension in her fingers against the string caused them to shake. While her bones had healed, perhaps her tendons were not ready for the strain after all. *Even so,* she thought, *this is no time for coddling.* She would be gone for three days at most, she figured, but on her return, whether she was successful at procuring reinforcements or not, they would need to be ready for a fight. She took aim and released, finding herself pleasantly surprised to hit the rim of the bull's-eye, closer than her other attempts.

Adella pulled another arrow from the ground beside her, where several more were stuck tip-down at the ready. She was alone at her make-shift archery range, while most of the other residents of Elldon slept peacefully. Adella's belongings were packed and ready; she only waited on Misses Asher so they may leave together.

Savoring the fresh, cool air, and the peace of her surroundings, she drew a deep breath, then nocked the arrow and took aim. The rustle of grass caught her attention and, glancing over her shoulder, she recognized the large silhouette of James approaching, his long work-coat billowing out behind him. Adella groaned to herself and prepared for another argument.

"I've been looking for you," he remarked as he stood beside her. Adella didn't turn to face him, but lowered her hands, relaxing the string while she listened. "I wanted to apologize," he continued. "I've been giving you a hard time lately."

"I hadn't noticed," she replied over her shoulder.

James let out a laugh. "I just want to be sure you've looked at things from every angle. You might be the Lady Governor Grimless now, but that doesn't mean you are infallible."

"You're really good at apologies," she commented. Lowering the bow, she looked at him thoughtfully. "Do you remember when we were younger," Adella began, "you and Jacoby would come to visit Greywood with your mother, and stay for tea? You'd whisper horrible jokes to make me laugh whenever I took a drink."

He smiled. "It would come out your nose."

"And my father would make me leave the room," she added with a smirk. "You used to get me in a lot of trouble. But I learned how to keep a straight face, at least." James had always enjoyed picking on Adella since she first moved to Elldon, and his antics had taught her a lot about keeping her natural impulsiveness under control. She used to hate him for it but, over the years, she had learned not to take it personally. At times, she even wondered if it was his way of showing familiarity. Either way, she had to concede that his mild antagonisms had made her stronger of character.

"You're welcome," he said proudly, patting a heavy hand on her shoulder. As he looked down at her, his expression softened. "It's time to go." Adella threw an uneasy glance westward, then turned to follow James through the manor.

Misses Asher joined them in the gravel courtyard outside the front entrance, where Jacoby stood with their horses already saddled, their travel bags secured behind the cantle. Misses Asher's horse, a piebald cob named Bixby, stomped his feet impatiently. The other horse he held was a tall, blue roan, aptly named Blue, that had belonged to Adella's mother.

James steadied the animal as Adella mounted up. "Thanks," she said. Settling into the saddle, she took up the reins. "Take care of the place while we're gone." Though she tried to keep her tone light, there was no hiding her discomfort at leaving Greywood behind.

"We're counting on you, Lady Grimless." His voice was solemn, almost pleading, and his grim expression mirrored her own anxieties. "Don't let us down." She looked him in the eye and nodded, then James stepped clear of the hooves while she urged her horse forward. "The place is ours now, Jacoby," he called out loudly as the two women departed, clearly intending for them to hear. "Let's drink up all the wine and race the horses!"

5

Pentz

Adella and Misses Asher arrived in Raymouth under a bright morning sky, as the weather had cleared during their travel. Misses Asher walked the horses to the livery stables while Adella proceeded down the cobblestone streets, wasting no time while she headed straight toward the docks on the west side of the city. Raymouth was less crowded today than it had been in years past, but she still had to work her way around groups of people gathering in front of shop windows or side-step teams of horses trotting by with their carriages in tow. Passing by the Ivy Crown, she briefly wondered if Armand might be inside, and hoped that was the case. *He would be safe there, at least,* she assured herself.

Adella came to the city's port, situated on the north shore of the River Ray. The docks here were protected by two long jetties of piled stone jutting far out from the land on either side, calming the waters within. She searched the ships that were already moored, with their crews busy loading and unloading their cargo. Not seeing the striped sails of *The Tigress,* she searched for them among the vessels that were coming and going over the glistening waves of Belgrand Bay. *That's odd,* she thought. *Rogero said he would be here for another week...*

She pulled his letter out from her haversack, smoothing the wrinkles carefully. *That's what he wrote, anyway.* It sounded as though he planned to stay for a while, since he had invited her to a game of cards in his room at the Ivy Crown. *They must've set sail early,* she thought. *What could have caused them to depart so quickly—?* She shook the thought from her head. *No matter.* She wasn't sure she wanted to see him, anyway. Her anger rose up again now, thinking about his invitation. *He must think I have nothing better to do than wait around for him, and drop everything when I'm summoned... A game of cards, indeed!* She huffed. *That's what you said last time.* Her jaw clenched as she remembered waking up in the Ivy Crown alone, wondering where he'd gone and if she'd ever see him again. *Not this time, Rog!* Adella stuffed the paper back into her bag. Though she had tossed his letter at the hearth after reading it, she had found it the next morning, flattened out on her writing desk. Unable to bring herself to destroy it after her anger faded, she had packed it away in her bag.

Adella stopped by each vessel to inquire if it was available to charter, but they each turned her down for various reasons. Some had only just come into port and wouldn't be ready to depart again any time soon, and others refused to sail to Pentz even before she had a chance to offer payment. After being sent away from the last ship, she took a seat on a bench at the waterside to wait for Misses Asher, setting her tapestry bag down by her feet.

"Adella!" a voice called out. She turned to see a young man in a blue sailor's jacket walk down the wharf toward her, a canvas market-bag slung over his shoulder.

"Yul?" she asked, standing to greet him. She had first met Yul Childric aboard *The Tigress* in the spring. After recognizing his family name, she had looked through her mother's ancestry book on her return home, and discovered the young man was a relation of hers. Now, whenever letters had to be delivered to Greywood Manor, Childric would use the occasion to visit. His presence was always welcome, as he reminded her somewhat of her brother Lucas, in the happier years before his painful betrayal. "What are you doing here? Where is *The Tigress?*"

"I'm on shore leave," he explained. "As for *The Tigress*, I don't know, I've been upriver. They must've set sail early." He shrugged. "What about you; what brings you to Raymouth?"

"I need to sail to Pentz, and quickly," she replied. "But none are willing to take on passengers."

Childric looked seaward, where a little schooner maneuvered its way through the boulders that broke the surface by the northern jetty. "*The Bluebell* may take you," he nodded toward the incoming vessel, "if you can manage to bring up Captain Declan in the conversation. Captain Loring owes him a debt or two, as do many other Valennian sailors."

"Thank you so much," Adella said, relieved to hear she may yet have a chance.

He eyed the ruby hanging from her neck. "I wouldn't flaunt that, if I were you," he warned. "It's terribly gaudy."

Adella laughed in surprise at his candor, and tucked the necklace beneath her cloak. "Good advice."

"Ah, I see my friends," Childric said, spotting a group of young sailors across the wharf. "I must hurry and catch them." He gave Adella an earnest smile. "It was good to see you, cousin! Take care of yourself. Be safe."

Adella bid him goodbye and waited for the schooner, watching the crew flake the mainsail as the dock boats brought the vessel into port. Finally, they finished mooring and began to unload cargo while Adella waited for an opportunity to speak to one of the mates. As one sailor concluded business with the dock porter, Adella stepped forward to inquire if the ship was available to charter.

"Depends on where you're heading," the sailor replied. She was older, and dressed in a crisp, black jacket with polished silver buttons, her dark hair tied back in a queue like her fellow crewmen.

"I need to get to Pentz," Adella replied. "It's a matter of urgency."

"Pentz?" The sailor gave Adella an appraising look. "We just came from Pentz, and were glad to make it through."

Adella furrowed her brow. "What do you mean?"

"You haven't heard?" the sailor asked incredulously. "A reaver ship has taken to stalking the Isles there, hiding out in the Folly. Fortunately, we did not catch sight of it."

"I need to get there quickly," Adella replied. "Reavers or no. Could I speak with your captain?"

"Yes." The sailor looked at Adella expectantly for a moment, then let out a laugh. "I am the captain of *The Bluebell*. Captain Loring."

"Oh," Adella replied. "I'm sorry, I didn't realize—"

"Understandable." Captain Loring smiled. "No hat. Lost it in a squall." She ran a hand over her hair. "I do feel quite naked without it." Loring paused in solemnity for her loss before continuing, "As to your question, I'm afraid it's too dangerous. My answer will have to be no."

"I see," Adella sighed. "It's too bad *The Tigress* left already. Captain Declan would have taken me."

"You know Captain Declan?" Captain Loring asked.

Adella nodded. "I've known him a long time," she admitted, unable to hide a note of sadness.

"You must be Adella Grimless?" Loring guessed.

Adella blinked at her in disbelief. "How did you know?"

Loring shrugged one shoulder. "Anyone who knows Declan has heard your name."

"I must get to Pentz, and quickly," Adella insisted. "A lot of people are depending on me to bring back help; I can't let them down."

"I won't endanger my crew by going back," Loring replied with a shake of her head.

"I understand you're responsible for their safety. However, you did say you just made it through safely," Adella countered. "You could do it again. But if I go back empty-handed, my people won't be so lucky."

"I'm sorry," Loring said, waving a hand dismissively, "but I can't help you."

"Listen," Adella began firmly. "The people of Elldon are all that stands between Valenna and the Sornian army. Raymouth is still reeling from the plague. If the Sornians make it here, it'll fall easily. Then where will you flee? We are fighting with our lives to keep the war off your doorstep, and we need help. Badly."

Loring pressed her lips together, considering her answer. "Maybe we can make a deal."

The Bluebell set sail in fair winds. Adella and Misses Asher spent most of their time on the main deck enjoying the cool breeze under the hot, summer sun. Soon, they came upon the many forested islands that dotted the coast in the area. Pentz was located on the easternmost shores of Belgrand Bay, the sea receding so far into Valenna that the famous port city was situated nearly in the center of the country. The waters, therefore, were usually calm and easy to sail, but the crew kept a watchful eye as they passed through the Isles. There had been no sign of sea serpents, or reaver ships, or even of *The Tigress*, though Adella wouldn't admit to herself that she was searching for its striped sails over the bright blue waves.

While the crew dropped anchor and readied the ship's longboat for shore, Adella and Misses Asher waited on deck with their bags in hand. The wind had picked up significantly by the time they arrived, and Adella had to clutch at her light, summer skirts to keep them in a respectable order. Beside her, Captain Loring surveyed the horizon to the southwest as a squawking flock of large, white seabirds soared above them, heading inland.

"What is it?" Adella asked.

"Seems there's foul weather rolling in," Loring replied. "Mind you don't get caught in it."

Adella looked toward Belgrand Bay. Though the sun was sinking low, the sky appeared clear over the water as far as she could see. Shrugging to herself, she tucked her bag under her arm and followed Misses Asher to the longboat. They said their thanks to the captain and crew as they disembarked and were rowed to shore. As Adella and Misses Asher walked down the wharf heading toward the city, they could hear Captain Loring giving orders to batten everything down.

As they entered the city, tall brick buildings rose high above them, their red facades starkly contrasted by pale windows, dormers, and columns. The buildings were so tall and grand, their designs so uniform and clean, that Adella couldn't help but let out a small gasp as the sheer scale of the city made her feel small and inconsequential. The surrounding architecture was of a newer, simpler style than that of the Capital, which had more ancient and ornate decoration, and yet it was much more refined than the plain fieldstone buildings that she was accustomed to seeing in Elldon. The streets were lined with massive, symmetrical terraced houses with entrances that opened directly onto the cobblestones, giving the city a very closed-in feeling that made Adella more anxious the further they went.

As they passed a wide lane, they caught a glimpse of the sprawling grounds of Lord Endlebridge's Estate not far off, with its long, sloping front lawn that led down to the main street that edged the shore. Misses Asher nudged Adella as they passed, pointing out the estate to her as they continued through the city.

Turning down one of the narrow side-streets, they came to a modest inn. A creaking, wooden sign hung by the entrance, depicting a wooly sheep, laying with a loaf of bread between his forelimbs, and the name The Lamb's Quarters written beneath it in red. The inn was crowded inside, and it was getting dark by the time the innkeeper showed them to their chamber. Adella tossed her tapestry bag onto the floor and retired to one of the bedsteads, eager to be done with the day.

Waiting for the sun to rise the next morning, Adella sat at the edge of the bedstead in the glow of the lantern and wrote in her notebook. Soon, faint light illuminated the edges of the curtains, and she peeked between them to view the early morning sky when rustle of fabric behind her caught her attention. "Misses Asher?" she asked quietly, turning to look. "Are you awake?"

"Awake enough," Misses Asher muttered. She rubbed her face and sat up, her eyes staring sleepily at nothing in particular.

"Good! No time to waste," Adella began, digging through her bag and pulling out a handful of hair pins. She gathered up her waist-length, auburn hair and secured it into a hasty bun. "I'm going to head over to the governor's estate and see if I can track him down." She took her traveling clothes from the foot of the bed and pulled her riding breeches up beneath her shift.

"Not so fast," Misses Asher replied, grabbing her rucksack and pulling out pieces of clothing. "It's Saturday," she said pointedly, but Adella only blinked at her. "The estate is open to the public in the summer months, with formal events at the end of the week," she explained. "We could walk right into the estate, sure. But only if we're dressed for it. Not to mention," she added, "you're Lady Grimless now; you'll need to look the part if you want to be taken seriously."

Adella sighed in resignation. "Right." Rifling through her own bag, she pulled out the red bodice and petticoat and dressed quickly without bothering to remove her breeches. She exchanged her patched-up leather riding boots for little ivory shoes with a wooden heel and pointed toe. *Let's hope I don't have to get anywhere in a hurry,* she thought, slipping them on over her stockings. Then, fishing around in her bag, she pulled out a small knife in a leather sheath.

"Is that really necessary?" Misses Asher asked, wrinkling her nose in disapproval.

"It's better to have a blade and not need one," Adella assured her, "than need one and not have it." It was a habit she had learned from Kol, who always had his own knife handy. The one time he had lent it to her, she had certainly ended up needing it. Turning her own blade over in her hand, she wondered how he was faring. A burning sensation gripped her chest when she hoped he would make it back safely. Adella couldn't help wondering where he was and what he was doing at that moment, worrying if he was safe or had been injured somehow. After all of her losses lately, she couldn't bear the thought of anything happening to him, too. *Oh, quit!* Adella scolded herself, trying to push her anxieties away. *If anyone can make it safely across the Campos and back, it's Kol.*

"You'll not be needing that in Pentz," Misses Asher replied, packing her things away. "So hide it well."

"Right, then." Adella tucked the sheathed knife into her bodice, then set her wide-brimmed straw hat on her head and tied it on with ribbon, making a bow at the back of her head. She then stuffed the notebook into her haversack and, pulling the strap over her shoulder, turned to leave. "Let's be off."

Passing a mirror on the wall, Adella stopped as her breath caught in her throat. For just a moment, she thought she saw her mother looking back at her from the glass, with the ruby necklace gleaming on her chest. It had been a while since Adella had dressed in such finery, since she'd lately been wearing more practical clothes at Elldon, and her reflection had caught her by surprise. The image before her now was one of a proper Valennian Lady with her head held high, standing primly in bold scarlet. *Misses Asher was right about the clothing,* she conceded. *It does make a difference.* Blinking tears away, she took a deep breath and straightened her hat. *Perhaps this will go well, after all,* she thought.

Adella and Misses Asher pushed through the crowds outside in the market square toward the open gates of the Governor's Estate. Adella glanced westward where the sea edged the city along the wharf, but the sky still looked clear. Putting Belgrand Bay behind them, they turned down the lane to the estate. Ahead of them stood the tall, symmetrical building, composed of red brick and embellished with white-painted dormers along its slate roof. They passed beneath two rows of broad linden trees that lined the way, sheltering the approaching guests from the sun. Other people walked to and fro, or chatted in idle groups. For others, it might have been a lovely day, but Adella steeled her nerves and walked onward with determination. *I will meet with Endlebridge and hire his troops,* she told herself, tugging on the red sleeves of her bodice to smooth out the wrinkles. *No matter what.*

They passed through the tall gate, made their way up steps and through open doors, where they entered a spacious reception hall, covered in well-polished walnut paneling. Brass candelabras lined the walls between massive portrait paintings in gilded frames. Overhead, a winged staircase echoed with the sound of footsteps as several young women in aprons made their way downward.

"Aunt Bea!" one of the girls called out. Passing the bundle of linens in her arms to another maid beside her, she ran over to greet Misses Asher. "What a surprise! Did I miss your letter?" she asked. There was a strong family resemblance; the girl had the same large, brown eyes as both Misses Asher and James.

"No, we didn't have time to write first." Misses Asher turned toward Adella. "Lady Grimless, this is the niece I told you about, Noella Fitch."

"You can call me Nell, if you like," the young woman said, smiling warmly. "I've heard so much about you, I feel as though we've already met." Nell watched the other young girls disappear down the corridor. "Come with me; I'll give you a tour of the estate."

"No time for that," Adella countered. "I need to speak with Lord Endlebridge urgently."

"He's out on the green," Nell replied cheerily, guiding Adella with a touch on the arm. "Follow me."

They followed Nell through the dark paneled corridor, passing by doorways that led into grand, formal spaces, until they came to the rear entrance. They stepped out into the bright light of day once more and into a large, grassy courtyard, where well-dressed ladies in colorful silks stood about holding wooden mallets, with ribbons fluttering from their sun hats on the light breeze. The rich, clipped grass of the court was embedded with small, metal hoops and little flags arranged in rectangles, with striped pegs at the center. In the distance beyond the lawn, the land swelled upward, with a high view of fields and trees further out from the brick buildings of the town.

Adella took in the sight, then searched the people nearby. "And where is he? Lord Endlebridge."

"Oh, this isn't the green," Nell replied. "This is the courtyard." She pointed up toward the rise beyond the lawn, where a long, low building sprawled under tall trees. "The green is further out, past the stables and barracks on the hill, there. He's gone riding, you see; we'd best wait for him here."

Adella let out a long breath, shoulders falling. "Oh, you can't be serious..." she muttered to herself.

"Will you play a game of croquet with me while we wait?" Nell asked her with a grin, nearly giddy at the idea.

"Shouldn't you be working?" Misses Asher suggested.

Nell shrugged. "Then who would entertain our esteemed guest here?" she asked, smiling innocently and gesturing toward Adella.

Adella glanced sideways at Misses Asher. "You're certain he will return here?"

"Of course," Nell replied. "He always comes to greet the guests at tea. I promise, you'll see him soon."

"All right then," Adella replied. "Might as well."

Nell gave a little cry of delight and scurried over to a wooden rack that housed the mallets and colorful croquet balls, returning with her arms full of equipment. "Do you know how to play," she asked, handing over a mallet, "or should I explain it?"

"I think I remember well enough." In truth, Adella hadn't played croquet since moving to Greywood Manor years ago, and she wasn't really sure she remembered the rules. It was a game for well-tended lawns, not the horse pastures and open prairie of Elldon. The contrast reminded her how out-of-place she felt at Pentz.

"Guest's choice," Nell offered. "Red is first."

"Red then, I suppose," Adella replied, and Nell handed her the red and yellow balls, leaving Misses Asher to keep score.

Placing the red ball before the first hoop, Adella swung at it with her mallet and hit only air. "Just a bit rusty," she admitted with a sheepish smile. She tried again, this time making contact with the ball, though it rolled feebly across the grass at an unintended angle, stopping short of the first hoop and too far to the right.

Nell smiled blankly at Adella, then proceeded with her turn, rolling up her sleeves with a look of determination on her face. Her strike sent the blue ball crashing beside Adella's. Nell walked over to where they lay and stepped on her own ball, knocking it hard with the mallet, and the impact sent Adella's red one rolling off the court. Then, she proceeded to hit her ball straight through the first hoop.

"I'm not sure that's how—" Adella began to protest, then, frowning, watched Nell continue to knock the ball through each of the hoops around the court. Adella wondered if they used different rules in Pentz than the ones she had learned.

"She's a known cheater," Misses Asher commented wryly.

"Perhaps we should head in," Adella suggested, her patience waning. "Take our seats."

"We can't quit now; I haven't won yet," Nell pleaded. "I very much wish to tell my friends I beat Your Ladyship at croquet." She pressed her palms together in supplication, pouting her lower lip.

"Oh, all right," Adella huffed. "But make it quick." With that, she struck her yellow ball; it missed the hoop entirely, rolling far beyond the boundary of the court. "Ugh," she groaned, rubbing her face with her hand.

Nell snickered, and readied her mallet. Before she could strike, the chime of a large bell rang out over the lawn, and she looked at Adella with widened eyes.

"What's that?" Adella asked.

Nell, apparently pretending not to have heard, continued to quickly knock the ball around the courtyard until it finally struck the peg. "Ha!" she cheered to herself, hopping in celebration. Around the lawn, the other guests looked in her direction as they made their way toward the entrance. Nell dropped her mallet and ran toward Adella and Misses Asher. "Hurry!" she urged, pulling them by their elbows. "We must get to the ballroom."

She led them through the halls and into an airy room with high-vaulted ceilings, its cream walls lined with pale, grey-green pilasters and wainscoting. Round tables were set with porcelain and silver. "Oh good," Nell said, looking around the room. "He's not here yet. Let's have tea, shall we?" she asked. Not waiting for a response, she directed them to take a seat at one table, then joined them with a tea tray from the sideboard that stood beneath a wide, arched window. The view looked out to the west toward the street that lined the wharf, with the Bay glimmering just beyond.

Nell placed a silver strainer over Adella's cup and poured tea into it from the pot. "This is a blend of Madorran black tea, rose petals, and vanilla, which has been brought all the way across the Greater Sea..."

Outside the ballroom, footsteps echoed from the hallway. Adella turned her head in time to see a large group of well-dressed men and women pass by the open doorways. *Is that the Governor?* Adella wondered. Overcome by frustration, she rose from her seat. "I'm sorry," she began, turning back toward Nell, "but I really must—"

Her words hung in the air as movement caught her eye from outside the nearby window. Across the wide lawn, a rider in the street struggled with his horse as it refused to go forward. The man kicked the animal's sides relentlessly, but still it balked. As he smacked its rump with a riding crop, the horse spun on its haunches, and man clung desperately to its neck before falling on his backside onto the cobblestones. Bolting away from the water, the horse galloped between the linden trees of the lane, then turned, hooves slashing marks in the perfectly manicured front lawn of the Governor's Estate, before disappearing from view. Adella was relieved to see the rider pick himself up off the ground and trudge off sullenly after his mount, apparently unharmed, though perhaps deserving of the tumble. She wondered what had spooked the animal, as all seemed peaceful outside. Even the waters of the Bay looked unusually low and calm.

"Sit, please," Nell said, motioning to the chair. "He will be here soon, I promise." She waited until Adella sat back down before pouring milk into her cup. "So what brings you both to Pentz?" Nell took a sip from her teacup, blinking her doe-like eyes at them expectantly.

"As I said, I need to speak with Lord Endlebridge," Adella explained. "I intend to offer him whatever payment is necessary in order to hire his regiment, or even half. We are in a bad situation on the border."

Nell nodded sympathetically. "I heard what happened to Elldon. I'm so sorry. But your arrival here is perfect timing." She leaned in to whisper, "I overheard that the estate just lost a shipment to reavers in the Isles; Endlebridge will be looking for ways to make up for such a heavy loss."

Adella nodded. Taking a sip, she inhaled the fine fragrance of expensive tea and willed herself to relax. "So, Nell," she ventured, making conversation. "It must be wonderful to live so near to the beaches?"

"Ah," Nell replied, a little bashfully. "It is, but... I can't swim," she admitted. "Though I do like to walk the shore at sunset."

"That sounds lovely," Adella replied.

"Are your parents liking their new place?" Misses Asher asked her niece. "They moved uptown to the market district, is that right?"

"Mhm," Nell replied, swallowing her tea. "One of the townhouses up in Battle Alley. Further from the water, but the rent is better for them now, with my father being out of work. They like it well enough, though Papa always complains of the echoes from the blacksmith in the early morning..." The two women continued to discuss family matters while Adella poured herself more tea.

Setting her cup down, Adella noticed a delicate clanking sound issue from the porcelain. Each dish on the table began to rattle; the clatter grew until the dishes shook violently and the table trembled. Above their heads, the massive chandelier swayed back and forth on its chain.

"What's happening?" Nell asked, her eyes widening while she looked around.

"Tremors," Adella replied. Rising to her feet, she motioned for the others to follow. "Come, let's get clear of the chandeliers."

Everyone huddled in small groups lined up against the walls, listening as the porcelain and crystal clanked around them. Adella stood with Misses Asher and Nell as they pressed against the wainscoting beside the window.

"You've seen this sort of thing before?" Nell asked, twisting the corner of her apron in her fingers.

"It's been happening in the Campos," Misses Asher replied. "It should calm—"

Her words were interrupted by a large crash as Adella's heart leapt into her throat; on the far side of the room, a massive brass chandelier fell to the floor in a shattering of crystal. Screams erupted as people scattered away from the pile of broken metal and glass, edging their way along the walls. The cries of alarm tapered off into nervous muttering as the clinking and rattling around them abated, all eyes fixed on the ceiling. Adella watched, pulse pounding loudly in her ears, as the swinging of the chandeliers gradually began to still. Searching over the room, Adella breathed a sigh of relief to see no one appeared to be injured.

"Is it over?" Nell asked as people began to leave the safety of the walls and disperse around the room once more, talking fervently amongst themselves.

"Looks like it," Misses Asher replied, and the two turned to head back toward their table.

Adella began to follow, but stopped when she heard a low, distant roar. "Do you hear that?" she asked, looking around. Turning toward the window, her stomach dropped. A massive wave of dark water rose up in the distance, churning over the Bay, breaking white and foamy over the jetties. The room around her erupted in screams as people dashed for the door. Adella stood frozen.

She watched the oncoming flood overturn and engulf the small fishing boats along the shore, then crash over the wharf and into the street, sweeping away carriages and trees in an instant. As the roiling waves bounded over the front lawn of the governor's estate, she knew they wouldn't have time to get out of the building before the water hit. She turned back toward the crowded doorway, urging the others through calmly though her heartbeat hammered in her chest. The room darkened around them. Glancing behind, Adella saw the wall of inky water just outside the window.

Glass shattered as seawater burst into the room, flooding across the floor and nearly knocking Adella off her feet. Her shoes were swept away while she trudged her way forward. She pressed in behind the others as they finally cleared the threshold, and then followed at the back of the group down the dimly-lit hallway as cold water tugged at her ankles, rising higher with each step. Ahead, the wall to the left gave way to a narrow staircase. Adella grabbed Misses Asher's elbow. "The stairs!" she yelled over the roar of the water. "Go up the stairs!"

They crowded at the base of the stairway as people, shoving and tripping amid frantic screams, made their way upward. Seawater rose to her knees while Adella waited for the others to ascend, looking up and down the hall to be sure no one was left behind. As she urged Nell and Misses Asher up the steps, a sudden surge hit her in the chest, knocking her into the stair rail. As she clung to it, gasping for air, Nell's foot slipped and she dunked downward. With one hand gripping the rail, Adella grabbed the young woman by her arm and, fighting against the current, pulled her back up.

Adella pushed upward against Nell's back while the two fought their way through the rushing flood and up the first few steps. Another wave crashed down the hall and buffeted against Adella, pulling her stockinged feet out from under her. Cold, murky seawater crashed over her head, overtaking her senses; it flooded up her nose and into her ears, filling her mouth with the taste of salt. Pain wrapped around her ribs as the leather strap of her haversack dug into her side and she rose up through the water.

Adella gasped as her head broke through the surface, and looked up into the face of Misses Asher, who, with a grip on the strap, desperately pulled her against the current.

"Grab my hand!" Nell shouted beside her aunt, straining to reach out to Adella without losing her grip on the handrail. Adella flung her arm as far out as she could, scrambling to get a foothold. Their fingertips brushed together as another surge of water battered her with debris. A jagged piece of broken furniture rammed into her back, scraping across her shoulder, tearing at her clothes and skin. The strap around her broke free of her body, and Adella was pulled down into the deluge.

"No!" Nell yelled. Beside her, Misses Asher was left holding the broken haversack as Adella was swept down the dark hallway, disappearing beneath the water.

6

The Campos

The skewbald mare mouthed at the bit, her hind end swinging around while she pranced in place. "Calm down, will you?" Kol muttered, adjusting the bow slung over his shoulder.

"Are you ready, Mister Kol?" Martin called out from atop a lanky chestnut, trotting in impatient circles around them. Kol noticed Martin was also armed with a bow and a quiver of arrows, along with a large hunting knife. He wondered if the merchant knew how to use them. Looking toward Greywood, Kol searched the windows for a familiar silhouette. He didn't want to head out into the Campos without seeing Adella first, not only to say goodbye, but also to lend her his knife. She had knives of her own, of course, but this one was different. It always made its way back to him and, if Adella had it on her, that meant she would, too.

"I can't hold this creature back any longer," Martin shouted over his shoulder and trotted off westward.

Kol's horse let out an anxious whinny. "All right, hold still," he chided as he placed a foot in the stirrup and swung up into the saddle. He threw one last glance toward the manor, but still there was no sign of Adella. He slacked the reins, and the horse didn't wait to be cued before trotting off after Martin.

They traveled across the tall summer grass, with the horses eventually settling into a brisk walking pace. The Campos stretched out wide before them, a sea of endless green waves rippling gently in the warm breeze. The monotonous scenery and the droning hum of insects lulled Kol into a sense of peace, but he refused to let his guard down, knowing there could be Sornian soldiers lurking beyond any rise in the landscape. He considered that they may come across Misses Asher's party on their travels, as they'll be passing Compass Point. The large rock formation was a favorite waymarker, as well as camping spot, due to its high vantage point.

Kol kept a careful lookout as they traveled, but his mind began to turn back to Greywood Manor. He wondered what message Armand had been tasked with delivering, and to whom it was addressed, which brought to mind the crumpled up ball of paper Adella had left by the hearth. Kol had gone to bed after she had discarded it, leaving Armand in the parlor alone. The next morning, it was gone. *Did Armand pick up Declan's letter?* he wondered.

"What do you think?" Martin asked, interrupting his thoughts. Martin was looking at him expectantly, and Kol realized he had been inadvertently ignoring the man's attempt at conversation while lost in his own musings. "Did you hear what I said?" Martin prodded.

"No," Kol replied. "What did you say?"

"Ah, nevermind." Martin shifted in the saddle.

They continued to travel in silence. Kol's backside was becoming sore, and he released his feet from the stirrup irons to stretch his muscles. Then, he remembered the mare liked to suddenly dump people in the grass and bolt back home, and quickly put his feet back into the stirrups. Once more, he lost himself in his thoughts, and it occurred to him that the message Adella sent Armand to deliver might have been an answer to Declan's letter. His brow furrowed tightly as the thought left a heavy, sinking feeling in his gut.

"Isn't that amusing?" Martin's voice interrupted Kol's thoughts once more.

"What?" Kol looked over at Martin, realizing he hadn't heard anything the man said.

"It's not important," Martin said dejectedly.

Kol sighed. "Tell me about yourself," he prompted, feeling guilty and trying to make amends. "Do you have family in Raymouth?"

"No," Martin answered. "I'm on my own. Since my mother passed, I've put all my efforts into the mercantile, I've never really had time for much else. Of course, I've spent my nights now and then with some decent women, but I'm not the marrying sort." He fell uncharacteristically quiet for a moment. "How about yourself?" Martin asked finally.

Kol shook his head. "No, I don't have family." He was surprised to find he no longer felt ashamed to admit it.

"Oh," Martin replied. "Well, what an exciting life you must have. Out here on the frontier, galloping through the wilderness, fighting back the raiders..." he trailed off wistfully. "I've never ridden this much in my life," he admitted with a grin. "How am I doing?"

Kol laughed. "You're doing just fine."

"That's good to hear," Martin said, brightening at the encouragement. "Like I was saying before," he continued one of the stories he had previously abandoned, "as the Madorrans don't care to speak our Modern Andolinian, and very few Valennians have had the chance to learn Madorran, it's given us all a load of trouble filling out our dock books. I've resorted to hiring a translator I'm fairly certain is, in fact, a smuggler—" He grimaced nervously. "I hope I don't regret it. Anyway, I had to give explicit instructions that the cargo be unloaded in my presence only, no one else will be permitted to sign for me." He looked over to see if Kol was still paying attention. Kol nodded in his direction, which was encouragement enough to keep the man going. "Not even my agent, Mister Kerchaw," Martin lifted a finger in the air for emphasis. "He's aboard *The Evarro*—that's the Madorran ship," he explained as an aside, "in my stead, as I've only recently got over the ague. Which is a whole other story..." he droned on.

The late afternoon grew hotter as the gentle wind tapered off completely. Black flies hovered over their heads, swooping down to take bites of flesh whenever given the chance. Pulling the brim of his hat lower over his face for shade, Kol surveyed the wide landscape for signs of other travelers who might have passed through the area. He had redoubled his efforts to listen to the merchant's chatter, nodding or smiling at what he guessed would be appropriate moments, but it was hard to pay attention when he had no idea what the man was talking about. As the sun moved lower in the west, shining clear and bright in their eyes, he turned his thoughts toward finding a place to camp for the night.

"...that's how I know Captain Declan," Martin said, and Kol's attention returned immediately to the conversation at the mention of a familiar name. "Through his father, rest his soul, back when I hired him to command my tea runners. Declan and Lady Grimless, can you believe it?" Martin mused. "Poor fellow."

"Why do you say that?" Kol asked. "'Poor fellow?'"

"Well—" Martin began, momentarily at a loss for words. "That's aiming a bit high, isn't it? Even for a sea captain." He shook his head. "It won't last. She'll move on as soon as someone of a higher class comes along."

Kol's expression soured. "Don't speak ill of Adella in front of me," he said flatly. He wasn't sure if any of what Martin said was true, but he didn't want to hear it either way.

"Forgive me," Martin's gaze shifted downward as he fiddled with the reins in his hands. "I didn't mean anything by it." He sat silently in the saddle as their two horses continued walking side-by-side.

Kol let out a breath. "Go on with your story," he prompted. "You were sick with the red ague?"

"I've told that one already," Martin replied. "Don't you remember?"

Kol looked blankly at him. *I volunteered for this,* he reminded himself. He couldn't help but give a tired laugh, though it was loud enough that Martin began to chuckle sheepishly along with him.

Finding scant cover beside a patch of shrubs and brambles, they stopped to make camp for the night. They weren't far from Compass Point and could see its dark form rising out from the undulating plains to the west, like the prow of a ship in a sea of green. Kol noted their good luck that the skies were clear and the ground dry beneath their feet, though he had packed for foul weather. He'd been given a lot of good clothing and useful items when Adella cleared out the rooms in Greywood, including a large oilskin cloak and a selection of weapons and hats. He knew they likely had belonged to her father or brother but, not wanting to cause her pain, he didn't ask. Though she was able to mention her parents without being overcome by grief, whenever her brother was mentioned, she would change the subject quickly, so Kol was always careful to avoid it.

"Shall we make a fire?" Martin asked, pulling his longbow off over his shoulder. "I've heard there are wolves out here."

Kol shook his head. "The wolves have never bothered us. It's the Sornians you should watch out for."

"But..." Martin began hesitantly. "You are a..." He trailed off, looking a bit worried for himself.

Kol rummaged through one of the saddlebags, searching for his waterskin, but stopped at the distinct sound of rustling leaves from behind him. His mare began to snort, the whites of her eyes showing in fear. He grabbed the reins to steady her, but she braced and pulled against his hand. "Shh, Ember. Calm yourself," he coaxed, to no avail. The horse stamped at the ground, preparing to rear. Kol looked over at Martin, who was nocking an arrow already. Kol knew if Ember were to get loose now, she would head straight back to Greywood, and he would be horseless the rest of their journey. She was a fast and tireless mount, which had made it worth the risk. At least, it seemed worth it when he chose her. Now, he wasn't so sure.

"It's probably just an animal," Kol said. "But we need to get away, or I'll lose my horse." He led the mare away from the patch of shrubs and toward the open field. Glancing back, he could see Martin reluctantly go to collect the chestnut horse, with bow and arrow still in hand.

A long, shrill squeal sounded from the shrubs. Kol looked to see a large shadow dart out of the bushes and head straight toward them. Ember jerked her head up, snorting loudly through her flared nostrils as she tried to bolt out of hand. It was all Kol could do to keep hold of her, turning in tight circles.

"Don't let go," Martin said. "I've got this."

Kol wasn't sure he believed that, and prepared himself for what might happen next. The animal charged across the grass, pale tusks jutting sharply upward from its jaw as it headed straight at him. He knew he would have to let the horse go to draw his cutlass to defend himself, and he had held off long enough.

As Kol released the reins, an arrow whizzed through the air, lodging into the charging beast's head with a sharp crack. Kol grabbed the reins again before Ember could bolt away, and watched as the creature fell over on its side, its sharp little hooves clawing helplessly at the ground for a moment, then lay still.

"Ha!" Martin said loudly, walking his horse over to where the animal lay motionless. "Got it."

As Ember quieted, Kol brought her over to join Martin. He looked down on the dark form lying in the grass with the arrow sticking straight out of its broad, hairy forehead.

"I've never seen boar out here before," Kol commented, crouching down to inspect the animal. He looked up at Martin in disbelief. "You hit it right between the eyes."

"Well, that's where I was aiming," Martin said blankly.

Kol laughed. "You're pretty good with that thing."

"My father taught me how to use a bow when I was very young," Martin explained. "We would often go hunting together." He smiled at the memory. "If we make a fire," he suggested, "we could have a nice supper."

"No fire." Kol turned to lead his horse back toward their camping spot. "We've packed enough provisions." He hated to leave the meat behind, but the smoke would announce their presence to any enemies for leagues around.

Martin frowned, then sighed sadly and followed along, catching up to walk beside him. "All right, let's go eat cold bread."

Kol smirked. "You'll get used to it."

Kol awoke and looked around, trying to get his bearings. He couldn't tell the hour or even the direction he was facing, since he found himself completely surrounded by a dense, white fog. "Martin?" he called out. They had taken turns at watch in the night, Kol taking the first shift and Martin the second. "Are you there?" He rubbed his eyelids and squinted around again.

"Uh, yes," Martin's voice called out tentatively. Kol squinted at a dark form barely discernible in the fog. "I've really got to, uh, relieve myself, but dare not wander," Martin continued. "I think I would get lost." The man came into view as he approached, fumbling around in his travel bag. "I can't seem to find my compass... Suppose we'll just have to stay put until it passes."

Kol shook his head. "We don't have time for that. I don't want to be away from Greywood any longer than necessary." He pulled the knife from his boot. "We're just going dead west today until we hit Compass Point." Holding out a thumb, Kol carefully placed the tip of the dagger onto his thumbnail. With Martin watching closely, he rotated the blade until a faint line of shadow showed itself on the surface of the nail. "Ah," Kol said with satisfaction. Casually spinning the knife in his hand, he pointed it westward. "It's that way."

"Fascinating," Martin commented. He walked ahead while Kol readied the horses, which they had hobbled with rope before nightfall. Kol gave them each a handful from the bag of grain he had spared for them from the pantry at the manor, then led them in-hand to catch up with Martin. Eventually, the fog turned into drizzling rain, clearing the air somewhat as they rode toward the massive rock formation, now a hazy shape in the distance.

Martin shifted in the saddle as their horses walked side by side. Even Kol was starting to feel a bit bruised in the seat, but he hoped to make it past Compass Point to the little pool on its northwestern side before nightfall.

"So," Kol began, filling the gap in conversation. "Adella mentioned you're the richest man in Raymouth. Are you one of the nobility, too, then?"

"No, in fact," Martin replied. "My family came from little means, my father was a soldier. I heard you were a soldier as well?" Kol nodded and Martin continued, "After he was killed at the battle of Enth, Mother opened a little courier service to make ends meet, and as I got older, I helped her with it. We barely got by, for the most part..." His brow tensed. "Until, during one particularly high-paying job, I met the man who would become my mentor, Lord Heffield, of the Belgrand Bay Company." Martin looked over to see if he was still listening.

Kol felt a twinge of guilt at that. "Go on."

"Well," Martin continued, "I don't know why really, perhaps it was out of pity—" He pursed his lips. "But, he taught me everything he knew about the merchant business, and soon I was printing catalogs and chartering ships to haul cargo of my own. My mother's courier service became the Royal Westward Trading Company, a proper mercantile, though she didn't live to see it. With the King's backing, it grew large enough to rival Heffield's own Belgrand Bay Company. Heffield and I drifted apart after that, but I've always been grateful for the opportunity he gave me."

Kol waited until Martin's tale had come to an end before speaking. "A soldier's son, now the richest man in Raymouth?" Kol scratched his stubble. "Do you think I could do something like that, too? Make something more of myself."

"Certainly," Martin answered. "You don't want to work for Lady Grimless?"

"It's not like that," Kol replied quickly. "Believe me—" He stopped himself, catching the curious look Martin gave him. Kol pulled the brim of his hat lower against the rain. Though he had attempted to tie back his hair, much of it hung loose, damp and clinging to his forehead. "What I mean to say is..." He exhaled loudly. "She won't need to keep a guard forever. When the war is over, then what will I do?"

"Only you can answer that," Martin replied with a shrug. "But the most important thing, no matter what sort of business you take up, is learning to keep meticulous records. You will live or die by the accuracy of your ledger..." he carried on with his discourse in the misting rain, and Kol listened attentively this time.

They rounded Compass Point from the north side. Its prominent rocky face, dark with rain, loomed above them like a sentinel over the plains. They stopped to dismount and stretch their sore limbs beneath the high precipice as Kol looked about for signs of passers-by. He recalled, somewhat wistfully, this was where he first met Armand, along with Teressa, when he and Adella had camped here for a night.

"Over here," Martin said, pointing to the ground.

Kol came to investigate and found the remains of a campfire, now nothing more than a patch of white ash in the bare soil at the base of the stone precipice. Crouching down, he stuck his finger into the soft white powder, and found it was still warm beneath the wet surface. "It's a day old, perhaps," he guessed.

"Sornian?" Martin asked.

Kol looked around at the ground, at the footprints in the soil. They were marred by the rain, but he could still make out some tracks. "Valennian," he said, motioning toward one clear print that was much smaller than the others. "The Sornians don't allow women in their ranks."

"Must be our Misses Asher," Martin guessed. "That's good news."

"We could've passed right by them in the fog," Kol mused with a smile. It was a relief to think the missing party would soon be back at Greywood to help in its defense. Compass Point lay roughly halfway between Elldon and the Sornian army's main encampment in the western Campos, and was only a few days' journey from either location. As it was still too early to make camp, they hopped back into their saddles and headed northwest, following along the path that Kol and Adella had taken on their way to Sornia in the spring. Their next waymarker would be the small pool where Adella had caught an eel, and the freshwater had oddly turned brackish overnight. He wondered if it still would be.

7

A Turn of the Blade

Kol leaned over the edge of rock and peered down into the darkness that lay just below his feet. The air that wafted up from below was cold and briny, smelling of fish. "Stay back," he warned.

"What's down there?" Martin wondered aloud. A pebble slipped out from beneath his boot and rolled along the slanted ground, then downward through the wide opening, disappearing into the abyss.

"I don't know," Kol admitted. "But the area isn't stable." The two men stepped backward from the edge. "This was a freshwater pool when I came here last." Kol sucked his cheek, remembering. "Adella broke it." A smile curled one side of his mouth. "Broke the bottom out. Then, it became brackish."

"She did not," Martin muttered pensively. "That doesn't make any sense. Where's the water now?"

Kol shrugged. "Come on," he motioned, shepherding Martin away from the ledge. "If you fall in, I'm leaving you to the eels."

"The what?" Martin asked. Kol merely chuckled to himself as the two men mounted up into the saddles again and continued westward.

Kol and Martin rode through the high scrubland until dusk, then dismounted and hobbled the horses. They sat amongst the fragrant prairie sages and shared some dried-out bread, then Martin brought out a flask from his waistcoat. He offered it to Kol. "Tell me," Martin began, "how did you get burdened with taking me to Smuggler's Port?" He cracked a smile, "Lady Grimless bribe you?"

Honey-sweet liquor burned Kol's throat as he took a swig, then shook his head. "She needed someone to do it, so I offered."

"You offered?" Martin asked, rubbing his chin pensively.

"Of course," Kol admitted, looking down at nothing in particular. "I would do anything for Adella." He had noticed that her responsibilities were starting to weigh heavily on her, and he wanted to help in any way he could. Glancing up, Kol caught Martin giving him a peculiar look. "What's that face for?" Kol asked, pointing at him.

Martin raised his brows innocently. "What face? I'm not making a face." He took a long pull from the flask. "So..." he began hesitantly, handing the flask to Kol again. "What about Declan?"

Kol frowned. "What about him?"

"I just thought," Martin said with a grimace. "The two of them..."

Kol took a drink before responding. "It's none of my business," he replied. "Or yours. But... I don't think it's true."

"I see," Martin said quietly.

"I'll take the first watch," Kol offered, eager to change the subject.

"Good." Martin spread his jacket over the grass to lie down, then folded his hands behind his head and yawned loudly. "I've never been so tired in my life." He closed his eyes and went to sleep.

It was Martin's turn to keep watch, and he passed the time searching the stars for familiar constellations. He often had taken up the role of supercargo aboard the ships that he chartered for his mercantile, and had developed an interest in navigation during his voyages as a way to pass the time. He crossed his arms and let out a sigh, staring up into the clear night sky. The air was warm and still, with the gentle chirrup of crickets lulling him into a feeling of serenity. He stood upon a small hill, not far from where he left Kol and the horses.

He searched for the constellation of the Wagon, and then found the North Star. Under the moonlight, he rifled through his haversack and brought out a little navigational instrument made of brass and wood. He lifted the quadrant to his eye, lined the eyepiece up with the North Star, and adjusted the brass fittings.

Martin had nearly gotten the alignment just right when he heard the snap of a twig close behind him. Turning, he saw the glint of metal in the moonlight as a dark figure behind him raised an arm. Martin fumbled around for the handle of his knife, but didn't have time to draw it before he heard a hoarse cry of pain. The man's body dropped down into the grass, with the shadowy form of a man standing over him.

"You didn't hear him coming up behind you?" Kol scolded, his voice quiet but heavy with reproof.

"No," Martin admitted. "What happened?"

"He didn't hear *me*." Kol wiped his knife on his breeches. "Pack up, we're heading north."

"Was that a Sornian?" Martin asked, following quickly after Kol as they headed back to their camp.

"Just a scout," Kol replied in a low voice. "An inexperienced one, thankfully, but that means there's a squadron nearby. So keep quiet until we reach the coast."

Dawn finally rose as the two travelers came to the high bluffs that formed the coastline. Kol reined in his horse and looked over Belgrand Bay, with its turbulent waves nearly black in the grey light of an overcast morning. The sea always seemed so cold and unwelcoming, he wondered how anyone could bear to spend their days sailing upon it, let alone prefer it to any other way of living. The bleak view of the sea turned his thoughts to the warm comforts of Greywood, which felt more like home to him than any other place he had lived. Kol hoped that, when the hostilities between the two countries ended and their town was rebuilt, he could find a way to stay.

They continued along the bluffs westward, stopping only briefly to stretch their legs or give the horses a handful of grain. As evening fell, the wind changed, bringing with it the scent of rain. Martin, riding beside Kol, inhaled the damp air and cracked a smile. "I'd say we're in for it," he commented. "Do you think we'll arrive before the storm hits?"

"Maybe," Kol replied. "We're nearly there."

Martin watched the sea grow darker in the evening light while the horses plodded along the coast. "You know," he began thoughtfully, "I've never really had the time to slow down and take in my surroundings... I've always kept myself busy with the mercantile—catalogs and records, and the like. I may have saddle sores," he joked, "but I think this has been good for me. Though," he added, "it certainly will be nice to get back to civilization! I could do with a hot cup of tea." He rubbed his lower back. "And maybe a feather mattress."

Rain began to sprinkle on their faces, and Kol drew his cloak tighter around himself. "We might have different ideas of civilization."

Kol stood at the threshold of the Hare and Dove, shaking the rain from his hat. Thoroughly soaked under his oilskins, his clothes clung heavily to his sinewy frame. The night air had turned chilly when sheets of rain dumped down on them for the last hour of their journey. Their horses stood tied to a post by the inn's entrance. Perched at the end of the pier, the dilapidated old building's three slightly-crooked storeys teetered precariously over the Bay. Martin stood unusually quiet, wringing out the hem of his shirt with a frown.

"Now, remember," Kol warned, "this isn't Valenna. Don't trust anyone, don't talk to anyone." He put his hat back on his head and streams of water trickled down his brow. "Don't go anywhere, do anything, or *say* anything unless I tell you to. Do you understand?"

"Dangerous," Martin replied. "Got it."

Kol pulled the door open and they entered the dimly-lit space, hazy with smoke in the light of a hearthfire. An old woman with a candlestick greeted them. She stood tall enough to look down on Martin, and she did so with an appraising look. Martin shifted uncomfortably under her scrutiny.

She turned her attention to Kol. "You're wanting lodgings, I take it?"

"We'll take two of your best—" Martin began.

"One room," Kol interrupted him. "The cheapest."

"I suddenly regret bringing you along," Martin muttered sadly while the woman showed them the way, the two men leaving rain puddles on the stairs as they went. When she pulled out a key and opened the door, they looked in on a small, dark room with only a couple of thin mattresses on the floor on either side of a single window. Kol handed her coins and she passed him the candlestick and left.

"We have to sleep on the floor?" Martin asked with disappointment.

"Only for one night," Kol replied, setting the brass candle holder on the table. "I have to take the horses to the livery. Stay in this room. Don't even so much as go *downstairs* until I return," he instructed. "I'll be quick." With that, he left, closing the door behind him.

Martin shrugged off his haversack and cloak and sat down on a mattress in the dim candlelight. "All right," he said to himself, crossing his legs. "I'll just wait here, then. On the floor."

Kol had only been gone a few moments when Martin heard a knock on the door. He opened it to take a peek, and the innkeeper pushed her way in, carrying folded linens. "Can you believe this weather?" she asked, shoving the bundle into his arms. "It's been relentless since spring." She looked him over in the candlelight. "You just going to sit in here, sopping wet? If you care to come downstairs, I've got a hot stew ready."

"Oh," Martin began, thinking it over. "I shouldn't..." Kol had been pretty adamant about not leaving the room. *Though, he does seem to be a rather overstrung sort of fellow...* Martin reasoned. *This old woman clearly doesn't think it's dangerous.* His stomach growled loudly.

"How about a cup of tea?" she offered. Martin wavered, then gave in and followed her downstairs.

She directed him to sit at a table and brought out a bowl of thick stew, then a tray with a steaming pot of black tea before disappearing into the kitchen. Martin took a deep breath, inhaling the warm aroma of beef broth, and shoveled a spoonful into his mouth. The hearty stew was a welcome change from the dry bread and soggy cheese he had gotten by on while traveling across the Campos. *I don't know what Kol was worried about,* he thought, taking a sip of strong tea. Then, a faint sound came from across the room, and Martin realized he wasn't alone.

He looked around and noticed cloaked figures sitting at a table far in the corner, barely discernible in the deep shadows outside the glow of the lantern. One man rose to his feet and stepped into the light. Fine clothes showed from beneath his oilskins, and Martin caught the scent of lavender.

"Heffield, is that you?" Martin blinked in confusion as he recognized his old mentor. He set his teacup down. "What are you doing here?"

"Oh, I'm just here on business..." the older man said casually, but his voice was as cold as steel. At his cue, the other men rose and edged toward Martin.

Martin stood quickly, knocking over his chair and backing away. A bolt scraped into place on the kitchen door behind him, and panic rose in his chest.

One man reached under his cloak, and Martin heard the slither of metal. He threw himself backward just in time to see the blade of a knife narrowly miss his gut.

Martin drew his hunting knife. Brandishing it frantically, he held the men at bay. "What is the meaning of this?" He looked at Lord Heffield in disbelief. "Why?" Martin asked, unable to hide the pain in his voice. "What have I ever done to you? We were friends."

"Yes," Heffield replied flatly, the lines on his aged face deepening beneath a powdered wig. "We were. And that was my mistake." He stepped backward to give his men space. "Consider this your final lesson," he said, turning to leave. "How to handle competition." Then, Heffield walked out the door, leaving Martin to face the others.

Martin held out his hunting knife, slashing it back and forth through the air to hold back the four men who had come from the shadows at Heffield's bidding. "Whatever he's paying you," Martin pleaded, "I'll double it."

The only response was the cruel laughter of the foremost man as he raised his arm; the dagger in his hand gleamed golden as it reflected the lantern light. The man made to slash down on Martin, but his arm stopped in the air when a hand grabbed his wrist from behind. A blade punched through cloth and flesh. The man dropped to the ground, revealing a tall silhouette behind him, the dark-cloaked form blending in with the shadows.

The two nearest men turned on the cloaked figure between them, as the man to the far right lunged toward Martin with his blade. Martin felt the man's knife cut through his shirt, nicking the flesh beneath at the same moment Martin lunged forward, plunging his knife deep into the man's belly. Martin pulled the blade back, and the man crumpled onto the floor, writhing.

"Martin, go!" Kol shouted, and the urgency in the order compelled him to obey. Jumping clear of the blades, Martin skirted around the fray, but stopped when he found himself on the unguarded side of one of the men, whose attention now was entirely on Kol.

Rather than fleeing, Martin lunged toward the man, thrusting his blade toward his open side. Just when was sure his strike would hit home, he felt a hand clamp down around his wrist. His target had turned and twisted Martin's arm in a painful, vice-like grip. His flesh panged as cold metal drove into his side, sinking into his gut.

8

The Seaborn

Armand opened his eyes and, finding nothing but blackness, promptly shut them to try it again. His head throbbed. Blinking, he looked around once more. He could see nothing at all, but slowly, he became aware of the gentle noises that surrounded him. He could hear the deep breathing of others, and a slight but constant creaking sound that accompanied a swaying motion he had only just begun to notice. Putting a hand to his left cheekbone, a burning pain blossomed from the touch, and he realized he must have a black eye. The sensation was nothing new to him.

Armand searched his memory. He recalled riding into Raymouth, stabling his horse, and heading for the docks to search for Captain Declan. *Or did I?* he wondered. He couldn't remember. Surely, taking a look around would jog his memory. Armand sat up and immediately toppled over, swinging upside-down before hitting the hard floor with a thud. Groaning, he rubbed a palm over his pounding forehead. Footsteps came from the darkness, and soon the golden glow of lantern light illuminated his surroundings. Sleeping sailors filled hammocks that hung from the beams, and one swung empty above his head. *I must be aboard The Tigress, then,* he reasoned.

The lantern bearer approached with measured steps, and stopped directly in front of him. "You're awake," a deep but feminine voice said. "Finally."

Armand squinted in the sudden brightness, trying to make out the face. "Who are you?"

The woman laughed. "Come, Benramil. Let's not wake the others." Her voice had a foreign lilt to it.

Armand followed her up and across the weather deck. The way she called him by his first name in her soft accent seemed both strange and familiar. Even in the darkness, he could see her braided hair was stark white. A sword hung in a sheath at her side atop her ragged petticoats. He liked her already. They continued aft, Armand moving quickly to keep up as they passed under the dusky sky, dotted with stars.

She led him down into a private cabin. Judging by its location on the ship, Armand figured it must be the captain's cabin, though his head was spinning too much for him to care. In the center, several people sat at a table looking over a large, tattered map of Belgrand Bay. The woman motioned for him to take a seat and set down her lantern.

Armand plopped into the chair unceremoniously, grateful to take a rest as his stomach began to turn. A sour taste rose up within his throat, but he forced it back again.

"This is the man I told you about," the woman said.

"Ah," came a reply from across the table. "Glad to have you join us, finally." Armand looked up to see an unfamiliar face, glowering from beneath a large cocked hat.

"Where's the captain?" Armand asked, looking around the room for Declan but finding only strange faces.

The man in the large hat laughed heartily. "You were right, Lizabeau," he said after catching his breath. "He does have a sense of humor."

"How do you know we can trust him?" a new voice interjected from across the cabin. A large, muscular man stepped forward out of the shadows. His accent was similar to Lizabeau's, but the voice was cold and harsh. *His accent...* Armand realized. *He sounds just like Kol!* Armand looked the man over. Though he appeared intimidating enough, with a fierce scar cutting through one brow, there was nothing in particular about his appearance that reminded him of Kol, save, perhaps, for his impressive height and apparent disregard of personal hygiene.

"The plan," Lizabeau replied, then nodded toward Armand. "It was his idea." At her words, the others of the room fell silent, gaping at Armand with various looks of surprise or admiration.

"I've got what we need right here, Captain," the Sornian said, pulling a large flag from inside his dirty shirt. It unfolded as he presented it, its design stitched in bright colors of scarlet and gold. Armand recognized it as the ensign belonging to the Royal Family of Valenna. As Valenna's navy had, over the course of many peaceful years, become relegated to purely ceremonial purposes, the flag was a symbol of diplomacy and an assurance of goodwill when encountered at sea. This was much unlike the Sornian Navy, which patrolled its national waters aggressively against foreign vessels.

"Remind me," Armand began, uneasiness growing in his gut. "Which of my many ideas are we talking about?"

There was an awkward pause until the captain laughed, then the others joined in. "Listen up," the captain quieted the crew. "We've made good time, thanks to the fair winds. Soon, we will be coming to the Northwesterlies, which we will follow across the Bay," he pushed a small, wedge-shaped piece of wood over the map, "until we come to Leveret's Folly." He grinned. "That's our pinch-point, and they'll never see us coming. But, if they do—" The captain nodded toward the Sornian. "Well, thanks to Ferras, we've got that sorted."

"Begging your pardon, Captain Russo," a younger man started hesitantly. The captain nodded at him to proceed, and the young sailor turned to Ferras. "What if they don't fall for it? How many caravels have they got in Valenna, anyway?"

"It doesn't matter the type of ship," Ferras countered. "Flags are official. It works every time."

"It won't hurt to prepare for contingencies," Lizabeau interjected.

Ferras stuffed the flag back under his armpit with a frown. "We've already thought of everything."

"What if they make it through the Folly too soon?" she asked. "If we sailed through the Isles of Pentz instead—"

"For the last time," Captain Russo interjected, "we're not going to Pentz."

"I wouldn't mind seeing the Isles myself," the younger man added.

"We can discuss sight-seeing later," the captain chided, and a few of the others snickered. "Benramil," he said, turning toward Armand. "A fine Andolinian name, that. It's good to have you aboard. Quarter Mistress," he said, turning to Lizabeau. "Please take our friend here under your charge, and find him some work. He must be eager to take the night watches, since he slept the entire day."

Lizabeau nodded and led Armand back up to the weather deck, where he stopped to clutch at the rail and vomited overboard. He wiped his mouth on his sleeve and looked around in the light of the hanging lanterns. The vessel was much smaller than he realized, with lateen sails of plain canvas rather than the square-rigged, red and black sails of *The Tigress*.

He patted his waistcoat pockets, suddenly remembering his urgent mission. Armand was certain the envelope he was sent to deliver to Captain Declan contained matters of the heart, and such things were, in his estimation, of the greatest importance. After Adella had left Declan's letter in a ball on the floor and Kol had retired for the night, Armand had given in to his curiosity and retrieved it. Though it had been circumspectly written, the note clearly laid plans for a tryst, but Adella's hot-tempered reaction to the offer told him her answer would disabuse the captain of the idea. Though he didn't look forward to breaking Declan's heart, Armand took his role as messenger very seriously, as it signified a great amount of trust in him on Adella's part.

The letter, however, was nowhere on him, and an icy panic flooded through his gut at the realization. "I was looking for *The Tigress*," Armand muttered in a daze of worry.

"I know," Lizabeau replied. "You mentioned that many times."

"I had a letter on me," he continued urgently. "I needed to deliver it in Raymouth. Where is it?"

"Any outgoing letters you turned in are on their way," she assured him. "Along with the rest of the mail headed for Valenna. We loaded it all onto *The Kestrel* as we passed at sea earlier today. They will take it onward to the Capital."

"Shit," he said, realizing the letter was heading in the wrong direction. Not only that, but he was supposed to deliver it himself, Miss Adella was counting on him. "I've got to get it back, Lizabeau," he said, remembering the name he heard the other man call her. "Quarter Mistress," he added respectfully.

"Why so formal now?" She leaned in close, lowering her voice. "You were calling me Lizzy last night."

Armand coughed and sputtered. "Right. Lizzy." He cursed himself for drinking so much.

Her smile fell away. "Don't you remember?"

"Maybe you could... jog my memory?" He raised his brows hopefully.

"Here?" she laughed, apparently mistaking his meaning. "I don't want to get flogged, do you?"

Armand didn't want to press his luck, but had one more question. "What's the name of this ship, again?" he asked, attempting to sound nonchalant.

"*The Seaborn*," she replied. "Stop playing games, or you'll get us both in trouble."

The morning sky above *The Seaborn* shone bright and clear blue. Armand busied himself at the starboard bow, recoiling a length of spare line to give the appearance of being useful. All the while, however, he mulled over his situation. He kept a close watch on the sailors around him for any clues that might jog his memory. *I should keep an eye on Lizabeau especially,* he decided, *since she's apparently the reason why I'm here.* The fact that he liked her, he told himself, was irrelevant. He would see her pass by now and then, a cutlass always hanging at her side. In fact, the crew were all likewise armed with various mis-matched blades. *Reavers,* he realized. *They must be reavers.* He watched as Lizabeau stopped to speak with Ferras. Armand tried to listen in on their conversation, but they were too far away for him to understand their Sornian accents.

He looked up at the masts, then across the length of the ship to-ward the prow. No flags or pennants hung in the air to identify their country to oncoming ships. The unpainted timbers of *The Seaborn* looked weathered, with fresh gouges of bare wood hacked from nearly every surface. That was much unlike Declan's *The Tigress,* which often flew an array of colorful pennants strung along the bow, the ship al-ways freshly painted.

"Cheese and biscuits!" he swore in dismay. *It seems I really have taken up with reavers...* He spat at the deck. *Sornian ones, too.* He lamented the fact that this made Lizabeau an enemy, with their two countries at war. He finished coiling the line and straightened his aching back. He stepped toward the rail to look out over the water, and noticed a dark shape in the waves up ahead.

It was a ship, too far in the offing to make out much detail, but he could see it bore square-rigged sails. *The Seaborn* followed behind at a distance, but seemed to be gaining on them. Soon, Ferras joined him at the rail.

"We're coming up on them," Armand commented. "According to the plan," he guessed. "Right?"

"Aye, the plan." Ferras glowered down at him. "Lizabeau seems to trust you well enough, but just know," he narrowed his eyes menac-ingly. "I'm watching you, Andolinian."

"Fine, but I'm not—" He shut his mouth quickly. *They think I'm Andolinian!* He didn't want to find out what would happen if they learned he was Valennian.

"You're not what?" Ferras asked in confusion.

"I'm not..." Armand's words fell away as his mind scrambled to think up something else to say. "Watching you," he improvised. He forced a wide grin, "I trust you completely." Ferras groaned in disgust and walked away. Armand rubbed his face with his palms. *That was close,* he thought. *I have to be more careful.*

Armand set his bowl down on the mess table, noticing with disappointment that it contained what looked to be burgoo. He was soon joined by Lizabeau, along with Farras and other sailors whose names he hadn't yet learned. The company made him uncomfortable, and he hoped he could make it through the meal without slipping up and saying too much. When the conversation turned toward the ship they now sailed on, however, he decided he had to try to learn more.

"That was back when *The Seaborn* was a merchant vessel," Ferras said, referring to a comment Lizabeau had made.

"Under its current captain?" Armand ventured.

Ferras shook his head. "Our captain took command of this ship when it was captured by *The Kestrel*. Before that, it sailed under the command of Captain Declan."

"Did you say 'Declan?'" Armand sputtered through a mouthful of food. "You can't mean Rogero Declan of *The Tigress*?" he asked, his curiosity momentarily overcoming his sense of caution.

"No," Lizabeau replied. "Arturo Declan. His father."

"I heard he was murdered," Armand replied, setting his spoon down into the bowl. "Gutted by reavers."

"That's not the whole story," Lizabeau explained. "Every sailor on Belgrand Bay knows it. They weren't merely reavers."

"It was all on account of the ship's owner, Seaborn," Ferras interjected.

Armand raised a brow. "The ship was named after its owner?" he asked.

Lizabeau nodded. "A Sornian merchant turned smuggler. A brute of a man. Twenty-some years ago, he hired a Valennian sea captain by the name of Arturo Declan to command his merchant ship, which was supposed to be hauling tea but was found to be smuggling Madorran poppy. Eventually, the scheme was discovered; things went badly and a fight broke out, half the crew siding with the owner and half with the captain. They were unable to take the ship, but Declan and his men escaped with a lot of stolen gold. Seaborn, of course, was out for revenge after that, but Declan used the gold to buy a ship of his own, always keeping just out of Seaborn's grasp... That is, until about five years ago, when Seaborn finally caught him." Lizabeau looked down at her hands. "Cut him down mercilessly; gutted like a fish. In front of Declan's own crew."

"And his son," Armand replied. "Right there on the deck of *The Tigress*—or so I've heard," he added hastily.

Lizabeau nodded. "It was named *The Hopewell* at that time," she corrected, "but what you heard is true. A gruesome tale."

"And where is this Seaborn fellow now?" Armand asked.

"No one knows for sure," she said with a shrug. "He was caught by the Valennians and imprisoned, but I've heard rumors that's no longer the case. They say he's gone now. Either dead, or escaped."

Armand shuddered at the thought of such a man roaming free.

Rain pummeled Armand's face as he stood watch at midships, when suddenly he heard an uproar from the larboard side. He crossed the deck in a hurry, his boots slipping on the wet planking as he stopped to look over the rail with the others who had gathered there. Peering down into the dark and choppy waves, he saw a sailor struggling to keep his head above the water. *The Seaborn* was running along at a fair pace, and though they tossed lines out to the man overboard, each try fell just out of reach, and he was quickly getting left behind in the water. Armand thought the sailor would be lost.

Finally, the sailor caught a line thrown from the stern and he was dragged along as the waves crashed over his head, forcing him under the surface. They worked to try to pull him in, struggling against each swell of the sea. At the rear of the group, Armand helped to pull in the waterlogged line as it gathered on the deck at his feet.

"Look, there!" A voice called out over the rain. "What is that?"

Crossing to the rail, Armand spotted a massively long creature, glossy black with barbed, spiny fins running down its back, cleaving through the water as it wove in and out of the waves before disappearing below the surface. It headed right toward the sailor that floundered in the ship's wake, clinging desperately to the heavy line.

"Get him out of there!" Armand shouted, hauling at the line along with the others, throwing their weight backward against the drag of the water. Sweat dripped down his brow, mingling with rain, while he pulled with all his strength until the line gave a sudden tug in his hands, burning as it pulled through his palms, then went slack.

"What in the fathomless hell was that?" a young crewman asked beside him.

"Sea serpent," Armand answered. "It's not the first I've seen of them."

"There it is again," the young man said, pointing into the distance. "And more of them." Sleek, dark shapes undulated in and out of the surface, twisting and turning back and forth among the waves. Then came the ragged sound of a man's scream.

"Ugh," Armand cringed at the sight of the creatures feeding on the sailor. "The poor bastard," he muttered sadly, placing his tattered old hat over his heart respectfully.

"What sort of creature do you suppose they are?" the young man wondered. "Are they sea snakes, or fish?"

Ferras shoved through the crowd to get a better view. He pulled a dingy red kerchief from his bald head, putting it over his chest as though it were a hat in a moment of silence before speaking. "No,

Danny. They are too large to be snakes," he reasoned. "They must be whales." They watched as the creatures vanished into the dark water.

"They're clearly not whales," Armand retorted, wiping rain from his brow. "When was the last time you saw a fellow being eaten by whales?"

"They've turned against us. The whole damn sea has," Ferras said. "They're whales."

"Or," Danny interjected. "Perhaps they're an ancient breed of beast not seen for a millennium, brought forth from the briny depths by a strange and unnatural force to punish mankind for its transgressions?"

"That's stupid," Ferras reprimanded. "Stay off the grog."

"They're fish, anyway," Armand muttered.

Armand made his way toward the bow, holding his hat down to keep the wind from blowing it away. He searched the endless, heaving water for a sign of more creatures, but something else caught his attention. Straight ahead, he noticed a familiar shape. A Valennian-style vessel, its three masts square-rigged with striped canvas, crept closer into view. *The Seaborn* appeared to be gaining on it, with the direction of wind more favorable to its fore-and-aft sails. Panic hit him like a punch to the gut. *No, it can't be,* he pleaded silently. *Not* The Tigress, *of all things...* His legs swayed beneath him and he clutched the rail for support, his knuckles turning white. *We can't be going after Declan's ship!* Groaning in despair, he slunk to the deck.

"What's the matter with you?" Lizabeau's voice came from behind him. "Seasick?"

"I, uh—" Armand stopped to think. "Right, seasick."

They watched silently as *The Tigress* changed direction, sailing to the northwest. Overwhelmed with anxiety, Armand wanted to ask her about their destination, but kept quiet. If he raised suspicion about where his loyalties lay and brought trouble to himself, he would be unable to help his friends on *The Tigress*.

"It won't be long," Lizabeau said, keeping her eyes on the sea. "Ben," she began softly. "No matter what happens..." She turned to face him, smiling sadly. "I'm glad to have met you." Then, she left.

As the day wore on, *The Seaborn* approached the Isles of Pentz. Ferras was true to his word, and never let Armand very far out of sight. Though Armand had awoken in the forecastle with the other sailors, he hadn't been assigned to a watch, and he wasn't sure exactly what his role was. Lizabeau would occasionally come by to check on him, though it seemed to be out of personal interest rather than official duty. Armand's role on the ship didn't seem to be merely as a passenger, however, since he was often put to various tasks throughout the day. He tried to keep his head down and blend in with the other crewmen while he worked, biting back on his anxieties while keeping an eye on *The Tigress* in the distance ahead.

They sailed between rocky islands of various sizes, some barely high enough to break the surface while others were larger, topped with trees and underbrush. He knew they were drawing nearer to Leveret's Folly, a narrow channel between two ridges of rock that jutted out from the waters of Belgrand Bay. He had sailed through the Folly in his younger years while completing his required two-year service in His Majesty's Navy, before being assigned to Lord Grimless in the Cavalry. He had been awestruck to see the massive rock formation that featured in the Old Andolinian tales he had heard as a child, and he still remembered the sight vividly.

When Armand headed to the mess deck for dinner, he intended to get through his meal without speaking to anyone, lest he accidentally give himself away as Valennian. His plan, however, was foiled when he was joined by Lizabeau, Ferras, and a few others of the crew, already talking amongst themselves.

As they finished eating, Lizabeau turned toward Armand. "Why so quiet?" she prodded. "Nerves?"

"No, not at all," Armand bluffed. "Can't wait to... do the—" He tried to think of something vague to say that wouldn't give him away. "Plan," he concluded lamely.

"Ha!" Ferras said, slapping the table in excitement. "*I* can't wait to see the look on their faces when we come up behind them." He grinned at the idea, revealing jagged, chipped teeth. "They won't see it coming!"

"We won't be close enough to actually *see* their faces," Lizabeau corrected. "And, well, they will see us coming after a certain point. But yes, we'll certainly catch them unprepared."

"And what a prize!" Ferras went on. "Just imagine all that loot on board..." he trailed off in contemplation, staring into his plate.

"You know," Lizabeau began, turning to Armand, "there was an old story about how Leveret's Folly got its name. Something about a man fighting with a sea serpent."

"Not just any sea serpent," Armand replied, eager to relate the tale. As the Old Andolinian legends weren't well-known in Valenna, he rarely got a chance to discuss them. "Leveret fought with the Guardian," he began. "The very embodiment of Mundil herself. With the Heart of the World in his hands, Leveret was unstoppable. One day, he set sail across the Bay to reunite with his true love, Paloma. That's when Mundil sent her Guardian to attack Leveret's ship and wrest the Heart from him. But, the creature was no match for Leveret, with the unnatural abilities bestowed upon him by the Heart. With each blow he dealt to the beast, droplets of its blood spattered the sea, forming the Isles of Pentz. With one massive punch to the beast's face," Armand jabbed at the air dramatically, "its many, massive teeth were knocked far across the Bay, and can still be seen to this day, sticking out from the waves. Then, finally, Leveret grabbed the Guardian by the tail and whipped the creature back into the deep. A great chasm rose up where it fell, forming the channel we now know as Leveret's Folly. According to legend, it was his defeat of the Guardian that sealed the fate of the Andolin Empire."

"I've never heard the whole story before," Lizabeau said in admiration. "When this is over, I think we'll keep you around." She cleaned up her dishes and left to return to her duties.

Great, Armand thought. *I just had to open my big mouth...* He might have been more worried if he wasn't already concerned for his friends on *The Tigress.* He was the one who put them in danger, so it would be his duty to get them out of it. *No matter what,* he vowed. Though he had no idea on the particulars of the plan that the reavers spoke of, a new one was forming in his mind. *If I can just save my friends, at least...* he pleaded silently. *But... if I manage to live through this, I swear—I'll never drink again in my life.*

9

Into the Folly

At daybreak, a thick, misty rain stretched across the Bay. The red and gold Valennian flag fluttered high above the deck as Lizabeau raised the spyglass to her eye. "This is it," she said, passing the glass to Armand with a slight smirk.

Armand watched Lizabeau's face. Her steely blue eyes were to him as deep as the sea, and she had a stately calm that seemed to belong to mountains and horizons rather than one person. He had truly loved only one person in his life, and though it had been unrequited, it was a love that had burned strong throughout the decades before being torn away by tragedy. He would never meet the likes of such a one again, he knew. *But this woman,* he thought, *perhaps if things were different...* Lizabeau left, and Armand shook his head to clear the thought away. He lifted the spyglass to his eye.

Slowly, he inspected a large mass of rock protruding from the sea, forming a great, dark wall that blocked the horizon. White plumes crashed against it. He could just make out a ship ahead of *The Seaborn,* approaching the chasm of Leveret's Folly. Though the weather limited the visibility, there was no mistaking *The Tigress's* red and black sails, even as they were being raised in preparation of entering the narrow channel. *What in the briny hell is he doing?* he wondered. *Declan, you fool!* He bit his lips and closed the spyglass. *Don't go in there!* Anxiously, he watched *The Tigress* sail out of sight, disappearing behind the rock. *Damn!*

Orders to shorten the sails were given as *The Seaborn* approached the Folly. *Are we chasing them?* he wondered. *Why follow them through the Folly, rather than meet them round the other end?* Unable to bite back on his questions any longer, he turned to interrogate a nearby crewman, but stopped himself when he realized it was Ferras. The Sornian sat upon the windlass, throwing him an intimidating glance while sharpening his cutlass on a whetstone. Armand thought better of asking him anything.

The Seaborn slowly crept its way into the channel of rock between the immense, forbidding walls. The crew was hushed, with only Captain Russo's commands breaking the silence. They could not see far ahead, as the channel's turns limited their view. High above the water, small, rugged plants clung for life in the cracks of the rocky walls. At times, the surrounding cliffs closed in more, requiring a very close watch on their heading to keep from scraping the hull. Other times, the passage gradually widened, allowing room enough for several ships to sail abreast before narrowing once more. At one such opening, Armand was bewildered to see a small ship's boat that seemed to have been left behind, bobbing in the waves. As they passed the boat close to starboard, Armand noticed its lines were thrown carelessly in the hull, and a felt hat had been left on one of the thwarts.

As *The Seaborn* turned to sail through a wide bend, Armand's gaze was drawn up toward one particularly large ledge. Caught on the promontory was a little, weathered fishing boat with its single mast broken, the sail long since gone. It sat high and dry, wedged up on the cliffside above the sea, now merely serving as a perch for seagulls. Armand wondered what had become of its crew when a sailor beside him spoke.

"Look," the crewman said, pointing to another shelf of rock on the cliff, just below the boat. Squinting, Armand searched until he saw what had caught the man's attention; a sun-weathered skeleton dangled from the rock's ledge, picked fleshless by gulls but still wearing the remnants of a sea-blue jacket.

"How do you suppose he got all the way up there?" another voice asked.

Their somber contemplation was broken with Captain Russo's order of "All hands on deck!" Armand followed behind the others, lifting up onto his toes to see over their heads. "We're approaching the Crucible," the captain began, striding leisurely across the quarter deck. His tall hat overshadowed a grimly-lined face and added height to his stature, giving the man an imposing look. "This is the center of Leveret's Folly, and the narrowest part of the channel. This is where we overtake them. Arm yourselves well, our opponents will be fierce. This will not be an easy take, I assure you—we will earn our gold," he grinned. "Make ready the ballista!"

At that, Armand's blood ran cold. He froze, lost in thought, as the captain finished giving his commands and the crew dispersed to their tasks.

"There you are," Lizabeau said, approaching with her arms full of various weapons. "Here, take arms." She offered him a cutlass in its scabbard.

"That's it," he said, reaching instead for an axe she carried. "That's just what I need." She gave him a curious look, but walked away to resume her duties.

As the other crew members all worked at their orders, Armand inconspicuously hurried down the companionway steps and into the dark hold, trudging through the stinking, fetid bilge water toward the center. Gripping the axe handle tightly, he took a deep breath. Then, he raised the axe and began hacking away at the grimy boards. As he chipped the wood away, the sea began to pour in, first a trickle, then a fountain spraying out through his handiwork. He kept chopping and prying, unconcerned for his own fate.

Cold water cascaded over his chest as he continued to hack away. The ship jolted suddenly and he slipped, plunging down into the water. Scrambling to regain his footing, he spat and wiped at his eyes. "No!" he pleaded desperately, hoping the impact didn't mean what he thought it did.

He sloshed through the rising water and stomped up the steps, coming out to the main deck in the grey morning light. Toward the bow, crew members crowded at the rail, throwing lines back and forth in the rain as they swung across to the other ship.

Armand stood staring open-mouthed. The vessel the crew was swarming was unfamiliar to him; its plain canvas sails were fore-and-aft rigged rather than square. It was not *The Tigress* they were attacking, but rather another caravel. Just beyond the vessel being boarded, *The Tigress* lay at anchor on the other side, blocking the channel diagonally. His mind reeled. *Three ships?*

"Shit," he grimaced. "What have I done?" His pulse pounded in his ears, muffling the shouts and clash of metal while he ran toward the bowsprit, desperate to be off the sinking vessel. He shoved his way forward and, biting down on the axe handle, caught a line as it was sent over from the larboard stern quarter of the other ship.

Armand swung, the open waves sloshing below him for a moment, then landed on the enemy deck into the center of the fray. Immediately, the flash of a swinging blade came at him, and he ducked just as it whisked over his head. Armand slashed at the man's leg with his axe, slicing through boot leather. The enemy reaver dropped to the deck, screaming and clutching his shin as Armand sprang up and shoved through the tumult.

He hurried down the steps of the quarterdeck, but froze when he came to the bottom. Blocking his way stood Lizabeau, her white hair swept to the side in a braid, a bloodied cutlass in her hand. She raised her sword as he had approached but, with a smile of recognition, stayed her hand. Armand grappled with his thoughts over what to do. *She's the enemy,* he reminded himself. Tightening his grip, he lifted his axe.

Confusion flashed across her face. Enemy or not, Armand couldn't bring himself to do it. For whatever reason, when he looked at her, he only saw a friend. His glance shifted from her to two dark figures who had come up behind her, blades drawn.

Armand threw his axe. It sailed through the air over Lizabeau's shoulder, lodging deep into one man's chest. Lizabeau turned and parried the other's blade with an ease that could only be acquired from many years of experience. Armand left her to it, retrieving his axe before sprinting to the forecastle in the driving rain.

Crossing amidships, he was accosted by reavers on either side. He dodged the swing of the cutlass from his left, and found himself stepping into the path of the blade on his right. Armand hoisted his axe up to block his face just as the blade edge hacked into the handle, barely missing his fingers. He shoved the axe forward into the man, who stumbled backward. Taking his opportunity, Armand swung it back down upon his attacker, sinking the blade deep into his shoulder.

A sudden blow struck on his left, and realized his shoulder had been slashed; a sharp pain flooded through his body. Screaming through clenched teeth, Armand wheeled his axe around, burying it in the man's side with the sickening crack of bone. His opponent fell to the deck with a shriek of agony as Armand sprinted off again.

Before he reached the forecastle steps, Armand was knocked sideways onto the deck by a man who, dodging blades, collided backward into him. Armand squinted upward, nearly blind with the rain falling into his eyes, and watched the brawny sailor cut down two reavers with a slash and a jab of the cutlass before Armand even had time to retrieve his dropped axe. He hastily grabbed the axe handle, hoisting his weapon in the air just in time to block the edge of the man's swinging blade as Armand was rounded upon by the sailor.

Armand held the axe with both hands, groaning as he pushed against his assailant's weight, pain searing through his body from his wound. Just when he thought his strength would give out, the sailor drew away his cutlass.

"Armand!" the man exclaimed cheerfully. "Forgive me, I didn't realize it was you." He extended his hand in assistance. Armand wiped the rain from his eyes and found himself looking up into a familiar and handsome face, smiling from beneath a large cocked hat.

"Captain Declan?" Armand took the offered hand and rose to his feet, wincing at the strain on his arm. "What in the deep, blue hell is going on?"

Declan gave him a concerned look. "Everything is going to plan, is it not?"

Armand stood speechless as a wave of sheer panic rose within him at those words, tightening in his lungs like a vice. Their conversation was interrupted by the swing of a blade as an enemy sailor came down the forecastle steps. Metal clashed loudly as Declan deflected the blow with his cutlass in one hand, then grabbed the reaver by the jacket with the other and, yanking him by the clothes, sent him careening into a group of oncoming reavers. Declan gave a little laugh as he watched them stumble over one another, but his amusement tapered off when he looked upward.

Seeing the smile fall from Declan's face, Armand looked to see what it was about. "Damn..." he muttered breathlessly. In the distance, a massive swell of turbulent water bounded down the channel, rushing toward the line of ships.

At that moment, two reavers came at them, swords swinging. Armand lifted his axe to meet them, but Declan drew his dagger and stepped in to parry. Straining to hold both blades against theirs, he looked back at Armand. "Get to *The Tigress*," he ordered. "Cut away the anchor. Go!"

Armand gave a quick nod and darted up the steps. He ran across the the forecastle's slick planks as fast as he could, climbed the rail with the heavy axe clamped between his teeth, and leapt through the air over the jostling waves to catch himself on the ratlines of *The Tigress*, all the while trying not to think about their impending destruction. Dropping to the main deck, he ran to the bow.

He skidded to a stop, slipping in rain puddles when he came to the windlass. Hoisting the axe over his head, he swung the blade down upon the anchor rode where it lay across the deck. One strike would not do it, the cable was too thick. Ignoring the sharp pain in his shoulder, he chopped at it again furiously; his mind set on succeeding at this one task to make up for everything he'd done. A scream sounded out from his lungs, though he was insensible to it in his panic. He unleashed all the emotions he had held back since awakening on *The Seaborn* onto the line that tethered the ship to the seafloor.

The deck tilted beneath his feet as a surge of water lifted the ship's stern. With one last axe blow, the taut anchor rode was cleaved into two, one end vanishing through the hawsehole as the bow of *The Tigress* pitched violently upward. Though his accomplishment had given him a glimmer of hope, it was quickly snuffed out by the fear of being smashed on the cliff.

A strong voice called out as the ship uprighted once more. Looking back, he spotted Declan at the helm, shouting orders to the crew members who had stayed behind with *The Tigress* or had made it quickly back on board.

The sea continued to rise, pushing the ship helplessly up and forward through the dusky channel, the jagged rock at their sides flashing by at a terrifying pace. Armand clung there, watching breathlessly as the vessel hurtled helplessly down the chasm, narrowly missing the cliff sides with each jostle of the rebounding waves. A sudden jolt hurled Armand hard against the rail as a sharp crack of splitting wood sounded across the ship. He glanced back to see another vessel's sails looming above as its prow rammed the stern of *The Tigress*. At the helm, Declan struggled to turn the wheel as quickly as he could.

Armand's heart sank. Straight ahead, a wall of rock materialized through the hazy rain as the channel before them veered sharply to the right. As the great force of the rising current pulled them toward the cliffside, he could see no way to save the ship from imminent destruction.

Armand braced himself against the rail, preparing for the inevitable collision. Just when it seemed the ship's bow would be crushed to splinters upon the rock wall, a great force heaved the ship upward, and his stomach lurched. Water rushed onto the deck, washing his feet from under him and nearly tearing his grip free. Clutching the rail, he regained his footing, and gaped.

The Tigress now sailed on a vast, endless sea, with only the stormy horizon stretching out in every direction; Leveret's Folly had disappeared beneath the swell.

He was surprised to see that, behind *The Tigress,* the two other ships had survived the ordeal as well, though they rocked wildly on the frothy waves. Cheering sounded over the deck as some of the crew threw their hats in the air.

Armand breathed a sigh of relief. "Sweet sea-mother," he muttered to himself, closing his eyes to savor the cool, damp breeze. He made his way to midships, and was surprised to see Captain Declan among the crew.

"There you are, my good man!" Declan called out, opening his arms wide. "Your plan worked perfectly!" He clamped Armand's arms to his sides and embraced him heartily, squeezing the rain out from their clothes to pool on the deck at their feet. Armand cringed at the pain in his shoulder. "We've put an end to *The Warbrand's* pillaging of Pentz once and for all," Declan said, releasing him. "And a Sornian ship-of-war will make a fine addition to our fleet." He took a step back to look around the weather deck. "Let's hope your friend, Quarter Master Swift, made it back onto *The Seaborn.*"

Speechless, Armand wracked his brain to make sense of what he'd heard. "Quarter *who?*"

"Lizabeau Swift," Declan replied. "Did you forget? Well, you were three sheets to the wind at the time," he continued. "The two of you seemed to be getting on well enough," he added with a smirk.

"I delivered the letter?" Armand asked, and Declan nodded. "With the Sornian reaver?"

Declan let out a laugh. "Sornian, yes, but fellow privateer, of course. *The Seaborn* sails under commission from the Crown."

"*No—*" Armand said under his breath, as a sinking feeling overtook him. Declan made his way back to the helm, calling out orders to set the course east to Pentz.

Frantically, Armand searched the waves for sight of *The Seaborn*. He spotted the vessel in the distance off the larboard rail, as it had hastily opened its sails and veered westward. Already, the ship sat low in the water. *Damn me,* he scolded himself, slumping down onto the deck. The sting of his wound pulsed up and down his arm, but he tried to push it out of mind. *I deserve much worse. Drank myself to oblivion, put my friends in danger, doomed a whole ship full of Valennian allies...*

The sharp piping of a boatswain's whistle pierced through the rain, drawing Armand out of his despair. He pulled himself together and followed the crew to starboard. Drawing slowly alongside *The Tigress* was the third ship, which was rigged with a mix of fore-and-aft and square sails in a style Armand did not recognize. Its freshly-painted black hull was adorned with gilded embellishments and emblazoned with the name *The Warbrand* across the bow. He spotted the source of the whistling as his eyes settled on a figure at its rail, waving a hand in the air.

"Ahoy!" a familiar voice called out over the distance.

"Lizabeau!" Armand elbowed his way to the rail, coming up beside Declan. "What happened?"

"The reavers," she replied. "They escaped on *The Seaborn*. Shall we go after them?"

Declan turned to Armand. "This is your plan," he said. "What do you say?"

Armand shook his head. "No need to go after them," he admitted with a nervous chuckle. He turned to look westward, where *The Seaborn* slunk low in the water, bobbing to one side with the waves already crashing over the main deck. "See for yourself."

After a late breakfast, the captain and some of the crew of the newly acquired ship, *The Warbrand*, which had sailed up alongside, were permitted to come aboard under the guise of dividing loot and sharing supplies. In fact, however, they spent most of their time on *The Tigress* celebrating their success and good fortune with the aid of a barrel of Madorran spirits that had been discovered on the new vessel. Armand sat at the table in the captain's cabin, surrounded by Captains Declan and Russo, along with a few officers from both crews, including Lizabeau. Armand also recognized the young navigator Hugo Jon from his previous time aboard *The Tigress*, whom he remembered by the name Nutmeg Jon.

Declan held a pewter goblet which had been overfilled with wine, and a little red rivulet dribbled down from his hand onto the table as he rose from his seat. "The Sornian Navy is now one warship fewer," he proclaimed proudly. "Though we had to give up an old prize for it. Captain Russo, congratulations on the procurement of your new vessel. May your command of *The Warbrand* be long and glorious." The officers chimed in with their congratulations, and Russo nodded his gratitude.

"Our thanks, of course, must go to our good friend, Ben Armand," Declan said, turning toward him. "I admit, when you first came to me with your plan, seeming about as drunk as anyone could be, I had my reservations. Poor Quarter Mas—" Declan stopped himself. "Quarter Mis—" He looked pleadingly at Lizabeau.

"Quarter Mistress, if you please," she offered.

"Quarter Mistress Swift had to explain it to me again before I caught onto its brilliance." Declan lifted his cup in the air. "To Armand, and his plan." He took a drink, and the others at the table did likewise. "Though I must say, that was one of our narrower escapes," Declan added with a laugh.

"If it hadn't been for the rising tide," Captain Russo replied, "it would have gone better. The sea has been unruly lately, but there's no accounting for the whims of Mundil."

Leaving the two captains to discuss loftier subjects, the others were dismissed to do as they pleased. Armand found himself absent-mindedly following Lizabeau down to the mess deck where the barrel of spirits served as a scuttlebutt of sorts, with the crew gathered round it in groggy conversation.

Armand watched idly while she filled a tin gill-cup with the amber liquid, his attention slipping to the voices of a group sitting at the table nearby.

"So I said to him," one man went on, "'The last thing I want to do is hurt you; but it's still on my list.'"

"Ah," another sailor exclaimed, pushing a bottle toward him. "You made a face! I saw it."

"I know this game," Armand remarked as they took a seat. Lizabeau set a cup before him, and he considered it before remembering his pledge to give up drink. Soon, the dice passed to them. Lizabeau made her roll, then offered them to Armand. "I, uh…" he hesitated.

"Go on," she nudged him. "I think you'd be good at this."

Armand gave in and rolled the dice. Seeing that he won the draw, he thought for a moment. "Have you seen Ferras?" he asked the group. "He's so ugly, he has to buy flowers for his own hand." He was surprised to hear loud laughter coming from behind him, and turned to see who it was.

"I have to admit," Ferras said, still chuckling as he wedged himself onto the crowded bench, "I had my doubts about you, but I'm glad to say you proved me wrong."

"Ah, well…" Armand replied. "I'm sorry for the loss of your ship."

"Better to lose it to the deep than to see it in enemy hands," Ferras affirmed. "Though our captain will be taking it hard, I'm sure. The capture of *The Seaborn* had made his reputation; with it gone to the depths, and Seaborn the man missing as well, Russo will have nothing left to show for it. And it was a fine ship."

"To *The Seaborn*," Lizabeau began solemnly, raising her cup. "And all who were lost this day."

"To those lost," Ferras said, lifting his glass.

Armand couldn't, in good conscience, refuse the toast. He clinked his cup with theirs and drank with them while the dice passed around again.

"I've got a good one," a young crewman said in a heavy Valennian accent. "Why is a Sornian like a lampfish?"

"Why?" Armand prompted. Beside him, Lizabeau leaned forward on her elbows as Ferras, unblinking, stared at the young man expectantly.

"Actually," the crewman demurred, looking down into his cup, "I can't recall." He knocked back the last of his drink.

They all rolled again, and Lizabeau won. "As I was wracked with labor pains," she began slowly, "my husband came to my bedside, sobbing. 'It hurts me to see you suffer so much on my account,' he told me." Lizabeau pursed her lips to keep her composure. "'Don't worry,' I assured him. 'It's not your fault.'" The others all laughed at that. When she saw it was safe, Lizabeau, who had been struggling to keep a straight face, joined in.

They played a few more rounds until Armand turned to Lizabeau, emboldened by the spirits. "You're an exceptional woman, Lizzy. Why don't you come back to Elldon with me? Give up the fighting, leave the sea behind..." he left his words hanging in the air, anxiously awaiting her reaction.

She blinked at him, then cracked a smile. Armand thought it was a good sign, until she burst into raucous laughter. Ferras joined in, then, one by one, the entire table. Dabbing at her eyes, Lizabeau stopped to catch her breath. "Oh, Ben," she sighed. "You have the best sense of humor."

Soon, *The Tigress* was underway again, heading for the nearest port at Pentz to make repairs with *The Warbrand* following behind. Armand, preparing for their arrival in the affluent port city, stood before the little mirror that hung from the bulkhead, smoothing his hair. He was eager to see land again, and to return home to Elldon. Armand hoped his young friends at Greywood had fared well enough while he was gone.

Coarse shouting came from above deck, interrupting his musing. He stopped to listen but, as the ship continued to sail smoothly, he put it out of mind. Armand set his hat on his head, then pushed it jauntily to one side while he inspected himself in the mirror. Not quite satisfied, he took a small comb from his pocket and ran it through his bushy sideburns. As he adjusted his shirt collar, an eerie feeling began to settle over him.

The ship creaked gently, rocking in placid waters. Even his own breathing seemed to have grown louder in the muffled stillness of the cabin. Holding his breath, he listened as the hairs on the back of his neck raised.

Armand heard nothing at all. A shiver ran through him when he realized the voices from the weather deck had stopped; not even Captain Declan's loud commands issued overhead.

Above decks, Armand didn't know what to make of what he saw. Debris littered the sea all around the ship; splintered pieces of wood, trunks of broken trees, the wreckage of small boats and other things floated on the water's surface.

"Heavens above," he muttered, looking around. As *The Tigress* passed through a particularly wide mass of drifting debris, its prow wedged through wooden crates, barrels, and whole or broken fishing boats adrift on the tide. Armand looked down upon one small boat that bobbed aimlessly in the waves as they passed and saw a woman's body, lying lifeless in the hull, her flesh ashen, her limbs and brow battered with gouges and scrapes.

10

Smuggler's Port

"Dammit, Martin!" Kol shouted, slamming the chamber door behind him. He slid the iron bolt into place, then turned to point a finger at his companion. "I told you not to leave the room! They'll be back—" Kol stopped when he noticed Martin holding his side, and lowered his voice. "Are you injured?"

"Just a scratch," Martin winced. "It's fine."

"Are you sure?" Kol stepped forward, reaching toward him. "I'd better have a look."

"No, I'm fine," Martin held a palm in the air to fend him off. "Really," he insisted.

"Two of them escaped," Kol warned. "This won't be the end of it."

"I know." Martin eased himself down onto one of the mattresses.

"Do you mind telling me what it was about?" Kol raised a brow as he wiped his blade with the edge of his cloak. "Those weren't Sornian soldiers."

"Lord Heffield," Martin replied. "I'm sorry, I…" He lowered his head. "I didn't see it coming."

Kol let out a long breath. "Nothing we can do tonight," he said, sheathing his sword. "Try to get some rest." He opened the punched-tin lantern and blew out the candle, then stood watch at the window.

Below, the waves of Belgrand Bay lapped against the pier in the moonlight.

"Martin." Kol nudged the man's shoulder with the toe of his boot. "Wake up. There's a ship coming into port, I think it might be your *Evarro*."

Blinking, Martin pulled the blanket off himself and tried to sit up, but fell back again with a groan. He lay on the mattress in the early morning's golden glow. A deep, red stain soaked the side of his white shirt.

"You said it was just a scratch," Kol scolded. Crouching, he pulled the cloth away from the flesh to reveal a puncture from a thin blade, small but deep. "You need a doctor."

"No," Martin insisted, trying to sit once more. "We must get to the docks. Elldon needs that shipment, and I gave the Lady my word."

Kol straightened. "She'd rather see you back alive."

"Not if it means losing the war, Mister Kol," Martin replied. "I'd made my fortune out of other people's pockets, and now I have a chance to put it to good use. I utterly insist." He held out a hand. "Help me to the docks."

Kol pulled Martin to his feet, then helped him down the inn's steps and out into the cool morning air. A heavy breeze blew in from the sea, laden with moisture and salt, making the waters choppy. Ahead, a foreign ship with fully battened sails was moored at the dock. A large flag, quartered with indigo and white, billowed from its stern; the colors of a Madorran vessel.

As they approached, they were met by a middle-aged man, neatly dressed in a black velvet jacket. "Mister Martin!" The man lifted his hands in welcome as he stepped off the gang-board. Beneath a wide-brimmed hat, his brown hair was tied back; a clean-shaven face bore marks that attested to the survival of the pox in his younger years. He glanced from the stain on Martin's shirt up to Kol, then back to Martin. "What happened?"

"Lord Heffield," Martin answered. "He wants a monopoly, and I am in his way."

"Indeed." The man's mouth flattened into a line. "Thank goodness he has failed."

"He needs to see the ship's doctor," Kol interjected.

"We have no doctor on board," the man replied. "But we'll do what we can for him."

"It's not so serious. Come, Kerchaw," Martin held out a hand. "Help me to the hold. We must make ready to sail as quickly as possible."

Martin, with Kerchaw's help, boarded the *Evarro*, leaving Kol to the task of retrieving the horses from the livery stables. Making his way back to the dock, Kol glanced at the people around him. Some were striding purposefully to or from the ships, or moving cargo, while others huddled about in small groups here and there in conversation. His gaze moved over one particular group, and he noticed a pair of eyes watching him. Kol pulled his hood over his head and quickened his pace.

Kol made his way down the hard-packed dirt road, keeping an eye on the shadows between the squalid buildings around him as he approached the stables on the far side of the town. Though the large manors and inns in Sornia and Valenna each had their own livery stables, Smuggler's Port, inhabited primarily by sea-farers, only had one for the entire town, situated on the edge by the fields of the Campos.

He came to the long brick building and walked through the open doors of the arched entrance, turning down the corridor. Stalls lined one side, and Kol occasionally had to dodge the muzzles of horses that reached out curiously toward him as he passed. At the far end, a man stepped out from a stall, and latched it shut as Kol approached.

"What do you need?" the man asked gruffly.

"I'm here to take my horses." Kol recognized the stablemaster from his previous visits. The man was, like himself, from Sornia, and spoke in the same accent.

The man squinted up at him from beneath bushy eyebrows. "I'll have them brought out."

"I will also be taking the four my friend had left here some weeks ago," Kol continued. "Under the name of Armand. Two small bays, a grey draft, and a black sporthorse. I need them all brought to the docks."

"It's about time!" the stablemaster replied. "The coin he left me ran out; I sold one of the bays to make up for it." He shrugged. "The rest are in the back pasture. You'll have to catch the black one yourself." He handed Kol a lead rope and walked off.

Kol made his way to the furthest pasture and climbed over the fence rails, spotting the horses grazing. The black mare, which he had named Madigan, raised her head at his approach. He remembered her to be of a good disposition, and so was pleased when she began to walk toward him. "Here, girl," he said and held out his hand while she lowered her gracefully arched neck, her long mane and tail streaming in the wind. He admired the animal's beauty as she trotted gamely over to him, spun in place, and kicked her back legs up toward his head.

He dodged sideways just in time, air rushing by his face as a hoof barely missed his ear. Kol scrambled to get clear before she could give it another try. "What's wrong with you?" he shouted while she galloped away, tossing her head.

Kol waited until she returned to graze with the others before approaching once more. He was greeted with the same reaction, this time a hoof striking his arm as he threw himself sideways. The mare ran off again triumphantly. Baffled, he retreated to lean against a fence rail and watched one of the stablehands pass through the gate, catch the bay and grey draft and lead them away without any trouble. Kol slumped down into the grass to think. It was tempting to leave the mare behind, but she was worth a small fortune, and he didn't want to give up the finest thing he'd ever owned.

He watched the horse graze, and noticed marks in her coat where the hair was missing. Her ribs made shadows along her sides. "Did they treat you badly?" he wondered aloud. The mare twitched an ear in his direction. Kol let out his breath, releasing the tension in his shoulders. "I know how that is," he said softly. "You probably think it's easier now to chase everyone off, and be on your own," he plucked the grass mindlessly as he spoke, "rather than let anyone get close and risk getting hurt again." The mare raised her head, giving him an appraising look before resuming her meal. "But if you do that," Kol continued, "you chase the good ones away, too. Like me, for example," he added with a small laugh. The mare began to walk toward him.

"It's a risk, certainly," he mused, more to himself than to the horse, unsure if she would attack him again. "But it's worth it to find someone who cares for you." Kol reached into his pocket and pulled out a dried heel of bread, then held it out on his palm. The horse sniffed hesitantly at the offering, then ate from his hand. Carefully, Kol slipped the rope loosely around her neck. "There's a good girl," he said, rising cautiously to his feet. The black mare put her soft muzzle to his face and blew gently, her warm breath mingled with his in an affectionate display of recognition, and allowed herself to be led out of the pasture.

With the horses loaded onto the ship, Kol returned to the inn to retrieve their belongings. Even with many dock porters working with *Evarro's* crew to transfer the cargo onto the next ship, Kol understood it could take a while and so he had ample time to spare. When he came down the stairway into the crowded dining room, he spotted the innkeeper clearing dishes from the table.

"Could you tell me," Kol asked as he approached, "where can I find a doctor?"

The innkeeper laughed. "Not anywhere here, I can tell you that much." She set a pile of redware plates on her forearm. "They've all gone to Valenna to treat the plague."

"Isn't there a surgeon around?" Kol prompted.

She shook her head. "I can find you a barber, if you like. They're good with herbs and leeches."

Kol swore under his breath. "Leeches won't do it," he replied, walking away. As he crossed the room, he noticed the emerald green of a Sornian soldier's jacket, and his eyes met the man's briefly. *Great,* Kol thought bitterly as he recognized the face. Mercifully, the soldier seemed to be alone, and Kol hoped he'd let him pass without comment.

"So the traitor lives," the man said loudly as Kol made his way to the door. "Hiding away here, with the other criminals?"

Groaning to himself, Kol turned to face the soldier. "Jais. How's the nose?" he asked, forcing a grin. "Shouldn't you be in the Campos, licking Blackburn's boots?" His eyes shifted from the man's freshly-shaven head to the plate sitting on the table in front of him, which was loaded with bread, cheese and fried bacon.

Jais sneered at the insult. "It's Lieutenant Rett, to you," he said smugly. "And I'm on leave rotation. But I could ask you the same thing." He took a bite of bread. "I heard you were dead."

"What's it to you?" Kol asked, mulling over the situation. "Unless you're looking for the reward money."

"Not yours," Jais replied, his mouth full of food. He took a long drink from his cup. "That woman you were with before," he continued. "Do you know where to find her?"

Kol narrowed his eyes. "Which one?"

Jais let out a sharp laugh. "You're joking, right?" He shook his head in disbelief. "The only woman who's ever gone anywhere *near* you. The Valennian captive."

"What do they want with her?" Kol demanded, unable to hide the tension in his voice.

"Prince Matei wants his property back." Jais leaned forward, resting his elbows on the table. "He's rather set on it, for some reason. Offered a lot of gold for her return."

"Matei is alive?" Kol muttered, but Jais only shrugged. "Well, I have no idea where she is," Kol said. "And it looks like you came here alone."

He moved his hand to the hilt of his sword, and the other people in the inn glanced in his direction. "We both know you're outmatched."

Jais glowered at Kol's assessment, but didn't argue. "I'm not looking for trouble," he replied. "As I said, I'm on leave. Let's call it a truce for now. We'll meet again soon enough."

Kol noted that the next time he crossed paths with Jais, he'd have to kill him. "I look forward to it." He took a piece of bacon from Jais's plate and stuffed it into his mouth as he walked away.

Kol returned to see Martin standing by the gang-board of the *Evarro*, writing in the ship's manifest. Beside him, Kerchaw directed the crew in transferring the cargo onto a massive Valennian brig that was moored on the other side of the dock.

"Ah, Mister Kol," Martin said at his approach. "Excellent timing, as usual; this is the last of it."

"Why didn't the *Evarro* just take it onward to Valenna?" Kol asked.

"I'm not sure," Martin replied. "I don't know Madorran. My translator only said the captain refused."

Smugglers, Kol thought. *Some of their other cargo must be contraband.* He watched as crates were loaded onto the Valennian ship. Its hull was painted a bright yellow, with the name *The Canary* painted in black on its bow. Looking further down the wharf, he noticed old-fashioned caravels moored at the docks, which he supposed once belonged to the Sornian Navy, but now must be in the hands of reavers. "Which is Heffield's ship?" Kol asked.

"*The Poesy* departed already," Kerchaw replied. "Sailed east early this morning."

"'*The Poesy*?' Really?" Kol raised an eyebrow at the name. "Which port would it be heading to?"

"Raymouth, of course," Kerchaw stated. "Same as us."

"Great," Kol said grimly. His gaze drifted to the churning waters of the Bay. "Have you heard of a ship called *Seaborn*?"

"Ehh..." Martin scratched his head. "Sounds familiar, but I can't place it."

Kerchaw shook his head. "Is that a merchant ship?"

"I don't know," Kol replied.

"Perhaps Captain Willis will know of it," Martin offered. "It's something of a Valennian tradition for the captain to have tea with the passengers before a voyage; you can ask her then."

* * *

"This man is Sornian?" Captain Willis scowled, setting her teacup down with a clank as they all sat around the table in the small passenger cabin.

"In fact, Captain," Martin contested, "he is Valennian, according to the Queen."

"Well, if the Queen vouches for him..." Captain Willis grumbled, pouring herself more tea.

"I've had more trouble from my fellow countrymen lately, than from Sornians," Martin replied.

"Yes, I heard you've run afoul of Heffield," Willis replied. "And outside of Valenna, too. That's unfortunate." Taking a sip from her cup, she threw a glance at Kerchaw. Martin nodded but didn't reply.

"Do you know of a ship by the name of *Seaborn*?" Kol said at length.

"Certainly," Willis replied, pushing back the long braid of her ginger hair, which was mingled with so much grey it was nearly the color of parchment. "*The Seaborn* is a notorious reaver ship, manned by nationless vagabonds. Of what interest is it to you?" She lowered her weathered brow, eyeing him askance.

"That's personal." Kol looked down, swirling the dregs left in his cup. "Was it a reaver ship twenty years ago?"

"Do I *look* that old?" she asked sharply.

"Well, if you're asking—" Kol began.

"You have a fine ship here," Martin interrupted, looking around the well-furnished cabin. There were several berths adorned with tasseled curtains for passengers to sleep in, and cedar trunks in which to store belongings. "The finest I have seen, truly. What an honor it must be to be captain of it."

"Thank you. It is a fine vessel, isn't it?" Willis said, brightening at his words. She then went into a long and detailed story of how she worked her way up through the ranks on *The Canary* until she earned the command. They finished their tea and Captain Willis departed. Kerchaw soon excused himself as well to inspect the stowage.

"She hated me before I even opened my mouth," Kol commented with amusement.

"Yes," Martin agreed. "And more so after."

Kol leaned forward on his elbows. "How did she know I was Sornian just by looking at me?"

"The cut of your hair, most likely," Martin guessed. "Any proper Valennian man wears a long queue. But, there is something about your face..." He squinted, inspecting Kol's features. "The nose, I think."

Kol put a hand over his rather prominent nose. "What about it?"

"Nothing," Martin shrugged. "You should worry more about your manners."

"I've no idea what you mean," Kol replied dryly. "As far as I know, I'm charming." He drummed his fingers on the table. "Who knew you would be coming to Smuggler's Port?"

"Kerchaw, of course," Martin replied.

"This captain," Kol lowered his voice to a whisper, "did she know you would be here?"

"Well, yes," Martin admitted. "The captains of both ships knew to expect me, but I know for certain neither would collude with Heffield. If they had any allegiance to him," he reasoned, "they wouldn't have contracted with me in the first place."

"What about Kerchaw?" Kol prodded. "Do you trust him?"

"Absolutely." Martin braced his side with a hand and leaned back against the chair. "Kerchaw's been my agent nearly from the beginning; I couldn't run the company without him." He shook his head, "Heffield was probably here on business of his own."

"Hm." Kol rose from the table, but had to catch himself on the back of his chair as the ship lurched into motion. A queasiness welled up in his gut when he realized he would be stuck on this ship for several days. "Ugh," he cringed at the thought.

Martin reached out to steady his sliding teacup. "Seasick already?"

"Something like that," Kol muttered.

Kol sat at the table, sharpening his knife with a whetstone. Across from him, Martin pored over the pages of his ledger, making marks in it with quill and ink. A couple of days had passed quietly at sea, aside from patches of rough weather that kept them mostly below deck.

"Shouldn't that be sharp by now?" Martin asked.

Kol tested the edge of the blade with his thumb, then packed his things away. "When's tea?"

"Three," Martin said without looking up from his work. "Ten, and three. Same as yesterday. And the day before that." He turned a page. "And everyday." Martin let out a breath and slumped in the chair. "If you're that bored, then come here," he gestured to the seat beside him. "Help me balance the ledger. Do you know your numbers?"

"I know the basics," Kol replied. "Counting and adding, and the like."

"That's all you need." Martin pushed the book over as Kol took a seat. "See this column?" He pointed with the quill. "Take the prices listed for each item, and add them together. Write the sum here." He handed the quill to Kol, then took a brass pencil with a thick lead from his waistcoat pocket. "You do that page while I work on this one, and we'll be done in half the time."

They worked for hours, Martin pausing to explain each part in detail whether it was needed or not, until Kol felt as though he could finish the rest of it on his own.

Martin inspected Kol's work. "Good, very good. Now," he turned the page, "label this sheet 'Raymouth.'"

Kol's hand wavered above the page, then he slowly wrote, 'Ramith.'

"Uh," Martin blinked at Kol's blocky handwriting. "You do know how to write, don't you?"

"I just did," Kol tapped the sheet with a finger. "Read it."

"Raymouth," Martin sighed in defeat.

"See?" Kol dipped the pen into the inkwell and continued to work. After a time, he broke the silence. "To be honest, I didn't really know how to make letters before I came to Valenna," he confessed. "I'm still learning."

"On your own?" Martin asked, though his voice sounded faint.

Kol shook his head. "With Adella's help," he admitted. Martin didn't respond, and Kol looked up to see he had grown pale, with beads of sweat glistening on his temples. "Are you all right?"

Martin set his pencil down and rubbed his face. "I'm fine," he insisted. Rising from the table, he made his way toward one of the berths. "I just need to—" Before he could finish, he collapsed onto the sole.

"Martin!" Kol rushed over and rolled him onto his back.

"I'm fine," Martin murmured as Kol helped him sit up. "I just need to get some rest."

Kol walked along the weather deck, taking in the cool sea breeze that cut straight through the worn-out linen of his shirt. A sky full of summer constellations, glittering white against the black, moonless night, stretched out in every direction. He had been unable to rest in his berth deep within the hull. The thought of being beneath the waterline as he tried to sleep was too unsettling for him, like being in the womb of the fathomless sea. It brought to mind images of the strange, serpentine creature he had seen much too closely the last time he'd sailed, so he went above deck to find solace in the vast expanse of the heavens. Instead of bringing him peace, however, it made him feel insignificant and alone. He was reminded of the stories he'd heard when he was a small foundling in Hedda. *Each star a heaven,* he remembered. *A world of its own.* It was said that those who passed from this world found a new home in the heavens. *Where we will be reunited with our loved ones that have passed away from this world...* He gazed up at the twinkling stars in the smattering of galaxies that seemed to swirl in the dark void above, and wondered if there was anyone up there waiting for him.

He shook his head, clearing his mind. His contemplation turned instead to Greywood, and he hoped all was well there. He thought of Adella, and wondered if she was thinking of him, too.

The Canary came into port at Raymouth in the morning. Kol followed Martin, leaving Kerchaw to oversee the unloading of the cargo. Martin hunched forward as he went, with a hand over his side, though the man still insisted he was fine. They waited at the gangway while the crew offloaded the horses.

There was an unexpected solemnity among the people coming and going briskly from the docks, as well as a battered appearance to the many vessels that crowded the waters. One blue-hulled schooner, moored close by, had a crooked mast which had apparently been jury-rigged after some trouble at sea, with the new mast lashed to the stump of the old one. He watched as the crew brought a litter down the gang-board, bearing a dark, soft form on its surface. Squinting from across the pier, he realized the burden they carried was a body, lying motionless save for an arm that dangled limply over the side.

"Damn," Kol uttered, catching up to Martin on the gang-board.

"What do you suppose happened?" Martin asked over his shoulder.

"I'm sure we'll find out soon enough." Kol nearly bumped into Martin, who had stopped suddenly. Something had caught Martin's eye and, as he looked to see what it was, Kol noticed a stately barque flying an assortment of flags moored on the far side of the docks. One large, white pennant fluttering from its mast displayed the image of a five-petaled flower, and its hull was painted in bands of black and white. "Heffield's ship?" Kol guessed.

Martin nodded. "He won't have the gall to cause trouble here in Valenna," he stated, though Kol noticed a waver in his voice. "Let's stop by the Ivy Crown; we have a while yet before the cargo is all loaded onto the wagons, and I'm dying for a beer."

They made their way across the bustling street to the inn, which was only a short walk from the water. While the Hare and Dove Inn at Smuggler's Port had been an ill-constructed, sprawling hovel on the verge of tumbling into the harbor, the Ivy Crown at Raymouth stood tall and dignified. Its sturdy face of pale grey stone, carved with intertwining floral embellishments, seemed capable of withstanding any storms that might blow in from the Bay.

As they entered, Kol looked over the crowd that was gathered inside. Many huddled on benches with sailor's blankets drawn tightly over their shoulders, looking bedraggled and somber. He and Martin took seats at a table. "What's going on?"

"They're bringing the survivors here," one old man muttered into his stoneware tankard. He was apparently a sailor, judging by the bright blue of his wool jacket.

Kol leaned in to hear over the voices of the people around him. "Survivors of what?"

"Of Pentz, man! Where have you been?" the sailor reprimanded. "The entire city was destroyed, washed into the sea."

"Pentz?" Kol searched his memory. "Never heard of it."

"A wealthy port city," Martin informed him, "on the easternmost shores of the Bay, where it cuts into the middle of Valenna." He shook his head sadly. "How awful."

Kol looked around to see if he recognized anyone. He noticed one young man in sailor's blues tending to the wounded whose face seemed familiar, though he couldn't quite place it.

The innkeeper came by with a pitcher and tin gill cups, and Martin got his longed-for beer. Kol sat tapping his cup absent-mindedly with a finger.

"Not long now, my friend," Martin began. "Then you'll be back home at Greywood. Is there someone in particular you're eager to see?" he hinted archly.

Kol couldn't hide a smile. "Perhaps."

"I'm sure she'll be happy to have you back as well." Martin started to drink from his cup but stopped abruptly, setting it aside as he put a hand to his gut with a groan.

"What is it?" Kol asked, raising a brow at the pained look on Martin's face.

"Nothing," he insisted. "The beer isn't sitting right, that's all."

"You don't look well," Kol replied. "Do you need to rest? I have plenty of coin left for a room."

"No need," Martin said. "My townhouse isn't far. I have to stop by there anyway; that's where I keep my records."

Just as they were rising to leave, the inn door swung open and two women entered. To Kol's surprise, he recognized one of them. "Misses Asher," he called out over the noise, hailing her with a wave of his arm. As the two women approached, he noticed they looked disheveled, their clothes stained with seawater and eyes rimmed with red. "What are you doing here?" he asked. "I thought you were at Greywood."

"Lord Endlebridge found us," Misses Asher replied. Her voice was hoarse, and there was a distant look in her eyes. "On the roof. He brought us into his boat, and we were taken up on *The Bluebell*. He stayed behind to look for survivors."

"What are you talking about?" Kol asked, furrowing his brow. "What happened?"

"We were at Pentz..." she began softly. "Waiting to meet with Endlebridge. Then, the sea came in. It was too much, too quickly. She stopped to help Nell—" Her voice broke as she nodded toward the young woman beside her. "But the water, it took her instead. She went under, and didn't come back up..." She shook her head. "There was nothing we could do."

"Who?" Kol demanded, grabbing her shoulder. "Who went under?"

Misses Asher looked tearfully up into his eyes. "Miss Adella."

Her words hit his gut like an icy dagger. "*No.*" He took a step back. "No, that's not possible. She's at Greywood."

Misses Asher turned to open a bag hanging at her side. She pulled something out and presented it to him. "I'm sorry," she whispered, handing the object over.

Kol took it, turning it over in his hands. It was a notebook. Though the leather cover was damp and salt-stained, the pages wrinkled and yellow, he recognized it still. When he opened it, he saw Adella's handwriting, and his stomach clenched, breath catching painfully in his lungs. Clutching the journal to his chest, he backed away and leaned onto the table. "No!" Kol groaned through tightly clenched jaws. Lashing out, he swiped his arm across the surface, sending the cups clattering and spilling beer over the floor. Slumping to his knees, he hid his face in his palms.

Misses Asher came and knelt beside him, placing a hand on his shoulder. "I'm sorry," she whispered.

Kol drew a shaky breath. "I should have been there with her."

"Here," she said, offering Kol a flask from her bag. "Poppy spirits. This will help calm your nerves."

"Uh," Martin stammered, his eyes fixed on something across the room. "We should leave."

"Give him a moment, for goodness' sake," Nell admonished.

"Heffield's here," Martin whispered to Kol, who was taking a deep swig from the flask. "I'd rather not risk him seeing us here. Come, we must get to my house."

11

Matters of Business

Kol rubbed his face, pushing back the dark, tangled curls that hung in his eyes. Warm afternoon light shone on him from a large window, which framed a view of the sun shimmering on the Bay's blue waters. It took him a moment to remember how he came to be lying on a sofa in the small sitting area. When his memory cleared, a dark and heavy emptiness settled over him once more. He watched the waves crest and crash, foaming onto the shore until footsteps on the stairs brought his attention back into the room.

"Oh good, you're awake," Martin said. "I worried you drank too much of that stuff."

"How long have I been asleep?" Kol asked.

"A while," Martin replied. "Misses Asher sent for the physician; you just missed him."

Kol leaned forward, elbows on his knees. "What did he say?"

"Not much." Martin shrugged. "He plastered me with a poultice. If I'm not better by tomorrow, he said he would bleed me." Bracing his wound with a hand, he lowered himself into an armchair. "I'm so sorry about Lady Grimless," he said gently. "What will you do now?"

Kol looked down at his hands. "Doesn't matter."

"I still have some business matters to attend to here in Raymouth, but the wagons will be leaving for Elldon soon," Martin offered, "if you'd like to go home."

"No," Kol muttered. He had promised Adella he'd look after Martin. *And I failed at that,* he thought, guilt boiling up beneath his grief. But his task wasn't done yet; he couldn't abandon his wounded friend now, and the thought of returning to Greywood when Adella wouldn't be there was too bleak for him to bear. "There's nothing there for me now."

"Then you'll be my apprentice." Martin let out a breath, leaning his head back against the upholstered chair. His face still looked pale, with deep shadows beneath his eyes.

Kol nodded. Soon, a knock sounded from the door in the entryway, and he looked questioningly at Martin.

"That will be Kerchaw," Martin predicted.

Kol grabbed his sword in its scabbard from his pile of belongings on the floor and, unsheathing it quickly, went to answer the door.

Before Kerchaw could say a word, Kol seized him by the shirt and dragged him across the room. "Please—" he pleaded as Kol threw him down onto the carpet. Kerchaw struggled to regain his footing, but froze as cold steel pressed against his throat.

"Kol!" Martin rose from his seat, eyes widening. "What's this about?"

Kol pushed the blade beneath Kerchaw's upturned jaw. "Go on. Tell him."

Martin put a hand out to stop him. "That's enough—"

"He's right," Kerchaw interjected. "I told Heffield you'd be there alone. He—" His scarred face contorted in sorrow. "He threatened my family. Forgive me, I... I was afraid."

Kol dug the tip of the blade into Kerchaw's throat, and a ruby-red droplet trickled down his neck. "How do you feel now?"

"Stop," Martin's voice was strained and weak. "Let him go."

Kol watched the little rivulet of blood run down the man's skin. *It's not enough*, Kol told himself. *After what he did... It's not enough.* His muscles tensed, ready to run the blade deeper through the flesh.

"Stop!" Martin shouted, drawing Kol out of his thoughts.

Kol sheathed his sword. "Fine."

Rising tentatively to his feet, Kerchaw pulled a piece of folded paper from within his waistcoat. "Here—" He held it out to Martin. "For your records."

Martin let out a breath, then took the paper. "Thank you," he said flatly.

"Mister Martin, please," Kerchaw begged, "I—"

"Just go," Martin interrupted. "Notify me when the cargo is ready." With a nod, Kerchaw turned and left. Martin stood, tapping a finger to his lip, then turned to Kol. "Come with me. We have matters of business to attend to."

Kol followed Martin down a sidestreet, passing beneath colorful shop signs hanging by the doorways of the mismatched buildings. Finally, Martin stopped at a door and knocked. As they waited, they watched a man balanced precariously on a step-ladder while he took down an old, weather-worn sign bearing the name of Willems. Setting it aside, he picked up a freshly-painted new one, carved in the shape of a shield and bearing the name Larsin, and hung it in place of the other above the window. Martin watched with a distant look, engrossed in his thoughts.

The door before them opened, revealing an elderly man peering at them through a pair of bridge spectacles. "Ah, Mister Martin." White, wooly curls surrounded his face; his hair blending seamlessly into beard all around, save for a bald spot on top of his head. "I was just wondering when you might stop by. Please," he stepped aside to allow them entry. "Come in." He led them down a walnut-paneled corridor to a small study; shelves full of leather-bound record books and stacks of paper filled the walls. He motioned for them to sit at a polished mahogany table, already prepared with an inkstand and sheets of parchment.

"Sorry to come by without notice, Higgins," Martin began, "but there've been some pretty dire happenings of late, and I need to make some quick changes. To start, I've just taken on Mister Kol here as my apprentice, and we'll need the proper paperwork drawn up for that, if you please."

"Ah, yes," Higgins peered at Kol through little round lenses. "Welcome to the Royal Westward Trading Company, young man." He leaned over and presented his hand, and Kol shook it. "I am Rodbury Higgins, the lawyer for the Company. Nice to meet you."

"A pleasure, thank you," Kol replied, remembering Martin's earlier rebuke of his social skills.

Higgins dipped the quill into ink and set to work. "Now, let's see... Please spell for me your full name."

"K, O, L," he replied plainly. Higgins looked up, waiting for him to continue. "That's it," Kol said. "Just Kol."

"But what's your first name?" Higgins prodded.

Kol's shoulders drooped. "That *is* my first name. It's the only name I've got."

"Ah, hmm..." Higgins muttered, the lines on his forehead deepening. "I've not encountered that before." He twitched his mustache. "Very well then."

"You should know," Martin warned, "Heffield sent his men to attack me; he wants a monopoly. Avoid him, and anyone from the Belgrand Bay Company, at all costs."

"That scoundrel!" Higgins wheezed, his spectacles sliding down his nose. "I'm not surprised; I've always heard he was crooked. They say he pays the Royal Guards to look the other way when his ship comes in—Sign here, please," he muttered to Kol, tapping the paper with a finger before turning back to Martin. "Tell me what happened."

Martin related his recent experiences, beginning with his return to Elldon and his offer to supply the town, through his arrival at

Raymouth and Kerchaw's betrayal. Occasionally, his narrative was interrupted by Higgins' requests for signatures or questions on certain shipping details, as the lawyer continued writing up records. Kol sat patiently, writing his name whenever instructed to do so, engrossed in their discussion.

"Do you think I should go to the authorities with this?" Martin asked.

"Yes, absolutely. But..." Higgins ran his fingers over his beard. "He could just bribe his way out of it, as he does with all the smuggling charges. You'll have to be very careful who you talk to; Heffield's a powerful man."

"But the Royal Westward is backed by the Crown," Kol reasoned. "Doesn't that carry any weight?"

"Not in Raymouth," Martin sighed. "Higgins is right. We're a long way from the Capital. If I provoke Heffield here, I'll be giving him a good reason to finish what he began in Smuggler's Port." He picked up the quill and signed a paper that Higgins passed to him. "It'll have to be done carefully."

"I'll ask around," Higgins offered, "discreetly, of course, and find one who won't truckle to Heffield."

Kol sat once again on the sofa, staring out over the city as it awakened under the clear light of early morning. The previous day had been spent attending to various business matters, as he and Martin returned to the townhouse to update the records that were kept in the small room of his study. Martin had retired early in the evening, feeling unwell. Though Kol had been given a spare chamber upstairs for his own use, it was much too quiet for his liking, preferring the sofa beneath the bay window that sat at street-level. The clopping of hooves and voices of passers-by helped to distract him from the deep abyss of his thoughts. Even so, he had been unable to fall asleep, and spent the small hours of the morning in the little parlor by the entryway. In his hands, he cradled Adella's journal, its salt-stained leather rough under his fingertips. He hadn't summoned the courage to open it again, but kept it with him nonetheless. Kol set it down on the damask cushion when a knock echoed from the entrance.

He opened the door, and a portly man shoved a large porcelain jar into his arms. "Take this, will you? Thanks. Come along now," the man ordered and marched into the house. Kol found himself carrying the heavy jar up the stairs behind the man's flapping brown coat.

They entered Martin's chamber, waking him at their sudden intrusion. The physician pulled a chair from the nearby writing desk and sat beside the bedstead, opening a bag that hung from his shoulder. "You've no idea the trouble I had in acquiring these fine fellows," he intimated while he pulled out a pair of tweezers, nodding toward the jar in Kol's arms.

"The what?" Kol asked.

"You've got an excess of fluid in your abdomen," the doctor explained to Martin. He peeled away the dressings from the skin, revealing a small cut, the flesh around it swollen and red. "It's stopped up your organs; it needs to be drained." With that, he turned to Kol and motioned for him to come closer.

The physician lifted the lid of the jar and reached in with the tweezers, pulling out a small, squirming object. He held it up to peer at the little creature as it wriggled around in the air, its legless body mottled with a pattern of black, red, and green. "Yes, these little fellows will do the trick," he mused, then lowered the animal, situating it delicately onto the flesh around Martin's wound. The leech eagerly clasped onto the skin.

After placing several more onto the swollen flesh, the physician sat back in the chair to watch them at their task. The jar in Kol's arms grew heavy while he stood by, waiting. Eventually, the leeches began to release, one by one, and wander away, at which point they were taken up again in the tweezers and placed back into the jar with their squirming brethren. The physician poulticed the wounds and bandaged Martin's torso, then took his jar and left with a promise to return the next day.

As Kol carried a tea tray up the stairs from the basement kitchen to the dining room, he heard voices coming from the entryway. He set the tray carefully onto the table, sat and pulled a kitchen rag off the steaming teapot. Having taken great care to brew it exactly the way Armand had shown him at Greywood, he was eager to see if he'd succeeded.

He poured the tea into his cup, watching bits of leaf swirl around in the dark liquid. "Dammit," he whispered, realizing he forgot to place the strainer on the cup.

"No time for tea," Martin said as he appeared in the doorway. "Kerchaw is here and the cargo is awaiting our inspection." Then, without waiting for a reply, he left.

Grumbling to himself, Kol shoved his chair back and rose to follow. He walked behind Martin and Kerchaw as they made their way toward the port, the fresh seabreeze playing on their faces. Several large wagons were lined up along the wharf, hitched with sturdy draft horses and loaded at the ready.

"Thank you, Kerchaw," Martin said coldly. "We'll handle it from here."

Kerchaw's face contorted. "But—"

"You are dismissed from your duties," Martin ordered. "Permanently."

Kerchaw looked pleadingly at Kol, but found no sympathy. Slowly, he turned to leave, glancing back over his shoulder before finally walking off.

Martin began his inspection of the cargo, ensuring that every barrel and crate was accounted for and secured properly, while Kol marked it all in the ledger, checking it against the bill of lading. The work was tedious and the bright, summer sun shone in their eyes, drawing sweat from their brows. Just as they were tying the tarpaulin back in place on the last wagon, Misses Asher approached from the direction of the Ivy Crown, bag in hand. "You're looking better," she said to Martin. "Will you be coming with us to Elldon?"

"I'm afraid not," he replied. "I still need to meet with the notary yet today, but I promise you," he bowed slightly, "I won't deprive you of my company any longer than necessary."

"Good," she replied, smiling. Then she turned to Kol, and her expression softened. "Surely, you'll be going back home to Greywood now?"

Home. The word struck him in the heart. He knew it would never feel the same to him; he couldn't face the emptiness waiting for him there. Kol shook his head, "I can't." His voice was hoarse and faint, barely a whisper.

"That's too bad," she commented. "We really need you."

Kol couldn't summon his words, only cast his eyes downward.

"I see," she said gently. "Well, good luck to you both." Misses Asher then turned and climbed into one of the wagons, settling onto the seat beside the driver. Soon, a whip cracked in the air and the foremost wagon began to roll away, with the rest following one by one. Kol swallowed hard, trying to tamp down a burning sensation that rose within his chest when he watched the last wagon turn out of sight, heading toward the home to which he could no longer return.

"Why don't you go ahead to the Ivy Crown?" Martin suggested, the lines in his face deepening with concern. "Take the rest of the day off. I have a few things to finish up first, but will join you soon."

Kol nodded.

He sat in a dark corner of the inn, far from the hearth where the seafarers liked to gather and entertain each other with their stories. Kol watched as one in particular gave a dramatic performance, hands gesturing wildly in the air while he related some undoubtedly exaggerated tale to his companions. Though the sailor's voice was loud enough to be heard from across the inn, Kol wasn't listening; his thoughts were elsewhere. The stoneware tankard was heavy in his hand and still mostly full; the foam on the surface of his porter beer had long since flattened. He lost track of how long he had sat there, eyes shadowed beneath the hood of his cloak despite the warm surroundings.

A solitary figure entered the inn, briefly flooding the space with golden light from the evening sun before being eclipsed by the closing of the door. The newcomer's stride was quick, his demeanor was one of agitation, his gaze roved from table to table while making his way toward the back where Kol sat. As he came closer, Kol was surprised to see an unmistakably scarred face. Pulling back his hood, Kol stood and the man's eyes widened with recognition.

"Where's Martin?" Kerchaw demanded as he rushed over, with fresh blood smeared across his forehead.

"What do you care?" Kol retorted. "Trying to get him killed again?"

"Heffield's men are looking for him right now," Kerchaw warned. "I just managed to escape. Where is he? He's in danger."

"At the townhouse," Kol guessed.

"No, I just came from there." Kerchaw grimaced. "Damn! Where else would he have gone? We have to find him," he pleaded desperately, clutching at Kol's arm.

"He said he would meet me here..." Kol searched his memory. "Ah, right! He mentioned the notary."

"Come on," Kerchaw urged, pulling Kol by his shirt sleeve.

Leaving the inn behind, they ran through the cobblestone streets, dodging carriages and pushing past groups of people milling about by the shop windows.

"This way," Kerchaw prompted, breath heaving as they turned down a narrow alley.

Kol followed as they approached a small brick building, his heart pounding when he noticed the door hung ajar. Pausing to draw his sword from its sheath at his side, Kol steeled himself and stepped toward the threshold. He nudged the door with his foot and it swung inward.

With his blade at the ready, Kol entered, walking cautiously through a long entryway as his eyes strained to adjust to the dim candlelight. "Martin?" he called out, peering into every corner and shadow cast from the lit candles in the wall sconces while he approached an open doorway, with only darkness visible beyond. Kol pressed himself against the wall to the side of the opening, motioning for Kerchaw to do the same. They stood in silence and listened. From the other side of the threshold, a floorboard creaked.

As a figure emerged from the doorway, Kol lunged forward, blade raised to strike. He stopped his hand when he heard a feeble gasp emitted from the small, bent frame of an elderly man. The edge of the blade stopped just in front of the man's face.

"Oh good heavens!" the man squeaked. He put his trembling arms up defensively, his voice frail and crackling with age.

"It's just the notary," Kerchaw sighed.

Kol lowered his weapon. "Where's Martin?"

"He just left," the notary replied. "He'd got a message to meet with someone at the docks."

Sheathing his sword, Kol threw Kerchaw a dark glance before the two turned and ran off down the hall.

They sprinted across town, now and then colliding into people coming out of shops or walking haplessly in their way, knocking off hats and jostling parcels as they went. As Kol and Kerchaw reached the street leading to the shore, they stopped to look around.

The sun was lowering into the Bay, painting the waves in bright gold. The ships sailing to and from the docks were merely black silhouettes against the sunset, and shadows hid the features of the people coming and going. Kol searched the figures to find any who could be Martin, when his eyes spotted frantic movement by the southern jetty. It wasn't very far down the beach, but the fading light made it difficult for him to make out details over the distance. Squinting, he saw a group of people by the shore whose quick, exaggerated motions indicated a struggle.

"There!" Kol said, looking toward the action and drawing his sword. They ran onward.

Over the roar of the sea and the drumming of his own heart, Kol heard a cry carried on the wind as a figure collapsed onto the ground. When they reached the group, Kol was immediately met by fists armed with glinting knives.

Kol caught one wrist in his hand and, blocking the other with the hilt of his sword, threw his head forward, smashing into the man's face. He heard the brutal crack of bone when the sharp bridge of his attacker's nose gave way under his forehead. The man yelped, covering his face with his hands, while Kol drew back his arm and drove his sword into the man's belly.

As he pulled the blade out, a sudden force slammed to his side, knocking him flat onto the sand; his sword was knocked just out of reach. A great weight bore down upon Kol's chest, immediately followed by a hard blow to his face, cracking against his cheekbone and shooting pain through his skull. He opened his eyes again in time to see another fist flying toward him.

Instinctively, Kol caught the fist in one hand and braced the elbow with the other. Using the locked arm as leverage, Kol threw his hips upward and tossed the man to the side. Rolling over in the sand, Kol grabbed the man's throat and squeezed with all his might. His opponent's fingers clawed and dug at his arms until Kol felt the tension give way beneath his fingertips. The man lay still.

Kol grabbed his sword and scrambled to his feet to see Kerchaw pressed with his back flat against the rocks by a hulking mass of a man. Kerchaw was gripping the man's wrists, struggling to keep the knife point at bay. The distance between the blade and his chest closed gradually as Kerchaw slowly lost strength.

Kicking up sand behind him, Kol rushed over. With all the strength he could muster, he slammed his shoulder into the ribs of Kerchaw's attacker, and they both fell with a thud onto the ground. Kol scrambled to wrest the knife from the man. Finally wrenching it free, Kol sunk the blade deep into the man's gut. A harsh scream rang in his ears as crimson blood pooled out over the sand. Kol hopped to his feet and turned to face the remaining men.

The last two men pulled the weary Kerchaw in front of them; one held a knife firmly against his throat. "Stop," the man warned as he stepped backward, pulling Kerchaw. "One move from you and he's dead."

Glancing at Kerchaw, Kol saw fear in the man's eyes, the whites of his eyes bright in the dying sunlight. Kol froze, watching Kerchaw's captors drag him tentatively backward, step by step, then disappear behind the rocks.

Kol turned quickly, scanning the bodies on the ground. In the orange light of sunset, he recognized one man who sat propped up against a massive sea-worn boulder. "Martin!" Kol fell to his knees beside him, cold dread flooding through his gut.

A faint gasp issued from Martin's lips. His eyes fluttered briefly, then closed altogether. Below his chin, a wide slash across his throat spilled a dark cascade of blood that blanketed his chest, staining his white shirt a deep, ruby red. Martin's muscles relaxed, and his head drooped to the side.

"*No*," Kol gasped. He pounded his fists into the damp sand. "No!" he shouted, a guttural scream that carried down the beach.

* * *

Bejeweled rings glittered on Heffield's thin, knobby hands as he marked a tally in his log. He looked over the cargo as it was hauled on board *The Poesy*, the weather deck illuminated by lanterns hanging above him in the growing gloom of twilight. "Haul it in quickly," he instructed the crew, who were hoisting a crate onto the deck from a boat that had drawn alongside. "We have a lot more to stow yet."

One brawny sailor, who had been helping to lower a barrel onto the ship, lost his grip, and the barrel fell with a sharp crack.

"Watch what you're doing," Heffield reprimanded. "If that turpentine leaks, I'll stick your head in it." Behind him, a young crewman approached and cleared his throat. "What is it, Fernsby?"

"The sea's getting rough, sir," Fernsby began meekly. "The captain wants to move out of harbor before the storm blows in."

"Tell him to hold off," Heffield replied. "We have more naval stores coming, and these scrubs are going slow enough as it is." Fernsby nodded and Heffield left him to it, returning to his private quarters below deck.

Heffield sat at his cluttered desk, scratching letters onto parchment with a quill in the warm light of the chandelier overhead.

Fernsby appeared in the open passageway. When Heffield didn't acknowledge him, the young man cleared his throat. "Sir."

"What is it?" Heffield demanded.

"Your men have brought someone on board," Fernsby said in a low tone. "From the Royal Westward Trading Company."

"What?" Heffield snapped. "Is it that weasel, Kerchaw?"

"Yes, that's the one," Fernsby replied. "They've taken him hostage, as insurance. Martin is out of the way now, but one of his men has proven to be quite the fighter. They couldn't best him. "

Heffield groaned. "Bring him in."

Kerchaw twisted his wrists against the ropes that bound his arms at his back, but the knot held tightly. Bracing against the hands that pushed him by the shoulders, he stepped quickly down the companionway and into a lavishly furnished cabin. A well-dressed elderly man sat working quietly at his desk. The gallery windows at his back were pitch-black with night. As Kerchaw was shoved forward, the man set down his quill and looked up.

"I'd hoped to never see you again," Heffield frowned.

"Likewise," Kerchaw replied hoarsely.

"Take a seat." Heffield nodded at the two guards and they forced Kerchaw into a nearby chair. Heffield took up his quill once more. "I'm told there's one from the Royal Westward who's been making trouble for me," he stated plainly. "Care to give me his name?"

Kerchaw snorted, drawing phlegm from his throat, and spat.

Heffield set his pen down. "Do you want to play this game again?" he asked, leaning back against the chair. "I know where your family resides. You have a lovely wife, and a child… A little girl," he added, his voice like steel. "Tell me where to find him."

"You'll never find him," Kerchaw said darkly. "He has no name. Holding me here won't make a difference; he cares for no one, has no one. A highly-trained mercenary, he can kill you with his bare hands, and he never sleeps," he added with a grin. "No, you won't find him. He'll find you, and then it will be too late."

"Sir," a young voice interrupted as a crewman appeared from the entranceway. "We found this man sneaking around the cargo." He stepped aside as two guards dragged a tall figure in by the elbows, though the captive didn't seem to be struggling against them. Kerchaw groaned in disappointment when he recognized who it was.

* * *

Kol, still in the grip of the guards, glanced around the cabin. "Nice ship," he commented dryly, trying to tamp down his seething rage long enough to figure out a way to get Kerchaw out safely. He'd stolen a small boat from the docks and snuck aboard the ship under the cover of darkness, but he didn't exactly have a plan. It's not that he felt any real responsibility for man's life; he just wanted to deprive Heffield of the satisfaction of taking it. *And if I can find a way to avenge Martin while doing it, all the better.*

"Thank you, Fernsby," Heffield nodded to the crewman, dismissing him. Heffield's gaze shifted to Kerchaw, who was unable to hide a look of dismay. "You were saying…?"

Kerchaw rolled his eyes upward, shoulders dropping with a sigh.

"And what have we here?" Heffield mused. Eyeing Kol, he rose from the desk, leaning on a brightly polished cane as he approached.

"This man," Kerchaw nodded toward Kol, "is Martin's apprentice. I'm sure you're aware of Martin's fate," he said bitterly. "I think you can figure what that means."

Kol, still firmly in the grip of the guards, threw a questioning glance at Kerchaw, who nodded resolutely.

"So, you're Martin's apprentice?" Heffield asked dubiously. "I didn't know Martin bothered with apprentices."

Kol stood, unflinching, as Heffield looked him up and down.

"The man wasn't very clever, of course," Heffield continued, finally turning away. "He was far too trusting. But then, I suppose I had been, too, once." He began to pace the length of the cabin. "It had always been my calling in life to build an empire upon the Bay," he mused. "I knew that. When I met young Martin, working so hard to gain so little, I felt pity for him. He reminded me of myself. I took him under my charge, I taught him the trade. Made him into the man he became. And the thanks I got?" His footsteps quieted when he turned to face them again. "Betrayal." He shook his head. "He struck off on his own; wanted to be his own man. We could have had a monopoly. We could have owned Belgrand Bay; we could have been more powerful than the Crown itself!" He rapped his cane forcefully onto the planks. "No matter," Heffield sighed. "I get what I want in the end."

"What's your point?" Kol snapped.

A smile played on Heffield's wrinkled lips. "With Martin out of the way, I'll be able to build a truly formidable empire. Without competition to slow its growth, the Company will expand exponentially. And factor in the profit we'll make on this war, now." He waved a hand in the air, frills of lace dangling limply from the cuff. "I will say, your coming down here did take some audacity. I'm assuming that you're both in need of work now, correct?" He chuckled quietly to himself. "I could use bold men like you." He turned directly toward Kol, leaning on his cane and looking him square in the eye. "If you join me, your compensation will be far greater than anything Martin could have given. If you refuse..." He turned away with a shrug, "Well, you know how that will go."

"You think I'd join you?" Kol asked, voice laden with disgust. He shook his head. "No. I'm familiar with snakes like you; used to work for those men. I won't make that mistake again."

Heffield laughed sharply. "You're in no position to be so condescending." He gave a small nod to the guard behind Kol

Kol caught a flash of movement from the corner of his eye, but hardly had time to even flinch before a blow struck his jaw. His head jerked sideways with a crack as his teeth struck together, knuckles crushing his lip. The bitter taste of blood spread through his mouth.

"Well?" Heffield urged. "Have you reconsidered my offer?"

Kol prodded around in his cheek with his tongue. Locking eyes with Heffield, he spat out a shard of tooth. Seeing that Kol refused to answer, Heffield nodded to the guard once more.

A fierce blow to his side knocked the breath from him. Doubled over in pain, Kol caught himself on his hands. Once again, movement flickered on the edge of his vision as the guard kicked out to deal him another blow.

This time, Kol grabbed the man's foot and twisted it violently, toppling the guard down onto the planking. As the man rolled onto his back, Kol flung himself out toward him, bringing his elbow down hard on his throat. Kol hopped to his feet, leaving the man gasping and rolling in pain. The other guard drew a cutlass and lunged for him, but moved too slowly. Kol grabbed his wrist and twisted, wrenching the cutlass from his grip. He spun it in an arc and buried it in the man's side, the flesh giving way with a popping sound as the tip plunged through cloth and skin. The guard let out a hoarse sputter, mouth falling open as he dropped to his knees, with the blade skewered through his middle.

"Stop him, you idiots," Heffield shouted. Kerchaw's two guards released him and drew their swords on Kol.

"Go," Kol ordered Kerchaw, and turned to face the advancing guards. Footsteps retreated behind him as he sidestepped the thrust of a blade. Catching the guard's outstretched arm under his elbow, Kol smashed his fist into the man's nose with the sound of crunching bone. The cutlass clattered onto the planks as the guard yelped, cradling his face in his hands.

The second guard came at him, and Kol shoved the first guard at him bodily. Stumbling backward, they collided into Heffield, knocking his cane out from under him. Uttering a sharp cry, Heffield fell, sprawling out onto the sole as his cane rolled away. Desperately, he stretched out his hand to retrieve it, to no avail. It was out of reach.

Kol spun on his heel and ran up onto the weather deck and into the cool night air. Footsteps pounded behind him. "Stop him!" a voice shouted. The crew around him flew into action, chasing after Kol as he sprinted across the deck.

Scrambling haphazardly around piles of stores and sailors coming and going, he rounded past crewmen passing barrels down into an open hatch amidships, its wooden grate temporarily set aside while they loaded the hull. In the dim lantern light, Kol nearly ran into one barrel as it rolled vigorously toward the hatch, and made a quick leap over it. A commotion of shouts and oaths erupted behind him as one of the men chasing him collided into it.

Kol pushed past a group of sailors by the rail who were working to haul a hogshead barrel, suspended by a line from the loading boom, onto the ship from a boat alongside. Footsteps, falling quick and heavy, pounded after him.

He passed below the dangling barrel, darting by one crewman holding an iron grease lamp from a chain and calling out orders to the men holding the line.

"Ho!" a sailor shouted as one of Kol's pursuers ran into him. The line he was holding slipped briefly through his hands, and the massive barrel hanging above them plunged downward. The crewmen holding the line groaned as it slid roughly through their hands until they were able to regain their grip. The barrel swung wildly, inches above their heads.

"Out of the way!" the man with the lamp ordered as the men pushed past him, advancing on Kol with brandished blades.

Kol rounded again, ducking behind the sailor holding the barrel line, using the man's body to block his attackers.

"Ack!" the sailor exclaimed, stepping back as a sword slashed by his face. "Get away!" Hauling on the line, he moved backward to get out of the fray, and the barrel over their heads inched upward.

Kol lunged sideways to avoid one swinging blade, moving once more behind the sailor with a grip on the line. He darted to one side, then another, using the man as a shield until one misplaced blow caught the sailor in the shoulder. With a shout of surprise, the line ripped free from his grasp, and the barrel came crashing down.

Wood splinters flew through the air as a pungent liquid flooded over the planks. Kol recognized the resinous aroma of turpentine spirits while the dark pool coursed across the ship, cascading down into the open hatch. His eyes stung as the vapors wafted upward.

The edge of a blade flashed in the light of the grease-lamp, slashing downward toward Kol. He threw himself sideways just in time to feel air rush past his cheek, but the blade sliced through his shirt, grazing his shoulder. Groaning loudly, Kol smashed his fist upward into the man's jaw.

He spun again, edging backward until the lamp-bearer was just behind him, and faced the others. He was unarmed, surrounded on all sides; there was no chance of escape now. Steeling himself, Kol raised his fists. The turpentine vapors burned in his nostrils, stinging his lungs as the men stepped toward him, their feet sloshing in the puddle of acrid spirits that seeped over the planking toward the toes of his boots. Then, he had an idea.

Turning, Kol jabbed the man behind him in the gut, ripping the iron lamp from his grip. With one last glance at the widened eyes of the men around him, he dropped the grease lamp into the pool at their feet.

12

Aflame

Kol didn't stop to watch the liquid ignite. At the clank of the iron lamp as it hit the turpentine-covered planks, he spun and ran across the deck, leaving the crew to deal with the consequences of his actions.

At the larboard rail, he searched for a sign of Kerchaw, finally seeing his frantic silhouette running, arms akimbo, in his direction as a growing light behind him illuminated their surroundings.

"What's going on?" Kerchaw panted when he joined Kol, looking around for the source of the orange light.

"Uh," Kol muttered, looking back at his work. A bright blaze was spreading across the deck of the ship, flames mounting higher and higher as they surged toward the open hatch of the cargo hold. The crew ran from the encroaching flames, shouting warnings to the other sailors below. *Shit!* Kol thought. *The barrels!* "We've got to get off the ship," he urged. "Now!"

They ran toward the bow, scrambling up the forecastle steps. At the rail, their shadows danced in the firelight. Feeling heat at his back, Kol glanced behind to see the main mast aflame, tongues of fire running eagerly up its tarred surface toward the sails. Deep within the ship, an intense inferno rumbled amid screaming as men fled the companionways. Thick, black smoke billowed out from behind them. All over the ship, the crew was in a panic; some ran below to try to help their fellow crewmen, others ran to the davits to lower the boats, or threw themselves into the water.

Turning back toward the sea, Kol gripped the rail. Below, black waves pounded against the hull; the foamy crests glowed orange beneath the blaze of the ship.

"We have to jump," Kol shouted over the roar of sea and fire, to himself as much as to Kerchaw.

Though he nodded in agreement, Kerchaw wavered as he looked down onto the dark, turbulent sea. The waves whipped to a frenzy in the rising wind, with heat and embers scorching their backs.

"Go!" Kol yelled. Kerchaw, with shaking hands, pulled himself up onto the rail and jumped, disappearing beneath the raging sea. Then, Kol climbed the rail and dove.

The pitch-dark water, frigid after the blazing heat, enveloped him, shocking his limbs as he plunged beneath the waves. He surfaced, blowing out the seawater, and searched for Kerchaw. Spotting him just ahead, swimming toward the shore, Kol followed.

Violent waves crashed over his head, pushing him below the surface as he struggled to keep afloat. *The Poesy* wasn't anchored far from shore, but the muscles in his limbs burned with exertion and began to cramp. Fighting against the tide, he wondered if he would make it.

Finally, Kol collapsed onto the shore beside the docks, gasping with exhaustion. In the firelight, he found Kerchaw and, coughing up seawater, watched the fire blaze in the distance.

Kol turned over on the sofa; the first light of dawn softly illuminated the sitting area. He had spent the past few days lost in his thoughts alone in the townhouse that had fallen into his care since Martin's death. Despite his silent, solitary surroundings, however, he could find no reprieve in sleep.

He got up and crouched at the hearth to make a fire. Though the air was warm enough, as the summer nights had turned balmy, he wanted the light. He struck the iron and flint, blowing gently on the spark that ignited in the tinder he had placed in the cold ash of the unkempt fireplace. A small flame sprouted, and he fed it kindling from the tinder basket beside the hearth. Watching the fire grow, the image of *The Poesy* ablaze arose, unbidden, in his mind.

Blinking it away, his thoughts turned once again to Adella. His heart gave a sharp pang each time he thought of her; he preferred it to the emptiness he felt otherwise. *I didn't even say goodbye.* He rubbed his face, pressing his palms over his eyes as tears rose. *So much I wanted to say...*

Kol reached for his haversack, which he had left carelessly by the hearth. Upending it, he scattered the contents over the floor. Folded papers spilled out along with his borrowed copy of *Mother Tigress*, until finally, Adella's leather notebook fell at his feet. He lifted it reverently, turning it over in his hands. The leather was dappled with salt stains, and the pages inside were yellowed and wrinkled. At Greywood, he had merely meant to tease Adella about reading her journal; he never would have done it. Now, it didn't seem to matter. Kol untied the leather strap that secured its cover and flipped through the pages, glancing over the graceful script until his own name caught his eye. He stopped to read.

For Kol's pay, I shall take the standard wages for a Lieutenant in the Cavalry, since his experience and ability are a match for that rank, or better. Then I'll double it, as he is new to Valenna and must build a life from nothing.

As for his character, though his manners might seem rough at first, I've found him to be an admirable man in every regard. I hope he stays at Elldon. With his military experience and intimate knowledge of the Sornian army, I know he will prove indispensable in our survival of this war. But more than that, he deserves a home, a place to belong. I hope he can find that here.

Kol closed the notebook. *Home.* The word stabbed his heart with hopeless longing. He had stayed in Raymouth to help Martin because that was the last thing he promised Adella he would do. After Martin was killed, Kol continued on his work with the Royal Westward Trading Company not only because it was all that was left of his friend's life, but mostly because he couldn't bring himself to go back to Greywood and face the emptiness that waited for him there. Keeping himself busy at Raymouth had kept his mind off the pain. *Admirable*, Kol thought bitterly, guilt gnawing in his gut. *You're wrong about me, Adella.* He let out a guttural shout and threw the book against the wall. *You hired me to protect you, and I left. Now you're gone—* He pressed his hands into his wet eyes, his breath coming out in ragged gasps. *And then Martin...* His jaw clenched. *I've failed at everything.* He looked through his belongings until he found the flask Misses Asher had given him. It was still mostly full. *If the small amount that I had was able to knock me out for so long...* He pulled out the cork. *I wonder what would happen if I drank the whole thing?* Slowly, he raised the flask to his lips.

A knock sounded at the front door. "Go away," Kol called out.

"No," came a muffled reply. The door unlocked with a metallic click, and Kerchaw entered, pocketing a brass key, and holding a large redware dish in the other hand. He looked at Kol, who still sat on the floor amid a scattering of belongings, half-dressed with hair disheveled, and frowned. "Get up," Kerchaw ordered. "There are matters of business that need your attention."

"Leave me alone," Kol muttered. "I don't want to be a merchant."

"Well, that's too bad," Kerchaw lifted his brows, feigning a sympathetic tone as he crouched down beside Kol, "seeing as you're now the sole owner of the largest mercantile in Valenna." He took the flask from Kol's hand. "Here," Kerchaw said, handing him the cloth-covered plate instead, "my wife made this for you."

Kol blinked at the dish in his hand. It was warm, and a savory fragrance wafted up from it. "What is it?"

"It's a meat pie," Kerchaw explained. "It's her specialty." He grabbed the cork from the floor and straightened. "Oh," he commented in surprise, sniffing the air above the flask. "Is that Madorran?" Kerchaw took a small sip, then licked his lips with satisfaction. "Mm, that's the stuff." He corked the flask and slid it into his waistcoat pocket. "Now, let's get to work. You've got a shipment coming in this week. From Sornia, by way of Smuggler's Port."

"I remember Martin dismissing you from the Company," Kol countered, setting the pie aside, then rose to his feet and straightened, towering over the other man. "After you betrayed him to Heffield."

"I didn't know he meant to kill him," Kerchaw pleaded, his pitted brow crumpling with emotion. "Please, the Royal Westward is my life; it's all I know. You can trust me; I swear it."

"I know I can," Kol replied darkly, and Kerchaw gave him a questioning look. "It would be stupid to provoke me," Kol warned. "I've got nothing left to lose."

On the dock, Kol stood in the bright morning sun looking at the furled but ragged sails of a Sornian Navy caravel. Bits of shredded canvas fluttered from the yards. Judging by its unkempt state and lack of a Royal ensign, it had been acquired by a different sort of owner and put to other purposes.

"A bit old-fashioned, isn't it?" Kerchaw asked. "Why do Sornians still use caravels?"

"They're traditional," Kol replied with a shrug. In truth, he knew very little about sailing, since he had avoided the water for most of his life.

"Shall we?" Kerchaw said, waving his hand in mock affectation.

With the large logbook under his arm, Kol strode onto the gangboard and *The Daringuard*.

As soon as he boarded, an older man in a dingy, cockaded hat and faded black coat came to greet him. "Welcome, my good sir," the man said in a heavy Sornian accent, bowing slightly. His face seemed to bear a permanent squint. "You must be the new owner of the Royal Westward. Mister Kol, is it?" he asked, and Kol nodded. "I'm Captain Jakim; the Westward and I have done a lot of business together," he explained. "But come; there will be plenty of time to chat later. This way, this way," the man prompted chipperly. Though he had a slight limp, his steps were lively.

They followed him into the dark cargo hold, dimly lit by lanterns hanging from the beams. Jakim took one down and handed it to Kerchaw while Kol opened the log book and, taking out a brass pencil, began to check the cargo against the bill of lading. They worked quietly for some time, scrutinizing the quantity and state of the goods until Captain Jakim broke the silence. "Nice to see a fellow Sornian get out into the world and make something of himself," he commented, pulling back a tarpaulin. "Especially one from the lower classes."

"Thanks," Kol replied curtly. "Is it that obvious?"

"Your name," the captain explained. "It's common among the lowborn. In fact, there are three other Kols on my ship, all from the streets or auction. One with a K, one with a C, and the third doesn't know, since he can't spell."

"How do you give orders to one and not the others?" Kerchaw wondered.

"Don't matter which is which," Jakim replied. "So long as the work gets done."

"Right." Kol made a mark in the book and turned the page. "You've been at sea for many years," he guessed, looking at the captain's sun-wrinkled face. "Have you heard of a ship called *The Seaborn*?"

"Sure," Jakim replied. "Who hasn't?"

"What do you know of it?" Kol asked eagerly.

"It was a fine merchant vessel," Jakim replied. "Well, that is, until the mutiny."

Kol stopped writing. "What happened?"

"Well..." Jakim's squint deepened. "The ship belonged to a man named Adamas Seaborn, who made an honest fortune transporting tea. It was good work in those days; the Sornian Navy had the run of the Bay, and you'd never hear of any trouble from reavers. However, Seaborn came to misfortune when he made the mistake of trusting a Valennian to command his ship, begging your pardon," he said, nodding respectfully to Kerchaw. "It turns out," Jakim continued, "that the captain he hired—whose name I can't recall," he added, scratching at his wiry, white sideburns, "had planned treachery all along. As they sailed back across the Bay, the captain turned half the crew against Seaborn, and they staged a coup to take the ship." He moistened his lips.

"Go on," Kol urged.

"Like I said," Jakim continued, "the waters were safe in those days. Seaborn's family were all on board; his wife and young son were lost that day. Though Seaborn himself was terribly injured, they were able to defend the ship, but the Valennian captain and the rest of the scoundrels escaped."

"Young son?" Kol's blood ran cold as he remembered his dream. "What happened to him?"

Captain Jakim shrugged. "They never found him."

Kol swallowed, his mouth suddenly feeling dry. "What was his name?"

"I can't remember now," Jakim replied. "You'd have to look in the ship's records."

"*The Seaborn* still sails?" Kol asked impatiently.

Jakim shrugged. "As far as I know."

"And what about Seaborn, the man?" Kol demanded.

"He'd been captured by the Valennians," Jakim replied. "Tortured, they say. Then imprisoned. But—" His voice lowered conspiratorially, "I've heard he escaped, and can be found in Smuggler's Port, if you know where to look."

Kol thanked the captain for the information, and they continued to work in silence while he pondered what he'd heard, wondering if it might be connected to his dream in some way. *After all,* he figured, *it was the same name on the ship. It can't be a coincidence.*

Many hours had passed by the time they finished checking the cargo, and Captain Jakim escorted them above deck. Kol and Kerchaw thanked him, crossed the gang-board once more, and stepped onto the dock, making their way back toward the streets of Raymouth.

"What say we go to the Crown?" Kerchaw suggested. "Get a proper ale." Kol agreed with the idea, and they turned along the street that edged the wharves to make their way toward the Ivy Crown.

As they walked through the busy streets, a familiar shade of ruddy brown hair caught Kol's eye. A woman walked just ahead, her once-fine clothes torn at the shoulder. The strands of her auburn hair hung down her back, loose and disheveled from wind and water. He pushed his way through the people coming and going, or milling about in front of shop windows, all the while struggling to keep the small, elegant figure ahead of him in his sight. His heart pounded in his chest and thrummed in his ears; soon all he could hear was the sound of his own breath while he fought to catch up. *It's her...* He reached out a hand toward the woman just as a carriage barreled through a cross-street right before him, cutting her off from his view. When it had passed, Kol looked desperately around, but there was no sign of the woman. *Did I imagine it?*

"What is it?" Kol was surprised to hear Kerchaw's voice behind him, and turned to find that Kerchaw had hastily followed him.

"Nothing," Kol sighed, trying to calm his nerves. "I thought I saw something."

"You should probably stay away from the poppy spirits," Kerchaw advised.

By the time they made their way to the Ivy Crown and sat at a table, Kol was more than ready for an ale or two. The innkeeper must have read it on his face, since she immediately brought them a pitcher and stoneware tankards.

"I wanted to say," Kerchaw began, filling his cup, "I know it can't be easy for you; this wasn't in your plan, I'm sure." He took a drink. "The Westward, I mean."

Kol nodded in acknowledgement.

"And," Kerchaw continued, "I get the sense there's more to what you're going through than I realized."

Kol didn't reply, only looked down into his ale.

Kerchaw went on, "But I wanted to thank you for stepping into Martin's role, daunting as it is." He gave a slight smirk. "He would be proud of you."

"Thanks," Kol replied. "Truthfully, I wouldn't have been able to do it without your help." He drained his cup and refilled it.

The innkeeper eventually returned with stewed beef and onions and the two sat, eating and drinking. As the night wore on, people filled the dining area, leaving some to stand. Kol and Kerchaw each counted out their coins to pay the innkeeper, setting them on the table as they prepared to part ways for the night. Kol looked over the groups of people chatting and laughing loudly while he finished off the last of his ale. Much to his surprise, the reddish hair of a woman from across the room caught his attention.

Kol set his tankard down, hand trembling as he rose from his seat.

Without taking his eyes off her, he crossed the room toward her against his better judgment, compelled by a deep longing. The clothes she wore weren't the same as those on the woman he'd seen earlier; there was no tear in the fabric, no blood at the shoulder. *That hair...* It was the same shade of auburn. He stopped just behind where she sat, surrounded by companions telling raucous stories with slurred voices. He reached out slowly, then grabbed her shoulder. At his touch, she spun around.

The face he looked into wasn't the one he had wished to see; the woman was older, with a heavily powdered visage and an ink-drawn mole by her mouth. "Do you want something?" she asked coyly. "I can be good company."

"Sorry," Kol muttered, his shoulders falling in disappointment. "Not what I'm looking for."

"Then maybe you should lower your standards," she retorted, eyeing him up and down. "You don't exactly look like a gentleman, yourself." With a scoff, Kol turned to walk away. "You don't smell like one, either," she called out as he made his way toward the door.

Catching up beside him, Kerchaw laughed loudly. "Did she turn you away?" he wheezed. "Sorry to say, but..." He snorted. "She's not a picky woman."

"It's not like that," Kol replied sulkily, annoyed more at himself than Kerchaw. "I thought she was someone else."

13

Reunion

Kol stepped onto the gang-board, squinting under the hot, mid-day sun. "Ugh," he sighed, his resolve waning. The ship he faced was massive and imposing, the weathered wood of its hull oiled and tarred to a dark gleam that contrasted with its brightly gilded trim-mings. Beyond the ship, the indigo waves of the sea glittered as far as he could see in an endless, heaving plane, its wild, opaque surface con-cealing all the dangers that lay beneath, unseen but ever-present. His thoughts flitted back in time until he stood, in his mind, once more aboard *The Tigress*, watching helplessly as Adella sank beneath black, stormy waters.

Kerchaw stopped next to Kol, yanking him from his thoughts back to the present. "What is it?" Kerchaw asked, sounding more curious than concerned.

"Nothing," Kol replied, rather unconvincingly.

Kerchaw raised an eyebrow. "You needn't sail with the cargo, I've got it managed." He eyed Kol, who stared down into the waves, his pale knuckles clutching the strap of the haversack that hung across his chest. "You sure you want to do this?"

"You mean sail?" Kol asked, gaze moving from the water up to Ker-chaw's face.

"Find Seaborn," Kerchaw replied. "It could be a waste of time." He frowned. "Or worse."

"I have to do this," Kol insisted. "I've always wondered what happened to me—to my family." He released his grip on the haversack and wiped his sweaty palm on the dingy linen of his shirt. "If anyone can tell me, it'll be him." He took a deep breath and strode forward.

"If you say so," Kerchaw mumbled, following Kol on board.

They were soon met by the first mate and shown to a private cabin, which was generously equipped with exquisitely-crafted furnishings. Kol tossed his haversack onto the mattress in one of the curtained berths, then sat, looking around. "Damn," he muttered. "Now *this* is a nice ship."

"*The Eglantine* is the finest ship on the Bay," Kerchaw said, dropping his bag at his feet. "You should buy it."

Kol let out a sharp laugh but stopped when he saw Kerchaw's blank expression. "You're serious?"

"I know the owner," Kerchaw explained. "He's looking to sell. The Royal Westward can certainly afford it, and the business could use a ship of its own, now that it's grown so much in the Belgrand Bay Company's absence."

"My own ship..." Kol said under his breath, his voice trailing off as he considered it. He had to admit, the thought of owning something so grand was certainly appealing.

"Think it over," Kerchaw advised. Beneath their feet, the sole lurched as the vessel got underway.

Kol looked expectantly toward the companionway. "No tea this time?"

"The captain is Sornian," Kerchaw informed him pointedly.

Kol laughed to himself. "Right. I suppose I've gotten a little too used to Valennian customs."

The first day of their voyage was uneventful, as the weather was clear and bright and the sea calm. This allowed the passengers to spend much time above deck taking in the fresh air; however, the only excitement to be had were the few occasions when the crew would spot something moving in the water. Hearing the spirited chatter that ensued, Kol and Kerchaw would rush over to the rail each time, only to be met with a view of the unbroken waves and nothing more.

The next day, *The Eglantine* passed close by the rocky fangs of the Teeth that rose out of the sea along the southern coast of the Bay, which formed the northern border of the Campos. Kol stood at the rail, watching the dark, jagged shapes pass in the distance, though his mind was far off beyond the shore. Roaming over the familiar fields, it alighted on Greywood Manor. Grief and longing burned in his chest, tightening around his heart. Like picking at an open wound, though, he preferred the sharper, more immediate pain to the dull ache of emptiness that hid beneath.

Voices rose up from the other side of the ship, snapping him back to the present. Excitement shot through him when he realized the crew were shouting, "Sail, ho!" for the first time since leaving port. The voices were sharp and their tones urgent, though Kol couldn't imagine why the sight of another ship should cause such a commotion. Curiosity drew him across the deck, where he found Kerchaw already among the crew that gathered at the rail, straining to get a clear view.

Kol wove his way through the crowd and looked out over the sea. There was, indeed, another ship sailing the waters, but that wasn't what caught his attention. A huge, snakelike figure, swift and dark, rose from the waves, its massive head towering up on its thick stalk of a neck just above the deck of the small Sornian caravel. A spiny fin formed a long crest down its back, and its elongated snout bore sharp teeth that protruded menacingly, visible even across the distance.

Screams carried across the water as the beast lunged over the ship, jaws snapping at the caravel's crew as they fled. The creature threw itself forward again, stretching across the main deck as it caught one unfortunate sailor in its teeth. A shrill, frantic cry echoed over the sea, ending abruptly as the animal tossed its head back and swallowed the man whole. The sea serpent wrapped its coils around the caravel and the mighty weight of its enormous body lay upon the ship, pulling the larboard side downward toward the water. Kol winced as he watched; the crew all around him had fallen silent.

From the far side of the caravel, another great, serpentine form appeared, rising between the masts to join the other on the decks. Among the waves, more of the beasts gathered, rising up from the water until the little caravel was entirely surrounded by dark, sinuous shapes.

"Should we try to help them, Captain?" Kol heard a crewman beside him ask.

"There's nothing we can do," came the captain's resolute answer. "Keep on course and for goodness' sake, keep your voices down." Across the water, dark shapes continued to gather at the surface until the sea around the caravel was black and writhing. A strange, eerie sound carried over the waves, and it took Kol a moment to realize it was the hiss of the sea serpents, which were now so numerous their vocalizations buzzed in the air, carried on the wind.

"Heavens, have mercy," Kerchaw uttered under his breath beside Kol, his face ashen as he pulled off his hat and placed it over his heart. As they looked on with open mouths, the creatures in the water slithered over the decks of the ship one by one, snatching and tearing at the crew, fighting each other for their dangling limbs, until it was overburdened with their massive bodies as they coiled around the forecastle and masts. The ship's larboard side listed lower and lower until the weight of the serpents finally rolled the caravel over and waves submerged the decks. Hapless sailors tumbled into the sea as the caravel capsized. Then, only the hull remained, keel to the sky, among the thrashing of the sea serpents.

"Back to your watches," the captain ordered, turning away from the rail. "Keep quiet," he continued as the crew returned to their duties. "And don't use the seats of ease or the pissdales until we are in safer waters, or we'll bring the damned things down upon us as well."

Kol clutched the rail, watching as the caravel disappeared into the distance.

When *The Eglantine* sailed into Smuggler's Port late the following day, Kol was glad to step foot on land. The remainder of their voyage had been nearly silent, with hardly a word uttered above a whisper, save for the captain's commands. Leaving Kerchaw to attend to his duties among the cargo, Kol went off on his own to find the man called Seaborn.

He walked along the wharf in the dying light of evening, heading toward the Hare and Dove. The rising wind whipped the waves up until they sloshed over the planks of the walkway, wetting his boots. Dark, foreboding clouds hung low over the town, the sharp scent of rain filling the air as he came to the inn door.

Inside, he walked along the edges of the dining area, keeping to the shadows outside of the light of the tin lanterns that sat upon greasy tables. Upon benches, people sat hunched over their tankards in the smoky atmosphere. His eyes flit from figure to figure but never lingered long enough to draw attention, until one face lit up with a smile aimed in his direction.

"You, there!" her voice croaked, broken with age, while she gave a feeble wave. "Yes, you," she said as Kol turned in her direction.

"Uh," he began quietly, striding quickly toward the old woman. "Do you know me?"

"Is that my little Kol?" she asked, the heavy wrinkles of her face furrowing deeper. "Not so little anymore." She patted the empty space on the bench beside her. "Come, sit with me."

Kol glanced around the room, relieved to find that no one else appeared interested in his presence. Smuggler's Port was too close to Sornia for his comfort, and he had many enemies in his old homeland. He lowered himself slowly onto the bench, squinting as he peered into her face. Her small eyes were nearly buried under heavy eyelids, but they glimmered with joy. "Mama Tia?" he asked tentatively. "How did you get out of Sornia?"

"I raised half the soldiers in Hedda; they let me come and go as I please," she said and, face wrinkling, smiled proudly. "I remember the day you were brought to me. Those dark eyes, those black curls. Yes, you're the little boy I gave the name of Kol."

"I'm surprised you remember me," he admitted.

"Nonsense," she chided, swatting his hand weakly for emphasis. "You were my favorite."

He let out a small laugh. "I had no idea."

She shrugged. "No, the other boys were hard enough on you already. You didn't speak to anyone for nearly a year; I didn't want to give them any more reason to dislike you." She took a drink from her tankard with a trembling hand, then set it back down with a slosh. "You were always a lonely child," she reminisced, her voice softening. "You wanted so badly to find friends, but you didn't know how to do it."

"Right." Kol looked down at the battered surface of the table, prying at a splinter of wood with his thumbnail. Sometimes, he still felt like that lonely orphan from long ago.

"Well, you're grown now," she said, dismissing the memories with a wave of her hand. "You're not that lonely boy any more, are you? You must have found someone special to settle down with by now?"

"Almost." The word came out more quietly than he intended. He cleared his throat. "And what have you been up to?" he asked. "What are you doing out here?"

"The Hare has good beer," she shrugged. "I still help out at the Home for Boys when I can, but my mind isn't what it used to be; I get confused sometimes..." Her jowls lowered into a frown. "How is the soldier's life treating you?"

"It wasn't for me," Kol stated firmly. "I'm a Valennian citizen now, and a merchant."

"Good for you!" she said, her small eyes twinkling. "I knew you'd make something more of yourself. A merchant!"

"That's partly why I'm here," he admitted. "That, and I'm trying to locate a man named Adamas Seaborn. I think he can help me find..." He rubbed the back of his neck. "Something I'm looking for. Have you heard the name?"

"No," she said with a slight shake of her head. "I'm sorry I can't help you."

"Don't worry about it," Kol replied. "I always wondered," he began thoughtfully, leaning forward on his elbows, "but I never had the courage to ask; why did you name me Kol?" His eyebrows drew together. "Was it just because of my eyes, my hair?"

"No, dear," she replied, pity softening her voice. "It was my brother's name. He died years before you came to us, but you looked just like how I remembered him."

"You named me in memory of your brother?" His heart panged sharply with an emotion he couldn't name.

Tia nodded. "That's why you were my favorite." She smiled, though the edges of her eyes glistened.

"I had always thought..." Kol began, then shook his head. "Doesn't matter," he said more to himself than to her. Beside him, Tia yawned loudly, her heavy eyelids drooping. "I won't keep you any longer," he said quietly. "It was good seeing you again."

"Goodbye, Kol," she said, placing her thin hand over his. "I hope you find what you're looking for."

Kol lifted her hand and gently kissed it. "Goodbye, Mama Tia." He rose from his seat and approached the innkeeper, who was busy wiping a table with a rag.

"What can I get you?" she asked, tucking the rag into her apron while he took a seat close by.

"Brandy." He set down two silver pieces.

She eyed the coins, raising a brow. "Valennian coin?"

"Does it matter?" he grumbled. "It's silver."

She pocketed the coins, then headed toward the kitchen. Kol didn't wait long before the innkeeper returned, sloshing a small glass of golden brandy down on the table in front of him.

"One more thing," he added quickly. "I'm looking for a man named Adamas Seaborn; have you heard of him?"

"I might've," she said, raising her thick brows and jingling the coins in her pocket. Taking her meaning, he reached into his bag again and set a silver piece on the table. She cleared her throat pointedly, and Kol set another coin down.

"I'll see to it you find him," she whispered, swiping the coins off the table and pocketing them. "Wait here." She then returned to the kitchen.

Kol sipped his brandy and watched the pendulum swing on a large wall-clock nearby, its heavy brass weights slowly lowering with each movement. He turned the little brandy glass, rotating its fluted stem in his fingers absent-mindedly. Finally, the innkeeper returned, clearing plates and trays from the dining area. When she passed, she slipped a piece of paper down onto the table in front of him. Kol studied the words written on it, then stuffed it in his haversack. Downing the last of his brandy, he headed out the front door.

Outside, a gust of wind blew tendrils of hair in his eyes. Walking along the wharf, Kol's hand moved protectively to the hilt of his cutlass when he came to a narrow alleyway that ran between the rows of buildings. Slowly, he made his way down the dark passageway, counting the number of doors on his way.

Kol's footsteps echoed down the empty alley as he came toward the rear entrance of one building. Aside from the muffled voices coming from within the other ones that lined the alleyway, he could hear no other sounds. He seemed to be alone in the narrow space, yet he was keenly aware of each doorway, each dark opening that led to other passages.

At his approach, the door creaked open, revealing a young man holding a chamberstick. "You the one looking for Seaborn?" he asked in a heavy Sornian drawl, even more pronounced than Kol's own.

"I just want to speak with him," Kol assured the man. "Personal matters."

"Personal, is it?" he replied, the lines of his face scrunching up to make odd shadows in the candlelight. "You work for the Valennians?"

"I *am* a Valennian," Kol stated. "But as I said, I just want to—" A hard blow smashed into his ribs, forcing the air from his lungs. He spun in time to catch a fist in his hand, this time aimed at his face.

Jaws clenching, Kol twisted the man's fist in one hand and, with the other, jabbed him with all his might just below the sternum. The man doubled over, wheezing as he struggled to take a breath.

A sudden force caught Kol around the neck. He struggled to breathe as his throat tightened, squeezed in the crook of an elbow. His fingers pried at the powerful, sinewy arm, nails digging and scraping at the sleeve as his vision blurred. Veins pounded in his neck and his ears rang as the world around him began to darken. Kol's legs buckled and he collapsed to the ground, pulling his assailant down with him.

Writhing on the gritty cobblestones, his hands finally clamped around the wrist that held him and, pulling it away, he gasped for air. As his sight returned in flickering spots, fingers grabbed his scalp, tearing at his hair and yanking his head backward. Kol reached for his boot and, fingertips fumbling inside, grabbed the knife.

He jabbed the tip of the blade into firm flesh beside his hip and a sharp yelp rang in his ear. A sudden blow hit his jaw and pain burst through his head, knuckles cracking against his chin. In a daze, he lost hold of his knife.

Kol jumped to his feet, head still spinning, as men rushed toward him and grabbed his arms. He wrenched and pulled against their hands, but there were too many. Once more, fingers grabbed his hair, holding tightly. Kol froze as the sharp, cool edge of a blade pressed against his throat.

"Hold him," a deep voice commanded. In the light of the lantern, one figure rose unsteadily from the cobblestones, pushing back loosened strands of grey hair. The old man limped toward him, one hand on his thigh, blood trickling darkly through his fingers. He stopped, inches from Kol's face and, with a pained grimace, drew himself up to his full height. He stood, peering eye-to-eye with Kol, their heights matched. "Let me see his face."

Kol squinted as the chamberstick, all too bright in the darkness of the alley, was held up toward him. "I'm just looking—" Kol rasped, blade still pressed against his throat, scraping the skin while he spoke, "for my family." The old man leaned further toward him, his sharp, piercing eyes crinkling as he scrutinized Kol's features in the candlelight. Undaunted, Kol held his gaze.

"You think I don't know a soldier when I see one?" the old man sneered. "Who sent you?"

Kol swallowed hard, and the blade dug further into his skin. "No one."

"We'll see if that's true," the man said with a scoff. "Bring him," he ordered to the others. "Let's continue this in private."

The next thing Kol knew was that he was being shoved into a dark room. "You've got great timing," the old man said sarcastically over his shoulder. "I was just about to pour a glass of brandy. Why don't you join me?"

Kol understood it was not a request. "Sure," he replied, trying to sound nonchalant with the tip of a sword pressed into his back. "I could use another drink."

Kol followed the old man into a small parlor, warmly lit by embers glowing from a humble brick fireplace. The old man took off his wide-brimmed hat and tossed it onto a nearby table, revealing coarse, iron-grey hair that had apparently once been cropped close but now hung below the ears. Two worn leather armchairs flanked the hearth, and he motioned toward one.

Kol was shoved into the seat and the cool steel pressed against his throat again. He watched as the old man filled two glasses from a decanter on the table, then pressed a glass into his hand.

"Drink," the man ordered.

Slowly, Kol raised the glass to his lips. Then, seeing the other man take a sip from his own drink, Kol knocked the liquor back in one gulp.

"Now tell me again..." The man winced as he lowered himself carefully into the chair and stretched out his injured leg. "Why are you here?"

"I'm looking for Seaborn," Kol replied. "I just want to ask him some questions."

"That's exactly what a soldier would say." The man took another sip, keeping his gaze locked onto Kol's. "So, who sent you?" he asked gruffly, setting his glass on a low table that sat between the chairs. "The Sornians? Valennians?"

"I told you, I'm not a soldier—" Kol leaned forward, but stopped at the touch of metal against his neck. "Not anymore. I'm just looking for some information about my family."

"All right, I'll humor you," the man replied, pulling a kerchief from his pocket. "Let's say you really are just looking for information," he continued, tying the cloth around his wounded leg. "What does Seaborn have to do with your family?"

"I don't know," Kol admitted. "That's what I want to find out."

"Well, you're wasting your time," the man replied grimly. "Seaborn is dead. Died long ago."

"*No*," Kol uttered, desperation in his voice. To think he'd come so far and gotten so close to finding where he belonged, finding out who he really was, and then to have that hope taken away so abruptly, seemed too cruel. "No..." he repeated, voice cracking, his stoic features twisting with despair.

The man eyed him curiously. "What's the problem?"

Kol leaned his head against the back of the chair, suddenly feeling very tired. "I think he might've been my father."

"What makes you think that?"

"A dream—" Kol began, then stopped himself. "No, a memory. I was a young child." The images from that night played in his mind. "Washed overboard from the decks of *The Seaborn*. I learned he lost his son the same way."

The lines of the old man's face deepened as his eyes narrowed at Kol. "Who are you?"

"As I said," Kol replied impatiently. "I don't know; that's what I wanted to find out."

"I wonder..." the old man began, then shook his head. "Doesn't matter, even if you are telling the truth. Maybe I believe you; maybe you really are looking for your family." He shrugged. "Do you know how many orphans end up on the streets in Hedda?" he scowled. "You're just one among many. Get him out of here," he snapped to his men. "But I'll be keeping your weapons," he added, motioning for them. One of his men handed over Kol's knife.

"No," Kol protested as he was pulled to his feet. "I need that back!" With his arms twisted up behind him and the blade still grazing his neck, he was dragged away.

"Didn't you hear?" one of them laughed as they shoved him toward the door. "Time to go." Another pulled open the door in front of him.

"Wait!" Across the room, the old man rose unsteadily from his chair. "Where did you get this knife?"

"I've always had it," Kol answered.

"Did you steal it?" the old man demanded.

"No!" Kol replied. "I had it when they found me on the street when I was little."

"So you could've gotten it anywhere..." Disappointment was heavy in the old man's voice. Reaching for his glass, he took a sip of brandy.

Kol shook his head. "My father gave it to me."

"What did you say?" the man asked breathlessly.

"My father," Kol replied. "He told me to keep it safe; he said..." Kol's tone softened as the words spoken in his dream came flooding back to him, "'Borrowed things always find their way back home.'"

Glass shattered as the old man's drink dropped to the floor. "Release him, all of you," the man ordered. "Leave us." The other cast confused glances at each other as they left, closing the door behind them.

The old man's eyes filled with tears. "I had a son, once," he began softly, cradling the knife gently in his hands. "He was just a little thing..." The tears finally spilled onto his cheeks, glistening in the golden hearth light. "His name was Kaias. We were sailing back from Valenna; it was bad weather, the day the crew turned on us. They—" His voice hitched. "They killed his mother; I couldn't stop them. And the waves were washing over—" His words cut off again, and he swallowed hard. "When I looked back, Kaias was gone." He turned to meet Kol's gaze. "Your eyes... They're just like hers. This—" His voice broke violently with emotion. "This was my knife."

Kol's heart raced, his mind fraught with questions. The initials on his knife, Kol remembered, *A S*... "You're Seaborn!" he replied, voice rising in excitement. "And I'm—"

"My son!" The man's countenance broke with overflowing emotion as he stepped toward Kol. "Kaias, my boy—" Opening his arms wide, he wrapped them around Kol, squeezing tightly.

Kol froze, bewildered by the sudden display of affection. Finally, he placed his hands tentatively on the man's back. A tight knot formed in his throat, burning with each breath. *Papa.* He blinked back tears that threatened to overtake his vision. "You were right," Kol said finally. "I did find my way back home."

In Kol's arms, Seaborn's injured leg gave out; Kol held him steady and helped him back to his seat.

"So many years lost," Seaborn said softly, lowering into the chair. "Come, tell me about yourself," Seaborn continued. "What do you do for a living?" He lowered himself into the chair. "And why did you claim to be Valennian?"

"I am a Valennian citizen," Kol explained. "I was a soldier in the Sornian army, but I realized we were being misled about the war—"

"You defected?" Seaborn interrupted, raising a brow. "To Valenna?"

"Yes." Kol crossed an arm over his body, rubbing his shoulder mindlessly and looking down into the waning embers. "I had my reasons."

"Of course." Glass clinked as Seaborn poured himself a new glass from the table. "And now?"

"And now I'm a merchant," Kol replied quickly, not allowing his thoughts to touch on the months he had spent in between, working for Adella. The pain of his loss was still much too raw, and he didn't want his father to read it on his face.

Seaborn gave a sharp, loud laugh. "A merchant! It must run in the blood." He grinned proudly.

"I fell into it under bad circumstances," Kol said. Creases formed between his eyebrows as the sight of Martin's gaping throat, dark blood streaming down his chest, flashed through his mind. He blinked it away, willing his thoughts back to the present. Before him stood the man Kol had always wondered about, always dreamed of meeting. Now, for the first time in his life, he was looking upon family, his own flesh and blood, after years of resigning himself to the ever-present, aching loneliness of being unwanted and unloved. "Tell me about my mother," he said, but the words came out hoarse and tight.

"Aristea..." Seaborn muttered dreamily. "She was beautiful." He swirled the glass in his hand carelessly. "Tall and strong, good at everything she put her hand to." A smile broke over his lips. "A quiet woman but always the first to laugh, and the loudest at it. And she had a fearsome, fighting spirit..." His voice faded away wistfully. "Come," he said, rising delicately from his chair. "Let's get out of this dreary hovel and celebrate. I know a place."

"But your leg..." Kol protested.

"Eh," Seaborn replied indifferently. "I've had worse."

Outside, the rain had begun to pour. Kol walked beside Seaborn, who limped somewhat as they wove their way through the muddy streets, the cool night air wicking through his damp clothes and into his limbs. Behind him, two of Seaborn's men had joined them, chatting between themselves, now apparently at ease with Kol's presence. The group stopped at the door of a low, sprawling building that seemed unremarkable in every way, save for the very loud voices that emanated from within, a stark contrast to the otherwise silent dirt lane overlooked by the dark windows of brick rowhouses. No sign hung above the lintel, and Seaborn didn't knock before swinging open the narrow wooden door.

They entered a spacious parlor room, where candelabras dripping heavily with old wax sat upon long tables, the warm light filling the space with a hazy, amber glow. Gaudy mirrors with tarnished reflections and peeling gilt frames hung along the walls, giving the illusion of never-ending space. Groups of men gathered at the tables, hunched around games of dice or cards amid intermittent laughter and tankards of foamy drink. The men looked old and coarse, especially when compared to the few women who sat amongst them; they were young, and might have been pretty under other circumstances, but their tangled hair and dingy clothing, well-worn and falling carelessly from bare shoulders, told Kol what kind of place this was.

They took seats at a table, taking up the dice and cup that had been left there among puddles of spilled beer. Their arrival caught the attention of an older woman, whose hair was piled in a high bouffant in the Sornian style and powdered so heavily that her natural hair color was inscrutable. She crossed the room to greet them.

"Adamas, my love, where have you been?" the woman asked, pouting her lips dramatically. "I've missed you."

"You keep letting them soldiers in here," he replied sharply. "You know a lot of us won't hold with that. Soon, they'll be all you get."

"Gold is gold." She shrugged a shoulder, her silk shawl slipping lower down her arm. "But there are none here tonight; let me make it up to you."

"The usual stuff," he replied gruffly. "And send some girls over; it's a special occasion." Seaborn waved ostentatiously toward Kol. "My son Kaias is back from the dead."

"How wonderful," she replied dully, her eyes lingering on a hole in Kol's faded shirt. "But I'll be surprised if he can afford anything more than a beer."

Seaborn looked at him expectantly, and Kol reached into his haversack and pulled out a leather coin purse. It clanked heavily as he dropped it onto the table.

"Well then," she said, brightening. "What'll you have?"

"Brandy," Kol replied. "Just bring the bottle." She nodded and left.

One of the other men dropped the dice in the cup. "How about a game of Hazard?" he offered. "Let's see if we can't lighten your burdens."

"I'm in," Kol replied. "If you're so eager to lose your money, that's your problem."

"Look, Hennet," Seaborn laughed, "he knows you so well already, and you just met."

Kol threw in some coins and Hennet matched them from his own purse, giving them over to Seaborn to keep track of.

"Seven," Hennet said. He rolled the chance, throwing the dice many more times before finally losing. "It's only a matter of luck," Hennet griped, dropping the dice back into the cup in disappointment as Kol took his winnings. "Whether bad or good, it runs as it runs. There's no skill in it."

"Maybe," Kol replied. "But some are luckier than others. Five." He shook the cup in preparation to roll, but a bump to his elbow from behind caused the entire cup and dice to fall with a clatter onto the table, spilling out a roll of twelve. "That doesn't count," he grumbled. He shot an annoyed glance at the figure crowding at the table beside him, and was surprised to find a young woman pressed close at his shoulder. Across the table, two more girls edged their way onto the benches; dark green glass bottles in their hands glowed softly in the candlelight.

Beside him, the girl poured an amber liquor into a small glass, then lifted it up toward his mouth. Her eyes widened as he grabbed the glass from her hand. "I can manage it myself," he said, then knocked it back at once. The brandy burned in his chest.

"Relax," Seaborn chided. "Maricella's girls are the best company you can get."

Kol set the glass down. "I'm not exactly in the habit—"

"What's the matter, not up to your Valennian standards?" Seaborn teased lightly. "Might take your mind off your troubles for a bit." His tone softened with concern, "You look like you have a lot of them."

Kol wiped the brandy from his lower lip with the back of his hand. He wasn't new to gambling nor was it his first time in this dicing-house, though, thankfully, no one seemed to recognize him. He had put the sort of man he used to be behind him, since he had become Valennian citizen. *Since meeting Adella...* He winced at the thought. Kol took the bottle and refilled his glass, liquor dribbling over the rim, and drained it again in one gulp. "Fine."

14

Choice and Chance

Kol unbuckled his belt, his fingers clumsy from too much drink, then tossed it with his sword and scabbard onto the foot of the bedstead. He pulled his worn linen shirt over his head and, wadding it up in his hands, looked down at the thick, white scar on the side of his abdomen. It seemed so long ago now, since the wound had healed. The memory of Adella's hands, pressing the cloth into the wound to stop the bleeding, came to mind. He thought of her face, so close to his own that he could feel her soft breath on his neck, remembering the look of worry that surrounded her pretty eyes and pouting lips while she leaned over him to change the dressings. No one had ever cared for him like that before. *No,* he shook the thought from his head, swallowing hard to keep the grief that gripped his chest from rising up his throat. *You can't live like this forever.*

Kol turned around to see the young woman set a chamber stick onto a small table, then begin to unlace her bodice. He stepped toward her. She was young, he knew, but now that he looked more closely in the candlelight, he could see she was much younger than he had realized. Wide, amber eyes looked up at him from beneath an array of chestnut curls. He hooked a finger under her chin and tilted it toward him. "How old are you?" he asked. Squinting, he searched her face for lines, but found only freckles.

"Old enough," she said, wrenching her chin from his grip.

"In that case—" Kol put a hand to the back of her neck, burying his fingers into her hair, and pulled her in close. He pressed his mouth hard against hers, and she let out a timid gasp. He drew back just enough to see the girl squeezing her eyes shut, cringing in fear. *What am I doing?* he asked himself, shoulders drooping. *This isn't who I am—Not anymore.*

Kol dropped his hand, stepping away. "You don't want to do this."

"I need the money." Her answer came out quick and sure, but her voice was nearly breathless.

He pulled a few gold coins from his drawstring pouch and tossed them onto the bed with a clink. It didn't seem like much to him now, but he remembered a time when it was far more than he'd ever had. It hadn't been that long ago. "Take it and go," he ordered. "But don't mention it to anyone."

The girl hesitated, eyeing the coins that glittered on the dirty, tattered quilt. Slowly, she reached out for them, then snatched them up, moving quickly away from Kol as though she was afraid he may change his mind. Watching him warily, she edged backward toward the door.

"You should find different work," he added, her eyes still fixed on him. "You're not suited to this."

Her hand found the door handle behind her. "Easy to say, for a rich man," she replied cuttingly, then disappeared out the door.

He let out a loud breath and flopped down on the bed, looking out into the blackness of the window. He had been so elated to find his father, the man he had always dreamt of meeting. He wanted so badly to be the son that Seaborn expected him to be, to make him proud. Now that he had the chance to fulfill that dream, Kol found his heart still ached too much from grief for him to truly appreciate what he had found. His head swirled. Crossing his arms behind his head, he closed his eyes and drifted off to sleep.

They sprung open as rough, raucous laughter echoed up from the street below the window. Kol rubbed his eyes, unsure of how long he had slept. Of the voices outside, one in particular sounded familiar, though he couldn't quite place it. Getting up, he went to the window and, looking down on the dark street below, caught a glimpse of several men just before they pushed open the door of the dicing-house and entered. In the faint light that spilled out from the casement windows, the glint of metal flashed at their sides. *Soldiers!* Kol's pulse quickened at the realization. He didn't know exactly why, but Seaborn had clearly wanted to avoid running into Sornian troops. *Something we have in common,* he thought. As a traitor to Sornia, there was sure to be a decent bounty on his head, and, somewhere far in the back of his mind, knew he was too drunk to put up a good fight. He grabbed his scabbard and buckled it onto his waist.

He hurried down the dark corridor to the top of the stairs, and could already hear Seaborn's deep voice. Kol pulled free the thin strip of leather that held his hair back in a short queue, shaking black curls over his eyes, obscuring his face.

At the top of the stairway, Kol clenched his jaw when he saw he was too late to give his companions a warning. The soldiers had apparently headed straight for their group just as they entered, and there seemed to be a confrontation playing out at the dicing table, with raised voices in hard tones. Aside from Seaborn and his men, and the newly arrived soldiers, the room appeared to be empty. Kol strained to catch their words.

"Just give us your gold, and we'll act like we've never seen you," a younger man said, his higher voice rising over the others.

"You can go to hell, whelp," Seaborn answered, and drew his sword. Metal rang as the men all about him flew into a frenzy, drawing swords as each of Seaborn's men took on one of the soldiers. Seaborn faced a flurry of strikes from his own opponent, retreating backward as the other hacked and slashed at him. Steel clanged against steel throughout the room.

Kol knew he had to act quickly or he would lose his newfound father the same way he had lost his friend, Martin. He couldn't let that happen; he just needed an opening into the fray. As Seaborn pressed backward against the wall directly below Kol's feet, he knew it was now or never. Licking his teeth, he drew the knife from his boot.

Just as Seaborn dodged a strike with a duck to one side, Kol hopped over the stair rail, sinking his knife deep into flesh and sinew as he landed on the soldier just below. The two of them hit the floor so hard that Kol heard the crack of bone, though he wasn't quite sure if it was his own or the other man's. It didn't matter; the fight wasn't over.

The hurried stamp of boots behind him was warning enough; Kol pulled his knife from the hollow of the man's neck and rolled sideways just in time to see the edge of a saber bite into the floor beside him with the crunch of splintering wood.

With a swift kick of his foot, Kol's heel met the soldier's jaw, sending him reeling backward as something small and hard skittered across the floor. The soldier hopped to his feet quickly and faced Kol once more, as fresh, scarlet blood dribbled down his chin.

The man barked out a crooked, split-lipped laugh, revealing a large, black gap in his teeth. He wiped his chin with his sleeve as he leveled his blade at Kol's chest. "You'll pay for that—" The soldier's words cut off and he collapsed to the floor, revealing Seaborn behind him, pulling his sword from the man's back.

Kol and Seaborn rounded to see Hennet holding the last soldier's arm, twisted up behind his back, sword to the man's throat. As Kol looked at the soldier's face, a shock of recognition shot through him. It was an older man with silver stubble on his craggy skin; his dark, beady eyes turned upward toward Kol, brows drawn together pleadingly.

"Garen," Kol acknowledged him coldly. "You should learn to mind your own business."

"Please, Kol," Garen begged him. "You're no stranger to a soldier's life. You know I'm just doing as I'm told."

"We can't let him go," Seaborn interjected. "He'll tell the others we're here."

Kol tensed, carving deep furrows between his brows. He opened his mouth, drawing a breath while he considered it.

Seaborn took a step back. "On your word."

"Please," Garen whimpered, eyes searching Kol's face. "I just got married last week; tell him to let me go." He struggled against the hands that held him, but to no avail. "You and me, we were friends, weren't we?"

Kol pursed his lips, pulling them to one side while he thought. In the years Kol had spent in the Sornian army, he had often found himself at odds with those around him. As a man with no family name, he had always been presumed a bastard, and was treated as such by those who were looking for someone to kick around. Though Garen had never been especially cruel—at least, no more than anyone else—neither did he ever offer a kind word or a helping hand. With the price on his head, Kol knew that if he were to let Garen go, the soldier would likely return with reinforcements.

But what if I'm wrong? Kol bit his lips, torn between his choices. If he killed Garen now, he would be no better than the Sornians themselves, no better than the men who killed Martin. *Martin...* Guilt burned in his chest, squeezing upward into his throat. *I promised to keep him safe.*

No. Resolve hardened within him. *If I let Garen go and he returned with more soldiers...* He wasn't sure he could protect his father then, and he couldn't take that chance. Kol looked Garen square in the eyes. "I have no friends," he said flatly. At his words, Hennet's blade slid through Garen's throat. The man gurgled a sputtering breath and dropped to the floor, dark blood pooling out around him.

"Out," barked a woman's voice. Behind them, Maricella stood, jaws clenched, and flung her arm out to the side, pointing across the parlor toward the door. "All of you."

Seaborn gave a chuckle. "Sorry about the blood—"

"Don't come back until you learn to behave," she snapped. "If you want to act like savages, go back to Sornia."

The four spilled out of the doorway and into the damp night air, tripping on each other's boots as Seaborn and his men laughed off the tension of the fight. A misty rain sprinkled on their faces.

"Damn, son," Seaborn said proudly, clapping a hand on Kol's shoulder as they walked along the muddy street. "You sure are handy in a pinch."

"Appeared right out of thin air," Hennet said appreciatively.

The second man snorted. "Pouncing on him like a... a cat," he added.

Kol laughed at the idea, shaking his head dismissively.

"Like a cat, is it?" Hennet scoffed. "Cats are little, fluffy things which couldn't kill a man. I think you mean a tiger."

"I know what a cat is," the other man replied defensively. "I mean like a cat on a mouse. The analogy holds."

"Ah, forget it, Livy," Hennet huffed. "Good thing you're not a poet."

"A tiger is a cat," Kol offered as they slushed through a large puddle.

"Nah," Livy replied. "I've seen the cats they keep in the stables for mousing, they're definitely not tigers. You can't keep tigers with horses; think about what you're saying."

Kol laughed at that. As his pulse began to settle from the excitement of the fight, he became aware of a stinging pain in his thumb. He shook his hand to dissipate the feeling, but that only made it throb.

"Do you have a place to stay tonight?" Seaborn asked, turning to Kol.

"I hadn't thought that far ahead," Kol admitted. "I could sleep on the ship, if I had to."

"Forget that." Seaborn waved the thought away as they turned down a narrow alley. "I have a room for you. Come on."

They neared Seaborn's home as the rain finally abated, leaving a pale mist hanging over the streets under the moonlight that had begun to peek through the clouds. They parted ways with Hennet and Livy, who apparently had more drinking to do elsewhere, and went in. Passing through the hall, they entered the main room, where embers were still glowing in the fireplace.

Seaborn stooped at the hearth, raking through the cinders with an iron stoker and feeding them with tinder from a nearby basket. As he rose, a spot high on his sleeve glistened a wet, ruby red in the light of the growing fire, where a slash ran through the fabric.

"Looks like they nicked you," Kol noted.

Seaborn put a hand to his arm gingerly and cringed. "I don't move as fast as I used to." He rolled up his sleeve, revealing a thin slice that ran across his upper arm. "Not too bad."

Kol flexed his right hand; his thumb felt stiff and painful. "I wonder if this is broken."

"Let's see." Seaborn took his hand and looked it over, pressing along the bones beneath the swollen flesh. "Just a sprain," he assured him. "It should heal up all right, but we'd better wrap it to keep it stable." He turned to fish around in boxes beside the hearth and pulled out a bundle of cloth, then set about gently winding it around Kol's injured hand. As the fire in the hearth crackled, filling the room with a comforting warmth, a lump grew in Kol's throat.

Seaborn tucked the end of the cloth under and paused, looking up into Kol's face. The sympathetic smile on his father's lips faded, a look of deep sadness dragging down his features. "My son," he muttered. "All the years that were taken from us..." Tears flooded the rims of his eyes.

"I wish it hadn't happened," Kol said, trying to keep his voice steady. "That I could have lived my life with you, and my mother." His brows furrowed against his will. "I don't even know what she looked like."

"Come, Kaias," Seaborn replied. "I'll show you." He took a brass chamberstick from the side table and lit the candle from the hearth's fire. Kol followed him down the long hallway and into a dark bedchamber. The low ceiling and small, curtained window gave the room a cramped atmosphere, the air stale and musty.

Seaborn crossed the room and held up the chamber stick, illuminating a painting that hung on the wall across from the little bedstead. Kol stepped closer, narrowing his eyes in the candlelight. A woman's image looked out at him from within the simple, wooden frame; her lips held a sly smile, and her piercing, dark eyes seemed to glitter with intelligence beneath angled lids much like his own. Straight, black hair framed her strong features in silky wisps; her skin, in contrast to Seaborn's pale complexion, was a warm, lustrous copper.

"My mother?" he asked quietly, and Seaborn nodded. Kol stared deeply at the painting, committing every detail of her face to memory. "How did you meet?"

"I saw her at the market," Seaborn began. "She was a prisoner of war, a rebel captured from the southern borderlands, skilled with horses. I got her from auction to oversee my live cargo, but instead..." A smile played on his lips. "I fell in love."

The truth behind his father's words made Kol uneasy. *Captured, sold at auction...* A tight knot grew in his gut while he wondered what her life must have been like, and if she had suffered violence. "Was she happy?" he asked, unable to hide the strain in his voice.

"She made the best of it, at first." Seaborn's reply was heavy with resignation. "When you were born, then she was truly happy. I always loved her, though, regardless." He set the chamberstick down on a little side table. "I still do."

Kol drew a deep breath through flared nostrils. "Who did this to our family?" he demanded, voice thick with emotion. "Who killed her?"

"It was that damned Valennian," Seaborn glowered, a distant look settling in his eyes. "He was the one to blame for her death—For what happened to you."

Kol turned to face him. "What Valennian?"

"The captain I hired," Seaborn replied. "Declan, that bastard. It was all his doing."

"Declan?" Kol's pulse quickened in surprise at hearing the familiar name. "I know a Rogero Declan."

"His father," Seaborn replied. "I got my revenge on the man, but it wasn't enough, for what he did." His hand clenched into a fist. "He took everything from me; my family, my legacy. I'm not done yet."

"What are you talking about?" Kol asked under his breath.

"I want to blot out his mark on this world," Seaborn growled. "Like he did mine."

Kol bit down on his lips, his mind racing with the new information.

"Enough about that, for now," Seaborn said, turning toward the door. "You should get some rest. It's been a long night."

15

Adrift

Adella clamped her mouth shut, holding her breath tightly as the cold water buffeted her against the floor, sweeping her down the dark hallway. Arms flailing about her, she tumbled along, bruising her elbows and knees as she desperately fought against the current. She couldn't tell which way was up, her senses were all but blank; she could only catch glimpses of dark objects flowing by when she squinted in the murky brine, with only the muffled sounds of water rushing around her ears while she dipped in and out of the surface.

Helpless against the pull of the incoming tide, Adella lashed out to grab at anything within her reach. Her fingers tore and scraped at the walls until she caught hold of a curtain, clutching the thick fabric against the pull of the water as her heavy skirts tangled around her legs. She struggled to kick free, trying to pull herself up out of the water until the curtain broke away from its fastenings. Adella plunged once more beneath the water and was swept away.

She came to a forceful stop when her body slammed against a wall. Scrabbling to find her footing, her head finally broke the surface, with the water sloshing just under her raised chin. Sediment stung her eyes as she looked around, stretching up onto her toes to keep her head above the waves.

The sea was pouring in fast, rising from her neck up to her lips while she turned about, searching the dark, flooded hallway for a means of escape. In the wall high above her was a small rosette window, glowing softly with morning light. She took a deep breath just as another surge crashed over her head.

Caught in the downward pull of an eddy, she tumbled around in the rising deluge, not knowing which way was up. Her lungs burned while she squeezed her eyes and mouth shut against the buffeting of filthy water. As the current began to abate, she swam upward, squinting through the swirling debris to find the dim light of the little window, now under water. Fumbling around the casement window frame, her hand found the small, iron latch and, pulling it, pressed against the glass. The round pane gave way, tilting on its central hinge as it opened to the dark sea beyond. Adella squeezed through, her shoulders and backside scraping against the window frame, but was stopped before she could get completely free. The waist of her skirts dug into her hips, and panic rose in her chest as she realized her clothes were caught on something.

She grabbed the fabric and tugged violently, trying to rip it free. Bubbles of breath escaped her nostrils while she braced her bare feet against the sill of the window and pulled, but to no avail. Reaching into the front of her bodice, she was relieved to find her small knife still secure in its sheath and pulled it free. She slashed frantically at the entangled hem to free herself, knowing she had only moments to spare. Finally, the blade bit through the cloth and the tension around her waist gave way.

Kicking as hard as she could, Adella swam upward, her arms burning with fatigue. The knife slipped from her hand and fell away, lost to the sea while she struggled upward. Her vision began to mottle black and her body ached for breath. Though she could see faint light filtering downward through the muddy seawater, she had no idea of how far the surface might be above her head. Soon, all she could hear was the pounding of her pulse in her ears as thoughts of drowning raced through her mind. Unable to control the spasms of her chest any longer, she exhaled.

As the last of her breath bubbled out, sunlight shimmered gold above her fingertips. She pressed her tongue tightly against the back of her throat to keep from filling her aching, empty lungs with seawater. Adella felt the cool pressure of the water on her face give way to warm, summer air and finally gulped breath into her burning chest.

Sputtering and choking on water that had gone down the back of her nose, she thrashed about in the dirty waves, the sea heavy with silt and debris. She had surfaced beside the governor's mansion; its white eaves hung above her head while she tread water in its shadow. Adella was relieved to find the building wasn't completely submerged. *Misses Asher, Nell—* she thought. *Did they make it?* She scanned the brick facade for signs of life, but saw no movement in the dark windows.

Struggling through the water, she swam toward the sheer wall of brick and reached out to grab onto a windowsill. Just when her fingertips brushed the damp stone, the powerful suction of the current pulled her away again with the shift of the tide, and pulled her out to sea.

Large pieces of wood, the remnants of items now unrecognizable in their ruin, swirled around her, jostling into her in the outgoing tide. Adella spun in the water in time to see a large, dark object heading right toward her. Taking a deep breath, she dove as it crashed over her head.

When she surfaced once more, Adella found herself in the dark hollow of a small, capsized boat, its interior filled halfway with a pocket of air. With the weight of her clothing pulling her downward and exhaustion seizing her limbs, she felt around until her hands found something to grab onto. Clinging helplessly to a thwart at the bow, she gasped to catch her breath. Outside, waves pummeled against the hull. Gripping the wood tightly, she braced herself against the jostling of flotsam that rammed into the sides of her shelter.

Adella floated beneath the overturned dinghy, dangling from the thwart in the cool waters of Belgrand Bay. While she let her weary muscles rest, she became increasingly aware of a stinging sensation on her back, searing across her bare shoulder where her clothing had been torn away. While tentatively prodding the ragged flesh, a sharp pain flared beneath her fingertips. She pulled her hand away quickly, sucking air through her teeth. *Don't look,* she warned herself. *Nothing can be done about it now, anyway.* The water sapped the warmth from her limbs while she waited, shivering in the turbulent sea.

After the pull of the tide had subsided and she no longer heard the hull crashing into other objects, Adella ducked under the water and resurfaced outside the dinghy. "Damn," she muttered when she saw how far the shore was, now only a dark shape in the distance. *Too far to swim.* She licked the bitter saltwater from her lips while she thought.

Turning back toward the boat, she reached up, straining to grab the keel at the stern as it bobbed low in the waves. When her hand finally caught hold, she kicked at the water and pulled herself up onto the hull, crawling across the belly of the dinghy. Balancing carefully, she slowly rose on her arms to get a better view of the horizon. It wasn't the horizon, however, that caught her eye.

A dark shape darted across the water, moving much too quickly to be flotsam. Though she squinted against the bright sunlight shimmering on the water, she could see it well enough. Her heart pounded against her chest when she recognized the serpentine form. *You again.* The memory of being dragged beneath the water by her foot suddenly surfaced in her mind.

She watched the creature snake through the waves, weaving around the bobbing litter as it gradually made its way closer to where she lay adrift. As it approached, a pointed snout broke the surface of the sea. Adella flattened herself against the hull, hoping to go unnoticed by its large, golden eyes.

The long form rippled as it turned in the water, circling the boat. Adella pulled her feet slowly away, careful not to disrupt the delicate balance of her perch atop the overturned dinghy. Her pulse quickened as the massive, serpentine head rose above the surface. Its mouth slowly parted open, displaying jaws cluttered with dagger-like, protruding teeth as the creature glided by. Its glossy skin was smooth and scaleless, of a dark grey color reminiscent of the porpoises she often saw hunting the waters of the Bay. *Pelkimund*, she said to herself, recalling the Old Andolinian symbols she had transcribed from the Codex. *That's what it was called.* Her eyes darted down to her left foot, now bare and dangling dangerously close to the water; a long, ragged scar stretched over the top, a reminder of the last time she saw a *pelkimund* so close.

With a splash, it disappeared below the murky water at some distance from the boat. Adella searched the waves for a sign of the creature's dark form, her eyes skipping over broken branches and wide patches of kelp and other debris to no avail. *Is it gone?* Looking down into the water, still dark and brown with silt, she realized it could be mere inches below her even now. Her pulse hammered at the thought.

As she stared, gaze fixated on the shadows that played on the waves in the light of the lowering sun, she thought she saw movement, a vague form sliding by just under the surface. Narrowing her eyes, Adella leaned further downward to peer into the murky depths, with the boat tilting lower into the water beneath her, and strained to get a closer look.

A flash of gold blinked up at her as one huge, golden eye opened just below the surface, its black slit of a pupil narrowing in the sudden sunlight. Adella sprung back in surprise, tipping the boat to one side. Unable to stifle a small scream, she slid over the hull, her hands and wet clothes slipping over the smooth wood, fingernails clawing at the boat's strakes while she desperately tried to keep herself from tumbling into the sea.

Finally, she caught hold of the keel, her fingertips clinging to their tenuous grasp as her bare feet splashed down into the water. Adella kicked and pulled herself upward but made little progress, her muscles still weak from her earlier struggles in the flooding manor. Her foot briefly struck against something large and fleeting in the water, and her mind raced with the memory of being dragged through the sea in powerful jaws.

Desperation spread through her, lending strength to her limbs. Finally able to draw herself onto the hull, Adella scrambled quickly up to lie across the keel. Hearing a loud splash behind her, she turned her head in time to see jagged rows of glistening, white teeth snap together before sinking back down below the waves.

The sun sank toward the horizon as Adella lay motionless upon the dinghy, legs astride the keel for balance, afraid to move lest she topple into the ink-dark sea and become fodder for sea creatures. She had been adrift for hours and her lips were cracked, the skin on her shoulders and arms tight and raw from salt and sun.

She held out her hand, arm fully stretched, aligning her palm across the western horizon. Only three fingers fit within the span between the sea and the evening sun. *Less than an hour until sunset,* she realized. *If I keep drifting with the tide,* she figured, *I will come to the Isles... But then what?* The Isles of Pentz weren't inhabited; being too small, they were merely used as waymarkers for ships sailing across the Bay as they headed toward the city of Pentz. If she made it far enough to reach the Isles, though, perhaps she could hail a passing ship. *If I'm that lucky.*

Or... Adella chewed her cheek, thinking over her choices. *I could start paddling toward shore now, and maybe reach Pentz before I die of thirst.* Already her mouth was parched, her throat gummy. *Or I could jump in, and swim for it...* The sea looked calm now, and there had been no sign of the *pelkimund* for some time. Though she was a fair swimmer, the shore looked so very far away now, and Belgrand Bay was home to many sharks. Adella knew the wound on her back was still bleeding, since she could feel the warmth of it trickling down her skin whenever she shifted. None of her options seemed promising.

The sky darkened into twilight as a few early stars blinked overhead. The sea stretched out endlessly all around, the shore long since lost to sight, as a feeling of hopelessness settled over her. *I'm not going to make it back home this time,* she realized, squeezing her eyes shut. *I promised I would bring back help,* she reminded herself. *And I utterly failed them. Kol, the people of Elldon, the Queen... I've failed everyone.* Adella clamped a hand over her mouth as a gasping sob escaped her lips, an unsettling sound over the constant, soothing shush of the waves. She shivered in the cool seabreeze that played over her raw skin and the long strands of wet hair clinging to her salt-encrusted clothing, and cradled herself for warmth. She looked up at the few early stars, already shining brightly above the darkening eastern horizon. *Mother, Father,* she thought, touching her fingertips to the ruby hanging from the chain around her neck. *If you're up there... I'll be with you soon.*

16

James

James paced the floor of Greywood's large parlor room as the antique grandfather clock gently chimed the hour. "No," he said adamantly, his voice echoing across the dim space. "I don't believe it."

"She couldn't have survived, James," his mother replied. "The dear girl is gone."

"We thought that once before," he reminded her, his voice distant in thought. He let out a breath of resignation. "Regardless," he waved a hand in the air, "Lady Grimless left me in charge, and so we will carry on as always. Until the Queen orders us to abandon Elldon."

"Right. Until then." She turned to leave.

"Be gentle when you tell Jacoby," he added. "You know he admired her."

She nodded over her shoulder and disappeared down the hallway, leaving him alone in the silence of the large room. "Shit," he muttered, crossing over the worn carpet toward the window. Once framed with lavish jacquard curtains, the windows of Greywood Manor now were all nailed over with boards. Squinting through a narrow gap, he looked out over the western horizon under the dim glow of first light. His glance passed over the stables, recently rebuilt after the attack by the Sornians earlier in the spring had ravaged the town, while he scanned the western sky. In the distance, far beyond the sleepy encampment that housed his neighbors, a pillar of black smoke rose up, tapering off northward on the wind.

It was closer, today. He didn't know what the Sornians were up to, but he was sure it wasn't good. "Adella," he said quietly to himself. "You promised."

He closed the curtain. *No,* he thought. *We can't waste time, waiting for help that will never come.* He turned, crossing the room to head outside. *We must act, while we can.*

James steadied the horse, a tall bay mare that had belonged to the late Lord Alfrin Grimless. Travia was a fearless creature, and high-spirited; if any beast could see him safely through a battle, it would be her. She pawed relentlessly at the ground, digging ruts into the dry, hard-packed soil with her hoof as she mouthed the bit. In his hand, he gripped his own short hunting bow, weathered but trustworthy. The weight of Lord Grimless' old cavalry saber pressed reassuringly at his waist: a treasure, now an heirloom of Adella's, borrowed from its place of honor on the wall of Greywood Manor.

James shifted in his saddle to look behind him, where a beautiful, young blonde woman, who had lately returned to Elldon, fiddled with her feet in her stirrups. Though she wasn't a confident rider, he knew Rosalind to be a prodigy with the bow. Her mount was suited to her inexperience; James had seen to that himself when he chose for her a stocky, even-tempered draft pony. Though fear shone in her wide, blue eyes, he saw resolution there as well. He gave Rosalind a nod of encouragement while she adjusted her fingers around her bow, already strung at the ready. To his right, rode Benson, his massive blacksmith's hands gripping the stock of a small crossbow, with the brass hilt of a newly-made saber gleaming at his hip. Though he couldn't see them from his vantage point, his mother and brother had taken positions at the rear of the formation. All around them, bridles jangled as riders mounted. Nearly fifty in number, though they were inexperienced in battle, the riders at his back had been hardened by want and desperation, tempered by loss and grief.

In the distance behind the rolling hills to the west, the Sornian encampment awaited. The column of smoke could be seen climbing higher and higher on the rising wind. James knew this was risky, but, in his estimation, it was their only chance to make a dent in their enemy's numbers before it was too late, and Greywood was overrun. *Adella would not approve,* he thought, feeling a wave of guilt for what he was about to do. *But she isn't here.* He drew a deep breath and, as the others looked toward him expectantly, squeezed his heels against the horse's side to cue her forward. She broke into a trot, then lunged into a working canter.

They rode hard over the grassy plains, each rider doing their best to keep in the formation James had instructed them to take, with the less experienced keeping to the center, armed with short horse bows, and the better riders to the fore and flanks, brandishing heirloom blades and make-shift polearms. The encampment appeared in the distance; judging by the number of tents and cookfires, he knew the enemy outnumbered them, but James's riders had the advantage of surprise. They would ride in and attack the enemy, causing as much havoc as they could as they swarmed the encampment, then gallop back homeward to seal themselves safely behind the stone walls of the massive Greywood Manor before their enemy had a chance to regroup. He was no soldier, but James knew his plan would work. *It had to.*

Though the air was still cool from the passing night, his shirt clung to him, damp with sweat from the hard ride as they neared the modest encampment. Across the wide, flat meadow of dew-pale grass, many small canvas tents were staked closely together, surrounding a single, large bonfire. Only a few horses could be seen tied here and there around the encampment, which was odd enough to catch his attention, but he gave no more thought to it than that. As it was early morning still, only a few soldiers could be seen traversing the camp, or relieving themselves in the open. As the long, swift stride of his horse carried him across the field, James dropped his reins to the saddle pommel and nocked an arrow onto the bowstring.

At the thunder of oncoming hooves, the soldiers in the encampment spilled out from their tents, frantically drawing swords or scrambling to string their own bows as the arrows of the Valennians flew down around them. One man, half-dressed and brandishing a gleaming saber high in the air, ran straight toward James at the head of the formation, a furious scream issuing from his throat. James released his arrow and it flew straight, plunging deep into the man's ribs through cracking bone. The soldier fell and, rolling limply in the grass, was lost beneath the horses.

The riders trampled over the encampment, barreling into tents as well as men. Soldiers threw themselves out of the way of their steeds, or were knocked down to then be trampled beneath hooves. Furious shouts and painful groans filled the air, mingling with the loud snorting of overwrought horses.

As they crashed through the center of the encampment, a group of soldiers, blades drawn and raised, banded together and turned upon the riders, running straight toward James at the front. An icy wave of fear shot through him when he realized how easily they could dispatch his mount, leaving him to face the attackers on foot or be trampled by his own formation. With trembling hands, he nocked another arrow and drew, taking aim at the nearest soldier.

Just as he released the bowstring, James was shoved sideways and the arrow sailed wide of its target. Glancing left, he saw Rosalind's horse jostling shoulder-to-shoulder into his own in the crowded formation. The soldier he faced raised his sword and lunged at the breast of Jame's horse, swinging the blade downward.

James's heart dropped into his stomach as his body heaved upward; he had to throw his arms around Travia's neck to keep from sliding out of the saddle. His fingers slipped on the foamy sweat of her short, summer coat as he inched backward over the saddle's cantle while the horse reared high into the air, striking out with her forelimbs. Her hoof came down upon the soldier's head, her iron shoe hitting his brow so hard it tore through the flesh. As Travia lowered again, the man disappeared beneath her hooves.

"Forward!" James shouted and dug his heels into the horse's flanks, sending her colliding into the melange of blades and limbs that pressed in upon him from the front. He slung the bow around his shoulders and reached for the hilt of his saber, but pain stopped him short. For a moment, all he was aware of was metal grinding against bone in his leg. When he turned to look for the cause, a bolt flashed past him and lodged into the neck of a man at his heel, its iron point protruding from the other side of his throat. With a stifled gasp, the soldier dropped his sword. Clutching his neck, he fell and was lost to sight beneath the horse. Beside James, Benson slung his crossbow over his shoulder by its strap and drew his saber. The riders pressed onward through the crowd, shoving, trampling, and hacking their way across the encampment as the soldiers fell beneath the hooves.

"Keep together!" James shouted as they finally broke free from the fray and galloped across the open grass. Air howled in his ears, muffling the thunder of the riders behind him while he spurred his horse onward. Her hooves kicked clods of turf high into the air as he led the formation in a tight arc, skirting the edge of the camp as they turned homeward.

As the riders tore across the wind-blown fields, a wide swath of thick trees came quickly into view up ahead, just to the north. James thought he caught a glimpse of movement from deep within its shadows, but, searching, could not determine its source. They galloped onward.

They approached the edge of the trees and James led the formation in an arc to the right, passing close to the wide copse. When James edged past the stately elms to his left, he heard the unexpected thunder of hooves from over a distance. For a moment, he thought his formation had split up behind him to go the other way around, but a quick glance revealed the truth. From the far side of the trees, a small group of horsemen barreled over the grass, picking up speed as they rode toward them with bows ready.

James swore loudly as panic soared through his body, jolting his heart into a pounding frenzy. *An ambush!* He cursed himself. The encampment, with its obvious columns of smoke, had been a trick to lure the Valennians out into the field. *They sacrificed their own men as bait?* The cruelty of it sent shivers down his spine. Leaning forward, he stretched his hands over Travia's neck and kicked his heels into her flanks. A glance backward showed a string of riders on fresh horses drawing alongside the formation, arrows flying between them. He watched as one of his own riders fell to the ground with a sharp cry, pinned through by an arrow shaft. Far to the rear, another fell, tumbling into the grass, and disappeared beneath the horses, then another, before the pursuing soldiers broke away and turned northward.

James pressed Travia onward, though her nostrils flared widely with each heaving breath, foam flying from her open mouth. "Nearly there, girl," he said, patting her sweat-soaked neck. Behind him, the riders began to lag, stretching out widely over the fields. They were nearing the manor, and James let out a breath when he thought they were in the clear.

As they passed by a rise in the land to the south, James caught a glimpse of a dark shape moving at the edge of his vision. Turning, he saw another group of horsemen emerging over the hill, heading directly toward them. He gritted his teeth as the enemy riders caught up to the rear guard. Arrows flew above the flash of blades in the slanting sunlight, and one horse fell to the ground, throwing its rider hard onto the grass. Though he could not see who it was, his throat tightened, jaw clenching as he thought of his mother and brother. The urge struck him to pull Travia around and come to the fallen rider's aid but he knew he had to stay on course and lead the others to safety; their horses were nearly spent galloping at speed much longer than they were used to. Glancing back, James could see several riders had fallen and were left behind, lying on the ground, though he could not tell, from the distance, if they were Sornian or Valennian. Then, as quickly as they came, their attackers veered away to the south, disappearing once more beyond the rise.

As the formation stretched across the fields toward Elldon, Greywood Manor appeared upon a hill on the eastern horizon, sheltered by tall elms that together formed a dark and imposing silhouette against the pink and golden clouds of sunrise.

James drew back on the reins, slowing Travia to a trot as they came to the outer fields on the western edge of the Grimless estate. The tents of his neighbors were all empty; the cookfires had died down to mere embers, abandoned when the people who stayed behind had gathered within Greywood.

James hopped down from the saddle, and nearly buckled when his injured leg gave out. The slash below his knee burned hot with pain. Riders came to the gates of the estate's paddocks, hastily dismounted, and led their horses into their pens before retreating into the rear entrance of the manor. Wincing, James limped toward the door and, standing by, urged everyone inside, then closed and barred it behind him.

He followed the group out of the mud room and down the service corridor. His breeches clung to his knee, damp with blood. "To your positions!" he shouted, pulling his bow off over his shoulder. "Make ready!"

James rushed through the manor as quickly as he could, hurrying up the foyer staircase, then entered one of the bedchambers. At the far side of the room, a large bay window that once framed a wide view of the Campos was now boarded up against attack. He peeked through a chink in the boards and, with his bow at hand, stood waiting, watching the horizon.

Time crept by as his muscles began to cramp. Blood seeped from his wound down his leg and pooled inside his riding boot, soaking his stocking. He began to wonder if no counterattack would be coming that day after all. Leaning back against the wall, he closed his eyes and breathed a sigh of relief.

After what felt like hours, he made his way back downstairs, and found the others seemed to have come to the same realization. Though they still kept their posts to await further orders, they threw him questioning glances, but he read hope in their eyes rather than trepidation.

In the main parlor, Rosalind and a few others stood at the boarded-up window on the western wall, keeping watch through a gap just wide enough to let an arrow through. At his approach, she lowered her bow. "We did it," she breathed. Golden curls framed her blue eyes as she searched his face. "Didn't we?"

Slowly, he nodded. "I think so."

Rosalind let out a laugh of relief, a smile spreading across her face. The muttering around them grew louder until cheerful voices filled the manor.

James watched his friends and neighbors flood in through the hallway from elsewhere around the estate. Soon, Jacoby followed, and joined them by the window.

"You did it, Jamie!" Jacoby said, clapping him excitedly on the upper arms. "It all went just as planned!"

James searched over the spacious room, now astir with activity as people gathered in groups, chatting exuberantly. "Where's Ma?"

Despite the sharp pain in his leg, James made his way down the long hallway that led from the manor's front entrance, past several rooms off the hall, to the kitchen. His mother hadn't been in any of the upstairs chambers, nor any other room he had looked in. The injured were still being brought to the kitchen to be cared for, and he was certain she must be there, if nowhere else. He opened the door and entered.

The room was crowded with the wounded, in their bloodstained clothes and bandages, and those who were caring for them. The sight of it soured his stomach with guilt. Rosalind had just finished bandaging the arm of a man in a chair as James approached. She rose, wiping her hands on her apron as the man in the chair said his thanks and left. "No sign of her?" she asked.

He shook his head. "She must have fallen in the field," he muttered, not daring to say it loudly lest that make it true. A pained scream came from the center of the room, where one man was being held down onto the table while Benson tugged at an arrow lodged deeply in his shoulder. James couldn't help but imagine his mother lying similarly in the grass, pierced with arrows.

"Don't worry," Rosalind said gently, seeing the look in his eye. "She may have only been unhorsed. We'll find her." She glanced down to the bright red stain on the hem of his pale canvas breeches, which was so heavy with blood it clung to his skin. "Why don't you let me look at that?" she asked, though it sounded more like an order than a question. He opened his mouth to protest but Rosalind didn't wait for his reply; she merely pulled him by the elbow and guided him into the chair, then went to fetch supplies.

Returning, she knelt beside him, pulled off his boot, then unbuttoned the knee of his breeches. While she worked, a flash of gold caught his eye on her left hand, and James was surprised to feel a twinge of disappointment when he realized it was a wedding band. She unbuckled his leather garter and, carefully turning down the top of his blood-soaked stocking, frowned at the deep slice through the flesh of his leg. After dabbing the wound clean with a wet cloth, she pulled a little sewing-tin from the pocket of her apron.

"Uh," James began nervously, remembering that she was a seamstress and not a surgeon. "Are you sure you can..." Rosalind shot him a warning glare, and he left the sentence unfinished.

"I know how to sew," she mumbled, holding a needle in her mouth while she pulled a length of thread from the spool.

"That's not really—Ah!" he shouted as the needle pierced his skin.

"Don't move!" she said sharply, wrinkling her nose at him.

"I can't help—Oh!" he groaned at another jab, putting a hand over his eyes and turning away.

"Heaven's sake!" she reprimanded, throwing a hand in the air. "Did you cry this much when you got the wound?"

"That's different," he replied sullenly, still hiding behind his palm. "This is worse." James clenched his jaw, groaning at the tug of the thread when she pulled each stitch through his flesh. The painful and unnerving sensation seemed more than he could bear.

"You can look now," she said finally, putting her sewing kit back into her apron. "Be careful with it," she warned. "I don't want to go through that again."

Slowly, he lowered his hand and glanced down at her work, with each stitch even and precise across the neatly-closed edges of skin. "Oh," he said in surprise. "Not bad."

Rosalind smiled. "You're welcome."

Looking out over the western fields, James shielded his eyes from the sun while he searched for signs of movement. The wide swath of summer-dry prairie spread out as far as he could see, dotted here and there with patches of trees and scrub like islands in a sea of gold. He strained to listen, but only the buzzing of cicadas filled the warm, balmy air, punctuated now and then by a snort or sigh from his horse.

Rapid hoofbeats from behind grew louder until Jacoby rode up beside him, drawing his horse to a stop amid a cloud of dust. "Benson's found another wounded," Jacoby said, breath heaving from the gallop. James raised his eyebrows hopefully at the news, but Jacoby shook his head. "No, it isn't Ma."

"Damn." James spit the dust from his mouth. "Any sign of her horse?"

"Nothing yet," Jacoby replied. "Not among the dead, or the stragglers we rounded up. Should we send scouts to the south, or to the east?"

James shook his head. "We don't have enough people to send in every direction. The Sornian activity has all been westward, and that's where she must've fallen. There's no reason to look anywhere else."

Jacoby drew a sharp breath through his nostrils. "Suppose she was captured?" he asked, worry cracking his voice. "Or suppose they—"

"No," James interrupted, looking steadily into his brother's watery blue eyes. "They were moving too quickly; they weren't taking prisoners." He shook his head firmly, "No, she's out here, somewhere..." He turned his face back toward the western horizon, not wanting to say the rest out loud. *Wounded or dead,* he told himself, *she's out here somewhere.* He pressed his heels into the horse's sides, sending her into a trot. "Keep looking," he called out over his shoulder.

James clicked his tongue in the side of his mouth to urge Travia on, posting the trot to keep from bouncing in the saddle when she picked up the pace. The pungent smell of sage and wild thyme, crushed beneath her hooves, scented the air while he traveled, his eyes scanning the landscape beneath the wide brim of his straw hat.

A dark shape in the grass ahead caught his eye. "Shit," he muttered under his breath as a sudden rush of blood tore through his veins at the sight. He nudged her behind the girth with his heel and Travia obeyed, springing forward into a canter, the sound of her hoofbeats mingling with the pulse pounding in his ears.

As he approached, James jumped out of the saddle. Wincing at the pain that shot through his injured leg at the impact, he led the horse forward. A heavy dread hit his gut like a lead weight when he recognized the large, still form of a dark horse stretched out in the grass, arrows protruding from its belly. Beside the animal, pinned halfway beneath it, lay the body of a young man. Stepping closer, James recognized the face, now broken and encrusted with dry blood, as belonging to one of the stablehands he had seen often around Elldon. The young man's brown eyes, once bright and animated, now stared, unblinking, up at the wide, blue sky. His hand still clutched the grip of a bow.

"No..." James whispered, brows drawn tightly together. He crouched and, passing his hand over the youthful face, pulled the eyelids closed. It was all he could do for him at that moment, until it was safe enough to return with a group to bring him home to his family. James's insides knotted with worry while he wondered if he'd find his mother in the same way. Travia lowered her head and sniffed, then let out a loud blow, nostrils flaring wide as she stepped back. "Shh," James said, gently patting her neck. Stepping into the stirrup, he mounted into the saddle once more.

He rode onward, scouring the fields around Greywood as far west as he dared. Tall columns of smoke rose up over the low hills that blocked the view of the Sornian encampment. While continuing to search for his mother, he came across several more of his fallen neighbors, their bodies riddled with arrows. Grief and guilt burned in his chest while he made note of each one he found, so that he may return to their loved ones and deliver the grim news.

It's all my own doing, James reprimanded himself as tears blurred his vision. His mother was missing, probably killed like others. More had been lost during the attack than he realized. Along with the gravely wounded, Elldon's numbers were down by a dozen. *Thirteen now, including—No,* he pushed the thought away. *She may still be alive. I just need to find her.*

He was too close to the Sornian camp to call out. Their scouts might have been watching him even now, hidden in the tall grass or among the small patches of stunted trees that dotted the landscape. Even so, James strained his ears to listen for a voice calling for help, or the whinnies of a horse searching for its herd.

Movement in the field ahead caught his attention. His skin crawled with goosebumps, nerves prickling with excitement when he recognized the dark form of a horse and rider, contrasted like a shadow against the pale grass of the Campos. Giving a quiet click of the tongue, he guided Travia toward a stand of trees to his left, which stood upon the crest of a hill.

When he came to the little copse, he kept the tangled branches and gnarled trunks between himself and the other rider. Approaching the far side, he drew the reins and brought his horse to a halt. From his vantage point upon the rise, shielded by the foliage, he watched the rider trot briskly southward. James was close enough now to see that the rider was much too tall, and the waist too trim, to be his mother, since she was a stout woman. The lack of a queue hanging down the back revealed the rider to be Sornian.

Now that he had a higher view, he saw in the distance a group of riders traveling in tight formation, too close together to get an accurate count of their number. *Where the hell are they going?* he wondered, his mind racing with possibilities. *Are they leaving?* They must have come from the encampment, he reasoned. *But why south?* There was nothing of note in the southern Campos, just more fields and, beyond that, impassable wetlands. Why they would be heading that way, he could not figure. *Maybe they're breaking camp after our attack,* he thought. *Good.* He watched the soldier catch up with the group as they passed behind a hill and out of view. Urging his horse forward with a squeeze of his heels, James followed.

He was careful to keep far behind and out of sight, knowing full well the dangers of doing such a thing alone. Whenever scouting parties were sent out from Elldon into the Campos, Adella had always insisted on their riding in groups for safety, but it was too late for that now. He couldn't risk losing the trail.

Following the swath of trampled grass left by the Sornian riders, he turned gradually southeast, then dead east. The path continued on for some time until, James reckoned, they must be directly south of Greywood Manor, having skirted around it at a safe distance, and out of the usual range of Elldon's scouts.

The heat of the late afternoon sun drew rivulets of sweat from his brow, his clothing damp through from top to bottom. He wriggled his toes in his swampy wool stockings in an attempt to disperse the heat trapped within his thick boots. Just when he was about to relent and head back to Greywood with no news to tell the others, the sound of voices carried over the field. Having held his horse back from the group of riders, he could not see what was happening up ahead, as the land swelled gently upward, blocking his view. He had to get closer.

Looking around, James spotted a patch of brambles at the summit of the rise, not far off to his left. He jumped down from the saddle, again momentarily forgetting about his injury until the sharp pain reminded him. Tying the reins up behind her neck, he left Travia to graze, knowing she would be too hungry from travel to venture very far. Then, he lowered into a crouch, biting back another groan. The stitches pulled painfully at his skin while he crept up the incline toward the thick tangle of briars.

Thorns tore his clothes, snagging the leather of his boots as he carefully picked his way up toward the crest. At the top, the plains beyond came into view, revealing the source of the commotion. James's heart dropped into his stomach at the sight. Spread out over the wide fields in the distance, marched hundreds of Sornian soldiers, all arrayed in emerald green jackets, the sun glittering on the brass and steel of their weapons. Flanking the infantry were groups of mounted soldiers, also in green uniform, armed with bows slung over their backs. James's mouth went dry, pulse pounding wildly, when he realized they were heading north, toward Elldon.

James hurried back toward his horse, heedless of the briars that slashed through his skin. His heart pounded as he fumbled to untie the reins and climb back into the saddle. Wheeling Travia homeward, he kicked her sides, clicking his tongue furiously to urge her into a gallop.

17

The Eye of the Pelkimund

Matei's senses swirled around him in a confusion of sound and darkness. Strange sensations filled his limbs: feelings of weightlessness, but also of resistance with his every motion, and a crushing pressure bearing down on every inch of his body.

He became slowly aware of a growing light ahead. Holding his breath, he watched it rapidly approach, and realized he was moving upward at an astounding speed toward a shimmering plane of light. Breaking through the surface, his vision cleared, and he beheld the bright blue of a vast, cloudless summer sky. Bobbing among the gentle waves, one dark object caught his eye. The breeze that blew his way carried the metallic scent of fresh blood.

Matei's consciousness was carried forward, borne upon the will of another, slinking through the water toward the shape that lay not far in the distance. Pangs of curiosity and hunger both stirred within him as a foreign and undeniable force pulled him forward. Nearing the unfamiliar shape, a brief motion atop the object attracted his attention. A figure lay strewn across its rigid form, prone and helpless, and, his instincts informed him, wounded. Sliding through patches of debris that littered the surface of the sea, he moved closer.

Within his own mind, Matei recognized the shape of an overturned boat, its curved keel protruding from the waves, and the figure of a young woman lying upon it. She seemed to sense his presence, since she sat up quickly and looked around. Finally, she turned in his direction and, even from his low vantage among the waves beside the hull, he beheld her face clearly, and recognized her. *Adella.*

Matei gasped, startled at the realization, and the connection with the creature broke. He dropped the heavy crystal; it clattered onto the floor as he fell to his hands and knees, lungs spasming as they fought for air.

"Matei!" he heard a voice shout over the sounds of his own retching. Finally, a chilly liquid spewed from his lungs, splattering and pooling on the floor, wetting his hands. He heaved, emptying his chest while the taste of salt filled his mouth. Firm hands clamped around his arms and he felt himself being lifted.

Slowly, he regained control of his senses. As his vision focused, he found himself once more in the familiar surroundings of the Royal Palace, with the sea breeze blowing in from the open balcony of his solar room.

"Are you all right?" Lucas asked, still gripping him by the arm. Teressa bent to retrieve the crystal that had fallen onto the colorful carpet at his feet.

"Don't touch that!" Matei shouted. She drew back immediately, her amber eyes widening as she looked up at him. He ripped his arm free of Lucas's grasp, and grabbed the softly glowing stone from the floor. "It's not safe," he murmured. He straightened and put a hand to his belly. The creature's hunger lingered uncomfortably in his gut.

"What just happened?" Lucas asked, brow creasing as he eyed the pool of water on the floor.

"I saw—" Matei huffed to catch his breath, wiping a trickle of saltwater from his lips. "I saw Adella."

Lucas and Teressa shared a glance. "What?" Lucas asked in disbelief. "Why? What's she got to do with any of this?"

Matei squeezed his fingers tightly around the cool, smooth facets of the large crystal; a gently thrumming energy pulsed through his hand.

He shoved the weighty stone into his waistcoat pocket. "That's what I intend to find out."

"What you saw, was it even real?" Lucas asked.

"I know it is," Matei replied.

"Look, we don't know what the Heart of the World is capable of," Lucas reasoned. "Only you can discover that. But whatever it is between you and my sister..." He wrinkled his nose. "If it's about the gold—"

"It's not about the gold," Matei snapped.

Lucas put his hand on Matei's shoulder and looked him in the eyes. "Just let it go," he urged. "Forget about Adella."

"No." Matei shrugged out of his grip. "I *will* find her."

"You don't look well," Lucas confided. "You've been putting so much of your attention into that crystal lately, I think it's exhausting you. You need to rest."

Matei pushed back a strand of ash-brown hair, which he had been neglecting to cut lately. "I'm fine," he replied, glancing toward a tall-case clock that stood against the wall. He let out a breath. "Besides, we are due in the garden for the procession."

* * *

With a hand on Lucas's elbow, Teressa stepped lightly down the high-arched corridor, her gaze passing from tapestry to tapestry along the alabaster walls. Groups of green-jacketed soldiers, with polished sabers resting against their shoulders, marched before and behind them as they approached the massive doors that opened out to the bright sunlight of the formal gardens.

On the wide lawn, a carriage waited, painted in bright colors of green and gold and drawn by a matched team of dappled greys that pawed at the ground, mouth working impatiently at their bits. Guards in emerald waited beside the doors of the carriage.

"There you are, my son!" King Berento's booming voice carried across the garden. "Come, take your seat. You may be Prince, but horses don't recognize crowns," the king handed him a small velvet cushion, "and these won't wait any longer."

"Then get better horses," Matei replied, climbing into the open carriage. He turned to Lucas and Teressa. "Come on," he motioned for them to follow. "You both must come."

"Why us?" Teressa wondered, climbing up the step behind Lucas and taking a seat on the leather-covered bench.

"Think about it," Matei said as the carriage rolled forward, with armed guards marching along either side. "The *Corelimun* is a symbol of the Andolinian Empire; and the Empire isn't complete without Valenna." He pulled the crystal from his pocket and set it on the tasseled cushion in his lap as the carriage turned, entering a long line of carts and various carriages decorated with floral wreaths and bearing other well-dressed nobility, as well as armed soldiers. As the parade rolled down a lane flanked by flowering shrubs, people gathered along the streets to watch them pass by. "With members of the Valennian nobility at my side," he went on, "the people will see that I am the rightful heir of Sornia—the one who can unite the Empire."

"I thought it was because we're friends," Lucas joked.

Matei laughed at that. "Of course," he admitted. "It would be dull to do this alone. But I'm not Matei the Bastard anymore, now I'm Matei the Crown Prince. Every action I take is symbolic."

"Uh," Teressa said timidly. "I'm not nobility though; I was a maid."

Matei grinned. "They don't know that." Setting the cushion aside, he stood and held the stone up toward the sky as cheering erupted in the streets.

"Where did the Heart of the World come from, to begin with?" Teressa asked while he took his seat again.

"It's always existed," Matei replied. "Even before Mundil formed. They say it was a star, and the world we know grew around it. That's why it's called the Heart of the World."

"They're just stories," Teressa shrugged. "You can't really believe them?"

"I do," Matei said. "And more importantly, the people of Sornia do."

"You'd think a star would be larger," she replied.

"It used to be," Lucas interjected. "That's how it's depicted in the ancient tapestries, anyway." He threw a sideways glance at Matei and leaned in to whisper to Teressa, "It's probably been dropped on the floor too many times." Teressa snorted as she stifled a laugh.

"There have been many versions of the legend," Matei stated plainly. "Sometimes the *Corelimun* is a star, sometimes it's a stone from the gizzard of a giant serpent. In some tales, it is the Guardian that kills Paloma; in others, the story is a bit darker..." His voice tapered off, his gaze drifting down to the crystal in his palm. "The tales of Leveret and the Heartstone have diverged over time, but, like all stories, they carry pieces of the truth within." Matei closed his fingers around the large, clear crystal. "And now, I will discover that truth for myself."

The carriage continued through the streets of Hedda, shaded from the bright summer sun by the tall linden trees that lined the way. The small kitchen gardens of the tightly-packed houses perfumed the air with a green, herbal fragrance that mingled with the smell of horse manure from the filthy cobblestones.

The procession approached the crowded port that served as the hub of the city, turning to follow the road that edged the shoreline of the Bay, with the many sailing ships coming and going in the glistening waters on their right. As they made their way along the shore, passing by throngs of sailors disembarking with their ditty bags on their shoulders or fishmongers calling out the day's catch, the crowds parted to clear the way, keeping a fair distance from the armed guards that walked alongside the carriages. Teressa noticed the people here seemed less interested in the pageantry that Matei indulged in; the cheers were fewer and less enthusiastic, with some people even giving scrutinizing looks that verged on disrespectful.

"Does it matter," Teressa wondered aloud, "if they think I'm nobility?"

"It matters to them," he replied, his voice cold and unwavering. "Class systems are in our very nature; no society can develop without some imbalance of power. Look at our herds of horses in their paddocks; they are always vying for rank. Or look at the bee, or the wolf—there is always one who rises to lead the others, one of stronger character. We are made to rule or to be ruled; we cannot avoid our own nature anymore than any other animal."

"But we're not animals," Teressa protested.

He turned away, his gaze settling over the crowded city streets. "Aren't we?"

Teressa looked to Lucas for support, but he seemed to be indifferent on the matter, though he watched the banter intently, one corner of his mouth pulled in a curious sort of smile. "What about the Madorrans?" she rejoined. "I've heard they have no kings."

"No," Matei conceded. "They are ruled by their priests instead, and are worse off for it. Why do you think they've come here, invading Belgrand Bay?" he asked, looking her in the face. "To get away."

"I thought it was for commerce," she muttered.

The carriage came to a stop in the busy street as too many people began crossing in front of the procession to continue. Their guards turned outward to keep the crowds at bay, fingers reaching toward their sword-hilts. Matei covered the stone protectively with his palms. Up ahead, shouting erupted, then the crack of a horse-whip sounded. Their guards craned their necks, edging forward to get a better look.

Teressa jumped in her seat as something dark flew through the air, landing right at her feet in a tangled ball of swirling motion. She pulled her legs up beneath her, pressing backward against the carriage wall and trying to get away from the squirming form. The mass unfurled itself slowly, and Teressa found herself facing a large, glistening eel, writhing on the floor, jaws snapping furiously.

"Guards!" Matei shrieked, crouching on the seat with a look of panic on his suddenly pale face. "Guards! Get—get that damned thing out of here!" he stammered.

One of the guards opened the carriage door and jammed the tip of his sword down into the creature, which still wriggled as he threw it aside into the street.

"Shit," Matei seethed, and sat back down.

"They threw it at us," Teressa said sharply. "What could it mean?"

"It means," Matei said, straightening his jacket, "we have work to do."

18

Visions

Adella drifted on the edge of consciousness, the expansive, heaving indigo waves under the twilight sky filling every corner of her mind, the roar of water ebbing and flowing in her ears. **What have you done?** A voice, as deep and cool as the sea, filled her thoughts. The blue horizon in her mind's vision split open, glowing bright like the sunrise, yawning wider until a massive globe, illuminated in shades of amber and gold, slashed with a pupil of black, blinked at her from across the darkness of the sea. **Return it,** the voice demanded.

Adella's thoughts, clumsy and muddled on the edge of sleep, scrambled to understand what was being asked of her. *Return what?* she wondered, her gaze sinking deeper into the black center of the eye until darkness enveloped her. The image of her hand, placing the golden disc of Leveret's Key into the lock high above the sea on the rocky wall of the Figurehead, flashed through her memory.

The answer echoed in her mind like the crashing of waves on the shore. **You must return the Heart.** In her stark black surroundings, Adella felt herself tumbling, her senses eddying around her.

Wake up!

Adella awoke with a jolt as she plunged downward, cold water rushing over her head. The overwhelming tang of salt filled her nose and mouth. She stifled the urge to gasp while she blinked and looked around in the dappled light beneath the sea, surprised to find herself surrounded by a bright, crimson glow which seemed to come from the water itself.

She floated, submersed in bright red light, still suspended below the surface. The entirety of the sea around her was illuminated, the shadowy forms of drifting kelp and passing fish the only darkness to be seen. She kicked her legs and swam upward.

As Adella broke through the waves, she blew the seawater from her nostrils and, treading water, looked around. Her mouth fell open at what she saw. The night sky stretched overhead, a crescent moon beaming among many white, twinkling stars in the cool night air, but they could not outshine the blood-red light beneath the sea. Spinning in the water, she searched for the dinghy and found it close by, bobbing low in the waves with the stern completely submerged. Kicking, she lunged up and grabbed the keel, then pulled herself carefully onto the hull.

After gaining her balance, she sat up and beheld the waves aglow, the surface of the sea glittering and shining like a field of bright embers beneath the stars. She had never seen anything so beautiful in her life, and yet the eerie sight struck her to the core with a rising panic. *'As the sea filled with fire...'* The words she had read in the Codex seared through her mind. *The seventh calamity!*

In the distance, the black shapes of islands contrasted against the strange light of the water. Between the shadowy silhouettes of the Isles, a dark form moved against the current. Narrowing her eyes against the red glow, her heart leapt into her throat when she recognized the distinct point of a prow. *A ship!*

"Wait! Wait!" Adella shouted, frantically waving her hands in the air. "Please," she added, a desperate murmur swallowed up in the wind. Around her, the crimson light of the sea began to dim, fading slowly away until all that was left was the pale moonlight shimmering on the waves. *Damn.* She hoped whoever might be on the night watch had seen or heard her; she thought she had heard voices on the wind, but couldn't be sure.

Not leaving it to chance, Adella rose tentatively onto her feet. The boat beneath her dipped side to side while she steadied herself, then tucked her tattered skirts into the lacing of her bodice and dove into the sea.

When she surfaced, the ship was out of sight, its silhouette lost in darkness. Arms paddling furiously through the water, she swam in the direction she thought it had been in, though she didn't know how far it was or if it had been real or merely a half-dream.

Her muscles burned and she gasped for breath, but she pushed herself onward through the waves as the chilly water leached the warmth from her limbs. A sharp cramp shot through her side, the pain hampering her movements while she sank lower and lower in the waves. She wasn't certain, but she thought she felt something smooth brush against her leg. Though blinded by the seawater in her eyes and waves that rose to block her sight, she caught a glimpse of a light ahead. Whether it was the glow of a distant lantern or merely a star glittering from the horizon, she couldn't be sure, but there was no going back now; she could only struggle onward to whatever fate soon awaited. As she struggled to keep abreast, the skirts she had tucked up came free and swirled about her legs, tangling around them until she could no longer kick free. She tried to take one last mouthful of air, but gulped only water as the waves crashed over her head. Her reaching hand was all that was left above the surface, grasping at the air in desperation.

A tight grip clasped around her wrist, pulling her head above the waves. She felt herself being dragged upward and drawn over a hard surface before toppling onto the softer form of a body. Adella rolled onto her side, coughing and heaving up water from her lungs, and gasped violently for air.

"My word," a man's voice began solemnly. "I hadn't expected to find anyone else." He helped her up and guided her to sit upon the thwart at the stern of the small boat. "Not this far out, anyway. Are you all right?" Adella opened her mouth to reply but could only cough.

"Turn about," came a voice from the bow, followed by the splashing of oars in water.

Adella wrapped her arms around herself, fighting to calm her breath through chattering teeth. The man shuffled around beside her while he removed his jacket, then wrapped it over her shoulders. She sucked air through her teeth as the wound on her back stung to the touch. "Thank you," she managed to say, though her voice was brittle and faint.

"Oh, right," he muttered apologetically, and rummaged around beneath the thwart. "Here," he said, pressing a waterskin into her hands. "You must be thirsty."

She uncorked it and gulped the fresh water, grateful to rinse away the taste of salt from her mouth. She let out a long breath, releasing the tension from her muscles. "I thought I would die."

"Many have," he replied quietly. "But I'm glad to have found one more survivor." He gave a wan smile, illuminated in gold by the light of a lantern hanging from a rod at the prow.

Adella bit her lip, watching him take up oars. She didn't know why, but his words struck her heart with guilt. "Did you see that strange light?" she asked hoarsely. "In the water."

"Yes," he said, nearly a whisper. There was a deep weariness in his voice that, at that moment, Adella knew all too well.

Releasing a long breath, she slumped with her elbows on her knees. "Oh, good." She huddled beneath the man's warm velvet jacket as the others rowed onward, drawing toward a ship that was moored among the islands ahead, its lanterns twinkling in the twilight of early dawn.

As the boat drew up alongside a tall, three-masted ship, the crew lowered a rope ladder. Adella was prompted to climb on board first and greeted by some of the crew, who all bore sober expressions. An older woman with plaited white hair came forward, offering a wool blanket. "Were you at Pentz?" she asked in a thick Sornian accent. "When the wave hit?"

Adella nodded, drying herself with the scratchy wool as the others climbed on board. "I was in the governor's mansion when it happened."

The man who had pulled her from the water stepped beside her. "You were?" he asked in surprise. "So was I."

"Come," the woman said, gesturing aft. "Let's get her below."

Adella was shown to a small cabin, the cramped space illuminated by a lantern hung over a small, round table. Heavy breathing filled the space from behind curtained berths. The woman who had led the way motioned for her to take a seat. "We've taken on a lot of survivors," she explained, "so we're short on space and supplies, but I'll try to rustle up something edible for your breakfast. I am Lizabeau Swift, Quarter Mistress here on *The Warbrand*."

"Adella Grimless. Thank you." Adella took a seat at the table, eager to rest her sore muscles. "Is *The Warbrand* a Valennian ship? I'd never heard the name before."

"It is now," Lizabeau replied with a wry smile, then left.

The man who had followed them below stood silently nearby, lines creasing his face while he regarded her curiously. His appearance was just as ragged and waterlogged as her own, with a torn white shirt and half-tied cravat hanging from his neck, his thick, brown hair loose and tangled. Drops of seawater still glistened brightly against the deep brown of his forehead.

The wound on her back began to throb, and she was sure she felt blood oozing through the fabric. "Oh, your jacket!" she exclaimed and began gingerly removing it.

"No, no," he said with a wave. "Keep it."

"Thanks." She pulled the warm velvet tighter around herself. "I'm sorry, I don't think I caught your name?"

"Endlebridge," he replied. "Sanjon Endlebridge."

Adella let out a small gasp. "Do you mean Lord Governor Endle-bridge?"

"Indeed," he said dimly, eyes looking through her. "The people of Pentz, they were mine to care for..." His voice faded to a whisper, "So many of them, gone."

"I was separated from my friend," she began. "I don't know if she survived. Did you see her?" Her voice rose hopefully, "Beatrice Asher?"

"Asher?" Wrinkles creased around his eyes as he searched his memory. "Older woman? She had a daughter with her... No, a niece," he corrected himself. "Yes, they were sent to Raymouth."

"Oh, thank heavens!" Adella let out a breath. "What do you mean, sent? What happened?"

"When the water broke through the windows," he began plainly, "I had just returned from the stables. We fled up the stairs, storey by storey, until we reached the attic, and were joined by others who had escaped the ballroom. Thankfully, the mansion never gave way to the water; we were able to climb out onto the roof from the attic window." He took a seat across the table. "Everything else around us was under water. Eventually, we were rescued by ships that had come to Pentz seeking anchorage, but finding only disaster."

"And Misses Asher and Nell?" Adella prompted.

"They were taken on board a schooner," he replied. "A blue-painted one, that changed course to Raymouth. I stayed at sea with *The War-brand* and another ship that accompanied it, searching the Bay for survivors."

She leaned forward on her elbows, lowering her voice. "What do you make of the light in the sea?"

Endlebridge shook his head helplessly. "I don't know; I've never seen anything like it."

"I thought I swallowed too much seawater and imagined it," she admitted.

"For a moment..." The muscles of his throat strained as he swallowed. "I thought the sea was blood."

Her gut clenched when she read the pain on his face. *He's lost so many people,* she realized, *that, to him, the sea might as well have been blood.* All the people who were lost to the sea; he felt responsible for each one. *Poor fellow.* She thought about her own neighbors at Elldon and the weight of her own responsibilities, however much smaller they were than his, and tried to imagine his heartbreak.

"I—" he stammered, voice low. "I overheard some of the sailors say it was an omen. Which is nonsense." He raised his eyes to her questioningly. "Don't you think?"

Adella crossed her arms for warmth as a chill swept over her. "What do you know of the legends of Andolin?"

"Nothing at all," he admitted. "That's the stuff of scholars and Sornians." His tone revealed how little he thought of either.

She leaned back in the chair. "Then, I wouldn't worry about it," she said off-handedly.

"Right," he agreed with a nervous smile.

A crewman entered the cabin, bearing a tray loaded with food and drink. "The captain offers his own fare for our distinguished guests," he said, placing the tray on the table.

The two thanked him, and eagerly reached for the tin cups. Adella gulped a mouthful of the cool liquid, and nearly spat it out at the taste of vinegar. "Ugh," she grimaced, managing to choke it down. "I think it's gone bad."

"It's supposed to taste like that," Endlebridge said with a slight chuckle. "It's switchel. A popular Sornian drink, I've been told."

"What's in it?" she asked, but he only shrugged. "Much of the crew appears to be Sornian," Adella leaned in to whisper. "Are we safe on this ship?"

"Safe enough," he replied. "The other captain vouches for them, anyway."

"Other captain?" Adella asked.

"Yes, a fine Valennian fellow," he replied. Endlebridge then turned his full attention to the salt pork on the tray, and so Adella did likewise.

"What will you do now?" she asked after they had finished eating.

He leaned back against the chair. "There's only one thing to do; we will rebuild Pentz."

"Even though the sea may come in again?" she asked quietly.

"It might." He shrugged. "That's always a possibility, living on the Bay. But, as I'm sure you've discovered already, there are always risks in life, no matter what we do or where we go. We can't let that keep us from carrying on, now can we?" His nutmeg-brown eyes rose to meet hers, gleaming with sincerity. "Some may decide it isn't worth the risk, but for those that wish to return, I will be there. I took an oath and I will fulfill my duty, no matter what."

Footsteps echoed in the companionway as Quarter Mistress Swift returned to the cabin. "I've got good news," she announced, waving a pair of buckled shoes in the air. "Captain Russo believes we've found everyone there is to find, and has decided we'll be setting sail in the morning. *The Warbrand* will be heading to the Capital," she went on while she approached, "but there is another ship anchored here among the Isles that will be making for Raymouth, and is willing to take on passengers." She set the shoes with a clunk onto the table before Adella. "You have your choice of port."

"Excellent," Endlebridge replied. "I am for Raymouth."

"As am I," Adella said, reaching for the shoes. "Out of curiosity, which ship will be taking us?"

Swift grinned. "You will be sailing with Captain Declan aboard *The Tigress*."

19

Captain's Quarters

*D*amn, Adella grumbled to herself while she watched *The War-brand's* crew lower the quarter-boat into the waves. Low, dark clouds had begun to blow in, blanketing the horizon. *I didn't want to meet with Rogero... especially not like this. Yet again.* Only a couple of months had passed since he'd discovered her, soaked and wounded, on the deck of his ship. *He's going to think I'm completely inept. Maybe I can keep my head down and escape his notice?*

Following Quarter Mistress Swift, Adella carefully descended the rope ladder and stepped into the small boat, with Endlebridge after her. Thunder rumbled in the distance as the oarsmen shoved away from *The Warbrand* and then worked against the waves, finally approaching *The Tigress* as drops of water began to fall from heavy rain clouds. Adella climbed aboard and searched the weather deck for a familiar face.

As crewmen gathered to welcome the new passengers on board, she was surprised to recognize one man in the group, though it wasn't Rogero.

"Miss Adella!" Armand exclaimed as he came forward, holding down his old rain hat as it flapped in the rising wind. "Heavens above, girl! What are you doing here?" He threw an arm around her affectionately.

"Ah!" she flinched as pain seared across her back. "Careful, please. But *really*," she scolded, patting his back with one hand. "I could ask you the same thing. I thought you were at Raymouth?"

"Uh, about that..." He stepped back, looking down at his boots.

"Adella!" a booming voice interrupted, followed by the sound of stomping boots. She turned to find herself looking up into familiar hazel eyes.

Adella groaned inwardly. "Rogero," she muttered. "Good to see—" Her words cut off when he threw his arms around her, pressing her face into the rough wool of his jacket. Once again, pain flared across her back. "Ah!"

"What is it?" he asked, taking a step back to look her over.

"Nothing," she replied. "Good to see you."

"Well, you all look like you could use a drink," he said, loud enough for the group to hear. He then turned to one crewman, "First Mate Jon, please see to it they are taken care of as best we can, given the state of things. I'll join you all as soon as I'm able." He prompted them with a flourish of his hand.

Adella, along with the others, followed Jon down to the mess deck, where crewmembers gathered around the tables in raucous conversation. One table, which held a cask of wine, seemed to be the center of attention.

"It's our honor to have two esteemed guests such as yourselves," the first mate began, "Lord Endlebridge, Lady Grimless," he bowed to each in turn, "upon our humble ship." Craning his neck, he searched over the crowd. "Let's have some music, shall we?" he called out. "Damn the boy, where's Childric?"

Adella was about to comment that she had seen him in Raymouth, but the screech of a violin silenced her.

"Thank you, Marley!" Jon shouted over the racket, then turned back toward them. "I was just about to rally a group for a game of cards," he said, pulling a deck from his waistcoat pocket. "Would any of you care to play?"

"All right," Adella agreed reluctantly. "But I must warn you, I'm not very good at cards."

"Even better," Jon laughed. "Miss Swift," he said as Lizabeau took a seat and a lively tune filled the air. "Good to see you again."

Armand wedged himself onto the bench beside Adella. "Where's Mister Kol?" he asked. "The boy's hardly left your side since you met."

"He's my personal guard; that's what I pay him for," she reminded him. "But he's on an errand to Smuggler's Port. Hopefully, his travels are going better than mine."

"It could hardly be worse," Armand reasoned as Jon shuffled the cards for a game of Briscola.

It wasn't long before Adella was out of the game, but she remained to watch, taking long draughts of wine to dull the ache of her sore muscles and bruised bones. As the game ended and the others dispersed to refill their cups, she took the opportunity to speak with Endlebridge.

"I forgot to thank you for pulling me from the sea," she began.

He dismissed the idea with a shake of his head. "No need for that."

Adella looked down at her hands, considering her words. "I must tell you the reason I was at Pentz," she continued. "I went there to ask something of you."

He looked at her expectantly. "What was it?"

"I wanted to hire your troops," she explained. "To protect Elldon. Not possible now, of course."

Endlebridge rubbed the back of his neck, blowing a strand of brown hair from his face. "Do you have the money for it?" he asked dubiously. "I heard what happened to your town," he went on, seeing her look of confusion, "and, believe me, I can sympathize with your plight. But I am responsible for the people of Pentz, and we've all just been displaced."

"Are you saying it's a possibility?" she asked, voice rising in excitement.

"The barracks on the hill were spared," he explained. "Along with the stables. I've already given them the order to regroup at the Ivy Crown in Raymouth."

"I'm prepared to pay whatever it takes," she began enthusiastically. "But I..." Her shoulders drooped. "I don't have any coin on me at the moment, of course."

"Right," he muttered. "Unfortunate."

"Wait..." she said, eyes widening as she remembered. "What about this?" Adella unclasped the gold chain around her neck and set it on the table. The large gemstone gleamed a fiery red under the lantern light. "A family heirloom—Andolinian ruby."

His eyes settled on the stone, unblinking. "How do I know it's not glass?"

"Test it." Adella watched him pull a coin from his pocket and run it over the surface of the ruby several times, inspecting it carefully under the lantern. Then, he pulled a large ring off his finger and pressed the large stone within it against Adella's ruby.

He looked at the green jewel in his ring and frowned, then slipped it back on his finger. "Your ruby is real," he admitted. "And worth an army."

"Then we have a deal?" she prodded.

He nodded. "We'll make the arrangements in Raymouth," he said, passing the necklace back to her.

Adella sighed with relief. "You have no idea what this means to me. Thank you."

"How about I bring you a fresh cup, and we can drink on it?" he suggested. She nodded, and he rose from his seat as Armand returned to the table.

"Miss Adella," Armand said, turning to her in all seriousness as he set down his gill cup. "I've decided I don't want to retire, after all. Ah," he waved a finger in the air when she opened her mouth to argue. "I know what you'll say, but it's my choice. I don't want to just sit and rot; I have a lot of life left in me and I want to make good use of it," he pounded his fist on the table. "Put me back to work."

"Well..." Adella pressed a finger to her lower lip. "I do need someone inside the Capital to be my eyes and ears; someone I can trust to inform me of the goings-on there, as I haven't received word from the Queen for some time. I'd ask Margavita—" She shrugged a shoulder. "But she's busy with her own affairs, and isn't very prompt at returning letters."

"Oh ho!" Armand rubbed his hands together, lowering his voice, "A covert mission? That's just the thing." He cackled mischievously. "Espionage..."

"Sh! Firstly," she leaned in to whisper, "I will need you to find a way into the treasury in the Ansebulet to see for yourself if Heart of the World is still secure."

"You can rely on me, my dear Lady Grimless," he assured her. "I delivered your letter to Declan, didn't I? With no trouble at all."

"Good." She smiled with satisfaction. "You'll need to be on *The Warbrand* when it sets sail for the Capital, so keep an eye on Quarter Mistress Swift; don't let her leave without you."

"That I can do," he said with enthusiasm.

"Lady Grimless," a young sailor began, approaching from the companionway. "The captain requests your presence in his cabin. At your convenience."

Adella's stomach knotted at the thought, but she could think of no graceful way out of the situation. "I'll be there shortly, thank you," she said. He nodded and returned above deck.

"You sure?" Armand muttered over his cup.

Adella fidgeted with the gold and coral ring on her finger. "I don't see what it would matter."

"Our actions affect more than just ourselves," Armand replied. "Even those not present."

"I have no idea what you mean," she replied coolly. "I think you have the wrong idea. I'm going to speak with an old friend, nothing more."

Armand shrugged as the others began to return to the table. Endlebridge passed a wine goblet to Adella and returned to his seat across from her.

"Did you all see the light in the water?" Lizabeau asked incredulously, returning with a newly-filled wine glass. "I've never seen anything like it."

"I was asleep when it happened," Jon replied, passing behind her. "The whole crew woke me with their uproar." He sat down on the bench beside her and sipped from a copper cup. "I went to see what it was about, but couldn't make any sense of what I saw. What was it?"

Lizabeau shrugged. "Who can say? But all this strangeness began with the appearance of the sea serpents, if you ask me. They're bad omens."

"Do you believe in omens?" Adella asked.

"You'll find seafarers are a superstitious lot," Jon interjected. "Especially Sornian ones."

"It was like that among the cavalry as well," Armand informed Adella. "Save for your father, of course. You know, they won't even wear green as they believe it's bad luck."

"Your father was Lord Alfrin Grimless, was he not?" Endlebridge asked, and Adella nodded. "I had met him on several occasions," he continued. "Outstanding fellow." He rubbed the stubble on his chin. "You know, I still hear the stories of his courage and recklessness from the Cavaliers. Your father's tales always made me wonder," he leaned forward on his elbows, "if he was truly that clever, or just very lucky?"

"I believe he made his own luck," Adella replied, a sad smile briefly crossing her lips. "But I've never been one for superstition."

"He was a clever man, for certain," Armand countered. "We were the lucky ones, for knowing him." He took a long drink. "Say," he began enthusiastically, turning to Adella, "did I ever tell you about the time he freed eighteen of our prisoners of war from the heart of the enemy camp at Enth with only a duck-call, a horseshoe, and a hat?"

"Uh, no," Adella replied, raising her brows in surprise. "I haven't heard that one. How did he manage it?"

"Wait—" Endlebridge interrupted. "That's not how I heard it. It wasn't a duck call, but a tin flute, and not a hat but a horse's feed bag…"

"No," Armand argued. "It was a hat. A woman's hat, in fact."

"But it couldn't have worked that way—" Endlebridge was interrupted by the sound of hurried footsteps pounding their way below deck.

"Listen up, fellows," a sailor yelled as he appeared from the companionway. "And ladies," he amended, bowing politely toward Lizabeau and Adella. "*The Warbrand* has given the signal for Russo's crew to return to ship." With that, Armand downed the remainder of his wine.

"Miss Adella," Armand began solemnly, turning to face her before he departed. "This may be the last we see of each other for a while. Times are different lately; there's more danger in the world…" He cleared his throat and started again. "I loved your father," he said plainly. "More than you know."

"Armand," she said gently. "I know."

"And you've always been like a daughter to me." He cracked a smile. "Or a really troublesome niece."

Adella gave a small laugh. "I know."

"What I mean to say," he continued, "is you're the closest thing to family I have and…" His eyes began to glisten at the edges. "I know I can't talk you out of staying at Greywood, but promise me—" He swallowed to clear a catch in his throat. "Promise me that you'll stay safe."

She nodded, touched by the emotion in his words. "Of course."

"And…" he added, "promise me you'll keep an eye on them at Elldon. Beatrice, and her boys; they never had much of a father. I did my best for them, while I could..." He sniffled, rubbing his nose on his sleeve. "Don't let them do anything stupid."

"I won't," she replied, straining to steady her voice. "I'll keep an eye on them." She took a deep breath and dabbed at her eyes. "No need to get sentimental," she said, more to herself than to him. "You're just going to the Capital. We'll meet again soon."

"Right," he replied, and gave a loud sniff. "The wine, you know?" At the rail, the sailors unrolled the rope ladder, and Lizabeau turned to them expectantly. Armand gave Adella a final embrace, squeezing tightly. "Don't go breaking any hearts," he added. "And tell Mister Kol I said farewell."

Adella nodded. "Goodbye, Armand," she said softly. He then turned and climbed down the ladder.

Adella watched as the boat made its way across the gentle swells of a now calm sea, the stars shining brightly in the heavens above. The salty breezes blew cool and invigorating over her skin. Despite all she had been through, despite all the dangers it possessed beneath its dark surface and the capriciousness of its temperament, the sea still held so much beauty for her. Looking around the ship, she watched the crew working at their tasks under the serene moonlight. She thought about what Endlebridge had said, that there would always be risks in life. Her duty bound her to Elldon, a small town on the edge of the frontier, and yet she was in no less risk of danger there than the crew were here. She may have survived the flooding of Pentz only to return home and face a violent death. *And these sailors*, she considered, *they have such freedom. To sail the world, see other lands. Elldon is so small... So isolated.* For a moment, she envied the seafarers.

Adella stepped quietly down the companionway to the captain's quarters. She looked around the familiar space, though it was a lot more disorderly now than she remembered. Papers and maps littered the table in the center, and the books in the case along the bulkhead were jumbled. The *Encyclopedia of Birds* lay open on the sole by her feet.

Across the space, Declan sat at his desk, quill in hand. His broad captain's hat hung from the back of his chair.

"I like to allow the crew a respite after each battle," Declan explained at the sound of her footsteps, writing in a large logbook. "It helps to keep things in perspective." A cup of wine sat on his desk, and he took a sip before turning a page. "Though I hope they weren't getting too disorderly," he added without looking up.

"Not at all," Adella walked hesitantly forward. "Even Armand was behaving himself."

Declan gave a slight chuckle. He set his writing quill into its stand and turned in his seat to face her. "So," he began, raising his eyebrows in a look of disappointment. "Pulled from the sea again, Adella? I'd tell you to stay away from the water, but if you did—" His stern face finally gave way to a smile. "Then I'd never see you."

"You know where to find me," she replied indifferently.

He frowned at that, then rose from his seat. "We will be arriving at Raymouth in the morning," he said, leaning back against his desk and lifting the wine glass. "I wanted to offer you the use of my cabin so that you may have some privacy."

"Thank you. But..." She chewed her lip. "Didn't you read my letter?"

"I did," he admitted, one corner of his mouth drawing upward.

She glanced downward. "I was angry when I wrote it."

"Yes, I... I noticed." Declan cleared his throat. "How are things at Greywood?"

"To be honest..." Her shoulders fell as she let out a breath. "Not great. But I'm hopeful things will improve soon."

"And yourself?" he prompted. "How have you been?"

Her fingertips found the gold and coral ring on her hand, and she spun it in contemplation. "It's hard," she admitted. "After losing my parents..." Adella's eyes shifted past him to the gallery windows that lined the back of the cabin, where her own reflection stared back at her. "Even though Greywood is crowded now, it feels empty without them. I try to keep my mind on other things—" Her words caught in her throat, and she took a deep breath. "How do you do it, Rogero?" she asked softly. "How do you deal with so much loss?"

"Like this," he said, raising his wine glass.

"It doesn't seem to be working for me," she commented.

He took a drink and set the glass on the desk. "No," he sighed. "To be honest, it doesn't get any easier. You just get used to it."

Adella pressed her lips together and looked up into his face, bronzed from years of sailing on the open water. His sun-bleached hair was as tangled with sea salt as her own; the stubble on his jaw and dark shadows under his eyes made him look, at that moment, older than his years. "I'm sorry about the letter," she said under her breath.

"Stay with me." His words caught her by surprise. "There's nothing for you there."

"You know I can't," she replied quickly. "I belong at Greywood, just as you belong on *The Tigress*. There's no reconciling that."

"Leave Greywood," he pleaded. "It's a lost cause; I think you know that." His voice lowered to an intimate whisper, "Sail with me."

His offer rekindled a longing in her heart, and she wondered if he was right. "Elldon is my home," she said, shaking her head to clear the thought away. "It's all I have; I can't leave."

"Listen," he stepped closer, standing just in front of her and looking her in the eyes. "I've loved you for so long. And I know you have feelings for me…" He reached up toward her face, but stopped his hand. "At least, you did once."

"Years ago," she countered. "I've moved on."

"You have?" His voice hardened. "It's not that Sornian, is it?" he guessed. "Kol."

"No," she said quickly. "He doesn't care for me."

He lowered his brow. "What makes you so sure?"

"He would have mentioned it by now, don't you think?" she snapped. "This isn't about Kol. I meant whatever it was between you and me—it's in the past."

Declan studied her face, his gaze shifting from her one eye to the other. "Is it?' He took her hand softly in his. "You and me..." He ran a thumb over her knuckles. "It might not be perfect, but it could be good."

Adella opened her mouth to speak, but stopped in surprise when she felt the roughness of his palm on the side of her face. Their breath mingled as he leaned down and pressed his lips against hers.

"Wait." Adella pulled away.

"What is it?" he asked, reluctantly releasing her.

"I can't." She threw her hands in the air. "I can't do this again. You broke my heart last time, and it wasn't worth it."

He flinched at that. "Adella, that was five years ago. I'm sorry," he pleaded. "I'm *sorry*; what more can I say? You said you forgave me."

"You were my friend. Or so I thought." She let out a breath. "Why did you ask me to marry you that night?" She shook her head. "Everything you said; was it all a lie?"

"No." His voice was earnest as he reached out for her. "I meant to keep my promise, but circumstances arose; I—" He dropped his hand. "I had to leave quickly."

"What circumstances?" she asked, narrowing her eyes. He opened his mouth to speak, but merely shut it again, turning away. "That's what I thought," Adella muttered, stepping around him to leave.

"Wait," he stopped her with a touch to the arm. Crossing over to his writing desk, he opened the drawer. Shoving papers aside, he pulled out a letter and handed it to her. It was battered and yellowed, its red wax seal crumbling with age. "I had meant to send this to you long ago, but I was too ashamed. If it doesn't change the way you feel..." His voice was almost a whisper, "Just say the word, and you'll never hear from me again." Declan turned and stepped hesitantly toward the companionway. "Please," he added over his shoulder, "don't read it until you are back at Greywood. I couldn't bear it." She gave a small nod, and then he was gone.

Adella flopped down onto the berth and let out a long breath, setting the letter aside. The wound on her shoulder pulsed. She pulled off Endlebridge's jacket and removed her damp bodice, then looked over her shoulder at the large patch of flesh that showed through the tear in her shift. The top layer of skin, in places, had been torn away, and the raw, red patches of scraped flesh still wept with blood, which diluted to a pink as it mingled with the seawater that dripped from her hair. Though the wound was shallow, it needed to be cleaned. "Ugh," she muttered; she didn't feel much like dealing with it at the moment. Picking the letter back up, she turned it over in her hands. *He said not to read it now,* Adella reminded herself. *But why? What's he hiding?* She bit her lip, wavering between following orders and giving in to curiosity. Finally, the latter won out.

The crumbling seal gave no resistance when she unfolded the paper, then smoothed it out to read the faded handwriting:

Dearest Adella,

No doubt you were surprised to awaken alone, and for that I am sorry. I had meant to return before sunrise. But everything went wrong.

I went to the docks to speak with my father on The Hopewell, *to tell him our happy news. However, as soon as I stepped on board, I knew the situation was dire. They were setting sail early to make a hasty departure. I had to go.*

No sooner had we lost sight of the shore, than we realized our ship was being followed. We did our best to outrun them, but it was no good. We were attacked and boarded. By the heavens, Adella, what happened then— My father was slashed, cut open. His innards—I tried to put them back in—He's gone.

We were able to save The Hopewell. *But that reaver bastard, he's still out there, hunting us. Beware* The Seaborn. *I'm sorry, but I must take* The Hopewell *across the Greater Sea. I know it's dangerous, but it's our only chance to lose him. I wish I could do more—I wish I could avenge my father, but I'm afraid, Adella. I'm so afraid, and I don't know what else to do.*

I will find you when I return.

Yours Always,
Rogero

The paper was dotted and smeared here and there with brown stains. *Blood,* she realized. *This letter must be five years old! All this time, I had no idea...* Guilt gripped her heart painfully, and she threw herself down onto the berth, losing herself in her thoughts.

Adella didn't know how long she had been lying there when footsteps woke her.

"I thought you'd be asleep already," Declan said apologetically when she sat up on the mattress. "I came to get something—You're hurt?" Concern lined his face when he finally caught sight of the wound on her back. "Why didn't you mention it?"

"It's nothing," she insisted. After recent events, it seemed insignificant.

Declan opened the trunk at the foot of his berth and rifled through the contents. "Here," he said, tossing supplies onto the mattress beside her. "Let's see what we can do." He sat down beside her and, running his fingers across her shoulders, gently brushed her long hair aside. Goosebumps rose on her skin at his touch. Carefully peeling the tattered fabric away from her bare shoulder, he inspected the damage, then turned to open a small tin. The warm scent of lavender and other herbs wafted up toward her while he dabbed a sticky salve onto the wound. She gasped sharply at the pain, but kept still. Looking over her shoulder, Adella watched him wrap clean cloth over her raw skin, and her eyes swept along the pale network of scars that slashed starkly over his tawny forearms.

Rogero glanced at the letter lying open on the mattress. "You weren't supposed to read that here."

"I've been wrong about you," she blurted out, turning to face him. "This whole time. I had no idea what you'd been through; I thought..." Her brow creased. "I thought the worst of you."

"I know," he said under his breath.

"Why didn't you tell me sooner?" she asked, looking up into his face.

"I didn't want you to know." He stood, eyes glistening, and stepped away. "I didn't want you to see me as a coward."

"You're not," she said, rising to her feet. Reaching out for him, she put a hand on his arm. "I'm sorry. For everything."

"Doesn't matter," he replied. "We're here now. Together." His gaze passed from her eyes down to her mouth. He brushed his hand along her jaw, then nestled his fingers into her hair. His breath was warm and smelled sweetly of wine as he leaned in, his lips meeting hers softly.

Adella wrapped her arms around him and kissed him deeper. Slipping a hand under his shirt, she skimmed her fingers over his ribs. The memories of years past flooded her mind as she traced the firm, knotty muscles. The pain of each cold night she had spent alone since their last together ached in some hollow corner of her heart. Now, the warmth of his skin soothed it as she pulled him closer.

Grabbing her around the waist, Declan pressed her against the bulkhead with his hips, then slid his hand beneath her skirts, running it up over her thigh. His hands were strong and callused, but gentle. Thinking about his offer, she wondered what it might be like to leave Elldon behind and sail with him over the wide and beautiful Belgrand Bay, or across the mysterious Greater Sea. *I could wake up beside him every morning,* she thought. *And see the world, instead of just the Campos...*

20

Home Again

Kol stood on the pier under the bright light of a warm, summer morning, watching the last crate, suspended from blocks and heavy line from the spar, inch down to *The Eglantine*'s deck. The ship itself was stately and imposing with its massive, dark form rising from the sea and contrasting against the pale sky. It looked to be a formidable match for any storm that Belgrand Bay may blow their way.

He had spent the previous week at Smuggler's Port getting to know his father better, trying to piece together an image of what their lives might have been like had they never been separated by tragedy. He hadn't been an unwanted bastard like he had always believed; he had a loving family, once. Somehow, knowing that made his past feel less cold to him now. Kol had come to realize that the day he was lost at sea had been a turning point in Seaborn's life. What followed after had been the result of choices made by a broken man who had lost everything. He hadn't wanted to press his father for details that clearly held so much pain for the man still. Even so, Kol understood it well enough; the same anger and resentment that entangled Seaborn's heart had long harbored in his own. Conversation about Declan clearly stirred up strong feelings in Seaborn, but Kol knew in his gut it wouldn't be the last he'd hear of the matter.

He turned toward Seaborn, who stood at his side. "You must visit me in Valenna," Kol offered. "I have a townhouse in Raymouth you're welcome to stay at."

"I would like nothing better," Seaborn replied. "I will write to you soon."

Kol smiled, heart swelling with pride. "Oh," he said suddenly. "I almost forgot..." He bent to pull his knife from its usual place in the top of his boot, and presented it on his open palm. "This belongs to you."

"I gave it to you," Seaborn said warmly, closing Kol's fingers around the handle. "Please, keep it with you." There was an unexpected gravity in his voice that reminded Kol of his dream. Chuckling slightly, Seaborn added, "For good luck."

Kol tucked his knife back into his boot, then stood and removed his wide-brimmed hat, smoothing back tendrils of hair that had fallen loose. "Goodbye, Father," he said, tentatively offering his hand, still carefully wrapped in bandage.

Instead of accepting it, Seaborn wrapped his arms around Kol's broad shoulders, embracing him tightly. "Goodbye, Kaias—" His voice broke with emotion. "My son," he added in a whisper. Then, he turned and, with one last look back, made his way down the wharf.

Placing his hat back onto his head, Kol looked up once more at the ship before him, admiring its beauty. Though he continued with Martin's company out of a sense of responsibility and obligation, his father's approval of the merchant profession gave him a new confidence in his choice.

The sound of footsteps caught his attention as Kerchaw walked down the gang-board. "The captain wants to set sail quickly," Kerchaw said, joining him. "Before the weather turns again."

Kol gave a nod. "You know, I've been thinking." He rubbed away beads of sweat that had begun to form on the back of his neck. "Perhaps the Royal Westward *does* need its own ship."

"That's the spirit," Kerchaw grinned. "I'll inquire about *The Eglantine* for you."

They boarded and checked the stowage in the hold, then returned to the weather deck in time to watch the crew set sail. Soon, the ship was underway and heading out into the open sea, homeward bound with fair winds under the bright, blue sky. Kol stepped toward the rail, filling his lungs deeply with the fresh, briny air as he watched the shore shrink slowly behind them.

Though the crew worked quietly, and orders had been given once more for the use of buckets in place of the pissdales, there was no sight of serpents in the calm, blue-green waters as they sailed. Steady breezes tempered the warm sunlight that shone on their faces. The terrifying sight they had passed on their voyage to Smuggler's Port was gradually put out of mind as everyone grew more at ease in the fine weather.

Kol passed the night aboard the ship much like each previous night since receiving Misses Asher's news about Adella. With the help of the poppy spirits or, in lieu of that, plenty of drink, he slept soundly no matter where he was, often waking much later in the morning than he had intended with a dry mouth and a pounding in his skull. On the second day at sea, Kol awoke at a reasonable hour, and the frightful images that managed to bleed through his dreams into his waking mind were nearly forgotten by the time he finished fastening the buttons of his fall-front knee breeches and buckling on his sword-belt.

When he came above decks to take in the fresh air before breakfast, he was glad to find clear skies again. Walking along the starboard rail, he looked out on the southern horizon, watching the peaks of the waves glitter in the early sunlight. Though the shore was too far off for him to see, he imagined that they were now passing by the sea caves that dotted the cliffs which lie between Smuggler's Port and the massive, rocky precipice known as the Figurehead; it was the Figurehead that marked the halfway point along the coast between Valenna and Sornia. *The Eglantine* seemed to be making good time, but soon they would be approaching the Teeth that guarded the coastline in that area. He knew the ship would need to either sail around them or reduce speed to weave carefully through them. Kol hoped the captain would choose to go around; in his experience, the Teeth seemed to be a breeding ground for trouble.

By early afternoon, dark clouds appeared along the western horizon, and blew in quickly. Kol breathed a sigh of relief as *The Eglantine* changed its heading to the northeast, changing course to sail around the Teeth. He and Kerchaw had just finished a quick meal that had been brought to their cabin before venturing above decks again.

They strolled across the main deck, keeping out of the way of the hardworking crew as they made their way up to the forecastle deck, and looked out over the bow at the vast plane of open water ahead. The cool breeze from this height wicked the perspiration away from beneath their arms, whipping strands of hair in their faces. A sudden gust snatched away Kerchaw's hat. He gave an indignant shout as he chased it toward the rail, then watched helplessly as it dropped into the sea. Kol caught up beside him and they stood, watching it bob tauntingly on the waves before disappearing below the surface.

"I liked that hat," Kerchaw sulked.

"That's too bad," Kol replied. "You can get a new one when we get back to Raymouth." He was just about to turn away from the rail when something caught his eye. A dark shadow, too deep below the surface to discern its shape, had appeared in the water beside the ship and seemed to be growing quickly larger. Instinctively, Kol leaned over the rail to get a better look and peered down into the blue waves below.

"What is it?" Kerchaw asked.

"Uh..." Kol muttered, squinting into the water. The shadow seemed very large now, and he could see it was much longer than it was wide. While he watched, a golden light flashed just below the surface as a large eye opened; its long slit of a pupil stared up at him. "Get back!" Kol hissed, trying to keep his voice down despite the panic that shot through him. He grabbed Kerchaw by the arm, pulling him along as they scrambled backward from the rail.

"Go!" Kol ordered, shoving Kerchaw toward the ladder that led down to the main deck. They clambered down and Kol searched for the captain amongst the crew, spotting him emerging from the aftcastle companionway. "Serpent!" Kol yelled. Drawing his cutlass, he crossed amidships to meet the captain, Kerchaw following at his heels. "Arm yourselves!"

"This is a merchant vessel," the captain retorted. His eyes roved the decks while he addressed the crew, "Make do with what you can!"

Kol looked at him incredulously. "What do you do when you meet reavers, then?"

"We outrun them," the captain replied, a look of understanding lighting up his face. He raised his voice to give an order, "Helmsman, prepare to—" The loud crack of splitting wood sounded from the bow of *The Eglantine*. Ahead, a strange, menacing form spilled over the forecastle, bringing with it water and slime. Immense jaws snapped at the crew as they scrambled and slid to get clear.

Just as Kol turned to run, he was barreled into by a fleeing sailor. Pain shot through him as he landed hard on his shoulder, his cutlass skittering from his hand and across the deck toward the larboard rail. Rolling over with a groan, he rubbed the bruise forming on his upper arm and looked toward the bow. "Too late," he muttered, terror sinking in his gut like a lead weight. Kol's breath hitched in his throat as a rancid, fishy stench fouled the air.

He jumped to his feet and ran after his cutlass. As he reached for the handle, it was kicked from his grasp and lost among a shuffle of feet as a group of sailors fled aft. One crewman, terror revealing the whites of his eyes, stopped and glanced down at Kol, then grabbed the cutlass from the planks and ran off, disappearing into the aftcastle. "Coward!" Kol shouted, clenching his fist. His injured thumb, still wrapped in bandages, throbbed painfully.

The cloying stench of rotting fish thickened the air, and he knew the creature was close. From somewhere behind him came a deep, grating scream that cut off suddenly, punctuated by the gut-turning sound of cracking bone. Kol spun and, frozen in place, watched the long, pointed snout of the serpent drag a crewman across the forecastle deck, pulling him in as its glistening body entwined around him.

Kol scanned the area, searching for anything he could use as a weapon. His eyes skimmed over a large coil of rope, an abandoned wineskin, and a wool hat before he finally noticed the long, wooden pole of a sailor's boat hook, lying by the forecastle on the other side of the deck.

Now that he had the chance to get a good look at the creature, he could see two sets of flippers low on its body, with the tail ending in a wide, barbed fin. The coils of its long, blue-black body lay between him and the boat hook, writhing in a puddle of blood as the animal tore at the sailor's limbs.

Kol's attention turned back to the boat hook. As he took a tentative step forward, the sea serpent's head jerked up into the air, rising high on its long stalk of a neck. The sharp spines that lined its back bristled upward as one wide, golden eye turned in his direction. A piece of mangled flesh fell from its jaws as they opened, and it landed with a squelch on the planks. The hair on Kol's neck rose while he stared into the unblinking eye and, for a brief moment, the world around him seemed to fall away, the sound of his heartbeat in his ears the only evidence of passing time.

In a flash, the creature lunged into motion, its body weaving back and forth over the deck as it bounded toward him. *Wait...* He stood motionless, pulse pounding so hard he could feel it drumming in his neck, while he waited for the right moment. If he moved too soon, the serpent would have room to turn and follow. If he waited too long, he would meet the same fate as the sailor. The stench of the animal was heavy in the air as it barreled toward him, the slits of its nostrils flaring wide.

Now. Kol dove forward, tucking into a roll as the beast's jaws skimmed by just above him. He sprang onto his feet, making a dash for the boat hook, with the scuffling of tail and fin on wood close behind him. He lunged for the pole, scooping it up as he slammed bodily into the bulkhead of the forecastle. Dropping into a crouch, he jammed the end of its pole against the base of the bulkhead where it met the planking, and shoved the brass tip of the boat hook up into the air, pointing it toward the oncoming jaws. The serpent sprang forward, its mouth open to snatch any part of Kol that it could.

The shock of the impact sent a jolt through Kol as the throat of the animal slammed down onto the brass hook. The pole shuddered in his hands as he strained to hold it steady and keep the serpent's jaws away from his head; his injured thumb pulsed as it threatened to give way. Braced against the bulkhead, the sturdy, wooden pole held fast as the hook head sank deep into the beast's mouth. Bone cracked and splintered as the long, needle-like teeth closed in toward him. He turned his face away and, squeezing his eyes shut tightly, steeled himself against the anticipation of pain.

The jaws went slack and the sea serpent's heavy head fell away; its long neck crashed sideways onto the planks with the boat hook still lodged in its mouth, the brass hook-head protruding from the top of its skull. Foamy, pink blood seeped from its head as the serpent lay dead at his feet.

Kol stood and looked around, rubbing his thumb to ease the pain as the captain approached, staring open-mouthed at the dead creature.

Kerchaw stepped down from his perch on the aftcastle ladder. "Well, I'll be damned," he said, voice breathy with awe. His gaze moved from the serpent's body up to Kol as he approached. "Didn't think they could be killed."

The remaining days of their voyage had been mercifully unremarkable, save for the unusual deference Kol had received from the crew and captain alike. Not wanting it to go to his head, he reminded himself that, if he hadn't noticed the boat hook nearby, he probably would be in the serpent's belly along with the unfortunate sailor. He tried not to think about that.

It had rained during the rest of their journey, keeping Kol and Kerchaw mostly below decks while the crew did what they could to repair the damage the sea serpent had done when it had thrown itself onto the ship. The bilge pumps were in use still when they made port at Raymouth in late afternoon. As the crew maneuvered *The Eglantine* through the choppy grey waters and moored at the pier, the dark clouds had begun to break up, with golden beams of sunlight cutting through the sky.

Kol and Kerchaw finished with their records and signed the bill of lading, then disembarked, walking along the gang-board under a brightening sky hung with a colorful ribbon of rainbow. As they went along the pier they passed the bow of the ship, revealing the extent of the damage that had been done to its hull. Several planks below the rail had been broken and splintered in places, the gaps temporarily plugged with oakum. Kol imagined the repairs would be expensive.

"On second thought," Kol mused, "let's hold off on buying *The Eglantine.*"

"Noted," Kerchaw replied. "Care to stop by the Crown for supper? I want to bring Annie home one of their cherry tarts."

They wove through the busy streets toward the Ivy Crown Inn, then pushed open the greasy door. Inside, many groups of people sat upon the long benches at the tables, engaged in loud conversation. Kol and Kerchaw settled at an empty spot at one table in the far corner.

Eventually, the innkeeper brought them bowls of hot beef stew and tankards of porter beer. As they sat and ate quietly, the other patrons around them carried on conversations of their own, and Kol inadvertently found himself listening in on them now and then. When he lifted his tankard and took a long draught, one husky voice at the far end of the table caught his attention.

"And with all this going on lately—plague, sea serpents, the destruction of Pentz, the death of the King—and now, we're at war with Sornia!" he scoffed. "I hope the people of Elldon can hold them off for a while, the rest of the country is still in bad shape."

"If Lady Grimless is anything like her father," another voice chimed in, "she'll do well enough."

Lady Grimless. Kol's mind raced with their words, the voices around him falling away until all he could hear was indistinct chatter, muffled by his own quickening breath. He slammed his tankard onto the table much harder than he had intended and rose to his feet. "Adella is alive?" he demanded, voice rising in excitement.

"Alive for now," the man replied with a sardonic smile. "And it's Lady Grimless, to the likes of you—"

Kol didn't wait for the man to finish speaking; he turned and headed for the door. Behind him, Kerchaw clinked a handful of coins onto the table and followed after him.

They hurried through the city streets, Kerchaw struggling to keep up but never asking where they were headed. Finally, they entered the livery stables, passing by the horse stalls until they came to the end, and stopped at the stall of a large, black mare.

Nickering softly, Madigan stuck her head out over the stall door, and Kol greeted her with a gentle hand on her muzzle. He then turned to face Kerchaw, unable to keep the flood of emotions from showing on his face.

"Go," Kerchaw encouraged. "I'll take care of things while you're gone."

21

The Rout

Travia's nostrils flared with every breath, foamy spittle streaming from her mouth as the familiar silhouette of Greywood Manor rose up before them, sheltered beneath the knotted arms of the tall elms. James reined the mare back to a trot as he wove through the tents that scattered the manor grounds, the sound of rapid hoofbeats drawing his neighbors out with curiosity. Searching their faces, he found the pale, blue eyes of his brother, whose face was drawn with concern.

"What is it?" Jacoby asked impatiently, grabbing Travia's reins as James dismounted. "Did you find her?"

"No," James huffed, struggling to catch his breath. He pushed back the straight, dark brown hair that had fallen loose from his queue and clung to his sweat-drenched forehead. "Not yet," he added quickly, trying to keep his voice light for his brother's sake. "But we have another problem." His brow knotted as he wished bitterly that his mother were there, and that Adella had survived. He didn't know what to do; the oncoming threat in the Campos was greater than he had anticipated, and more imminent. Elldon simply didn't have enough people to face what was headed their way. It was hopeless.

"James," Jacoby's voice was firm but pleading while he studied his brother's face. "What is it?"

"See to my horse," James ordered, "then gather everyone in the parlor."

Outside Greywood, while the early evening sun painted the landscape a bright gold, the interior of the manor remained stuffy and dim. With the tall casement windows boarded up, the only illumination came from the brass chandelier that hung from the center of the spacious parlor. The lit beeswax candles, which had recently arrived in Martin's shipment of supplies, perfumed the air with the sweet scent of honey, filling the room with a warm glow. Standing at Adella's writing desk, James set aside the many-tined seashell that served as a paperweight, then shuffled through the notes that had been left on the table surface. He had hoped to find some words of instruction or advice to guide him, but found only personal correspondence and work lists, none of which could help him figure out what to do to prepare for what lay ahead. He was on his own.

As he set the papers back onto the desk, a memory struck him. *There is a time for action and a time for patience,* Adella's words came to mind; *the hardest test of leadership is to discern one from the other.* He had been rash with the first attack, he knew that now. He had charged headlong into a situation without taking the time to fully understand it first. Adella had warned him of that, but he had been too impatient to listen.

This time, however, things were different. He knew the Sornian's plans now, for one. The pending attack by their reinforcements, he was sure, was meant to be a surprise. It was the culmination of all their subterfuge in the west, and would have been a clever move if it had gone as planned. However, knowing the Sornians' next move gave Elldon the advantage. As far as the Sornians knew, their army's presence in the south was still unknown to the Valennians. *To discern one from the other,* the words repeated in his mind, and he knew what needed to be done. He just had to convince the others.

James looked around as they began to file into the parlor, and his heart swelled with affection for his neighbors. He had come to know them better after the initial attack on Elldon in the spring, when they had rallied at Greywood to defend what was left of their town as their homes burned to cinders. He let out a breath, steadying his nerves against the dire news he was about to give them.

Glancing from face to face, he met Rosalind's steely blue eyes as she came through the doorway and stood attentively nearby. Her curly hair, the cheerful color of sunlight, was pinned up on top of her head, revealing the deep slice through her ear, now blackened with scab. Benson and his young son, Nicolas, made their way toward the sofa and took seats, the boy with his little dog in his arms. Jacoby entered with the last group and stood before him in the crowded space, watching him expectantly.

James stepped forward, sucking his teeth while he thought. "I will be frank with you," he began solemnly. "The Sornians have gathered reinforcements in the south and are already marching toward Greywood. After our last skirmish, we lost more than we could spare. It was our hope that Lady Grimless would secure help from the north, but," his gaze dropped to the worn-out floral carpet, "she never returned."

He cleared his throat, shifting his weight as his wounded leg began to throb. "We are on our own; there will be no help for us. We are already too few, and we've only just begun to rebuild. The injured and those unable to fight will be sent to Raymouth, but it will take some time for them to make it to safety. The army will be upon us by tomorrow; we need to buy our people some time to escape." He stopped and looked them over, meeting the others' eyes in turn. "If some of us stay and fight, it will give our wounded, our children, a chance to survive. If the Sornians reach Elldon first, they won't have a chance at all." A heavy silence filled the room while he waited for an answer. The eyes of the people around him darted away or turned downward, avoiding his gaze.

"How did it come to this?" an old man in a carpenter's apron interjected. "A whole army to the south, and no one noticed?"

"We weren't scouting to the south," James admitted. "We weren't expecting it, with the enemy encampment to the west—" He swallowed hard as he realized how wrong he'd been. The time he'd insisted to Adella that Sornians weren't clever came bitterly to mind. "It was a diversion."

"James is right," Benson said, rising from his seat. "There's no way we could get everyone to Raymouth before the army reaches Elldon; they will be dead in the street before they reach the bridge. But if we ride out to meet the Sornians, we can delay their attack. We need to buy our people, our children," he said, gesturing toward Nicolas with a broad palm lined with black, "the time to escape." He looked around at the others. "I know what we're asking of you, but it's the only way. Who will ride with us?"

"I'm with you," Jacoby said, eyes fixed on his brother's. "If we give up now, we lose whatever chance we have of finding Ma."

"So what's your plan?" a brittle voice said. Searching out the speaker's face, James recognized the stout, older woman as Misses Joley, the bakester who had volunteered to oversee Greywood's kitchen after her own shop had been burnt to rubble. Her grey hair was pulled back in a bun and covered with a kerchief, hands hidden in the pockets of her frilly apron.

James pressed his mouth into a tight line. Every eye looked toward him, awaiting his response. "We ride out to meet them," he stated plainly. "Like before. Only this time, they won't be expecting it. We've seen what a mounted attack can do against foot soldiers," his voice grew louder with determination. "If we bring the fight to them, we can stop them before they reach the manor."

"Your last plan cost us too many," the carpenter replied. "And now you're asking for more of us to die?"

"I—" The accusation stabbed him with guilt as James searched for the words to reply.

Rosalind spoke up, stepping forward, "I was new to Elldon when the attack came in the spring. Not many here knew me." She rubbed the chintz-patterned sleeve on her upper arm, voice softening as she remembered. "But my husband and I had saved up for years, and spent every bit of coin we had to buy our patch of land here. When the Sornians destroyed our home, we fled to Raymouth like many of you did. We didn't realize the ague—" Her voice cracked. "I survived it, but he and our baby didn't. I brought them back here to be buried." She had to force the words out through thick emotion. "On our own land. And whether it happens sooner or later, I plan to join them." She took a deep breath, steadying her voice. "If I can save some lives doing it, all the better."

James was touched by her story, hearing it for the first time. He could only nod at her answer, encouraged by her resolve.

"Just how many are they?" Misses Joley asked.

"Maybe two, three hundred infantry in uniform," James guessed. "Around two dozen cavalry. Thankfully, I saw no more than that. But I followed a group of riders from their camp in the west, and I'm certain more will be joining them the longer we wait."

"That's all?" Joley replied. "They must not think much of us."

"Even so," James said, letting out a breath, "that's plenty."

"We've never seen uniformed soldiers in the Campos before," Benson commented. "They must have come straight from Sornia. They'll be tired from marching that far, plus we'll have the advantage of surprise..." He scratched the dark stubble along his jaw. "If we use every horse we have left, it would amount to nearly half a troop. It could be enough."

"What do you say?" James looked around the room. The flickering candlelight cast dancing shadows on the walls, glimmering in the many eyes, wide with worry, that met his now. He was responsible for each life there, and though Adella wasn't able to keep her promise, she died trying. He should be willing to do the same. "Who's with me?"

The room filled with low muttering as the others discussed amongst themselves. At first, the quiet tones sounded apprehensive, dubious; then, the voices grew stronger and more certain.

"I am," Benson stated, giving a reassuring nod of his head.

Jacoby turned toward James. "Me too."

"As am I." Rosalind turned, eyeing the others expectantly.

Misses Joley came forward. "Count me in."

James waited, muscles tense in the following silence, not sure what the rest of the group would say. Then, one by one, they spoke up, pledging their service, with each voice more confident than the last, until nearly the entire room had agreed. When the room had quieted once more, he let out a breath. "Good," he said, shoulders falling with relief. "We'll prepare tonight, and ride out at first light."

The first grey tint of dawn blotted the horizon as James put his foot into the stirrup and pulled himself into the saddle. Holding back the reins as Travia danced impatiently in place, he turned to address the group, organized into a wedge formation behind him. "I know we're not soldiers," he began, voice echoing over the dewy grass in the quiet of early morning. "Our horses may not be battle-trained, or our weapons new. We are farmers…" He searched out his brother at the back of the group, then Benson and Rosalind at the flanks. "Blacksmiths, merchants and housewives. But we do have one advantage." He pulled his bow from his shoulders and hefted it in the air. "We are Valennians!" he shouted, words echoing over the silent, dewy fields of early morning. Voices cheered as blades and bows rose toward the sky. "And this is our home!" Amid their resounding answer, he swung the mare around to face the vast plains of the south. "Forward!" He slackened the reins and Travia burst eagerly into a gallop. The thunder of hooves followed close behind.

James checked her pace, drawing her back to a trot to conserve energy for the fight ahead. The southern prairie they traversed was flatter and more open than those to the west; there would be no cover for an ambush. Though he was certain he was taking the right action this time, he couldn't quell the fluttering of nerves that surged through him, causing his hands to shake.

They drew nearer to the low-lying fields where he had discovered the Sornian army, and James shifted nervously in the saddle. The cool, morning air swept over his face, neck and hands, raising goosebumps over his skin beneath his sweat-dampened clothes. Soon, they were mounting the rise he had crouched upon the day before, beyond which the soldiers gathered. The hooves of the horses trampled the briars at the crest as the vast fields below came into view. Soldiers in emerald marched over the wind-swept grass, much nearer than they were the day before, burdened with knapsacks and bedrolls as they began their day's march.

"Charge!" James shouted, spurring his horse into a hard run as they began their descent on the other side of the rise. The swift strides of the mare swallowed up the distance. Behind him, the rumbling of hooves echoed like thunder as the horses tore over the landscape, flinging up clods of turf, snorting and blowing in excitement.

James dropped his reins and, pulling an arrow from the quiver at his side, drew his bow and loosed it into the wall of soldiers. He drew again and again until the very last moment he could spare, then shouldered his bow and drew his saber.

Fanning out into a wide line on either side of him, the formation of riders crashed into the green-clad soldiers like a wave on the shore. James hacked at all he could reach from his saddle; slicing through shoulders, necks and emerald jackets. The wide-eyed look of terror as his saber slashed across one man's face burned into James's mind; he saw it still, felt the gritty drag of his blade against bone, even after the soldier fell into the grass, disappearing with a brutish shriek beneath the boots of his panicking countrymen. As Travia jostled between the soldiers and the horses of the other riders, a crack of pain flared through his body. He was unable to hold back a scream as his left ankle, caught between the barrels of the two horses, wrenched violently backward. Squeezing with his opposite heel, James jerked Travia's reins and she sprung to the right, ramming into the soldiers that hemmed her in.

All across the front of the formation, the Sornian soldiers broke rank and turned away, shouting as they fled from the onslaught. With a quick glance from left to right, James saw the Sornian cavalry moving forward from their position at the flanks as they galloped to their countrymen's aid, and he knew his riders would soon be surrounded if they didn't act immediately. Though they had all been aware of the danger they faced and rode into it willingly, James quailed at the thought of losing so many of them again. "Fall back!" he shouted to the others, holding the saber aloft and pointing northward. "Retreat!" He spun Travia around on her haunches, throwing a glance in each direction to be sure they'd heard. "Retreat!" he screamed again over the din, waiting for the others to follow his command before sheathing his blade and spurring Travia into a hard gallop.

The Valennian riders stretched out over the fields, some falling behind as the horses tired or slowed from injury. His own ankle pounded fiercely, though James didn't know how bad the injury was. He didn't dare to look at it until they reached the safety of Greywood Manor, but he could feel its strength was gone. His left foot slipped from the stirrup, dangling limply, and he grabbed Travia's neck, weaving his fingers through her mane to keep his balance in the saddle.

Glancing backward, he saw the Sornian riders following close at their heels, gaining on them with fresh horses. Though he had been prepared to die in this fight if need be, now that it seemed close at hand, he found himself only wishing to live another day. He shivered as a cold sweat enveloped him. With every muscle in his body tensed, he fought to keep from sliding sideways, knowing if he fell, he would surely be trampled by the hooves that rumbled after him.

As they sped toward the ridge, James felt his grip on Travia's neck slipping, his fingers slick and clammy. Travia was blowing hard, nearly spent, and the Sornians behind were quickly gaining ground, drawing weapons at the gallop. Ahead, a pale haze hung low in the air, though he didn't know the source since he couldn't yet see beyond the ridge. The echo of hoofbeats seemed to come from every direction, no longer just at his back. Disoriented and weak, James's hold on Travia's mane gave out as they crested the ridge. He slipped sideways down the saddle, held tenuously in place only by one stirrup as his fingers dragged uselessly across her sweat-soaked coat, when movement caught his eye on the other side of the rise. *What the hell—* he thought, squinting in confusion. In the field beyond, a spirited band of horses, tails and necks held high, galloped at speed toward them, each rider upon their backs arrayed in bright red. *Valennian scarlet!* he realized in astonishment. Emboldened by the sight, James rallied the last of his strength and, shoving his foot hard against the stirrup, pulled himself back into the saddle.

Travia heaved, her pace faltering. Ahead, the riders in red pounded across the field, kicking up a cloud of dust as they charged head-on toward James's formation. As they descended the ridge, his own riders were impelled faster down the slope, on a collision course with the oncoming horses. Glancing behind, James saw one Sornian horseman closing the distance toward him, while drawing a bow and taking aim at Travia's haunches. "Shit!" James muttered to himself, pulse surging through his limbs in a burst of panic. Danger was closing in on him ahead and behind.

There was nothing else he could do; James pulled Travia's reins and turned her suddenly to the right, hoping that the Valennians would be quick enough to follow suit. At the sudden change of direction, however, Travia stumbled, throwing him forward onto her neck, his body weighing down her front quarters until, with a sickening lurch, James felt himself sailing helplessly through the air. With the loud crack of breaking bone, he hit the ground, the rocky soil tearing at his cheek as his head collided with dirt, sliding for a moment until a massive weight fell down on top of him, crushing his injured leg and pinning him into place. Stars burst briefly across his vision, then the world turned black.

22

Riders in Red

Adella stood at the rail while the ship's boats towed *The Tigress* into port, and breathed a sigh of relief to finally have made it safely back to Raymouth. The voyage from Pentz had taken days longer than usual, slowed by the calm winds and the passage of other vessels, which caused long delays at anchor while the captains convened to share news and supplies.

As the ship drew closer to shore, she noticed a haze, faint but dark like a drop of ink suspended in water, hung over the harbor, accompanied by the acrid smell of smoke. Fear shot through her when she thought of the last time she had come to Raymouth under smoke, and the tragedy that met her there: the bodies in the water, the plague, the news of her parents' death.

Nearly home, she reminded herself and took a deep breath, steadying her nerves. She was aching to get back to Greywood and see Kol again, certain he'd have returned to Elldon with the supplies by now. More than that, though, she needed to tell him about the voice she thought she had heard, about the strange light in the sea and Paloma's writings, impatient to ask if he thought it might all be related to the Heart of the World, or if she was only losing her mind. She trusted Kol's advice more than anyone else's, and wanted him to be the first she spoke to about the matter.

As the crew lowered the anchor and the boats returned to take on passengers, Captain Declan approached. She hadn't had a moment alone with him since the night he gave her the letter. He had berthed in another cabin, letting her have the private use of his quarters to keep their personal affairs out of the crew's chatter around the scuttlebutt.

He stood beside her, arms folded at his back while he watched the crew below draw the ship's boats alongside. "You needn't go," he said, a tinge of regret seeping through his stoic tone.

"Yes, I do," she replied firmly. "I'm a member of the nobility and Valenna is at war; martial service is not only expected, it's required of me. You know that."

He turned to face her, his eyebrows drawing together. "In that case, I can't say when we'll meet again."

"I know," she sighed.

"But—" His face took on a hardened look and he lowered his voice. "Whether you understand it now or not, I know we belong together; and I'll get my way eventually."

"What?" she snapped, a shock of cold running through her at his words. She stood speechless, searching for a response, while he took her other hand and kissed her knuckles. Adella snatched her hand away as Endlebridge approached and stood beside her, waiting his turn to bid farewell to the captain. Adella searched Declan's face for a hint of his meaning, but his placid expression was inscrutable. Not wishing to have a private conversation overheard, Adella turned, putting Declan behind her, and walked toward the ladder.

She swallowed hard, her throat suddenly feeling dry. With her insides a torment of emotion, of longing and confusion, Adella threw him one last backward glance, then gathered her torn skirts in one hand and climbed down the ladder into the boat. Endlebridge followed and took a seat behind her as the crew took up the oars, heading for shore. She turned Declan's words over and over again in her mind, trying to decipher his intent. Whether they had been made lightly or if they were the product of deranged thoughts, she couldn't be sure, and hadn't had the time to ask. She and Rogero had been good friends once, certainly, but that had been years ago; she wasn't sure she truly knew him anymore. *No use dwelling on it right now,* she told herself. *There are more important matters at hand.*

Adella turned around to speak to Endlebridge. "You won't forget our bargain?" she asked him lightly, in an attempt to stifle her nerves.

"I'm a man of my word," he assured her, a smile pulling at his full lips. "But I must confer with the troop captains first. Let's meet at the Ivy Crown for supper."

Adella nodded, then turned to look landward. As they were rowed toward a small stretch of beach beside the docks, bordered on one side by large rocks, she noticed someone standing in the surf, watching them expectantly. Judging by his bright blue jacket, she knew he must be a sailor, though his lithe frame didn't fill it out completely. When the crew jumped into the water and pulled the boat onto the sand, the sailor waded out into the water to assist. He came forward, and Adella recognized the youthful face and energetic demeanor of Yul Childric.

"Yul," she greeted him with a smile as she stepped out of the boat. "Good to see you again."

"Good heavens, cousin!" he gushed, steadying her with a hand to the elbow. "You've no idea how worried I've been after hearing what happened at Pentz—for you, for *The Tigress* and my shipmates..." He took a deep breath. "When I saw those red and black sails coming in, I was so happy I nearly shat myself."

Adella laughed, and they moved aside to let the others behind them step out of the boat. "How've things been here?" she asked.

"The most outrageous thing, Adella," he confided, brows lowering. "A ship caught fire some nights ago as it lay at anchor. Good sailors were killed. Rumors are that it was deliberate."

"How awful!" Adella replied. "Why would anyone do such a thing?"

"There was a feud amongst the merchantry, from what I gather. The criminal that did it," he lowered his voice, "must still be loose in the city, and heaven knows the Royal Guards are useless, so be careful." He nodded a quick goodbye and turned his attention to the ship's boat, lending a hand to return it seaward.

Adella looked back at *The Tigress*, with black-and-red sails furled as it lay at anchor in the jostling waves. Her chest ached when she wondered if she'd ever see the ship again, or its captain. Memories of their years together surfaced; laughter in the formal gardens, whispers echoing down the vast hallways of the Ansebulet, the warm touch of their first kiss at the Ivy Crown all weighed heavily on her while she forced herself to turn away, stepping through the deep sand of the beach toward town.

Adella strode through the doorway of the Ivy Crown, which had been propped open with a stone to let in the cool breezes from the sea, and looked around. Inside, she spotted the usual mix of seafarers and merchants. She walked across the large dining area, an uneasiness growing in her chest as she passed by the crowded tables without the cue she searched for. She had spent the spare hours before supper milling about in the shops of Raymouth despite her empty pockets and ragged clothing, but now the time had come.

"Lady Grimless," a jaunty voice called out. In the corner, a man rose to his feet. "Please, join us."

Adella breathed a sigh of relief when she recognized the stately silhouette of Lord Endlebridge. It was then that she realized, in the dim light of the inn, that the group of men he sat with all wore jackets of Valennian scarlet. "Lord Endlebridge," she replied, looking them over. "Is this the troop I've hired?" she asked hopefully.

"No, these men are infantry," he replied, picking up a pewter goblet and taking a sip. "And I shall need their help in rebuilding Pentz. No," one corner of his mouth tightened into a playful half-smile, "I think I have something a bit more..." He searched for the right words. "Suited to your circumstances."

"What do you mean?" Adella asked dubiously.

He set his cup down and rose from his seat. "Why don't I show you?"

She nodded, then followed him toward the back of the inn and out the rear entrance. They walked down the cobblestone street toward the livery stables where she and Misses Asher had left their horses on the way to Pentz. A man in scarlet, who stood at a stall door patting the muzzle of a sleepy chestnut, turned and approached them.

His clothes were new and well-tailored; his black cockaded hat sat perfectly level over a ribboned queue.

"Lady Grimless," Endlebridge began, "this is Captain William Holcomb of the Pentz Standing Cavalry."

"I'm so glad to meet you," Adella said earnestly, offering her hand.

"The pleasure is mine," Holcomb replied, removing his hat to reveal heavily powdered hair above a freckled brow. He took her hand and, bowing, brushed her knuckles with his lips.

Adella quietly cleared her throat and drew back her hand. Though it felt odd to her to receive an intimate touch in such a formal manner, she reminded herself it was the customary greeting for a noblewoman of Valenna and, now that she had inherited her father's title, she'd just have to get used to it.

"I understand you are our new patroness," Holcomb continued, donning his hat again. "You are a countess, I believe?"

"Not exactly," Adella replied.

"The lady holds an older title from the days of the Empire," Endlebridge explained, shooting an apologetic look toward Adella on behalf of the captain. "That being the title of Equess Primorri, or First Knight in the Old Andolinian."

"But, as there is only one person who bears such a title," Adella added, "most people can't remember it, let alone pronounce it." She smiled and gave a slight shrug. "So I am simply called 'Lady Grimless.'"

"It's comparable to the modern title of marquess," Endlebridge explained. "Though she is the only noble that is not a member of the Royal Family."

Adella opened her mouth to explain that, though that was true of her father's side from which she inherited her title, she was, in fact, related to the late King Harrian through her mother's side, but thought better of it when she noticed the look on the captain's face.

"I see," Holcomb replied, brows raised and eyes wide with confusion. It was the usual reaction whenever Adella's father had tried to explain the intricacies of the distinction to anyone who inquired. "I'm glad I asked," he added unconvincingly. Behind him, hooves clattered on stone as figures in scarlet led their horses one-by-one out from the open doors of the stables. "Lady Grimless," Holcomb said proudly, "this is my troop."

The cavaliers, leading their horses in-hand on their right, walked along the cobblestone square, forming a wide circle before her as they returned toward the stables.

"Now, this isn't the cavalry troop you're familiar with from the days of your father's service," Holcomb warned. "Our ranks have been pared down, and each troop is fewer than they traditionally have been. Gone are the quartermasters and cornets and such—We have only captain and cavaliers. After all," he added with an embarrassed smile, "our regiment hasn't been needed for combat since the skirmishes at Enth, and those who had experienced that have since retired."

"And the number?" she inquired.

"Sixty-three," he replied, the confidence in his voice waning as he looked down at his polished boots.

"Sixty-three?" Adella repeated. *That's little more than half a proper troop.* She was grateful even for that amount, yet Adella couldn't help but wonder how it could possibly be enough. "I can't begin to express how grateful I am for your service," Adella said, loud enough for all to hear. "The people of Elldon will be glad to welcome you." The thought crossed her mind that Elldon might have been better off with infantry if they would have been a greater number, but she nodded her approval as the last cavalier disappeared through the stable doors. *No time to be picky,* she reminded herself. After all, the cavaliers' homes had probably just been destroyed by the flooding of Pentz; she was lucky any of them had agreed to go at all. *We'll have to make do with what we can get.*

"There are a few more preparations to make," Holcomb informed her, "but we shall be ready to depart at dawn."

She smiled at the thought of finally seeing Greywood again. "Very good."

The cavaliers, with Adella leading the way on a borrowed horse, arrived at Elldon with the morning sun still low on the horizon. As she rode up the cobblestone path leading to the entrance of Greywood Manor, Adella flung her leg over the saddle and stepped down from the stirrup. An ominous silence loomed over the estate, which was a sharp contrast to the lively state she had left it in. Pulling the reins over the horse's neck, she led the little, black gelding up toward the towering fieldstone building and secured him to the iron ring of a hitching-post.

Metal creaked, and Adella turned to see the twin doors of the manor's entrance cracking slowly open. A wrinkled face peeked through the gap, then the door flung wide.

"Lady Grimless!" an old man shouted, words rising with disbelief while he shuffled down the steps of the entrance toward her. "Bless me! You're alive?"

"Seems that way," she quipped, then stumbled backward in surprise when he threw his arms around her.

"And you've brought reinforcements!" he sobbed into her jacket. "If you go now, you may just make it in time to save them."

Adella steadied the man by the shoulders while he drew back, and recognized the white-bearded face of Elldon's carpenter, Mister Giles. "Save who?"

Adella urged her horse onward, leading the way over the troop's new and unfamiliar territory as they charged south across the sun-yellowed grass toward the ring of clashing metal and screams of wounded horses. Her torn, scarlet skirt billowed out on the wind behind her.

At her back, rode the sixty-three cavaliers that comprised the Pentz Standing Cavalry's troop led by Captain Holcomb, untried in battle but eager to prove themselves worthy of their scarlet jackets. Years of rigorous peace-time drilling and discipline had kept their movements nimble and their sabers sharp. Sparing a quick glance to her side, she shared a look of determination with her new acquaintance, the young Captain Holcomb, who led the troop proudly, straight-backed and smartly dressed. Though she had only met him briefly, she now must trust him, and his troop, with the lives of her neighbors. Adella hoped he, along with his troop, would measure up to her expectations.

Her left hand gripped a loaded crossbow, the very one which she had taken off a dead soldier's horse in the Campos the day after she'd rescued Kol from the Sornian camp; it was one of the few weapons that had been left behind in Greywood, since she kept it in her own bedchamber, and she had retrieved it quickly before heading out into the southern fields. Buckled to her waist, was a spare saber lent to her by Captain Holcomb.

As Adella and the troop galloped toward a slope in the land, a horseman appeared at the summit ahead, riding hard down toward them. She let out a gasp as more appeared behind, and soon a group of riders were racing down the slope toward them. She braced herself, assuming they must be Sornians on the attack. Her grip tightened on her crossbow; she heard the rasp of metal as Holcomb drew his saber.

Ahead, the leading rider, seeing the oncoming troop but unable to slow his steed on the downhill, yanked his reins to the side, his horse veering suddenly eastward. Confusion muddled her thoughts while she tried to make sense of the action. With a broadside view of the animal, Adella noticed the rider's tall bay horse looked very familiar. Then, the man's face turned her way for a moment when he fell forward onto the horse's neck, and she understood why. *That's James!*

"Valennians!" Adella shouted, widening her eyes at Holcomb beside her.

Holcomb reined his horse away immediately. "Right!" he bellowed out to the troop, saber shining as he hefted it in the air, pointing westward. "Sharp right!"

Adella watched in horror across the field as the mare, her late father's own beloved Travia, lost her footing at the sudden change of direction. The horse stumbled a few strides until a sickening crack rang out, audible even over the stamp of hooves, as the bone of the lower forelimb snapped. Travia toppled over, slamming sideways into the dirt; slender, brown legs flung up in the air as the mare collapsed onto her rider, the broken limb dangling loosely amid a fine spray of crimson blood. The horse tried to stand, rocking helplessly on its side with its other three hooves scraping uselessly across the red-stained grass. Adella's stomach turned violently at the sight as James lay with his own leg trapped between the flailing horse and the hard-packed ground. All around them, the field was in chaos as horses and riders scrambled to keep from colliding into each other.

As Holcomb's troop veered right, the oncoming group of plain-clothed riders rounded left. Adella hesitated, reluctant to abandon her first charge with the new troops that were now in her command, but she couldn't leave James and Travia to suffer. "Go on without me," she called out to Holcomb. He responded with a curt nod, and she galloped her horse toward where Travia lay, still struggling to stand.

Adella hopped from the saddle, crossbow in hand, and ran to Travia's side, dodging swinging hooves from the panicking animal. "Shh..." Tears welled up in her eyes while she pressed a hand into the mare's soft neck, guiding her head back down to rest on the ground. "Be still." At the sound of her familiar voice, Travia calmed, gazing up at her through a large, questioning eye. Adella's gut wrenched when she realized what must be done. Lifting the crossbow, she pointed the bolt at the hollow above the mare's eye socket, aiming carefully at an angle into the skull.

"I'm so sorry, girl," Adella whispered, voice caught deep within her throat, and squeezed the lever. Travia's legs gave one last spasm, then went limp. Memories throughout the years, of feeding her in the stables and grooming her soft coat, raced through Adella's mind and dizziness overcame her, her legs feeling as though they would give out. She pushed the thoughts away. *Not now.*

Setting the crossbow down, Adella stepped around and crouched beside James, patting the cold, damp flesh of his face, one cheek smeared with fresh blood. "James," she said quietly, but there was no response. "James!" she yelled sharply, shaking his shoulders. Finally his eyelids fluttered open and warm, brown eyes, the same shade that Travia's had been, strained to focus on hers. "What have you done?" she asked, though her voice was filled with worry rather than reproach. "Are you hurt?" Searching over his upper body, she found no obvious injury.

"Adella?" he murmured feebly, eyes closing once more. Hooves drummed loudly around them as cavalry in green passed dangerously close by.

"Dammit, James," she spat. Grabbing him by the upper arm, she tried to pull him free.

His eyes popped open again as he let out an agonizing scream, and she let go. "I think it's broken," he warned, voice husky with pain.

"Well, damn," she muttered, eyebrows drawing together with fear and grief. Looking around, the battlefield was in chaos, with some riders in scarlet, some emerald, and others, though fewer, in the duller colors of ordinary country clothes. Her eyes shot from face to face among the plain-clothed riders of Elldon, wondering if Kol was among them. The different riders that passed her by were swept up in struggles of their own, not even taking notice of Adella on the ground. It was up to her to get him out, and she needed to do it quickly, exposed as they were in the middle of a battle. However, she had no idea how. The only time she'd ever needed to turn a horse over was when she would happen to find one cast against a wall, which she'd free by looping a rope around the legs, rolling the animal onto its back and then over to the other side, but that certainly wouldn't work now with saddle still between James's legs; he would be crushed. Moving back toward her gelding, who had taken to grazing close by, she searched the saddle bags until she found a rolled-up length of rope, and ran it through the saddle-girth on Travia's belly. "This might hurt," she said to James, though she wasn't sure if he could hear her.

With trembling fingers, she tied the other end in a loop and, guiding her own horse nearer, slipped it over his neck. "Come on, boy," she goaded, pulling his reins to lead him forward. "Pull!" As she tugged at his reins, he stepped forward, pressing into the rope with his chest. His small hooves grated and slipped against the dry grass and soil. "Come on!" she urged desperately. Adella pulled again, clicking her tongue in her cheek as his hooves scrabbled uselessly against the hard-packed dirt. Releasing the reins, she slumped onto the ground, chest heaving tightly against the laces of her scarlet bodice, and rubbed the sweat from her face with her hands. *It's no use*, she told herself. *He's too small to do it.* The raw grief for her father's horse, yet another precious piece of her family lost, weighed heavily in her heart, dragging down her resolve.

A faint groan issued from behind Travia's back and she knew, for James's sake, she had to keep trying. Adella rose and went around to her horse's hindquarters, smacking him firmly on the rump. "Come on!" she shouted, pulling the reins as the little gelding pressed into the rope once more. His hooves dug into the rocky soil, slowly gaining purchase. As he inched forward, the girth around Travia's barrel strained with the weight of her body. Finally, Adella heard the grating of rock and soil as the bulky form behind her inched forward.

A piercing scream rang out close behind, but she continued to pull the reins. Travia's body slid slowly over the grass as the little gelding gained ground, and soon, Adella glanced back to see James's leg lying free, the ankle twisted at an unsettlingly wrong angle. She slid the rope from her horse's neck and led him to James's side, then crouched beside him.

The ground beneath her rumbled and a rush of air brushed her skin, hoofbeats pounding in her ears, as a rider galloped much too closely by, hooves nearly missing James's head. Adella let out a steadying breath as she fought to settle her nerves. "We've got to get you out of here," she said, pulling him by his arm to a seated position. She searched the ground around her until she found his bow, which lay nearby, broken in two.

She grabbed the pieces, then, ripping strips of fabric from her already-torn petticoats, made a hasty splint for his leg. When she carefully lifted his shin, however, James screamed in pain so loudly that it rang in her ears.

"Leave me," he pleaded, tears forming in his eyes.

"No!" she yelled, tying off the make-shift splint. Adella stood, taking a wide stance to brace herself, and held out a hand toward him. "Get up."

He shook his head weakly. "I can't..."

"Get up," she ordered. "You will get on my horse, or die here."

"Ugh," he groaned through tightly clenched jaws and clasped her hand. Moving delicately, he brought his right leg beneath him and, leaning heavily on Adella's shoulder, managed to stand, holding his injured foot above the ground.

As James took hold of the saddle for balance, Adella wove her fingers together, her hands forming a sling. "Come on," she offered, hunching down to brace herself against his weight. "I'll give you a leg-up." Groaning, he placed his knee in her hands and, with all her strength, Adella heaved him upward while he pulled himself into the saddle. Again, he bellowed in agony at the motion, then quieted, settling into place. Adella let out a long breath as he took up the reins.

"Look out!" James shouted.

She spun just in time to see the glare of metal in the sunlight as a blade slashed down toward her. Instinctively, she caught the soldier's green-clad wrist in her hands, the edge of a saber stopping in mid-air before her face. He was unbearably strong, and she knew she wouldn't be able to hold out for very long. "Go!" she called out to James as the soldier pressed downward, the edge of the blade inching closer toward her head. She heard the beat of trotting hooves behind her as James obeyed.

From the corner of her eye, she caught a flash of movement behind the soldier's back and, in an instant, he was shoved forward into her, a small moan escaping his lips while she felt his grip on the handle loosen, the strength leaving his arms. Adella had to step aside to keep from being caught beneath him when he fell, his saber falling uselessly to the ground. She looked to see what had happened, and a wave of confusion overtook her at the sight of a vaguely familiar face. A man stood before her with a bloodied sword, pulled from the back of the soldier who had attacked her. He was young, with strong features and a hard look in his eyes; though he wore ordinary clothes, his freshly-shaved scalp showed him to be Sornian.

"Jais!" Adella shouted, eyebrows jumping up when she remembered the soldier who had taken her to the auction block in Hedda only months ago. She looked down on the dead soldier's emerald coat, then up at him in bewilderment. "What in the *world* are you doing?"

"I need you alive," he replied darkly.

Adella blinked at him, not understanding his meaning at first. Then, as she reached for the grip of the borrowed blade at her side, his hand darted out, taking a painful hold on her wrist. She wrenched her arm to try to free it, but froze when she felt the tip of a sword press against her ribs in warning. Just then, an arrow whirred through the air, and Jais let out a sharp cry as it lodged into his thigh. Adella twisted her arm free while he doubled over in pain. Dust surrounded them, carried on the wind as a rider on a tall horse trotted up toward them and reined to a halt. She looked up to find Captain Holcomb in the saddle, drawing another arrow.

Adella braced herself, waiting for the release, then groaned inwardly when her conscience got the better of her. "Hold, Captain," she ordered begrudgingly. After all, whatever his intentions, Jais had just saved her life. "Leave him."

Holcomb shot her a dubious glance. "If the lady insists," he deferred, voice cool but polite. With the arrow still drawn and leveled, he looked at her and lifted his brows questioningly.

"I do," she replied. As Holcomb slowly lowered his bow, Adella turned back to Jais. "We're even now," she commented, grabbing her crossbow from where she had left it in the grass. "Let that be the end of it." Still gripping his injured leg, jaw clenched tightly, Jais glared up at her but didn't reply.

"Come," Holcomb offered, holding out an open palm toward Adella. "The Sornians are scattered; we're heading back." She took his hand, and he pulled her up into the saddle in front of him. Then he legged his horse to a trot, and they headed north.

Soon, Greywood Manor came into view in the distance, perched on its hill beneath the elms. The fields surrounding the estate were astir with the people and horses that had arrived before them, and Adella realized she and Holcomb were among the last to return. While she dismounted and held the reins for Captain Holcomb to do likewise, she was glad to see James had managed to stay in the saddle long enough to make it back, since he now lay upon the grass with Benson and Rosalind at each arm, trying to lift him.

Adella went and knelt beside him, helping the others lift him by the arms and assist him while he hopped on his good leg toward the manor. With some trouble, they were able to bring him into the large parlor and ease him onto the sofa. Rosalind placed a pillow behind his back as Benson carefully lowered the injured leg onto the cushions.

As Adella turned to leave, James grabbed her wrist. "I'm sorry—" He winced, face scrunching in pain. "I should've—"

"Don't," Adella interrupted. "Don't worry about that right now; you need to rest."

James dropped his hand, his eyes growing glossy. "My mother," he croaked. "She's out there somewhere. In the Campos."

"Don't worry," she assured him, putting a hand on his shoulder. "We'll find her. Just rest now."

He leaned back and closed his eyes.

23

Around the Map

"We're going to have to feed an army," Adella said, inspecting Greywood's larder room, which was now stocked full of supplies, with barrels stacked in the corners, rashers of bacon and braids of onions hanging from the beams. "I see Martin's shipment arrived safely."

"It did," Rosalind replied, hurrying to keep up with Adella's quick stride. "And it was quite generous. I've never seen so many cones of sugar in one place."

"I'll have to find him and thank him," Adella commented. "And arrange to pay him back," she added, pulling open the carved-oak doors of one of the large cabinets that lined the walls. "Oh," she gasped, finding it stuffed completely full with dry goods in bags, boxes and tins.

"Everything we could need," Rosalind assured her.

"What about tea? Spices? Flour?" Adella asked, rummaging around in the cabinet.

"Yes, yes and yes," Rosalind replied. "As well as biscuits, salt pork, honey—"

"Oh, Kol must be happy about the honey," Adella remarked enthusiastically, recalling his delight at finding a jar of it in a saddlebag when they had traveled across the Campos to find Lucas. It seemed like ages ago, now. "Is he around?" She looked up from the shelves to Rosalind. "I haven't seen him yet, and I'm starting to worry."

"Kol?" Rosalind repeated, eyes turning upward in thought. "Right, the Sornian. No, he isn't here. I haven't seen him since before you left for Pentz."

"What?" Adella blurted out, accidentally slamming the cupboard doors closed. "What happened? Is he—"

"Alive," Rosalind assured her. "At least, he did sign the waybill." Reopening the cupboard, she pulled out a packet of folded papers and held them out to Adella. "He apparently stayed in Raymouth with Martin."

"Martin hasn't returned, either?" Adella lowered her brow as she took the packet, then shuffled through the papers. "Hm," she said pointedly when she found Kol's signature. It was large and forcefully written, as the quill had pressed its path harshly into the parchment. Clearly, it was his handwriting; she knew it well from the many times she had helped him with his penmanship. Directly below his name was printed the title *Apprentice*.

"Perhaps it's for the best," Adella said coolly, trying to tamp down her rising emotions. "It isn't safe here, anyway." She tucked the papers beneath her arm.

Rosalind coughed politely. "Anyway, don't worry about dinner for the troops," she offered cheerily. "I'll see to it everyone is fed."

"I appreciate it," Adella said, smiling despite her sullen mood. "We're lucky to have you."

Making her way through the manor, Adella came to the dining room, and paused. Her Codex and workpapers still littered the table's surface, untouched since her departure. She couldn't help but recall this was the place she had met Kol for the first time, though it'd been a bad first impression indeed. Under his duties as a Sornian soldier, she had found him here during the attack on Elldon, attempting to capture Teressa. Adella had charged at him in an attempt to save her friend, then he left. Soon after, he switched allegiances and agreed to help her track down Lucas. *Perhaps Kol is like that,* she wondered. *Switching allegiances quickly, trying to better his station...* She wondered if Martin was paying him more as an apprentice than she had as a guard. *If so, how could I blame him? But still...* He had left without saying good-bye, and hadn't even bothered to write to let her know he was safe. *Was I not even worth a 'goodbye?'* The thought stung.

'Wherever you go,' she remembered his words at the Capital, '*I will go with you.*' Since he'd been a constant companion in the days since, Adella had come to believe he'd meant it. *But I've been wrong before...* She reminded herself of all the times she'd misjudged someone, and paid the price for it. Lucas's treason against Valenna, his involvement in the poisoning of the River Ray, had been completely unexpected. The pain of his betrayal was still too raw for her to speak of it to any-one. *My own flesh and blood, a traitor! Ruining our noble family name.* Her teeth clenched at the thought. *And I had no idea! Then Tess, Rogero, even Ballantyne...* She'd been wrong about each of them in different ways, and the memories kindled a burning shame in her heart. *No, I'm no judge of character. Clearly, I was wrong about Kol.*

Adella stomped her way back to the parlor where James lay on the sofa, eyes closed with sweat gleaming on his brow, his breath shallow. *Poor fellow,* she thought, worry knitting her brows. *I should've known better than to put so much on his shoulders.* Quieting her steps, she approached and stood beside him.

His eyelids flickered. "W—" he began feebly.

"What is it?" she whispered, kneeling to hear better.

"Wuh—" he sighed.

"Water?" she guessed, looking around the room for something he could drink. "Is that what you want?"

"Whiskey," he managed to utter.

"Oh," she huffed, rising to her feet. "Well, I suppose it can't hurt." She grabbed a flask that had been left on a nearby side table and handed it to him. He pulled out the wooden stopper and gulped the contents eagerly. "That's plenty," she said, pulling the flask from his hands. "Too much of that stuff and you might think you can walk it off." She corked it and set it aside.

"I was wrong—" he began hoarsely, then blew out a pained breath.

"What's done is done," she replied. "And it was done well enough. From what I hear, we've gained a substantial victory thanks to your actions."

"Have we?" he asked. Wincing, he tried to sit up.

"Mhm." She smiled. "Thankfully, we arrived when we did. But if you had only waited a moment before galloping off to battle, we could have gone with you."

He leaned back against the arm of the sofa and closed his eyes. "But you were dead."

Adella chuckled softly. "Oh, right," she conceded. At the sound of footsteps, she turned to see Benson standing beside her. "Will he be all right?" she whispered, leaning in toward him.

"He'll live, though he won't be walking for a good, long while." He shrugged his broad shoulders. "I set the bone as best I could, but I'm a farrier, not a surgeon. Oh, that reminds me," he added suddenly. "You should take a look in the stables; some of your horses have returned."

James's eyes popped open and darted in their direction. "I have to piss."

Behind Greywood Manor, Adella slid open the door to the stables. Inside, horses nickered at her presence. The rough-hewn building was still under construction from when it was burned by the Sornian army that spring. Only half the stalls inside were complete, with one of the three aisles still empty, save for work tools and stacks of lumber on the dirt floor. She peered into each stall, until one soft, brown muzzle appeared over the stall door and greeted her with a familiar squeal.

It was the little bay she had found in the Campos earlier in the year. She rushed over, throwing her arms around his head. The gelding put his muzzle beside her cheek and sniffed, sharing breath in greeting. She hadn't seen him since she had been captured by the Sornian army in the Campos that spring; the horses had to be left behind at the livery in Smuggler's Port when Adella had been taken aboard *The Accord*. Then, after she had returned home to Elldon, it hadn't been safe enough to cross the Campos to retrieve them yet. "Kol must've sent you back?" she guessed, her heart filling with gratitude while she ran her fingers through the animal's soft, brown coat. *If he's here, then that must mean...* She stepped back, looking at the stalls around until she spied one massive, dapple-grey head lift up from its hay and blink at her. *Patches!* She smiled to see Armand's old draft horse safely back home. *Armand will be so happy to see him.*

From the next stall, a finely-boned roan horse stuck out his neck, stretching his nose toward her. "Good to see you, Blue," she greeted him happily, then kissed the side of his warm muzzle. While at Raymouth, when she hadn't found either Blue or Bixby in the stables, she had inquired on the matter of the stablehands and was relieved to hear that Beatrice had returned with them to Elldon. "But where is your friend, Bixby?" she asked, running her hands softly down his muzzle. Misses Asher's horse was nowhere to be seen. *Beatrice must've been riding him,* she realized, *when she disappeared.* If she had simply been killed in the field, Bixby would've likely returned home on his own to the comfort of his herd, his dry stall, his bucket of oats. The fact that he hadn't was, oddly, both unsettling and encouraging. *If there's still a chance of finding her,* she told herself, *I must try.*

Morning light filtered through the cracks in the parlor room's boarded windows. Adella stood in front of a large, hastily-drawn map she had tacked crudely to one wall, peering at it and tapping her lower lip. Then, with her brass pencil, she scribbled some more marks in one corner. Behind her, boots shuffled across the mahogany-plank flooring, echoing off the high ceiling as the others ambled into the room.

"Good morning," Adella began chipperly, turning to greet the cavaliers and neighbors that had entered. "I asked you all to gather here so that I may introduce to you Captain William Holcomb, and his troop of the Pentz Standing Regiment. Captain, would you come forward?"

Captain Holcomb approached the map and stood at Adella's side. "Good to meet you all," he said, folding his arms behind his back. "Our cavalry troop has been hired by Lady Grimless to assist you on the warfront," he explained. "We shall do our utmost for our Queen and country."

"Why hasn't she sent us soldiers?" a craggy voice spoke up, one Adella recognized as that belonging to Elldon's carpenter, Mister Giles. "Does she even know we're at war?"

"I can't say," Holcomb replied. "But we must trust Her Majesty knows what she's doing. After all," he added, smiling pertly, "this isn't her first time on the throne."

"What do you know of it?" Giles replied. "You're too young to remember."

Holcomb cleared his throat to answer, but Adella stepped forward. "As soon as I receive word from the Queen on the matter, I will inform everyone. In the meantime, let's be grateful we have the cavaliers to assist us. Now," she said, striking the map with the point of her pencil, "back to the topic at hand: acquainting the troop with their new home."

Stretching up onto her toes, she drew a large circle in the center of the map. "Cavaliers, this is the area we call the Campos—contested territory consisting of vast, open fields between Valenna and Sornia, mainly to the west of Elldon. To the north, Belgrand Bay." She pointed with her pencil while she spoke. "To the far south, impassable fens. Do *not* venture there; the ground is very treacherous. Horses have been lost completely in the mire."

"Now," she continued, turning to face them with a grim expression, "the plains of the Campos are vast; you can travel for leagues without sight of an identifiable landscape feature to guide you. Not only is it very easy to get lost, but the area is also occupied by Sornian soldiers. They are adept at subterfuge, and have no qualms about using their own men as bait. Therefore, no one is permitted to travel alone. Any questions?"

"I have one," a voice arose from across the room. The group parted to reveal James with his hand in the air, still stretched across the sofa with his leg propped up on pillows. "Where did that map come from?"

"I drew it," she replied matter-of-factly. "This morning. While you all were sleeping."

"Is it accurate?" he asked.

Adella shrugged. "Fairly."

"What's that spot there?" He pointed toward the map. "Just north-west of Compass Point."

"That's the salt pool," she replied.

"There's no pool there," Giles interjected. "That's the Hole in the Campos. I've seen it myself."

"Are you certain?" Adella asked, forehead creasing in thought. "A hole?"

"Not *a* hole; *the* Hole," he replied. "It's where we lost Tobias."

"Hm." Adella turned to look closely at her map. "The water level must've dropped..." Her eyes scanned from her little triangle-shaped drawing of Compass Point, roving north toward Belgrand Bay until settling upon the steep peninsula known as the Figurehead, where she had used Leveret's Key to open a secret door in the cliffside. *And then the water rushed out...* As Matei's captive, she had taken a small boat from *The Accord* into the opening, rowing deep inland. *We were beneath the northern stretch of Campos,* she realized, remembering the glowing light above Paloma's tomb. *It all could be connected... The Hole in the Campos, the salt pool, Paloma's tomb... All one and the same!* The sudden realization left her frozen, deep in thought.

"The water was released from a cavern in the Figurehead," Adella explained. "Enough to reveal a cave system under the Campos."

"If that much water had flooded out," James replied doubtfully, "there would've been massive consequences elsewhere in the Bay."

Adella dropped her pencil. "Like, a wave?" The thought struck her to her core, draining the warmth from her face, then down through her body.

"Exactly," he replied. "Much like the quake had done at Pentz."

"No..." she uttered, more breath than voice. *The wave that killed my parents... It was my fault!* Her head became weightless as dizziness overcame her senses, her legs losing their strength. "Excuse me for a moment," she managed to whisper, stumbling through the group and out into the hallway.

Adella leaned against the wall, fingertips gripping the wainscoting for balance. The sting of tears gathered in her eyes, but she had been holding them back so often after her parents' passing that she wasn't sure they would fall now, even if she let them. After all, with her father gone, she was the Lady of Elldon. It was her turn to be the strong one.

* * *

A solitary hawk let out a shrill cry as it soared high overhead, wheeling in wide circles on the breeze. Adella's leather riding gloves creaked against the reins while she drew Blue to a halt. She took a deep breath; the warm, evening air was laden with the green, heady scent of wild herbs, mixed with the tang of distant rain. Her eyes, shielded from the early-evening sun beneath her palm, followed the grey-winged hawk, with tail feathers a blazing orange, along its path through the sky. *Hm,* she mused to herself. *I've never seen that kind of bird in the Campos before.*

Above the fields, clouds scudded low across the blue sky, painting moving shadows on the dry summer grass that billowed softly below. The sight reminded her of happier times, before her family had been broken apart by tragedy. Memories of racing ponies across the Campos with Lucas, picking wildflowers with her mother, hunting small game on horseback with her father during holidays when he hadn't been too busy with official duties, all came to mind while she stared distantly, taking in the landscape. Now, her beloved prairies were filled with the threat of foreign enemies, and the pain of her memories.

The shrill peal of a horse's whinny rang out from the west, where the fields in the distance were tinged with the bright purple of wild lavender blooms. Blue's ears perked as he jerked his head up, listening intently. Then, neck stretching low, he answered with a long, resounding neigh.

"What is it?" Holcomb asked, drawing up beside her. Behind him, more riders in red followed. They had been riding for hours in the hot sun, searching for signs of Misses Asher. They were all weary and soaked with sweat, eager to return to the cool sanctuary of their tents. Reluctance was clear in his voice, which Adella understood well enough; they were nearly back to Greywood, after all, and there was a barrel of perry waiting for them in the coolness of the cellar.

"Hm..." She pressed her lips into a line. "It's probably nothing."

Holcomb cued his horse to a walk, but Adella remained behind, staring westward over the fields. "Are you coming?" he asked over his shoulder.

"Go on," Adella replied. "I'll be right behind you."

Holcomb halted his horse. "Then I'll come with you."

A brief vision of James's crushed leg, with the foot twisted at a gruesome angle, burst into her mind, knotting her stomach with guilt. "No—" Adella blurted out. Lowering her voice, she added, "No, that's not necessary." She wouldn't allow such a thing happen to another person she was responsible for, if she could in any way prevent it. She'd rather risk going alone than to have that again on her conscience, or worse. *It could have been much worse...*

"I don't think—" Holcomb began, but stopped short as Adella raised a brow at his protest. "If you say so," he amended, spurring his horse to a trot. "Just be careful," he called out as he rode away.

* * *

Swift hooves clattered over the wide, blue span of the River Ray as Kol rode across the bridge toward Elldon. Leaving the crowded city of Raymouth behind, the black mare's long strides covered ground quickly, cutting hours off a journey that, for slower travelers, often took a day. When he came down the hard-packed dirt road toward Elldon, he passed by the charred husks of houses, barns, and shops that had once made up the town. His face burned with shame at the memories it roused of the part he had played in the attack. *If it hadn't been me leading the squadron that night,* he tried to reason with himself, *it'd have been someone else, and Greywood wouldn't have been spared.* The thought did little to relieve the guilt.

Greywood Manor came into view and he slowed Madigan to a trot, allowing the mare a little reprieve as Kol rounded the estate. If he knew Adella, she wouldn't be hiding out in the Manor. He came to the fields behind Greywood where the residents of Elldon camped, weaving through their tents and small cook-fires.

"Adella!" he called out, searching from one area to another, but there was no answer. Every unfamiliar face he passed ignored his presence, preoccupied with their own tasks. He approached one old man in a leather apron tending to a pot that sat on a bed of coals. "Where's Adella?" Kol asked, but a shrug was the only response.

Making his way through the camp, Kol was puzzled to see a group of riders approaching from the west, all in bright scarlet jackets. *Is that the Royal Guard?* he wondered as they dismounted, leading their horses toward camp. *What would they be doing out here?* He trotted toward the group.

Kol halted his horse before the foremost rider, blocking his path. Though the man appeared to be of some rank, judging by his decorated jacket, he looked out-of-place at Elldon; he was crisply dressed with not a blemish on his pale breeches, his tidy hair held back in a silk ribbon. "Where's Adella?" Kol demanded as he dismounted.

The man looked Kol over, then narrowed his eyes. With a backward glance at the others, he made a quick motion with his hand. At his cue, two of the riders rushed forward and grabbed Kol by the elbows.

Kol pulled his arms free, but more men in red came forward, holding him back while he tried to break out of their grip. "Let go," Kol ordered. "What do you think you're doing?"

"I could ask you the same thing," the man replied, unsheathing a sword from his side. "You have a lot of nerve coming here, Sornian."

Kol tried to pull his arms free from their hands, but stopped when the tip of the blade pressed into his chest. "I'm no Sornian; this is my home." Kol couldn't hide a note of worry in his voice, "I just want to see Adella."

"Oh, you'll see her, all right," the man retorted, one corner of his mouth pulling upward. "Tie him up," he said to his men, sheathing his sword. "While your concern is misplaced," he said, stepping closer and looking high up to meet Kol's eyes, "*Lady Grimless* was right behind us and will be along shortly. She'll know what to do with you."

"You left her alone in the Campos?" Kol snapped.

"Well, I—" the man stammered. "I was following her orders." A high-pitched whinny rang out from the western fields as a horse galloped, riderless, toward them, barreling into the campsite. Men in red jackets rushed forward, trying to catch the wayward animal. An arrow protruded from its rump, streaking its flank with bright, crimson blood.

"You idiot!" Kol shouted. He wrenched his arms free, knocking some of the men to the ground while others tripped over them. Grabbing Madigan's reins, he climbed into the saddle and galloped westward.

24

Crushed Lavender

Adella watched the cavaliers disappear over the ridge, heading toward Elldon. Turning back westward, she searched the land until she spotted a patch of thick scrubland in the distance. It was too far to see the details clearly; she'd have to get closer.

Blue tossed his head, yanking on the bit. "All right," Adella whispered. "We'll take a quick look." She pulled her crossbow from her shoulder by its strap and, bracing her foot into the steel cocking stirrup, loaded it with a bolt from the carved-wood quiver on her belt. Then, she urged Blue forward.

"Just a quick peek," she said, patting his neck. "Then we'll head home." She knew the chances of finding Misses Asher out there were slim but she would never forgive herself if she didn't check right now, and it wasn't likely she'd run into trouble this close to Greywood. There had been no sign of the Sornians in the western fields; indeed, no sign of them at all since the Valennians had charged their formation, breaking their ranks and scattering them. Tracks showed the army had fled south.

Adella trotted across the sloping fields toward the grove of stunted trees, where she believed the sound had likely come from. She hadn't wanted the company of the cavaliers because, whatever she might find out there, she wanted to approach unnoticed, and that wouldn't be possible in a group. *Especially a group wearing bright red.* The dove-grey bodice and canvas breeches she wore now beneath her petticoats were much more appropriate for scouting. *Besides,* she figured, *it probably really is nothing; no reason to get hopes up.*

As she rode through the far field, searching the ground for signs that others had passed that way, her horse grew increasingly agitated, blowing loudly through flared nostrils with his head held erect. "Shh..." she whispered, patting his neck reassuringly. "Just a little farther. I don't see anything to be worried—"

Blue reared suddenly and Adella was thrown backward from the saddle, landing so hard the breath was forced from her lungs, the color knocked from her vision.

Stunned, Adella sat up and gasped for air, inhaling the heady scent of the crushed lavender as she rubbed her head to try to clear the stars from her sight. When her senses returned to normal, she looked around for Blue, but there was no sign of the animal. "Oh, *damn,*" she whispered, angry at her own stupidity, while she patted around in the tall grass beside her, searching for her crossbow. Thankfully, it landed nearby, though it had apparently shot its bolt somewhere into the field on impact. *Could've been worse, I suppose.* She grabbed it and, rubbing her sore backside, rose gingerly to her feet.

Undeterred, Adella crouched low in the tall, sun-bleached grass and crept toward the thicket of small trees and brambles that had caught her eye from the ridge, which was still a good distance away. Though she hadn't seen any sign of tracks or crushed grass aside from her own, she strained to listen for a stamp or snort that would reveal the presence of horses, but heard only the eerie silence enveloping the surrounding fields. *Nothing, not even birds...* The realization sent a chill through her.

A high-pitched squeal rang out nearby, sending a jolt of panic through her body; instinctively, Adella dropped down onto the ground, disappearing beneath the grass and wild herbs. Squinting through the foliage, she looked around for the horse the sound must have come from, but still saw nothing but the surrounding fields, and the copse of trees ahead. Pulling a bolt from the quiver on her belt, she loaded her crossbow and continued to crawl forward.

She peeked through the brush beneath the trees, and noticed the grove formed a circle around a grassy clearing. In the center of it, she could just make out a flash of black and white through the gaps in the foliage in front of her. Another shrill scream rang out through the trees, and Adella's heart raced when she understood. *That's Bixby!*

She trampled through the underbrush and into the clearing. "Ho," she said in a low, soothing tone as she approached the horse, who had apparently been left there, unsaddled but tied by the reins to the limb of a small tree. Bixby, in a frenzy, pulled, bucked and reared against the bit; pink foam spilled from his mouth, tinted with the blood that dripped from the corners, staining his white lips ruby red.

Shouldering her crossbow, Adella drew the borrowed saber from her side as she ran forward and hacked at the leather reins that held him. Finally, the tether broke free and Bixby burst forward in a flurry of mane, darting across the clearing with his tail tucked under his rump.

Adella searched for a sign of Misses Asher. "Beatrice!" she whispered as loudly as she dared. "Are you here?" She froze, listening intently. The wind gently rustled the leaves in every direction. Somewhere behind her, a twig snapped.

As she spun, brandishing her saber, a dark form crashed through the brush ahead toward her with a rattling snort. Adella let her breath out in relief when she recognized the mottled, grey coat of her mother's gelding. "Blue!" she said softly, sheathing her saber. "There's a good boy." Taking the reins, she patted his neck to settle him, then climbed into the saddle.

She urged him forward, but he balked, stammering backward and blowing in alarm. "Not again," she muttered. "Go on!"

The animal gave another sharp snort. Across the clearing, the branches rustled as a horse and rider stepped through the foliage, and

Adella found herself looking up into the hard features of Jais. "Found you," he said, a malicious grin spreading across his mouth. He lowered a coil of rope from his shoulder.

Her heart hammered in her ears as another rider appeared to one side, then the other. Each held bows with arrows drawn, leveled at Blue's chest. She pulled the right rein, kicking the horse's side, as he spun on his haunches and lunged forward into the trees.

Branches slashed Adella's face as Blue burst out into the open field, free to stretch his legs out into a gallop. Outside the shelter of the trees, dark clouds had begun to gather in the west, squatting low and heavy in the sky, scenting the air with rain. Adella leaned forward in the saddle, pushing her hands up Blue's dark mane to slacken the reins. Hooves pounded a rapid drumbeat across the yellow grass.

Adella glanced back to see Jais coming up quickly, the long legs of his dark bay swallowing up the distance behind her. The other riders followed after him. Ahead, lay the bright eastern sky, still blue and cloudless before an approaching storm. Behind her, thunder rumbled.

Adella dug her heels into Blue's body again and again, clicking her tongue loudly while her pulse pounded wildly through her veins. She felt a hot puff of breath on her hand and turned to find Jais's horse reaching over, teeth bared and snapping at Blue's neck. Setting the reins on the pommel, Adella leveled her crossbow at the other horse.

A hand clapped hard around her wrist, the force of the impact knocking the heavy weapon from her hands. It fell to the ground and was quickly left behind as the horses galloped onward in the direction of Greywood Manor. "What the hell are you doing?" Adella spat. "Let go!" She wrenched her wrist around, ripping it from his grip as she drew her arm away. With all her might, she swung her elbow at his face, and it met his nose with a resounding crack. Pain flashed up her arm.

Jais screamed, covering his face with his hands. "You bitch!" he yelled, voice unusually muffled as blood poured profusely from beneath his hands. His horse fell behind as Adella urged Blue faster.

Droplets of cool rain sprinkled her cheeks and forehead as Adella rode back across the field of undulating grasses. They weren't far from Greywood now; past a small stand of trees and over the next rise, she would see its familiar shape in the distance, silhouetted against the darkening eastern sky.

A whirring sound hummed in her ear; Blue jerked his head up high in the air as an arrow flew past them, landing harmlessly in the grass. "Shit!" she hissed, pulling one rein as she veered suddenly to the right and galloped toward the trees.

Blue was blowing hard and losing speed. Adella clucked her tongue desperately, slapping the ends of the reins against the horse's shoulder and legging him faster. *Just a little farther,* she told herself. *Then perhaps we can lose them in the trees.* She knew it wasn't likely, but it was her only chance. Blue was too winded to outrun them any longer.

A jarring shriek rang out as Blue shuddered, throwing Adella forward. The reins ripped from her hands as she hurtled through the air. She landed hard onto her side, pain rattling her bones, then tumbled roughly through the wet grass. When the ground was no longer a blur spinning around her head, she sat up, searching through her swirling vision for Blue.

She spotted him nearby, rising from the ground on trembling limbs. An arrow, with bright white fletches, protruded from his rump. With a stumbling first step, he shook his coat, then turned eastward once more and, blowing out a loud, panicked snort, ran off toward Greywood with the arrow shaft still lodged in his flesh. She hoped he would make it home.

Adella hopped to her feet and, with fumbling fingers, hastily drew her blade as the other riders surrounded her, pulling their horses to a sudden halt. Behind her, stood the thick stand of trees, close enough to provide some shelter from the increasing rain that now poured down in earnest, drenching her.

Jais stepped down from his saddle and turned toward her, his face smeared with blood, the bridge of his nose swollen and crooked. "You broke my nose!" he bellowed, voice muffled from the swelling. He held the coiled rope in one hand, and drew his sword with the other.

"Good." Adella raised her heavy saber, widening her stance the way she'd seen Kol do when he'd been practicing, and hoped she looked like she knew what she was doing. She regretted never having learned to use a sword. Unlike bows that were used for hunting, swords were weapons for times of war; her father had never thought it necessary for her to learn. She knew she couldn't win this fight; her only chance to get away would be to reach the cover of the trees at her back. As the other two riders drew their bows, she wondered if Jais still wanted to capture her alive. *He seems rather angry about the nose.* She glanced back at the foliage, a dark, welcoming shelter in the storm. *I hope his greed is stronger than his anger,* she thought. Lifting the sword higher, she lunged toward him. As he flinched, bracing his blade for impact, she spun and ran for it.

The feint had bought her a few strides before shouting erupted behind her. She tore through the underbrush; the cool, damp air beneath the canopy chilled her wet skin as she ran as best she could, limping from the pain that stiffened her joints. Pounding footsteps followed her, crashing through leaves, snapping branches. *Looks like his greed won out, or I'd be stuck with an arrow by now.* Her chest heaved for breath as tree trunks flashed by, black shapes in the growing darkness. On her right, a thick clump of shrubbery rose up quickly from the shadows. Darting sideways, she ducked behind it.

Slinking down into the bushes, Adella readied her saber. Voices approached from the other side of her cover.

"Lost sight of her," she heard one man rasp, panting hard.

"Split up," Jais replied. "She can't have gone far." Then, boots shuffled through the leaf litter, tapering off in different directions.

Adella held her breath and strained to listen through the pattering of the rain in the canopy above. It was too dark now beneath the gloom of the trees to see much, but the crunch of breaking twigs on her left sent ice through her veins. After a pause, there was another slow crunch. *He's sneaking around the shrub.* She drew back her saber.

Leather brushed softly against foliage as the dark shape of a boot came down close by her feet. With both hands, she swung the blade hard through the leaves and it slashed across the calf, biting through leather into flesh. A sharp scream pierced her ears as she spun, scrambling away. Behind, there was a soft thud, then the ragged breathing and rustling leaves of a body writhing on the ground.

Through the trees ahead, the dying evening light showed a pale grey. Her chest heaved as she gasped for air, ribs straining against the laces of her bodice while she ran, dodging tree trunks, toward the dim twilight. When she approached the dusky fields, framed by the black trunks and branches of the surrounding trees, a dark silhouette stepped out from the shadows, blocking her path.

"Enough," a man's voice snarled, the dark lines of a drawn bow visible against the fading light at his back. "If you so much as twitch a finger, I'll put an arrow in your gut."

Slowly, Adella raised her arms, though one hand still clutched the hilt of the saber, pointing it skyward. Footsteps shuffled behind her.

"Drop it," Jais ordered behind her back.

Hesitant to obey, Adella loosened her fingers around the hilt, letting the blade begin to slip slowly from her grip, the point tilting downwards, as she gradually lowered her arm. A sudden force knocked it from her hand as rough fingers clamped around her wrist, twisting her arm up behind her back.

He grabbed her other wrist and wrenched it backward. Adella braced herself, pulling against the motion, but it was no use; his grip held tight. "You're going to bring me a pretty profit," he whispered, his foul breath brushed against her hair, warming her neck. "Unlike that other woman we've got back at camp. She'll only be good for bait." He chuckled softly into her ear.

Adella stiffened. *Misses Asher!* The sudden realization left her stunned; she was barely aware of the coarse rope that slid around her wrist, the scratching and pinching of her skin while he wound and tightened the coils around her arms. She scrambled to form a plan. *If they take me,* she figured, *then they will likely take me back to wherever they've got her.*

From the shadow of the trees, a small, dark shape flitted across her vision. The man before her jerked backward, struck by the object that had whizzed through the air, and a short rasp of breath was knocked from his lungs. The arrow flew limply from his bow, skittering off at an angle toward the ground as he collapsed with the glint of metal at his throat.

"What was that?" Jais muttered behind her, his grip on her wrists loosening while he looked around, searching into the darkness. Then, he released her entirely and drew his sword.

Adella stepped away, edging cautiously toward the field beyond the trees as she pulled and twisted against the ropes that clung to her wrists. Where the trees met the open field, the other Sornian lay dead, a dark, crumpled shadow in the grass. Still working her wrists against the binds, she ran toward the prone figure.

"Who's there?" Jais asked from behind her, with a faint quaver in his voice.

Adella was pleased to find that he hadn't fully tied the ropes as they finally gave way, falling from her wrists. She crouched over the other man's body. The whites of his lifeless eyes shone pale in the twilight; the handle of a small knife protruded from his neck, its blade lodged deeply in his throat. Over his shoulder, a clutch of arrows stuck out from the quiver beneath his back, and she grabbed one.

"Forget the gold," Jais called out, voice echoing through the trees. "You're too much trouble. I'll just kill you and be done with it." The scuffle of his boots grew louder as he came closer.

She grabbed the dead man's bow from the ground and, rising to her feet, nocked the arrow. Turning to face Jais, who was striding toward her with sword raised, she drew the arrow back and took aim. Her two fingers, which she had broken in the spring while fighting on the island of the Cairn, trembled at the tension. Just as she released, a tendon in her hand popped, stinging sharply as her grip gave out and her arrow flew wide of its target. "Ah!" she yelped, shaking the pain from her hand.

Jais let out a smug laugh and came toward her, his raised blade shimmering in the last dull dregs of daylight. Adella tightened her grip around the bow as she took it in both hands. It wasn't much, but she was out of options. She raised one end into the air, ready to meet Jais' sword.

In a flash, he lunged, his blade slashing through the air. Adella swung the bow to meet it, cracking it against the sharp metal just in front of her face. She shoved away, the edge of the cutlass sliding down the length of the well-polished elmwood, and Jais swung his blade around in the air to try again.

Once more, Adella hefted up the bow to block the strike, but the force of the blow was too much. She fell backward, dropping the bow when she hit the ground hard on her backside. She let out a groan at the pain that surged up her spine. Above her, she could just make out the dark shape of Jais' blade as he raised it again, preparing for a final blow.

Adella shuffled backward, her fingers clawing through the damp grass and wet dirt as she inched away from him, until her hand touched something hard and cool—it was her saber.

His blade whirred through the air above her head. Adella grabbed her saber and shoved it upward with both hands to brace against his blade. The clash of metal sang through the air as the force of the blow shuddered through her arms. Though it now was too dark to see much around her, she felt the weight that bore down upon her hands let up as Jais let out a sharp cry, then a sputtering gasp. With a loud thud, he fell to the ground at her feet.

Still clutching the saber, Adella spun to the side and scrambled behind the trunk of a nearby tree, which was nothing more than a black shadow in the surrounding gloom. She listened intently. Through the whisper of wind in the leaves, there was the faint pat of a boot on grass, the soft, low huff of a man's breath close by, then silence. The hairs on the back of her neck raised when even the wind seemed to hush, and the darkness in front of her face grew deeper.

She slashed the blade in front of her and was surprised to hear a sharp ring when it met steel.

"Adella?" a voice whispered. There was an edge of raw emotion in the deep, familiar tone.

She let the saber fall from her grip as warm arms wrapped tightly around her rain-soaked shoulders. "Kol?!"

25

Confessions

Kol tried to steady his shaking breath as he pulled Adella close, burying his face in her soft hair. "Adella," he murmured, squeezing his eyes shut against the tears that welled up and threatened to spill down his face. An overwhelming sense of relief washed over him as the heavy burden of grief lifted from his heart. His arms tightened around her.

Her stiff posture softened and she leaned into him, releasing the tension from her body with a small sigh. "Kol..." she said gently. "What is it?"

"Wherever you go, I go," he replied, remembering his promise at the Capital. "That was the plan."

"What are you talking about?" she asked, her breath warming his neck.

"You were gone." He moved his hands to her shoulders and, drawing back, peered into the dark shadows that covered her face. "I..." His voice was little more than a whisper. "I thought I lost you."

Beneath his fingers, her shoulders tensed. "Me, gone? You're the one who didn't return." She took a step backward, bumping awkwardly into the tree behind her. "What are you doing out here, anyway?"

Kol picked up his sword from where he dropped it, sliding it into the sheath at his side. "Saving your life."

"I had it handled," she said pertly.

"Looked like it," he commented.

She bent and retrieved her saber from the ground. "How did you find me?" she asked over her shoulder.

"Finding you is easy," Kol replied, fighting a smirk. "I just look for trouble, and there you are."

"Well—" she began sharply, but stopped herself. "Thank you," she said, her tone softening.

"Adella..." His voice was grim. "Martin is dead."

"What?" she blurted out, rounding on him. "No—" Adella shook her head, though the motion was barely visible in the darkness. "You've been working for him in Raymouth."

"Is that what you thought?" Kol bristled at the idea. "That I would just leave like that, without a word?"

"Uh," she stammered. "Well, I—"

"They told me you were dead," he interrupted.

"I'm sorry." Adella turned her face away. "I didn't know."

"It doesn't matter now," Kol replied. "Let's go home."

As they left the cover of the trees, the darkening sky opened wide above them. The clouds had begun to break. Low above the eastern horizon, the full, white moon hung like a lantern, bright enough to leave shadows on the grass as they walked. Not far ahead, a large, black shape revealed the spot where Kol's horse obediently waited, grazing.

"Is that Madigan?" Adella asked as they approached; the smile in her voice was audible. She put a hand to the mare's head, caressing the muzzle. "I lost Blue in the field."

"I know," Kol replied, untying the knot behind the mare's neck that had kept the reins safely off the ground. He pulled Madigan into position beside Adella. "Get on."

"Ugh..." she groaned. "I've fallen twice today. Everything hurts."

"All the more reason not to walk back. Up," Kol prompted, and lifted her by the left knee while she pulled herself into the saddle. Then, they headed east, toward the rising moon.

They rode silently, surrounded by the chirrup of crickets and the jingle of the bridle on the balmy night air. As they came toward the fields surrounding Greywood Manor, loud voices from the encampment made a stark contrast to the quiet of the Campos. Bright cookfires cast their orange light over the tents and people going to and from the manor. At the edge of camp, several figures steadied horses, preparing to mount up.

As Kol halted Madigan, a figure approached, holding a punched-tin lantern and leading a horse at his side.

"Lady Grimless?" a voice asked, and Kol recognized the clipped, precise cadence of the soldier he had spoken to earlier. "We were just about to search for you. What happened?"

"Captain Holcomb," Adella greeted the man curtly. Ran into a bit of trouble," she admitted, "but it's handled now. Where's Blue?"

"Your horse has been cared for," Holcomb replied. "We removed the arrow, and the wound looks clean. I think it'll heal well."

"Very good." She swung her leg over the saddle and dismounted. "Thank you, Captain."

"That was quite a risk you took," Holcomb remarked. "Going out alone like that." He glanced toward Kol, mistrust evident on his face.

"I've found out where Misses Asher is. I'd say that was worth the risk. Captain Holcomb—" She stepped forward, pulling her riding gloves delicately from her fingers. "This is my good friend, Mister Kol. Be sure he is treated with the same respect that is given to me." Then, she took the lantern from his hand and walked off.

Kol passed Madigan's reins to Holcomb. "Brush her down for me," Kol ordered brusquely, and Holcomb's proud expression dropped to a weary frown. Kol chuckled to himself and followed after Adella.

A wide ring of plain canvas tents surrounded the encampment, providing a sense of seclusion from the wilderness beyond. On the far side stood a large pavilion tent with its front panels tied back, forming an open-air awning to the leeward.

Ahead of him, Adella lifted her skirts and stepped over a log that stretched across the ground, serving as seating for several figures in red jackets. Kol walked behind as they made their way toward the pavilion, and the warm smell of simmering stew that emanated from a pot on the coals made his stomach growl. As they entered the tent, the lantern that Adella carried illuminated the space, and Kol was surprised to see it filled with enough furniture to comprise a comfortable bedchamber; there was a cot covered with sheepskins with a large storage trunk at its foot, waxed tarpaulins covering the bare ground, even a small writing desk and chair. Adella hung the lantern on a standing iron hook.

"This is *your* tent?" Kol asked.

"Mhm." She lifted the lid of the trunk, then began untying the strings of her damp skirts. Kol opened his mouth to say something, though he wasn't sure what, but stopped when he saw she wore breeches beneath. She bundled the skirts up and dropped them into the trunk. "My father's old campaign tent," Adella continued. "The bedchambers in the manor are being used for storage." She rummaged through the contents. "Including yours," she said with an apologetic wince. "Sorry."

"Great."

Adella handed him a piece of clothing. "It's all I've got that might fit you, but it's dry."

Kol held it out and saw that it was a large shirt. While he pulled his own off over his head and worked his arms through the sleeves, she glanced in his direction, then quickly away. He smiled to himself as he pulled the fabric over his head and down over his lean waist. "'No one travels alone,'" he reminded her. "That was the rule."

"It's my rule, I can break it if I wish." She closed the trunk with a soft thud. "I'm starving, how about you?"

"The same."

They returned to the campfire, and a young man in a red jacket pressed bowls of hot stew into their hands. Adella thanked him, then she and Kol stood, eating silently, for some time. "The Pentz Standing Cavalry," she began at length, nodding toward a nearby group of figures clad in red. "While you were gone, I went to Pentz to ask the Lord Governor there for assistance, and was fortunately able to hire Captain Holcomb's troop."

"Is this all of them?" he asked, looking around for others he may have missed in the darkness.

"There are a few out on picket duty," she said, pushing her spoon around in the bowl. "But for the most part... Yes."

"Do you know him very well?" Kol asked. "Captain Holcomb."

"Only met him recently," she replied. "Why do you ask?"

He shrugged. "I don't like him."

Adella laughed. "You don't like anyone."

"That's not true, what about Armand?" he reasoned. "Where is he, anyway?"

"I sent him to the Capital, I think he'll be safer there..." As she spoke, raindrops began to patter on their faces. "Oh, not again," she huffed, setting her bowl down by the fireside. "Come on," she urged, pulling him by the elbow toward the manor as the rain turned to a downpour. "There's something I need to show you."

They ran toward the rear entrance of Greywood Manor, taking shelter from the rain as they stepped through the threshold.

As they made their way through the candlelit manor, Kol and Adella came to the main hallway and were approached by Rosalind. The glow of the chamber stick she carried painted black shadows in the deep worry lines on her face.

"What's the matter?" Adella asked.

"It's James." Rosalind wrung the corner of her apron. "He's in a great deal of pain. He keeps asking for whiskey, but he's had too much already."

"I'll see what sort of herbs we have in the kitchen," Adella replied. "But his leg is in such bad shape, I doubt we have anything strong enough to make a difference."

Listening, Kol put a hand into his haversack. His fingertips met the cool glass of the flask that Misses Asher had given him. Though he had been taking some each night, there was still a good amount left to offer them, but Kol wasn't sure he could sleep without it. If he gave it over, he'd be in for a rough night. Inside the bag, he tapped the glass with a finger.

"Here." Kol pulled the flask from his bag and held it out. The liquid within shone a burnished gold in the candlelight. "Give him just a little at a time. It'll help him sleep through the pain."

Rosalind uncorked it, and a bitter, medicinal aroma wafted through the air. Her eyes shifted from the flask up to his face. "Thank you," she said, then hurried away.

"Madorran poppy?" Adella asked, raising her brows. "Are you a smuggler now?"

Kol laughed. "Are you going to report me to the authorities?"

"Hm..." She continued down the hall as Kol followed. "I'll have to think it over."

She led him into the dining room, where a large, leather-bound tome lay open upon the table, surrounded by scattered sheets of paper beneath the light of a brass candelabra. "You're still working on the Codex?" he asked.

She nodded. "From what I can figure, it's a patched-together work. Some parts are ancient and delicate, and tell of the old legends of Andolin. Other parts are newer translations of some of those stories, written in an early form of Modern Andolinian, or another unknown language. One whose writing seems to resemble Madorran."

Kol ran his fingertips over the smooth pages, tracing the simple lines of ink that somehow told Adella the stories of the past. He was no scholar; the feat seemed all but impossible to him.

"But that's not what I wanted to show you." She carefully thumbed through the Codex, and Kol's eyes moved from the pages up to her bare neck, where long, silky hair fell in loose tendrils over her delicate collarbone. The sight of her elegant silhouette in the candlelight filled him with a warmth, a sudden feeling of comfort, that told him the dark weeks that he had passed in grief and loneliness were over now; he was home.

"Here," she said, smoothing the pages flat, and his attention returned to the Codex. Across the parchment spread an illustration of the sea, with primitive galley ships sailing over roiling waves beneath dark clouds. Sea serpents coiled around the picture, forming a border. Though the pigments had clearly faded over time, the colors were still distinct. The sea was painted crimson.

"When I first saw this drawing," Adella continued, "I didn't think much of it. That is, until the night Pentz was destroyed."

Kol looked up from the page and met her steady gaze. "What happened?"

"When the water came in, I washed out to sea with the flotsam, sheltered beneath an overturned boat." Crossing an arm over her chest, she rubbed her shoulder. "By nightfall, I had been swept out to the Isles. And in the darkness, the sea started to glow. It only lasted a few moments, but..." Her voice grew solemn, "It was as bright as fire. Red as blood."

"Hm." Kol thought back on his time in Raymouth. He hadn't heard any talk of the sea changing color, though, truthfully, he hadn't been paying much mind to anything other than his own problems.

"I was picked up by a passing ship after that," she said matter-of-factly.

"What do you make of it?" he asked. "The light in the sea."

"In the Codex," she replied, "a similar event is recounted by a scribe named Paloma, during a series of catastrophes that lead to the fall of the Andolinian Empire. They began after Leveret acquired the *Corelimun*," she added, using the Old Andolinian name.

"The Heart of the World," Kol remembered. "Just like in the legend of Leveret I learned in the orphanage. Do you think it's an omen?"

"I wouldn't use that word," Adella replied, carefully closing the Codex. "But I can't think of a better one at the moment."

"And you believe it will all happen again?"

"You think I've lost my mind?" she asked with a nervous laugh.

"Not at all." He pushed the papers around absent-mindedly, looking from one glyph to another until one caught his eye. He lifted the paper to see it more clearly; it was the same spiral that Jago had shown them, inscribed beneath the skin of his wrist. "If the Heart of the World is safely locked away at the Capital, then why would this be happening now?"

"I don't know," she replied. "But when I was out at sea, I heard..." She bit her lip.

He set the paper down and met her eyes. "Heard what?"

"Ehh, never mind," she said quickly, waving a hand in the air. "It was nothing. I just know that, whatever's happening, I must stop it before it's too late."

"What do you mean?" His voice was harsh with surprise. "Why you?"

"Because *I'm* the one that let Leveret's Key fall into the wrong hands," she replied. "I'm the one that opened Paloma's tomb. It's all been *my* doing."

"That's not—" Kol began.

"The wave that killed my parents," Adella interrupted, "that was my fault. When I opened the sea cave."

Kol exhaled loudly. "You can't hold yourself responsible for the movements of the tides."

"You don't understand," she insisted. "It needn't have happened. None of it. I'm the one who told Lucas I had the Key, and he took it from me. I trusted him, and I was wrong."

"Why didn't you tell me this before?" he demanded, stepping closer. The thought that she hadn't confided in him earlier stung, and he couldn't stifle the hurt in his voice, or on his face.

"I'm sorry. I wanted to, but I—" She looked down at the floor. "I couldn't bear it."

He put a finger beneath her chin and tilted it up until he looked into eyes so blue and brimming with tears that he felt as though he were staring into the sea itself. "It's all right," Kol said quietly. He wanted so badly to comfort her. "We'll figure this out. Whatever it takes," he promised, "we'll do it together." A strand of hair, still damp with rain, hung in her face. He tucked it gently behind her ear as his eyes dropped to her lips.

"Listen," he pleaded, cupping her cheek in his hand. "I need you to know, I—" Kol took a deep breath. He knew the sudden surge of courage within him, bubbling to the surface, wouldn't last. He had to tell her while he could. "I love you, Adella." Now that he said them, the words sounded plain and small. His heartbeat hammered so wildly against his chest, he wondered if she could hear it.

"Oh, Kol..." Her voice was gentle, but something in the tone struck him like a dagger to the heart. He wondered if it was pity. His thoughts flickered to the girl at the dicing-house, remembering the way she had cringed at his touch, and felt the shame of it all over again.

Kol pulled his hand back from her face. "Don't—" he interrupted. "Don't say anything. Please." He stepped back. "I'm not telling you now because I want something from you. I just need you to know."

"All right," she said softly.

"Good." He let out a breath, letting his shoulders fall.

Adella turned toward the table and started gathering the papers, stacking them in a neat pile. "How did Martin die?"

"He was murdered." Kol stepped beside her and picked up a handful of scattered notes. "By another merchant; a man he thought was his friend."

She froze. "How awful."

"I should've been there," he went on. "I could've stopped them..." His hands clenched, the papers rustling as they wrinkled in his sweaty palms.

"His death wasn't your fault," she said, touching his hand lightly.

Kol unclenched his grip and drew a deep breath. He hadn't realized how badly he wanted to hear her say those words. All he could do was nod.

"Help me carry these to the study, will you?" she asked, piling a stack of papers onto the heavy Codex and balancing them precariously in her arms. "This work is far more important than I had realized."

He grabbed the rest of the papers and picked up the candelabra, filled with candles burnt down to stumps. Then, he followed her out through the hall and up the stairs, passing people coming and going as they made their way through the manor.

They entered the study, with its walls lined with built-in bookcases, all painted in a faded blue. Adella stopped to look around. "This was my father's study," she remarked, shifting the large Codex onto her hip in one arm. "Everything is as he left it. Sometimes, it feels like he's still here..." She put a hand to her bare neck, as if reaching for something no longer there. "As though there are pieces of the people we loved in the things they left behind." Adella set the Codex onto a small desk and began to sort through the papers, arranging them in some particular order known only to her. "Is that silly?"

"No. I know what you mean." Kol set the candelabra on the desk and watched her rifle through the papers. "Martin left his mercantile to me. It was his whole life... Now I'm responsible for it."

"Does that mean you'll be returning to Raymouth?" she asked without looking up from her work.

"At times," he replied. "But I want to live here in Elldon and open a shop. That was always Martin's plan, and now it's mine."

"Good." She smiled up at him. "I'm very glad to hear it."

"Besides," he continued, straining to keep a straight face, "someone's got to keep an eye on you. Keep you out of trouble."

She laughed and picked up the Codex. "Good luck with that." Crossing the room, she tucked the tome into an empty spot high on a shelf.

Kol looked over the books that filled the shelves, running his fingers over the spines to wipe the dust from the titles. "Which is the next *Jonny Reddin-Black* novel?" he asked. "After *Mother Tigress.*"

"Uh," she muttered, returning to the papers on the desk. "That would be *Blood Island,* I think. Over there." She nodded the direction. "He meets Clara in that one, but—"

"Sh!" He pulled the book from the shelf. "Don't spoil it for me," he said, turning it over in his hands. The cover bore a gold floral design imprinted into the rough, green cloth. "May I?" he asked, waving the book in the air, and she nodded. "By the way," Kol continued, tucking the book under his arm. "I met my father."

She turned to face him. "Your father? But I thought..."

"I was lost at sea," he replied. "My father was a merchant; my mother..." His mouth pulled to one side. "Well, I saw her likeness in a painting. She was beautiful."

"That's wonderful!" Adella said, her face brightening. "I'm so happy for you. I'd love to meet him someday."

"Uh, right. Sure." He wasn't sure how he felt about the idea; his father didn't seem the sort of person he'd want her to meet.

She continued to sort through the papers. "Does that mean you do have a family name, after all?"

"Yes," he replied. "It's Seaborn."

Adella stopped, and her back straightened. "Seaborn?"

"My name was Kaias Seaborn; my father is Adamas Seaborn," he went on, though she remained motionless. "Have you heard the name?"

"Isn't there a ship named *Seaborn*?" she asked.

"That was my father's merchant ship," Kol replied. "Years ago."

"Merchant, are you sure?" Her voice was uncharacteristically icy. "Not a reaver ship, was it?"

"No."

She resumed her work, her fingers running quickly through the pages. "So, should I call you Kol, or Kaias?"

He chuckled. "Kol is fine." Walking along the wall, he turned his attention to the various other books that filled the shelves. Save for the soft thump of his boots and the shuffling of paper, silence filled the room.

"About what you said before..." she began slowly. "How long have you felt that way?"

"It started the moment we met."

"But—" Adella spun and faced him. "We were fighting when we met. I attacked you."

A grin spread across his face. "I know," he replied, and she lowered her brow, looking at him in speechless confusion. Outside, the clatter of rain on the windowpanes faded away. "Sounds like the rain has stopped," Kol commented. "It's late, you should get some rest."

"Right," she sighed, setting the papers down on the desk. "We'll need to find you someplace to sleep. I'd offer a spot in my tent for the night, as it's plenty large enough, but I don't want any rumors started."

Kol raised his brow. "What sort of rumors?" he asked innocently, though he couldn't suppress the smirk on his face.

"Shall I explain to you what goes on between a man and a woman in private," she asked wearily, "or can you just use your imagination?"

"By all means," he replied with a broad grin and crossed his arms, "please explain it." Kol looked at her expectantly.

Color bloomed on Adella's cheeks, and she turned quickly away. "So you admit you have no experience in the matter?"

He laughed. "You know I'm only playing. Anyway, I doubt I'll get much sleep tonight."

"Why is that?" she asked. "Nightmares?"

He plopped down on a small sofa by the wall and opened *Blood Island*. "Something like that."

26

Letters

The blazing sun wicked perspiration from her brow as Adella strolled behind the line of archers. Though it was still morning, the air was still and stifling. Tilting back her straw hat, she wiped the beads of sweat away with the back of her hand, watching as each archer released an arrow in turn.

"Very good," she commented as Rosalind hit close to the center. Next, Jacoby let his fly, and it sailed just over the rope target, nicking the upper edge. "Close, Jacoby!" she said, trying to sound encouraging. "Your aim is getting better." While he grabbed another arrow, Adella stepped closer to speak to him privately. "How's your brother doing?"

"The leg is healing all right," Jacoby replied, "but it's killing him to be laid up like this."

"I'm sure." She would feel the same way in his situation. "I'll check on him when I return to the manor, and see if I can cheer him up."

"Thank you." Jacoby turned his attention back to the target.

A shadow fell over Adella's face as Kol stepped beside her, and they watched the next archer release an arrow in silence. He had dozed off while reading in the library the night before and she had left him there to sleep, retiring to her tent in the field.

At length, Kol glanced at the saber hanging at Adella's hip. "Do you know how to use that?" he asked, nodding toward it.

Pulling him by the elbow, she led him away from the others a step and leaned in to speak confidentially. "As a matter of fact, I don't," she muttered from the corner of her mouth. "I was wondering if you might show me how."

He quirked his lips to one side, apparently giving it some thought. "It's not a skill you can pick up lightly," he warned. "It took me many years of training and experience to get this far."

She smiled. "Then we'd better get started."

"Fine," Kol sighed in mock annoyance. "After tea."

"That's the spirit," she said brightly, clapping him on the shoulder. "Spoken like a true Valennian."

They walked together, returning to watch the archers at their practice. After several more misses from Jacoby, Kol stepped in to help him with his form, patiently showing him how to position the arrow on the string. Her gaze lingered on Kol; she had to admit he cut a dashing figure, with his stately height and broad shoulders.

As Adella waited, her thoughts wandered to the events of the night before. She remembered the earnest look on Kol's face when he told her how he felt, and the way he held her tightly beneath the shelter of the trees before that. *He was so relieved to see me,* she thought, absent-mindedly watching while he took the bow and drew it slowly to show Jacoby. *And he had felt this way for so long.* Guilt wrenched her heart when she thought back on all the time they'd spent together, with her oblivious to his feelings. *If only he had mentioned it sooner...* Whether she would still have resumed her relationship with Captain Declan if he had, she didn't know. Perhaps she wouldn't have been so hasty. *Now, no matter what she decides to do, one of them is bound to get hurt.* 'Don't go breaking any hearts,' Armand had warned. She wasn't sure if he'd meant Kol, or Declan, or both, but she was certain of one thing; *I should have listened.*

An arrow flew across the range and hit the target dead-center, pulling her out of her thoughts. Kol looked back at her, meeting her eyes, and a proud grin stretched across his face. Though he had a rather rough look about him, with dark, patchy stubble and stray curls hanging free from his short queue, it made him all the more endearing. *I'll have to tell Kol about me and Rog eventually,* Adella thought sadly as she returned the smile, nodding in approval. *But not today. Let him be happy for a little while longer.*

She glanced around and noticed Rosalind eyeing her curiously.

"Lady Grimless!" a voice called out. From the direction of Greywood Manor, Mister Giles hurried toward her, his leather apron jostling while he shuffled across the grass. "You have a visitor."

Her stomach fluttered with anxiety while she wondered who it could be. *Rogero?* she guessed, but that didn't seem likely. "Who is it?" she asked as Giles approached, trying to sound indifferent.

"A sailor," he replied. "With letters for you."

"I'll be right there." Then, she raised her voice to address the others, "Let's take a rest, shall we?"

James still lay upon the sofa, staring at the ceiling with his bandaged leg propped up on a stack of pillows. Remembering her promise to his brother, Adella stopped to check on him.

"How are you faring, James?" she asked. He replied with an indifferent grunt. "Can I get you anything?" she tried again. "Tea, perhaps?" Behind her, the others began to file in from the hallway.

"Whiskey, if you don't mind," he said quietly. "I'd get it myself, but..." He turned his head to look squarely up at her, and frowned. "I belong to the sofa now."

"Whiskey it is," she said, then turned to leave.

"And," he added, stopping her before she could take a step. "Could you put it in a teacup so no one knows? Rosalind says I've had enough." He frowned. "She's being too strict with me; it still hurts a great deal."

"I can do that," she replied, then made to leave again.

"One more thing," he said, catching her again before she left. "You might as well bring the pastries, too."

"We have pastries?" she asked, her interest piquing.

"Yes," he replied. "The little, colorful ones they make in the Capital. They arrived with the cargo from Raymouth."

"Why didn't you mention it earlier?" she joked. Clearly, they had all been busy with more serious matters.

James chuckled. "I'll keep it in mind next time," he replied. "Oh, another thing," he added, reaching for something beneath the sofa. "This belongs to you." He held out her father's saber.

"Thank you." The heft and coolness of the blade felt reassuring in her hands as Adella secured it to her belt, replacing the borrowed one.

Footsteps padded behind her as Kol approached. "Your visitor's waiting in the dining room."

She nodded. "I'll be back soon," she promised James, then turned and left.

Adella followed Kol into the dining room, where Yul Childric sat at the table in his blue sailor's coat and long, blond hair tied neatly in a queue. "It's good to see you again," she said warmly, taking a seat beside him. "How have you been?" Across from her, Kol pulled out a chair and sat, opening *Blood Island* as he reached for his cup.

"Perfectly well." Childric watched her pour fragrant lavender tea into the blue-and-white porcelain. "I've got a good deal of letters to deliver here at Greywood, now that the reavers in the Bay have been dealt with." He pulled a waxed-canvas haversack from his shoulder and opened the flap. "As for your own, there's one from the banker at Raymouth," he said, setting the envelope in front of her. "One from a Benramil Armand." He placed that one on the other. "And from Her Majesty, Queen Ellinora." Childric set that one before her as well, then poured tea into his cup. "That one," he commented proudly, "was brought with some urgency to me by her own personal courier."

Adella looked them over one by one. "Are these all the letters you have for me?" she asked, trying to hide the disappointment in her voice.

Childric picked up both cup and saucer in each hand and took a sip. "Yes."

She set the letters back down on the table and turned her attention back to her tea. "And is your captain well?"

Childric lifted his cup to his mouth again. "He is," he muttered into the rim.

"I suppose he must be very busy," she reasoned.

He sipped the tea, smacking his lips loudly. "Not particularly."

"Hm." She took a long draught, nearly finishing it all in one gulp.

"Things have rather calmed down in Raymouth," he went on, setting the porcelain down with a clink. "Though the murderer that set that ship afire was never caught." He picked up a piece of candied plum from a small bowl on the tray and popped it into his mouth. "My friend Fernsby, who was a member of the crew," he continued while he chewed, "told me he knows who did it. He was there; saw it for himself." He washed the mouthful down with tea.

Across from her, Kol looked up from the book, the color drained from his face.

"Who was it?" Adella asked.

"He's too afraid to speak of it," Childric replied with a shrug. "I can't say I blame him, after what happened. Who knows what a criminal like that is capable of?"

Kol released a breath and leaned back against the chair.

"How horrible!" A shiver ran down Adella's spine. "That such a scoundrel could get away so easily. I hope the Royal Guards find him and deal with him properly."

"What if it was an accident?" Kol asked from behind the open book.

"I don't think so." Childric's crisp tone brooked no argument.

As they sipped their tea in silence, Adella reached for one of her letters and broke the seal. Pulling out the contents, her eyes roamed over a brief message. "The banker wishes me to know he's returned to Raymouth," she said flatly. Setting it aside, she reached for another, and opened it.

It took her a moment to read through the sloppy handwriting, marred with blotches of stray ink. "Armand has arrived safely at the Capital." She picked up the letter from the Queen next. Opening it, she read silently:

Lady Grimless,

My dear girl, as I'm aware of the dangerous situation I've placed you in on the frontier, it pains me to inform you that the Council of Lords are vehemently against a war with Sornia. With my claim to the throne so tenuous right now, being merely regent until the rightful heir can be determined, I must placate them as best I can. Therefore, I can't at the moment send you support, and, officially, I must give you orders not to engage the enemy in combat in the Campos. You, as Lady of Elldon, are charged with the defense of Valennian land only; do not, by any means, provoke the Sornian army in contested territory.

However, unofficially, I remind you that, even though the Campos do not belong to Valenna, neither do they belong to Sornia. Your town is located at a strategic advantage point, situated as it is between our two countries—especially as it guards the Raymouth Bridge. If things go badly, you must protect the bridge with everything you can muster.

I, in the meantime, will begin diplomatic outreach toward the Azbarian family, particularly with Prince Matei now that he is the next in line for the Sornian throne, as we've just received word that Prince Gio has passed suddenly. Let's hope that Prince Matei is a more reasonable fellow than King Berento, though he could hardly be worse. I am hopeful that opening communications between our two countries will bring us a peaceful resolution before things get too out of hand. I trust a little diplomacy will save many lives.

I write this to you in confidence; please destroy this letter after you've read it.

Keep your chin up,

Ellinora

P. S. I have sent funds for your use at Elldon; the banker in Raymouth should be contacting you about it soon.

Adella's heart sank. "Wonderful," she grumbled to herself, then folded the letter and tucked it into her pocket. *No troops...* She blew a breath out of the corner of her mouth. *Well, at least she sent money.*

"I had been wondering..." Childric ventured at length, refilling his cup. "Do you know why your family relocated from the Capital to Elldon?"

Something about the abrupt question made Adella uneasy. "I wasn't privy to the reason, but I suspect it had to do with that business with Lord Hollen," she replied. "It'd been going on in the shadows for years, and everyone knows my family has always been loyal to the Haspen Dynasty. The conspirators likely wanted us out of the way."

"You don't say..." Childric muttered.

"Why do you ask?" Adella's eyes narrowed while she tried to decipher the meaning behind his tone. "Do you know something I don't?"

"Uh, no," he replied, taking another candied plum. "Just curious." He stuck it in his mouth and licked his fingers. "Well, I suppose I should be getting back," he said thickly, then thumbed through the remaining contents in his haversack and pulled out a handful of letters. "The rest of these are addressed to others here at Elldon," he went on, setting the stack in front of her, "if you would see them safely into their hands for me."

"Of course." Adella pushed her chair back and stood. "I'll walk you out—"

"Actually," Childric interrupted, "I was hoping Mister Kol here would be so kind."

Her eyes widened as she glanced toward Kol, who seemed equally surprised by the request, though Adella was sure she was the only one who could read it in his generally stoic expression. Calmly, Kol closed the book, then rose and led Childric from the room.

In the foyer, Kol slid back the thick iron bar of the lock and pulled open the front doors of Greywood Manor. Outside, the sailor's horse, apparently borrowed from the livery stable at Raymouth, waited in the bright sun of the gravel courtyard, tied to a nearby hitching-ring.

Childric crossed the threshold, then turned toward Kol. "I have some letters for you," he said, ducking to dig around in his bag. "Ah, here we are!" He presented them with a flourish.

"Thanks," Kol said, tucking them into the cover of his book.

"Oh, and one more thing," Childric continued. "The captain wanted me to relay a message."

Kol raised an eyebrow. "To me?"

"Indeed." Childric cleared his throat, his eyes rolling upward while he thought. "Captain Declan requests that you keep a respectable distance between yourself and Lady Grimless."

"What?" Kol asked flatly, brow lowering.

"He understands the nature of your regard for her," Childric explained, "and wishes to inform you she is already spoken for."

Kol's shoulders tensed, his fists clenching as he towered over the young man. "Declan is telling me to stay away from Adella?" he asked, clipping his words sharply.

Childric shifted on his feet. "Well, yes—"

"And he sent you to give me orders?" Kol snapped, his voice rising as anger burned in his face.

"Ah, no—" Childric replied, putting his palms in the air. "He merely asks for your word as a gentleman."

"Do I *look* like a gentleman?" Kol growled through his teeth, and slammed the doors shut in the young man's face.

Adella walked into the dim and smokey kitchen, ducking under bundles of dried herbs that hung from the ceiling beams, to the large cupboards and rifled through their contents, shoving aside bags and boxes for some time before finally giving up. "Have you seen the pastries?" she asked helplessly to Rosalind, who was busy at the hearth. "James asked for them."

"They should be in there," Rosalind replied, setting the fire iron down and coming to her assistance. "Here they are." She pulled out a small wooden box. "Right in front of you," she laughed.

"Oh," Adella replied sheepishly. "They usually come in a tin; I wasn't looking for a box."

"Odd, isn't it?" Rosalind mused, her voice taking on a dreamy tone. "That the thing we're searching for can be under our nose, and we'd never see it if it looks a little different than we expected."

"Right," Adella replied with a nervous laugh as she took the box. "How silly of me." She couldn't help but wonder if Rosalind was still talking about pastries, but the other woman's placid smile revealed nothing of her meaning.

Adella returned to the large parlor room, bringing James the pastries along with whiskey she pilfered from the kitchen when Rosalind wasn't looking. She set the pastry box onto a small table beside the sofa, where he seemed to be dozing. Pulling a flask out from the pocket in her petticoats, she poured a little whiskey into the cup and left it for him, then grabbed a handful of pastries from the box before turning away.

Crossing the room, Adella stood before the large map on the far wall, nibbling absent-mindedly on one of the pastries, when Kol approached with a glower on his face.

"Insufferable," he muttered.

"What is?" she asked, raising a brow.

"Nothing."

"Well, you look tense," she replied, eyeing him sideways. "Try to relax, if it's nothing." She offered him a pastry on her palm.

"I can't relax," he said dryly. "It's tension that's holding me together. If I relaxed now, my limbs would fall off."

"Hm," Adella muttered as he took the pastry and popped it into his mouth. Then, she turned her attention back to the map. "Do you see that bridge there?" She nodded toward a little scribble in the upper right corner that stretched across her depiction of the River Ray.

"Is that what that is?"

"Yes..." she replied defensively, pouting at the insult. "How best would you defend it from the Sornians?"

He studied the map, his eyes roving over its various markings. "Scouts, spies, caltrops, tiger pits, and ground spikes," he said, touching various points on the map while he spoke. "And guards," he added, tapping the location of the bridge.

"And if you wanted to make an offensive maneuver?"

"I would place a small group to draw the enemy out," he explained, "in an advantageous location between the two camps—one with plenty of surrounding cover; say, here—" He tapped an open area to the west, encircled by small markings that represented trees. "And stage an ambush."

"You would use your own people as bait?" she asked dubiously.

He shrugged. "That's war."

Adella peered closely at the spot on the map. *That's exactly where James said the Sornians ambushed his party,* she realized. *Just as Kol described.* She pressed a finger to her lower lip absently. "Now, how do we free Misses Asher from their encampment?"

Kol sucked his cheek, looking at the map. "That won't be easy."

The Hawk

A hawk soared high above the undulating fields, carried on a rising current of balmy air. Far below, a lone rider halted atop a ridge, overlooking the western fields. As the hawk looked down on the landscape, the colors of the world around him—the green of the grasses, the azure of the sky, the deep, warm browns of the horse's coat and the woman's hair—all shone in vivid hues he'd never before experienced. Even soaring high above, he could see every detail of the plains, down to each brightly-colored flower. The effect made him nauseous.

The woman's face he could also see clearly, and it was one he recognized. *Adella,* Matei thought with satisfaction. *I see you.*

Gliding eastward over the prairies, the hawk's keen eyes spied movement in the distance. Matei willed the creature to adjust its pinions, and his vision dipped lower over the grass as the wings carried him closer. Below, camp tents of plain canvas encircled bustling activity, with figures clothed in so vibrant a red, it was nearly shocking to the hawk's eyes. On the far side of the encampment, horses grazed in a make-shift wooden pen.

The hawk flew on. Ahead, the foreboding form of a stone manor rose from a hill top, enshrouded in the gloom beneath tall trees. Beside the manor, stood newly-built stables, the rough timbers still bearing the pale shade of freshly-hewn wood. A small movement below, nearly undetectable to Matei, caught the bird's attention, and he found himself being compelled downward toward the ground, the landscape around him fading to a blur of color.

Sickened by the sudden loss of control, Matei pulled back, drawing his thoughts once more to his physical form. How long he had soared over the Campos, he didn't know, but it was clearly too long. His mind clung to the bird still, reveling in the excitement of the hunt, unwilling to leave behind his newfound wings. Matei found himself caught in-between; he could faintly hear the voices around him in his solar room overlooking the noisy streets of Hedda, yet still felt the wind through his feathers and the warm sun on his back. The effort it took to draw him back into his own body was much too great. He closed his eyes, and let the bird carry him away.

"Matei!"

The voice called with such urgency, it broke through the beating of wings and the rush of wind. Summoning the last shred of his willpower, Matei centered his mind into his own limbs, ones which he could barely feel but knew must still be there. As his own form seemed to finally solidify around himself, he forced one eyelid open, and was relieved to see his own hand, resting on the colorful carpet close by his face. The glow of the *Corelimun* pulsed brightly between his knuckles like a raw and beating heart.

Deft fingers pried open his hand, and the smooth planes of the large crystal slid from his grip. Matei opened his eyes and, though his shoulder and hip pressed against the hard floor, the walls spun around him; his chest rose and fell with shallow, panting breath.

Propping himself up on an arm, his stomach churned and he doubled over, heaving uncontrollably. The acrid, half-digested contents of his breakfast burned up into his throat and splashed onto the floor. Pain drummed his skull with each rapid beat of his pulse.

"What happened?" Lucas asked, crouching at his side. "We kept calling for you. You looked—" Lucas's worry-lined face came into focus. "You looked like you'd died."

"I'm fine," Matei replied, grabbing the crystal from Lucas's hand. "I'm still getting used to it, that's all."

"Well," Teressa sighed, "at least it wasn't seawater this time; that was odd. I'll get a rag."

"Leave it." Matei rose gingerly to his feet. "The servants will clean it up." He took a tentative step, and faltered on trembling legs.

"Easy," Lucas said, grabbing Matei's elbow and steadying him. "What was it this time?" he asked eagerly, guiding him toward the sofa. "Where did you go?"

"I crossed the Campos." Matei lowered himself onto the cushions. "And I found her. I found Adella."

"Ugh," Lucas groaned. "You know how I feel about your obsession with my sister."

"It's not an obsession." Matei tucked the heavy crystal into his waistcoat pocket. "I see her in my dreams. We're connected somehow."

Lucas wrinkled his nose. "Like I said..."

"I mean when I sleep with the crystal beneath my pillow," Matei replied. "Our fates are intertwined in some way; I can feel it." He rubbed his throbbing forehead. "I saw everything, Lucas," he said, looking his friend in the eyes. "I know their number, the locations of their campsites, their defenses... I could see everything." He hopped to his feet with sudden resolution. "I need to get a message to General Blackburn."

To Be Continued...

www.ingramcontent.com/pod-product-compliance
Lightning Source LLC
Chambersburg PA
CBHW071304140726
47996CB00005B/1624